There can only be m...
Mayfair when a pro...
lady reads a scanda...
confession . . .

MW00753202

"Good evening, my lady."

$\mathcal{S}$he turned and realized that even if she hadn't known his voice, she would have known his eyes. They gazed at her through a black mask that covered the entire upper half of his face with the same heated intensity that stole the air from her lungs every time he looked at her. She'd have known his mouth as well. Not only because it was perfectly formed, the bottom lip slightly fuller than the upper, but because of how one corner tilted upward, skewing all that perfection with a hint of lopsidedness that shouldn't have been attractive, but was. Annoyingly so.

Her gaze skimmed over his all-black highwayman costume. He looked tall and dark and dangerous—as if he were prepared to abscond with whatever might take his fancy and the consequences be damned. A thrill she couldn't name raced through her. "Rather than good evening, shouldn't you say, 'Stand and deliver'?"

By Jacquie D'Alessandro

CONFESSIONS AT MIDNIGHT
SLEEPLESS AT MIDNIGHT
NEVER A LADY
NOT QUITE A GENTLEMAN
LOVE AND THE SINGLE HEIRESS
WHO WILL TAKE THIS MAN?

Jacquie D'Alessandro

Confessions at Midnight

AVON

An Imprint of HarperCollinsPublishers

This is a work of fiction. Names, characters, places, and incidents are products of the author's imagination or are used fictitiously and are not to be construed as real. Any resemblance to actual events, locales, organizations, or persons, living or dead, is entirely coincidental.

AVON BOOKS
An Imprint of HarperCollins*Publishers*
10 East 53rd Street
New York, New York 10022-5299

This book is dedicated with my deepest respect and gratitude to all those who have served and are currently serving in our Armed Forces. Thank you for the sacrifices you and your families make to keep our nation free and safe. I'd especially like to thank my dad, World War II veteran James Johnson, for not only serving in the Army, but also for instilling in me a profound love of our country. And thanks also to my mom, Kay Johnson, not only for being a wonderful mother, but for marrying that handsome former soldier.

And, as always, to my fantastic husband, Joe, for being The Most Patient Man on Earth, and my terrific son, Christopher, aka Patience Junior. Jegamesh, boys. I love you!

I would like to thank the following people for their invaluable help and support:

My editor, Erika Tsang, and all the wonderful people at Avon Books/HarperCollins for their kindness, cheerleading, and helping make my dreams come true, including Liate Stehlik, Carrie Feron, Debbie Stier, Pam Spengler-Jaffee, Buzzy Porter, Brian Grogan, Mike Spradlin, Adrienne Di Pietro, Mark Gustafson, Rhonda Rose, Carla Parker, and Tom Egner.

My agent, Damaris Rowland, for her faith and wisdom, as well as Steven Axelrod and Lori Antonson.

Jenni Grizzle and Wendy Etherington for being such great buds.

Thanks also to the wonderful Sue Grimshaw of BGI for her generosity and support and Kathy Baker, bookseller extraordinaire. If bookselling were an Olympic event, you two ladies would bring home the gold! And as always to Kay and Jim Johnson; Kathy and Dick Guse; Lea and Art D'Alessandro; and Michelle, Steve, and Lindsey Grossman.

A cyber hug to my Looney Loopies Connie Brockway, Marsha Canham, Virginia Henley, Jill Gregory, Sandy Hingston, Julia London, Kathleen Givens, Sherri Browning, and Julie Ortolon, and also to the Temptresses and the Blaze Babes.

My terrific book club buddies Susie Aspinwall, Sandy Izaguirre, Melanie Long, and Melissa Winsor for their kindness, friendship, and support.

A very special thank you to the members of Georgia Romance Writers and Romance Writers of America.

And finally, thank you to all the wonderful readers who have taken the time to write to me. I love hearing from you!

Chapter 1

His hand slipped beneath my gown to slowly glide up my leg. The muted sounds of the party came through the library door, and I knew we risked being discovered. But I simply did not care . . .

Memoirs of a Mistress by An Anonymous Lady

"When we chose this book to read, I had no idea it would be so . . . explicit," murmured Carolyn Turner, Viscountess Wingate.

She clutched her slim, leather-bound—and much perused—volume of *Memoirs of a Mistress* and glanced around her drawing room at her three guests, who, along with her, comprised the Ladies Literary Society of London. All three faces, she noted, bore scarlet blushes identical to the one scorching her own cheeks. Quite understandable, as one of her guests was only newly married and the other two were virginal innocents.

Virginal, yes. Innocents—no longer, thanks to the *Memoirs*.

Of course, in spite of having been married for seven years, she herself still had never *dreamed* of, let alone experienced, half the things described in the scandalous book that had recently taken Society by storm. Before her beloved Edward's untimely death three years ago, she'd believed they shared every conceivable pleasure with each other.

Based on her reading of the *Memoirs*, apparently not.

Her sister Sarah, the new Marchioness Langston by virtue of her recent marriage, cleared her throat. "Well, the entire point of forming our little Ladies Literary Society was to forsake the classics for more forbidden fare."

"True," said Lady Julianne Bradley, whose normally porcelain complexion now resembled a fiery sunset, "but there is forbidden, then there is *this*." She held up her own copy of the book and Carolyn noted that many of the pages appeared decidedly dog-eared. Julianne leaned forward, and although they were alone in the room, she lowered her voice. "If Mother ever discovered I'd read such shocking things, she'd . . ." Julianne briefly squeezed her eyes shut. "Oh, I cannot even imagine it."

"She'd fly into the boughs as she always does," chimed in Lady Emily Stapleford with her usual forthrightness. "She'd demand her hartshorn, then, once recovered, I wager she'd confiscate your copy in order to read it for herself." Emily grinned at Julianne over the rim of her teacup. "In which case you'd not only be confined to your bedchamber for the remainder of your natural days, but you'd never get your book back. So make certain she doesn't find out."

Julianne's color deepened, and she quickly added another sugar lump to her tea. "As I've absolutely nothing to which I can compare anything I've read in the *Memoirs*, I can't help but wonder if half the things the author describes are even . . ."

"Anatomically possible?" finished Emily. "Yes, I wondered the same thing." Her gaze bounced between Carolyn and Sarah. "Well?"

Sarah pushed up her spectacles then fanned herself with her napkin. "I'm hardly an expert, as I've only been married two months. But from what I can tell . . ."

Her voice trailed off, and Emily leaned forward so far she nearly tipped from her chair. "Yes?"

"Everything she describes is . . . possible."

Emily sat back and *whooshed* out a long breath. "Never say so." Her amazed gaze shifted to Carolyn. "Do you concur?"

Carolyn pressed her hands against her book, which rested in her lap. Snippets from the scorching story of the Anonymous Lady's sexual exploits sifted through her mind and she felt as if the pages set her gown on fire.

"Certainly possible," she agreed, even though she wasn't quite positive. But really, weren't most things *possible*?

"But are they . . . enjoyable?" asked Julianne, her blue eyes round. "Because I must say, some of them sound rather . . . messy."

An image flashed through Carolyn's mind . . . of Edward's handsome face hovering above hers, his flesh buried deep inside her. The indescribable joy of that intimacy.

"Definitely enjoyable," Carolyn and Sarah said in unison.

"Even what she describes on page forty-two?" Emily asked in a breathless voice, rifling through the pages of her book.

Carolyn didn't need to look at page forty-two to know what was described there—she'd read the highly sensual passage so many times she could recite it by rote. Still, she fell in with the group and opened her book. Her gaze fell upon the Anonymous Lady's vivid description of a quick tryst in which her lover took her against the library wall between courses at a dinner party.

"Possible," Carolyn murmured, picturing the carnal image of the lady's legs wrapped around her lover's hips while he thrust into her, hard and deep. Although Edward had never made love to her in such a rough and . . . ungentlemanly way, she supposed it was possible—provided the gentleman was quite strong and vigorous, the lady quite agile and filled with stamina, and they were both quite determined.

"And, um, definitely enjoyable," added Sarah.

Three gazes immediately flew to Sarah. Surely her sister hadn't—

But one look at her sister's dreamy expression glowing behind her spectacles made it clear that Sarah knew of what she spoke, a fact that unsettled Carolyn in a way she didn't quite understand.

Emily cleared her throat. "I . . . see. Well, what about that bit on page fifty-three? Surely a man wouldn't do *that* . . . would he?"

"And the other on page sixty-one?" added Julianne. "Surely a woman wouldn't do *that* . . . would she?"

Again Carolyn knew precisely to what her friends referred without looking at the book. Her face flamed hotter and she found herself shifting in her seat from the same disconcerting sensations that had plagued her during her entire reading of the *Memoirs*.

Readings, her inner voice interjected, emphasizing the plural.

She shot her pesky inner voice an inward frown. Very well, *readings*. Many, many readings. Alone in her bed, her mind overflowing with carnal images that left her overheated.

Although she again had no personal knowledge of the shocking goings-on described on pages fifty-three and sixty-one, she had no reason to doubt the word of the Anonymous Lady who clearly knew her way around a boudoir. And a library. And the stables. And even the dining room.

For starters.

Carolyn shoved the sensual images aside and stated, "According to the rumors, everything in the book is completely true."

Sarah cleared her throat. "Yes. Men *do* do those things. Um, women, too."

Carolyn blinked. Surely Sarah hadn't done *that*. Yet another quick look at her sister made it quite clear she had. And that she was deliriously happy about it. An odd mixture of delight and envy suffused her. Delight—that Sarah, who for so long had been overlooked because she wasn't classically beautiful and her interests tended toward scholarly pursuits, had found a deep and abiding love with Matthew Devenport, the Marquess of Langston. And envy—because Carolyn so profoundly missed the deeply satisfying relationship she'd shared with Edward, one she knew in her heart and soul could never be duplicated. She'd been fortunate to find her one true love. And sadly, had lost him to a sudden and unexpected illness.

After three long years of widowhood she'd finally accepted the fact that the ache of missing her beloved husband would never completely go away. So she kept him in a special corner of her heart where his memory burned brightly and always would. She might have remained forever in her state of mourning, isolated from everyone except her family and few closest friends, but several months ago Sarah had taken her firmly in hand and all but dragged her out, encouraging her to discard her solitude and black gowns and join the living again.

At first Carolyn resisted, but she'd slowly come to once again enjoy being out in Society, attending soirees, socializing with old friends, forging new acquaintances. She behaved a proper lady at all times, determined to never do anything that could besmirch Edward's memory. Achingly lonely though the long, silent nights remained, her days were now pleasantly occupied with visits and shopping excursions with Emily and Julianne—her two dearest friends, and of course Sarah, her dearest friend of all. Still, she had a great deal of free time on her hands here in London and wished to find something to occupy herself.

Something useful. A project of some sort. Most days she felt as if all she was doing in life was taking up space.

Not wishing to dwell any longer on her increasingly somber thoughts, nor on the more salacious parts of the book, parts that had reignited desires she'd thought long buried, she said, "I recently learned that the *Memoirs,* in addition to being the latest scandal, is also responsible for a new rage sweeping the ton."

Emily arched a brow. "Oh? Making love in a moving carriage?"

"Or in the billiard room—"

"No," Carolyn said with a laugh, cutting off Julianne's guess. "It's *the notes* the author describes."

"Oh, yes, the mysterious unsigned missives the Anonymous Lady received from one of her lovers," Julianne said in a breathless voice. "She'd arrive at the time and place in the note and they'd engage in a tryst."

"Exactly," Carolyn said. "Last night at Lord and Lady Lerner's musicale I heard several ladies say they've received such notes. And the results were very satisfactory."

"I would imagine so," Sarah said, her nod sending her spectacles sliding down her nose. "I'd very much like to receive such a note."

"Indeed?" asked Emily, her eyes twinkling with mischief. "From whom?"

Sarah blinked and pushed up her glasses. "Why, Matthew, of course. In fact, I told him so over breakfast this morning."

Julianne heaved a long, dreamy sigh. "I would *love*

to receive such a note. It's so . . . dashing. And romantic."

"Such a note would ruin your reputation," Carolyn said gently to her overly romantic friend.

"Yes, but to be desired so strongly . . ." Julianne heaved another sigh. "The *Memoirs* have taught me so many things. Things Mother certainly never told me."

"No one's mother would ever tell them such things," Carolyn said with a smothered laugh of horror. Certainly her mother never had. On the eve of her wedding, her mother had only offered the troubling and cryptic advice for her to close her eyes, brace herself, and recall that the ordeal would be over in a matter of moments.

Clearly Mother did not know of what she spoke, because her wedding night had been a beautiful, tender experience that marked the beginning of her and Edward's deeply satisfying and intimate bond.

"My mother has *never* spoken of such things with me," said Emily. "Indeed, if it weren't for the fact that she gave birth to six children, I'd be tempted to say she didn't know how we were conceived. I think it very fortunate that an Anonymous Lady wrote the *Memoirs* to drag us all from behind the shroud of ignorance. Someday soon some lucky, handsome, wealthy man will have the good sense to fall in love with me, and he will be very happy that I've read the book."

Carolyn glanced up at the portrait of Edward that hung above the fireplace and a flood of sadness swept over her. Love and intimacy were over for her. Edward had been such a wonderful, honest, kind and loving man. To this day she considered it a miracle that the very eligible, very handsome Viscount Wingate had singled her out for his attention. Indeed, if her father hadn't been a physician and the viscount hadn't happened to injure his hand in the same London bookstore where she and her father were browsing, they most likely never would have met. But from that first moment, she'd felt as if she found a piece of herself she hadn't even realized was missing.

Blinking away the memories, Carolyn forced a smile and said, "Well, perhaps we'll hear of more notes being received at Lady Walsh's masquerade tonight. It is rumored to be a gala event."

"I heard more than three hundred guests are expected," reported Sarah. "Matthew told me this morning that Lord Surbrooke is arriving in London today and will attend."

For reasons she neither understood nor cared to examine, Carolyn's pulse jumped at the mention of her new brother-in-law's closest friend. She'd met Lord Surbrooke several times over the years, as Edward had known him, but she herself had only become better acquainted with him earlier this summer during a house party at Matthew's country estate.

At first she'd categorized the handsome, charming earl as nothing more than another shallow aristocrat, spoiled by too much money, free time, and fawning women. Yet when he believed himself unobserved, his dark blue eyes turned pensive and seemed to harbor sadness. It was an emotion she understood well, and she couldn't help but wonder if some manner of tragedy had befallen him in the past.

But there was something else in his eyes . . . something that disrupted her calm and made her insides flutter in the most unsettling way. Something she wasn't quite certain she liked.

She was saved from commenting when Julianne chimed in, "Mother told me that Mr. Logan Jennsen will also attend the party."

Emily wrinkled her nose. "I'm certain he'll be easy to spot in the crush. He'll no doubt be garbed as a serpent. Or perhaps a wolf."

"I don't understand why you dislike him so," Sarah said. "He's very entertaining."

"I simply can't credit that he's invited everywhere," Emily said with a sniff. "Has no one besides me noticed he's an uncouth American?"

"He's invited everywhere because he's obscenely wealthy," Julianne said. "No doubt he'd like to find himself a peer's daughter to marry to ease his way into Society, and with his vast wealth he'll surely succeed." She gave Emily a teasing nudge. "Best watch out or he'll cast his eye upon *you*."

"He'd best not, unless he'd like to lose his eye. Perhaps he'll cast his net in *your* direction."

"He'd be wasting his time, as Father would never consent to a match outside the peerage, regardless of the gentleman's wealth. And there's not enough hartshorn in the kingdom for Mother to consider it."

Carolyn had no doubt Julianne's assessment was true. Julianne's mother, the formidable Countess Gatesbourne, was overbearing in regards to her only child in a way that made other overbearing mothers seem like tame kittens. She was determined to see Julianne make a brilliant marriage. On the basis of her stunning looks alone, Julianne could attract any man. Combined with her sweet disposition and her family's vast wealth, she was one of the most eligible young women of the ton. And sadly, very much under the crushing weight of her mother's heavy thumb. Carolyn prayed that Julianne's gentle, romantic nature wouldn't be trampled by some philandering, jaded peer, but she'd seen enough of the breed to know that men like her Edward were rare amongst the species.

Her gaze shifted to Emily and sympathy filled her. Emily had recently confessed that her family was suffering severe financial difficulties, thanks in part to her father's excessive gambling. She feared her father planned to arrange for her to marry some old, creaky lord with nothing to recommend him save a great deal of much needed money. Carolyn dearly hoped such a fate wouldn't befall her lively, spirited friend.

In order to break the silence that had descended, Carolyn asked, "What sort of costumes are you all wearing?"

"You're not supposed to tell," said Emily, shaking a finger.

"But how else will we find each other in the crush?" asked Julianne. "I need to know who to look for in case I get an opportunity to escape Mother."

"Matthew and I will be attired as Romeo and Juliet," said Sarah, "except in our version of the story clearly neither of them die, as we are older than the teenage lovers. And besides, I cannot abide unhappy endings."

Emily heaved a sigh. "I shall be the tragic Ophelia.

I wanted to be Cleopatra, but Mama said 'twas too scandalous." She grinned. "Perhaps I should go as the Anonymous Lady."

"Yes," Carolyn said. "For a costume you could wear your skirt ruched up about your waist and carry a copy of the *Memoirs*."

They all laughed. "I'll be dressed as an angel," said Julianne.

"Very appropriate," Carolyn said.

"And boring," Julianne said with a sigh. "But Mother insisted."

"Wait until you see Carolyn's costume," Sarah enthused. "I helped her choose it."

Carolyn shot her sister a mock frown. "More like you ordered it, had it delivered here, then demanded I wear it." She looked at her two friends. "Since her marriage she's become very domineering and demanding."

"My husband likes me that way," Sarah answered tartly. "If I hadn't helped you with your costume, you'd have dressed as a shepherdess."

"Most likely," agreed Carolyn. "I certainly would not have chosen Galatea."

Julianne's eyes lit up. "Oh, the beautiful ivory statue that comes to life. You'll be stunning, Carolyn."

"And feel as if I'm only half dressed."

"Be happy that you're wearing anything," Emily said with a devilish grin. "Galatea was nude, you know."

Carolyn shot Sarah a frown. "I think *you* should go as Galatea and I'll go as a shepherdess."

"Heavens, no," said Sarah. "What on earth would Romeo want with a Greek statue? As Julianne said, you'll be stunning. There is nothing the least bit improper about your costume."

"Of course not," agreed Julianne. "Indeed, based on some of the costumes worn at Lady Walsh's ball last year, you'll be overdressed." She lowered her voice to impart, "A shocking number of women dressed as harem members."

"And nearly as many men were attired in togas—men whose rotund figures most assuredly should *not* have been draped in sheets." Emily gave an all-over shudder.

"I'm almost sorry I missed it," Carolyn said with a smile.

"With a few minor adjustments we could turn you from Galatea into Aphrodite," Sarah said to Carolyn with a speculative air. "The goddess of desire is who I wanted you to be to begin with."

"Absolutely not," Carolyn said firmly. "What would people think?"

Sarah reached out and lightly clasped her hand, her brown gaze serious as it rested on her. "That you are a young, vibrant woman who deserves to enjoy herself."

"I'm a thirty-two-year-old widow who is too old and too sensible to parade about in an unbecoming fashion." She said the words softly, to take any sting from them. She knew Sarah meant well, and truly she appreciated her sister's efforts on her behalf. But ever since she'd reentered Society, she sometimes felt as if in her determination to get on with her life everything was moving too quickly. As if she were losing part of herself, of the person she'd been for the last ten years—Edward's wife. She occasionally had difficulty recalling images of him that used to be so clear in her mind. Couldn't precisely recall the sound of his laughter. The warmth of his touch. The slow leaching of those memories confused and saddened her. And frightened her. For if her memories of Edward faded away, she'd have nothing left.

"There is nothing unbecoming about you," Sarah said gently, squeezing her hand. Then she smiled. "And we are all going to have a grand time this evening."

Carolyn returned her sister's smile, although she wasn't as optimistic. The idea of a costume ball had sounded exciting when she received the invitation, but now that the day was here, she felt decidedly less enthusiastic. She'd allowed Sarah to talk her into the Galatea costume, because as her sister pointed out, Galatea was brought to life, just as she herself wanted to be brought back to life. What she hadn't pointed out to Sarah was that the statue of Galatea was only brought to life because Pygmalion, the sculptor, fell passionately in love with his work of art. Love had brought Galatea to life. At one time, love had done the same for her, but she knew in her heart it would not, could not, happen again.

Chapter 2

The note read only, "Midnight, the stables." I instantly knew who it was from. Heart pounding with anticipation, I arrived at the appointed time. He stepped from the shadows and without a word pulled me into his arms . . .

Memoirs of a Mistress by An Anonymous Lady

Standing in a shadowed corner of the crowded ballroom, Daniel Sutton, Earl Surbrooke, was about to sip from his glass of champagne when he saw her. His hand froze partway to his lips, his drink forgotten as he stared at the Greek goddess garbed in pure ivory across the room. Flickering light from the dozens of candles in the overhead crystal chandeliers cast her in a soft, gilded glow. Her costume left both slender arms and one shoulder bare. His avid gaze drifted over the exposed creamy skin, and his imagination instantly conjured his fingers skimming along the silky smoothness. His lips tracing a trail along her delicate collarbone. Her name whispered through his mind and he had to clamp his jaw shut to keep from saying it out loud.

Carolyn. . .

Desire, hot and fierce, gripped him. Even with her honey-colored hair powered white and a mask covering most of her face, he'd recognize those perfect, lush lips, that slender neck, the curve of her cheek, that regal posture anywhere.

She stood alone, scanning the crowd. He would have given a great deal to be the person she sought, but he knew she'd be searching for her sister Sarah or one of her close friends, Lady Julianne or Lady Emily.

Someday very soon you'll be looking for me, his inner voice promised. Yes, her gaze would seek him out just as his did her at every opportunity. He intended to see to it. For he'd wanted her with a bone-deep intensity from the first instant he'd laid eyes upon her.

To this day he recalled that moment with such vivid clarity it could have happened ten minutes ago rather than ten years ago. He'd seen her—a vision in a blue gown—across the ballroom during a party hosted by one of his Eton friends, Edward Turner, Viscount Wingate. For a few brief seconds it felt as if time had stopped. Along with his breath. And heart. A ridiculous, inexplicable, visceral, and unprecedented reaction. True, she was beautiful, but he was accustomed to stunning women. Of course, he'd prevailed upon his friend to introduce him. And Edward had obliged, presenting Miss Carolyn Moorehouse.

They'd exchanged pleasantries, and Daniel fell more deeply in lust with the blushing beauty with each passing moment—a state of affairs he couldn't understand, as innocents were not at all to his taste. But something about her grabbed him by the throat and wouldn't let go. He wanted her, in his bed, naked and trembling with desire, and by God he was determined to have her.

Perhaps the fact that she wasn't an aristocrat was what he found so utterly refreshing and alluring. Regardless of the reason, he'd never been so wildly and instantaneously attracted to any woman. He was about to begin his seduction by asking her to dance when Edward requested everyone's attention—then announced that Miss Moorehouse had consented to be his wife.

Now, a decade later, Daniel still recalled his dumbstruck reaction. It was as if all the color had leaked from the room, leaving everything painted in dull, dismal shades of gray. After shaking himself from the stupor into which the news had thrust him, he saw what he'd been too stupefied to observe earlier—that Edward adored Carolyn, and she clearly felt the same about him.

He'd attended their wedding two months later— an occasion that left him feeling empty. The marriage was obviously a love match, and Edward was a friend. And while Daniel's actions didn't always fill him with pride, he drew the line at cuckolding friends. He therefore forced Carolyn from his thoughts and kept his distance from the happy couple as much as possible, reminding himself that he had no real interest in her other than bedding her, and there were plenty of other beautiful women available to slake his passions.

But the truth was that every time he found himself in the same room as Carolyn, he had trouble concentrating on anything other than her. The sensual fantasies she inspired confounded him for his inability to dispel them. Luckily she and Edward didn't attend many soirees, so he rarely saw them. He'd gone on with his life and finally convinced himself that his inappropriate lust had been an aberration.

After Edward's sudden death three years ago, Carolyn had gone into seclusion, retreating from Society entirely. He was therefore stunned several months ago to learn she was to be a guest at a country house party at the estate of his best friend, Matthew Devenport—a party Daniel was instantly impatient to attend. Before he arrived at Matthew's estate, he reminded himself that the oddly fierce attraction he'd experienced all those years ago was an anomaly. That he'd no doubt take one look at her and yawn. Still, not wanting any distractions or possible encumbrances, before leaving for the house party he amicably ended his brief yet steamy affair with Kimberly Sizemore, Countess Walsh, knowing the gorgeous widow would quickly move on to the next man.

When he arrived at the house party, however, it only required one look at Carolyn to bring all the lustful urges she'd once inspired roaring back. Her mere presence rendered him befuddled and bemused and tongue-tied in a way he might have found amusing had it not been so utterly irritating, uncharacteristic, and bewildering. He didn't lack for expertise or confidence when it came to women, yet somehow this sedate, petite woman made him feel like a bumbling lad in knee pants. It required all his finesse not to simply gawk and babble in her presence.

He learned through their conversations—during which he managed not to gawk and babble *too* much—that she remained devoted to her dead husband's memory and had no desire to ever marry again. Which only made her more perfect, as the last thing Daniel wanted was a wife. No, he wished only to bed her, and determined then and there to do what he hadn't when he first met her—seduce her. A challenge indeed, given her continued worship of her dead husband. But he was a patient man and he'd never wanted a woman more, his every nerve ending heating with anticipation at the upcoming game of enticing her to his bed, where the fire she'd ignited ten years ago would finally be extinguished. They'd enjoy a quick, mutually pleasurable affair, unmarred by messy emotions, then they'd each go their separate ways. He'd established a nice rapport with her in the country, and now that they were both back in London, he was prepared to begin his seduction in earnest.

Starting right now.

He handed his untouched champagne to a passing footman, but before he could move, a man costumed as a pirate approached his quarry. Daniel's eyes narrowed when, after several seconds, Carolyn extended her hand to the masked buccaneer and smiled. He didn't know who the bloody bastard was, but realizing that he had tarried here in the shadows too long, he set a determined pace toward Carolyn. It was his intent to prod the pirate along—using the point of the bastard's own sword if necessary—yet before he took more than half a dozen steps, a feminine hand curved around his arm.

"You make a very dashing highwayman, darling," said a throaty voice he instantly recognized. He turned and found himself the subject of a thorough perusal through Lady Walsh's mask. His gaze flicked over her. Garbed in a revealing outfit, Kimberly looked wickedly desirable and stunningly alluring. And he wanted nothing more than to escape.

Still, she was his hostess and a former lover, and protocol demanded he be polite. It certainly wasn't her fault he was in a rush to cross the room. "Cleopatra?" he guessed, lifting her hand to brush a light kiss over her fingers.

"Indeed," she said, her voice a sensual purr. "I was hoping you'd come as her lover, Marc Antony. Did you not receive my note suggesting you do so?"

He had, but ignored the missive. They'd parted amicably before he left for Matthew's country house party, and he intended to keep things that way—amicable, and parted.

"I only arrived in Town this afternoon and didn't get all the way through the mountain of correspondence awaiting me," he replied, assuaging his conscience by reminding himself that it was the truth.

"Are you enjoying yourself?"

"Very much. Your parties are always entertaining." His gaze flicked over Kimberly's shoulder and he tensed. Carolyn was still smiling at the pirate, who was handing her a glass of champagne. Bloody hell, prodding the bastard along at sword point might be too subtle. Perhaps hanging him from the yardarm would be better.

"I'm glad." Kimberly leaned a bit closer and he caught a whiff of her exotic scent. Her hand discreetly brushed across his thigh and his attention snapped back to her. Through her mask, her emerald eyes glittered with sultry invitation. "I can think of something else you'd find entertaining."

He forced a smile and bit back his impatience. Perhaps at some other time or place he might have taken her up on her offer, but he simply wasn't interested. Still, he had no wish to offend her. Indeed, he prided himself on remaining on friendly terms with his former lovers.

He bowed over her hand then gave her a quick smile. "I'm certain you could think of several dozen entertaining things, but I wouldn't dream of depriving your other guests of your attention. Give my regards to his grace," he added, referring to the Duke of Heaton, the man rumored to be her latest paramour, and one reputed to be extremely generous with his lovers. No doubt Kimberly would garner a number of expensive baubles from *that* liaison.

Someone else claimed Kimberly's attention, and Daniel took the opportunity to melt into the crowd. He headed directly toward Carolyn and the soon to be rousted pirate. Strains of music drifted over the cacophony of voices and laughter as he made his way through the crush. He lost sight of the couple for several seconds and paused. The crowd in front of him shifted and his hands clenched. That bloody pirate was leaning close, as if whispering in her ear.

And she was bloody well laughing at whatever he was saying!

It required every ounce of his control not to shove people aside and stalk over there. To make like his highwayman costume suggested and steal away with her.

"You look as if you just bit into a lemon," said a familiar, amused voice beside him.

Turning, he found himself the subject of a costumed Romeo's perusal. "This is supposed to be a bloody costume party," Daniel muttered, his voice laced with the irritation rippling through him. "How is it that everyone recognizes me so easily?"

"I wouldn't have known you at all," Matthew-as-Romeo said, "except for two things."

"Which are?"

"One, you told me you intended to dress as a highwayman—rather a dead giveaway, that."

"Yes, I suppose," Daniel murmured, his attention firmly fixed on the laughing couple standing at the edge of the dance floor.

"And second, the icy glare you're shooting at Logan Jennsen made it clear. I must say, as much as I appreciate your enmity toward him on my behalf, it is no longer necessary. Now that Sarah and I are married, he wouldn't dare look at *my wife* with a lustful gleam in his eye. In fact, I'm considering a business venture with him."

Daniel slowly turned his head to stare at his friend. "That pirate is Logan Jennsen?" he asked slowly, in a low voice that even to his own ears resembled a growl. He didn't care if Jennsen *had* saved him a great deal of money by advising him against an investment that had ultimately proved unsound. In spite of Jennsen's financial acumen, before this moment he hadn't particularly liked the brash, wealthy American who seemed to turn up at every social function. As of now, however, he most particularly *dis*liked the man.

Matthew Romeo raised his brows. "Are you saying you didn't know?" He looked toward the pirate then stilled. He slowly turned back to Daniel. "No."

"No what?"

Matthew's lips pressed into a thin line and he jerked his head toward the corner. Muttering an oath, Daniel followed his friend to the less crowded area.

Lowering his voice so they couldn't be overheard, Daniel repeated, "No what?"

"If you didn't know that was Jennsen, that can only mean you were simply staring daggers at whoever was conversing with Carolyn."

Daniel didn't bother to pretend he didn't know the goddess's identity and met Matthew's gaze straight on. "What of it?"

"Damn it, I suspected something of the sort at my house party, but I was so involved in my own affairs I didn't pay much attention." Matthew blew out a long breath. "She's not the right woman for you, Daniel."

Again he didn't pretend to misunderstand. "Perhaps I'm looking for the wrong woman."

"She's not the type you usually . . . consort with."

"And what type is that?"

"The jaded, bored sort. The sort who wanders from one liaison to the next." He lowered his voice further. "She's a decent woman."

A combination of irritation and hurt rippled through Daniel. "Are you insinuating I'm not a decent man?"

"Of course not. Actually, you're a much better man than you give yourself credit for. But when it comes to women, you're . . ."

"Fond of shallow, short-term liaisons based solely on physical pleasure?" he provided helpfully when Matthew seemed at a loss for words.

"Precisely. And so long as that makes you and your partner happy, it's perfectly acceptable. However, it is not the sort of arrangement that would make Carolyn happy."

"Perhaps we should leave that for *her* to decide."

Matthew studied him for several seconds then said quietly, "She's Sarah's sister and I don't want her hurt."

"What makes you think I'd hurt her? The only way a person can be hurt is if their heart is involved. She's made it abundantly clear her heart belongs to her dead husband."

"Then why bother?"

Daniel shook his head. "Obviously your marriage has cast everything you see with a rosy glow. This situation with Carolyn offers the best of everything—an affair with a woman I need not worry will attach herself to me like a bothersome burr, yet there's no actual living man to take it into his head to challenge me to pistols at dawn." He watched her and Jennsen tap the rims of their champagne flutes and an unpleasant sensation that felt exactly like jealousy seared him. "We'll be discreet and no one will get hurt." Except, perhaps, for that pirate bastard Jennsen. Yes, *he* might find himself in the privet hedges. Head first. Or walking the plank. Into shark-infested waters.

"She's agreed to this arrangement?" There was no missing the surprise in Matthew's voice.

"No. Not yet."

"I thought not. I hate to be the one to break this to you, but I think you're in for a disappointment. In fact, I'm certain of it. From everything Sarah has told me, coupled with all I've observed, Carolyn is not the sort of woman to engage in a casual, torrid affair. There are dozens of other women who would welcome your attentions."

"At the risk of sounding conceited, there are. As you well know—or at least you did before you wrapped the matrimonial noose about your neck— being pursued by women comes with the territory of being titled, wealthy, and not hideous in appearance. Actually, being titled is really the only requirement. The other two are merely whipped cream on top of an already frosted cake."

"I always look forward to the cynical pearls of wisdom you cast before me."

"Any cynicism I possess is founded upon unvarnished truth gleaned from acute observations of human nature. And clearly someone needs to drag you down to earth." He shot his friend a speculative look. "Good God, you're practically . . . glowing."

"That's called happiness."

"How leg-shackling yourself to the same woman for all eternity could induce any sensations other than dyspepsia and nausea is beyond me."

"You say that because you haven't met the right woman."

"Of course I have. Many times."

"By right I mean a woman with whom you can share your life—not just your bed."

"Ah. Obviously our definitions of 'right' differ greatly."

"As recently as a few short months ago I might have agreed with you, but no longer. You'll feel differently after you fall in love."

"Are you foxed?"

"Not a bit."

Daniel shook his head. "My dear bedazzled, bamboozled, besotted friend—just because you plunged into the sticky quagmire that is love doesn't mean I plan to succumb."

"Ah, but that is where you shall meet your nemesis, because as I discovered, falling arse over backwards in love isn't something you can plan—or not plan. It just . . . happens."

"Perhaps to you. I, on the other hand, am extremely adept at sidestepping all manner of unpleasantness."

"Including sticky, messy emotions."

"Absolutely. If you'd kept your head about you, you'd still be an eligible man about town."

"Yes. And I'd be missing out on sharing my days and nights with the most amazing woman I've ever met."

"And where, pray tell, is your amazing woman? Why is she not keeping you occupied so you don't torment me?"

"She is chatting with Lady Emily and Lady Julianne, no doubt concocting some scheme or another."

"My sympathies."

"On the contrary, I find Sarah's schemes most entertaining. Especially one she mentioned to me this morning."

"And what is that?" Daniel asked without much interest.

"It concerns a note she wishes to receive from me, one that simply states a time and place."

"Good God, women request the most ridiculous things. For what possible reason would she want such a missive?"

"So we can meet at the appointed time and place, where I'll . . . remind her how glad she is to be my wife."

That got Daniel's attention, and he turned toward his friend. "Intriguing. Wherever did she get such an idea?"

"Some book she recently read which is apparently very popular with the ladies. A note of that sort was mentioned in the story and is now all the rage."

Daniel returned his gaze to Carolyn then said in his blandest tone, "Perhaps your wife suggested this little game because she's grown bored."

"I doubt it. I keep her quite busy. You, on the other hand . . ." He made *tsking* noises.

"What?"

"Do you even know *how* to seduce a woman?"

Daniel swiveled his attention back toward his friend then leaned forward and sniffed. "How is it that you don't reek of brandy?"

"I told you, I'm not foxed. On the contrary, I'm perfectly sober, and perfectly serious. Obviously you're experienced in the bedchamber, but have you ever had to actually work to get a woman there? From what I can tell, you've never needed to expend more effort than to crook your finger toward a female to entice her to do your bidding. One look at your exceptionally handsome visage, your devastating smile, and they fall at your feet like raindrops."

Daniel blinked, nonplussed. Bloody hell. Of course he'd had to charm and convince women to become his lover. Surely he had. Of course he'd been the instigator. Many times. Exactly when, he couldn't quite recall at the moment, but that didn't mean he hadn't.

Shooting his friend a glare, he said, "Why I converse with you remains a mystery, as I already have two annoying younger brothers."

Rather than looking abashed, Matthew grinned. "Neither of them possess my charm. Besides, you've clearly forgotten that I'm older than you."

"By a fortnight."

"Admittedly a narrow margin, but one that renders me older nonetheless. Which would actually cast *you* in the role of the annoying younger brother. Lucky for you I've always considered you a sibling."

"Yes, lucky is precisely what I'm feeling right now. As to your question, of course I know how to seduce a woman. And as soon as I manage to shake loose of you, I intend to get on with it."

"I don't believe I've ever seen you quite so undone." Matthew chuckled and clamped a hand on his shoulder. "You know, it's going to give me a great deal of pleasure to someday say 'I told you so' while watching you slip into the sticky quagmire."

"Absolutely, positively, not going to happen."

"Hmmm. Isn't there some saying about pride going before a fall?"

"Yes, but it doesn't have any bearing on this situation."

Matthew smirked. "I disagree. Care to make it interesting?"

Daniel narrowed his eyes. "How interesting?"

"Twenty pounds says you'll be betrothed by the end of the year."

Daniel stared, struck momentarily mute with amazement. Then he threw back his head and laughed. "Oh, by all means. Only please let's make it fifty pounds."

"Very well. Fifty pounds."

Daniel grinned, held out his hand, and they shook on it. "This is going to be like taking a sweet from a child."

Amusement glittered in Matthew's eyes. "Clearly you've never actually attempted to take a sweet from a child. I wish you luck."

"That fifty pounds is as good as mine already."

"We shall see. Now, if you'll excuse me, I'm going to ask my wife to dance."

Chuckling, Matthew moved off. Daniel turned toward Carolyn and Jennsen, but before he could take a step, a costumed Julius Caesar blocked his path.

"I heard you'd be garbed as a highwayman, Surbrooke," said a familiar male voice in a slurred undertone that hinted of bitterness. "How appropriate, considering all you stole from me."

Daniel resisted the urge to step back from the brandy fumes that pelted him with Lord Tolliver's every word. He'd heard the earl had taken to drinking heavily since his shipping venture failed, and clearly those rumors were true. "I've no idea what you're talking about, Tolliver."

"Of course you do. Been told you had a meeting with that bastard Jennsen just before you pulled out of our deal. I'd wager he's the one who told you not to invest with me."

"My decision was my own. And a wise one, as it turns out."

Tolliver's eyes narrowed behind his mask. "I know you, Surbrooke. Know *all* about you. You'll be sorry."

Daniel shot him a cold glare. "Blackmail and threats don't become you. Although you're so foxed you most likely won't even remember this unfortunate exchange. God knows I intend to forget it."

Without another word, he moved away from Tolliver. He could feel the earl's stare boring into his back, but Tolliver made no move to follow him. Daniel's attention returned to Carolyn and Jennsen, who stood less than twenty feet away. Determined not to be waylaid again, he headed toward the woman who'd ignited his fantasies for far too long.

Let the seduction begin.

Chapter 3

His seduction began with the simplest of words: "Good evening, my lady." By the end of the evening my appetite had been well and truly whetted. And thus commenced what would prove to be my complete and utter capitulation. . .

Memoirs of a Mistress by An Anonymous Lady

Carolyn stood near the edge of the dance floor with the dashing pirate. She'd recognized Logan Jennsen by his distinctive American accent the instant he spoke to her, and now she couldn't help but laugh at his disgruntled words and expression about donning a costume.

"Utterly ridiculous," he said, shaking his head and waving his hand to encompass his pirate garb, complete with tall boots, rakish hat, and a long black cape. "Wouldn't be caught dead wearing something like this in America."

"It could be worse," she replied in an undertone, nodding toward a rotund frog passing in front of them.

He tossed back a generous swallow of his champagne. "Good God." He turned toward her, and she felt the weight of his regard. "You, however, are stunning, Lady Wingate. Indeed, seeing you looking so lovely is about the only thing making this soiree bearable."

Carolyn blinked at his use of her name. "Thank you, Mr. Jennsen."

He winced. "I suppose my American accent gave me away?"

She smiled. "I'm afraid so. But I have no such accent. How did you guess my identity? I believed myself quite unrecognizable."

"Oh, you absolutely are. If your sister hadn't told me what you were wearing, I never would have known this exquisite creature was you."

"Because I normally look so *un*exquisite?" she teased.

"On the contrary, I've never seen you look anything less than stunning. However, you are normally less . . . uncovered." His gaze skimmed down her gown, which left one entire shoulder bare and hugged her body to her hips before falling in a straight column to the floor. There was no missing the appreciation in his eyes. "Your ensemble is extremely becoming."

Heat flooded her cheeks at his admiring assessment and compliment, followed by a sense of relief that he wouldn't have recognized her. She felt disconcertingly *bare* in her costume and had no wish for people to know that the normally demure Lady Wingate would don such a revealing outfit. Bother-ation, she should have dressed as a shepherdess. If she had, surely Mr. Jennsen would not be eyeing her in such a speculative manner. Although she couldn't deny the unexpected frisson of feminine satisfaction at his open admiration.

"Thank you, sir. And although you might not care for masquerades, you make an excellent pirate."

His eyes gleamed behind his mask. "Thank you. Perhaps because I've spent a fair amount of time on ships." He returned his attention to the swirling couples. "Forgive me for not asking you to dance, but I haven't yet learned the intricacies of your En-glish steps. I would only embarrass myself and bruise your toes."

"No need to apologize. Pirates are more renowned for their sea legs than their dance legs."

In truth, she'd been relieved to skip the dance. Despite her determination to move on with her life, she hadn't yet ventured onto a dance floor since Ed-ward's death, and she feared the first time she did so might prove emotionally draining. But she was enjoying Mr. Jennsen's company, as she had at Mat-thew's house party where she first met him. He was unpretentious, outspoken, and sprang from humble beginnings, as did she.

The first strains of a waltz lifted over the crowd, and Carolyn craned her neck, despairing of ever lo-cating her sister, Emily, or Julianne in the crush.

"You mentioned seeing my sister," she said. "Where was she?"

"I saw her outside, before I entered the house. A carriage bearing the Langston crest arrived just ahead of mine. If not for that, I wouldn't have recognized her, either." He smiled. "Although, the fact that Juliet wore spectacles over her mask was a rather broad clue."

Carolyn laughed. "I suppose so." Given his imposing height, she was about to ask Mr. Jennsen if he might be able to see a costumed Juliet, Ophelia, or an angel when a deep, masculine voice behind her said, "Good evening, my lady."

Although only four words had been spoken, the way her heart tripped over itself and a warm tingle skittered down her spine made her suspect they'd been said by Lord Surbrooke. She'd wondered if they would encounter each other this evening. Indeed, while searching the crowd for her sister and friends, she found herself examining the gentlemen as well, wondering which mask he might be hiding behind.

She turned, and realized that even if she hadn't known his voice, she would have known his eyes. Through a black mask that covered the entire upper half of his face, they gazed at her with the same heated intensity that stole the air from her lungs every time he looked at her. She'd have known his mouth as well. Not only because it was perfectly formed, the bottom lip slightly fuller than the upper, but because of how one corner tilted upward, skewing all that perfection with a hint of lopsidedness that shouldn't have been attractive but was. Annoyingly so.

Her gaze skimmed over his all black highwayman costume. He looked tall and dark and dangerous—as if prepared to abscond with whatever might take his fancy and the consequences be damned. A thrill she couldn't name raced through her.

"Rather than good evening, shouldn't you say, 'Stand and deliver'?" she retorted, proud that she sounded so calm when she suddenly felt anything but.

He made her a formal bow. "Of course. Although by 'Stand and deliver' I actually mean 'May I have this dance?'"

Carolyn hesitated, surprised at how much she wanted to accept his invitation. If this had been any occasion other than a masquerade, she most likely would have refused. She was well aware of Lord Surbrooke's reputation, and had no desire to say or do anything that might lead him to believe she would consider being his next conquest.

Of course, it was quite possible he didn't know who she was. Hadn't Mr. Jennsen stated he never would have recognized her? She gazed into Lord Surbrooke's eyes and detected only heat—not recognition. Surely a man with as many past mistresses as he was purported to have had looked at most women in such a manner. Most likely he was just attracted to her costume. Even more likely, she was the tenth woman he'd gazed upon so warmly and asked to dance this evening.

Still, the idea that they were completely anonymous ignited a strange thrill inside her. If she accepted his invitation for her first dance in the arms of a man who wasn't Edward, she could hide behind her mask.

Before she could reply, a large, warm hand cupped

her elbow. "Do you wish to dance with him, or would you prefer he go away?" Mr. Jennsen asked in a low voice close to her ear.

"I appreciate your concern, but I am well acquainted with him and believe I'll accept his invitation," she replied in an undertone. Then her lips twitched as she saw someone approaching. "Prepare yourself, Mr. Pirate. A damsel in distress is sailing toward your port side with a very interested gleam in her eye."

"Indeed? My favorite sort of wench. Do you know who she is?"

As the woman wore the slimmest of masks, Carolyn found her identity easy to discern. "Lady Crawford," she replied to Mr. Jennsen. "She is a widow and very beautiful."

"I'll leave you to your evening then, my lady." He made her a formal bow, nodded to the highwayman, then turned toward the costumed damsel.

Carolyn faced Lord Surbrooke. He was frowning at Mr. Jennsen's back, but quickly shifted his attention to her. Then he extended his elbow. "Shall we?"

She paused, assailed by doubt now that the moment was upon her. Torn between a sudden, nearly overwhelming need to run from the room, to return to the safety and security of her quiet existence, ensconced in her memories, and the equally strong desire to step from the shadows. *It's time to move on with your life*, her inner voice whispered. *You need to move on.*

"I don't bite," came the highwayman's amused voice. "At least not very often."

Her gaze settled on his lopsided grin, and for several seconds her lungs ceased to function. She shook herself from her brown study and smiled in return. "You merely pilfer and purloin."

"Only when the occasion calls for it. Tonight the occasion calls for waltzing . . . I hope." He lifted her hand and brushed his lips against the backs of her gloved fingers. "With the most beautiful woman in the room."

A heated tingle raced up Carolyn's arm, a reaction that simultaneously alarmed, annoyed, and intrigued her. It was ridiculous to feel flattered by the words of such a practiced rogue, yet a tiny, feminine part of her couldn't help but bask in the compliment. Drawing courage from both his open admiration and her anonymity, she inclined her head toward the swirling couples. "The waltz awaits us."

Once her feet touched the dance floor, she barely had time to draw a breath before she found herself drawn into strong arms and swept into the circling tide of dancers. She stumbled slightly, whether from the dance steps she hadn't attempted in so long or the shockingly unfamiliar sensation of being held in a man's arms again, she wasn't certain. But the highwayman held her securely and she regained her footing.

"Don't worry," he said softly, his warm breath brushing by her ear, shooting a pleasurable shiver down her spine. "I won't let you fall."

And with those words he swept her along, turning and spinning. The other dancers, the rest of the room, dissolved into a swirling blur of color that rotated around them. The only thing that remained clear was his masked face. His eyes, intent on hers. She felt utterly surrounded by him. And utterly exhilarated.

His long, strong fingers wrapped around hers, their warmth heating her even through the layers of both their gloves. His other hand, while resting in the exact correct position in the precise proper spot on her lower back, seemed to brand her skin. A breathless sensation seized her, and helpless to do otherwise, she simply allowed herself to be carried away. How could she have forgotten how much she loved dancing?

He led her expertly, effortlessly, and it seemed as if she were floating in the circle of his strong arms, her feet hovering several inches above the floor. A soaring, weightless, almost magical feeling raced through her and a breathless laugh escaped her. Conversation, laughter, and the music buzzed around them, but all of that faded into nothingness. All except him. The way his gaze never left hers. The movement of his muscled shoulder beneath her palm. The brush of his leg against her gown. How his slightly splayed fingers slowly stroked her spine as his palm pressed her just a tiny bit closer with every turn.

His clean scent invaded her senses, a pleasing combination of fresh linen and spicy soap that filled her with the unsettling, overwhelming desire to lean closer. To bury her face against his neck and breathe deeply.

Except that breathing deeply was proving a problem. Erratic puffs of air that coincided with her equally erratic heartbeat escaped her parted lips. A sense of pure elation, combined with a heady, heated awareness of him, infused her. She felt more alive than she had in three long years.

Lord Surbrooke drew her to a stop near the edge of

the dance floor, and to her chagrin she realized that the song had ended. How was it possible she hadn't noticed? For several seconds they both remained still, as if frozen in a posed, motionless dance, their gazes locked. The heat of his hands singed her and she couldn't move. Couldn't breathe. Could only stare. And feel . . . the sensation of him holding her. Her hand nestled in his. His palm resting against her back. His body close to hers.

The sound of polite applause broke through the trance into which she'd fallen, and he slowly released her. Snapping from her stupor, she dragged her gaze from Lord Surbrooke's to join in the clapping for the musicians.

"Would you care for a drink, lovely goddess?" his low, compelling voice asked close to her ear. "Or perhaps a turn around the terrace for some fresh air?"

Fresh air sounded not only very welcome but essential, although she suspected his presence would do nothing to help her breathlessness. The desire to go onto the terrace with him was so tempting it both stunned and unnerved her. Yet, why shouldn't she? They wouldn't be alone—surely other couples had ventured outdoors.

"Some fresh air sounds delightful," she murmured.

He extended his arm, and although she placed her fingertips very properly on the curve of his elbow, somehow nothing about this felt proper. Which was utterly ridiculous. There was nothing wrong with her talking to Lord Surbrooke. Dancing with him. Taking a bit of air with him. He was a . . . friend.

Still, an undercurrent of tension, of excitement, filled her, one she couldn't recall ever before experiencing. No doubt because of their costumes and the masks that hid their identities. She'd only attended one masquerade ball before tonight and it had been years ago, shortly after her wedding. So surely these unprecedented heated flutterings were merely the result of this new experience. Of course, it might also be because in *Memoirs of a Mistress* the author described a steamy encounter with her lover at a masque. An encounter that began with a waltz. One during which the author had felt a heightened sense of freedom due to her anonymity. . .

She pressed her lips together and frowned. Botheration, she never should have read that book. *You never should have read it half a dozen times,* her inner voice chastised.

Oh, very well, half a dozen times. At least. The blasted book had filled her head with questions she'd never be able to answer. And with sensual images that not only invaded her dreams but flashed through her mind with appalling frequency, suffusing her with an edgy, prickly sensation that made her clothing feel too tight and her skin feel as if it were about to burst, like an overripened fruit.

Exactly the way she felt right now.

She stole a quick glance at Lord Surbrooke. He appeared perfectly calm and collected, which served as a splash of cold water to her overheated skin. Clearly whatever was ailing her was affecting only her.

The instant they stepped outside, the chilly breeze slapped her to her senses. He led her to a quiet, shadowed corner of the terrace surrounded by a grouping of potted palms in huge porcelain vases. Several couples strolled around the small fenced garden, and a trio of gentlemen stood at the other end of the terrace. Otherwise they were alone, no doubt because of the unseasonably cool air, hinted with the scent of rain.

"Are you warm enough?" he asked.

Dear God, ensconced with him in the privacy provided by the potted palms, she felt as if she stood in the midst of a roaring fire. She nodded, then her gaze searched his. "Do . . . do you know who I am?"

His gaze slowly skimmed over her, lingering on the bare expanse of her shoulders and the curves she knew her ivory gown highlighted—skin and curves that her normal modest mode of dress never would have revealed. That openly admiring look, which still held no hint of recognition, reignited the heat the breeze had momentarily cooled. When their eyes once again met, he murmured, "You are Aphrodite, goddess of desire."

She relaxed a bit. He clearly didn't know who she was, for the way he'd said "desire," in that husky, gruff voice, was a tone Lord Surbrooke had never used with Lady Wingate. Yet her relaxation was short-lived as that desire-filled timbre pulsed a confusing tension through her, part of which warned her to leave the terrace at once. To return to the party and continue searching for her sister and friends. But another part—the part held enthralled by the darkly alluring highwayman and the protection of her anonymity—refused to move.

To add to her temptation was the fact that this anonymous interlude might afford her the opportunity to learn more about him. In spite of their numerous conversations during the course of Matthew's house

party, all she actually knew of Lord Surbrooke was
that he was intelligent and witty, impeccably polite,
unfailingly charming, and always perfectly groomed.
He'd never given her the slightest hint as to what
caused the shadows that lurked in his eyes. Yet she
knew they were there, and her curiosity was well and
truly piqued. Now, if she could only recall how to
breathe, she could perhaps discover his secrets.

After clearing her throat to locate her voice, she
said, "Actually, I am Galatea."

He nodded slowly, his gaze trailing over her.
"Galatea . . . the ivory statue of Aphrodite carved by
Pygmalion because of his desire for her. But why are
you not Aphrodite herself?"

"In truth, I thought costuming myself as such a bit
too . . . immodest. I'd actually planned to be a shepherdess. My sister somehow managed to convince
me to wear this instead." She gave a short laugh. "I
believe she coshed me over the head while I slept."

"Whatever she did, she should be roundly applauded for her efforts. You are . . . exquisite. More
so than Aphrodite herself."

His low voice spread over her like warm honey.
Still, she couldn't help but tease, "Says a thief whose
vision is impaired by darkness."

"I'm not really a thief. And my eyesight is perfect.
As for Aphrodite, she is a woman to be envied. She
had only one divine duty—to make love and inspire
others to do so as well."

His words, spoken in that deep, hypnotic timbre, combined with his steady regard, spiraled heat
through her and robbed her of speech. And reaffirmed her conclusion that he didn't know who she

was. Never once during all the conversations she'd shared with Lord Surbrooke had he ever spoken to her—Carolyn—of anything so suggestive. Nor had he employed that husky, intimate tone. Nor could she imagine him doing so. She wasn't the dazzling sort of woman to incite a man's passions, at least not a man in his position, who could have any woman he wanted, and according to rumor, did.

Emboldened by his words and her secret identity, she said, "Aphrodite was desired by all and had her choice of lovers."

"Yes. One of her favorites was Ares." He lifted his hand, and she noticed he'd removed his black gloves. Reaching out, he touched a single fingertip to her bare shoulder. Her breath caught at the whisper of contact then ceased altogether when he slowly dragged his finger along her collarbone. "Makes me wish I'd dressed as the god of war rather than a highwayman."

He lowered his hand to his side, and she had to press her lips together to contain the unexpected groan of protest that rose in her throat at the sudden absence of his touch. She braced her knees, stunned at how they'd weakened at that brief, feathery caress.

She swallowed to find her voice. "Aphrodite caught Ares with another lover."

"He was a fool. Any man lucky enough to have you wouldn't want any other."

"You mean Aphrodite."

"You *are* Aphrodite."

"Actually, I'm Galatea," she reminded him.

"Ah, yes. The statute Pygmalion fell so in love with was so lifelike he often laid his hand upon it to as-

sure himself whether his creation were alive or not."
He reached out and curled his warm fingers around
her bare upper arm, just above where her long satin
ivory glove ended. "Unlike Galatea, you are very
much real."

Her common sense coughed to life and demanded
she move away from him, but her feet refused to
obey. Instead she absorbed the stunning sensation of
his touch. The shocking intimacy when he slipped
one finger beneath the edge of her glove. Heat gushed
through her, rendering her mute.

"He showered her with gifts, you know," he said,
his glittering eyes studying her.

Carolyn managed a nod. "Yes. Brightly colored
shells and fresh picked flowers."

"Also jewels. Rings and necklaces. Strings of
pearls."

"I'd much prefer the shells and a flower."

"Than jewels?" There was no missing the surprise
in his voice. His fingers slipped from her arm, and
she had to clench her hand to keep from snatching
his and setting it back on her skin. "Surely you jest.
All women love jewels."

He sounded so positive, she couldn't help but
laugh. "Jewels are lovely, yes, but to me they lack
imagination and are impersonal. Anyone can visit
the jeweler and select a bauble. To me, a gift's value
is in how much thought went into selecting it as op-
posed to how much it cost."

"I see," he said, although he still sounded surprised. "So what would you have wanted Pygmalion
to bring you?"

She considered, then said, "Something that reminded him of me."

He smiled. "Perhaps diamonds and pearls did so."

She shook her head. "Something more . . . personal. I'd prefer flowers he picked from his own garden. A book from his own collection that he'd enjoyed. A letter or poem he'd written expressly for me."

"I must admit I never thought I'd hear a woman say she'd prefer a *letter* over diamonds. Not only are you exquisite, you're—"

"A candidate for Bedlam?" she teased. "Extremely odd?"

His teeth flashed, straight and white, accompanied by a low, deep chuckle. "I was going to say extremely *rare*. A breath of fresh air."

His gaze lowered to her mouth. Her lips tingled under his regard and involuntarily parted. A muscle ticked in his jaw and the air around them seemed to suddenly crackle with tension.

His gaze returned to hers, and even the dim light couldn't disguise the heat glittering in his eyes. "Speaking of letters," he said, "have you heard of this latest rage of ladies receiving notes that state only a time and place?"

Carolyn's brows shot upward. Clearly Lord Surbrooke had heard of the practice. An image flashed through her mind, of him and a woman who, dear God, looked exactly like her, engaged in a tryst, their bare limbs entwined—

She briefly squeezed her eyes shut to banish the unsettling picture then said, "I've heard of these notes, yes."

"Have you ever received one?"

"No. Have you ever sent one?"

"No, although I find the idea intriguing. Tell me, if you were to receive such a missive, would you go?"

She opened her mouth to emphatically state *of course not*, but to her surprise and chagrin found the words would not come. Instead she found herself saying, "I . . . I'm not certain."

And with a dismaying, unsettling clarity, she realized that she truly *wasn't* certain. Yet how could that be? It was as if she'd donned her goddess costume and become a different person. A person who would consider a secret rendezvous with an unknown admirer. What on earth was happening to her? And why would it be happening with this man? This charming, practiced, nobleman who was like so many of his peers—interested only in his own pleasures.

Botheration, clearly the *Memoirs* were to blame for filling her mind with these ridiculous thoughts and disturbing images. As soon as she returned home she'd toss the book into the fireplace and be rid of it.

Raising her chin, she asked, "Would *you* go?"

Instead of immediately answering yes as she would have expected, he considered for several seconds before replying, "I suppose it would depend on who sent me the note."

"But the entire point is that you don't know."

He shook his head. "I think you'd have at least an inkling of the sender's identity. A clue as to who desired you that much." He reached out and lightly clasped her hands. The heat of his palms seeped through her gloves, and she found herself wishing that no barrier separated their skin. "A desire that strong surely could not go unnoticed."

A reply . . . she needed to think of something, *anything,* to say, but instead all she could focus on was the word he'd just spoken, which kept reverberating through her mind.

Desire.

Before she could recover her usual aplomb, he said softly, "To answer your question, if *you* sent me such a note, I would go."

Silence engulfed them. Seconds passed, pulses of time that felt to her thick with tension and an almost painful awareness of him. Of everything about him. His commanding height. The breadth of his shoulders. The compelling intensity of his gaze. His scent, which seemed to intoxicate her. His touch against her hands.

His gaze flicked to her throat then returned to hers. Heat and mischief gleamed in his eyes. "I see you are not wearing any expensive baubles. That presents a bit of dilemma for a highwayman such as myself."

She swallowed and managed to dredge up her voice, no easy task with his fingers still wrapped warmly around hers. "You would steal from me?"

"I must live up to my costume, I'm afraid."

"You said you weren't a thief."

"Normally I'm not. But in this case I fear it cannot be helped." He glanced down at his black attire and heaved a dramatic sigh. "Here I am, all dressed up in my mask and cape, yet without a diamond in sight."

Amused in spite of herself, Carolyn said, "I must confess, I'm not overly fond of diamonds."

"I must confess that's something I've never heard

any woman say." He flashed a wicked grin. "You realize we've just exchanged midnight confessions. And you know what they say about those."

"I'm afraid I don't."

He leaned a bit closer and her pulse jumped. "They say that they're dangerous—but in the very best of ways."

Carolyn suddenly realized that this interlude was a perfect example of "dangerous in the very best of ways."

"The women in the ballroom are adorned with more baubles than you could possibly carry away," she pointed out.

"I've no interest in any woman other than you, my lady."

His words whispered over her, heating her, exciting her. In a way that both distressed and secretly thrilled her.

"I have no jewels," she whispered.

"You are the jewel. Still, in the absence of any diamonds or pearls, I am forced to improvise and will therefore steal . . ." He took a step closer, then another, until only a mere ribbon of space separated them. " . . . a kiss."

Before she could react, before she could so much as blink or draw a breath, he bent his head. And slowly brushed his lips over hers.

On the outside, her body went perfectly still. But on the inside . . . inside, it felt as if everything shifted and changed speed. Her stomach swooped downward, her heart stumbled then quickened its pace. Her blood seemed to thicken, yet somehow run faster through her veins. And her pulse . . . she felt it everywhere. In her temples. At the base of her throat. The folds between her thighs.

He lifted his head and their gazes met. No trace of amusement remained in his eyes. Instead they seemed to burn like twin braziers, igniting an ache, a yearning in her she hadn't felt in so long she barely recognized it.

He studied her for several seconds, then, with a low growling sound, he yanked her into his arms and slanted his mouth over hers. Her lips parted, whether from desire or surprise or both, and everything instantly faded into insignificance—except him.

Heat seemed to pump from his body. He was so incredibly, lusciously warm. Wrapped in his strong arms was like being enveloped in a fire-warmed blanket. His clean, masculine scent filled her senses, weakening her knees with a delightful sensation of light-headedness, one that encouraged her to skim her hands up his broad chest, to wind her arms around his neck and hold on tight.

And thank goodness she did because the first bold stroke of his tongue against hers turned her bones to porridge. A groan rose in her throat, half shock, half heated desire, and she pressed herself closer, absorbing every nuance of his passionate onslaught.

The darkly delicious taste of his mouth. The strength of his one arm that kept her firmly anchored against him—most welcome, as she otherwise would have slithered to the flagstones. The heat of his other hand as it slowly ran up and down her back, as if trying to learn every inch of her. The solid wall of his chest flattening her breasts. The unmistakable jut of his arousal pressing against her abdomen.

Desire, so long forgotten, sizzled through her, a bolt of lightning that ignited her skin. She opened her mouth wider beneath his, mating her tongue with his, desperate to know more of his taste, his touch. Her fingers tunneled through the hair at his nape and she cursed the gloves that prevented her from feeling the thick, silky texture.

And then, as suddenly as it began, he lifted his head, ending their kiss. This time there was no stopping her moan of protest. With a great effort she dragged her eyes open.

He stared at her, his breaths as rapid and erratic as her own, his eyes as glazed as she knew hers must be.

Lifting one hand, he gently cupped her face. "I knew it would be like that," he said in an unsteady whisper.

His voice penetrated the sensual fog engulfing her, and the reality of where she was—*who* she was—smacked her like a cold, wet rag. With a gasp she stepped back, out of his grasp. Her shaking fingers flew to her mouth, whether to wipe away Lord Surbrooke's kiss or to seal it to her lips, she didn't know.

Dear God, what had come over her? What had she done?

I'll tell you what you've done. Her inner voice dripped with condemnation. *You've tarnished Edward's memory.*

A cry of distress rose in her throat and she clamped her lips together to contain it. She desperately tried to recall the tender wonder of Edward's kiss, but it remained elusive and out of reach. How could she, when the taste of another man remained on her lips? When she still felt the imprint of his hard body pressed against her? When her mind, her senses, were still too inundated with the tempestuous, passionate kiss she'd just shared with—

A man who wasn't her husband.

A plethora of emotions, led by confusion, guilt, and shame, bombarded her, followed by the overwhelming need to escape. "I . . . I must go," she said, sounding as stricken as she felt.

"Wait." He reached for her, but she shook her head and backed away.

"No. I . . . please, let me leave."

Without waiting for his response, she darted around him and swiftly made her way back into the party, where she was immediately swallowed by the crowd. She didn't pause to search for her sister or friends, but hurried to the foyer, where she requested her carriage. The five minute wait felt like an eternity, one she spent in a nearby shadowed alcove with her hands pressed to her churning midriff.

The instant she was ensconced in the dark interior of her carriage, she covered her face with her hands, and the sob she'd managed to swallow until then broke from her throat.

What had she done? *How* could she have allowed that to happen?

Everything inside her cried out and reached for the memory of Edward she carried in her heart, of his gentle smile and tender touch, of the sweet love they'd shared. But the beloved memories proved elusive. Instead, all she could envision was a devilish highwayman with intense eyes and a captivating mouth who had weakened her knees. Despite her determination to move on with her life, she hadn't anticipated anything like *this*. Hadn't expected this overwhelming flood of unexpected passion.

Yet there was no denying it, and again she cursed her reading of the *Memoirs,* which had set her on this ruinous sensual path. So the question remained: What did she intend to do about it?

Chapter 4

Everything about him rendered me breathless. He could seduce me with a mere look, a single touch. His hands, with those long, strong, clever fingers, were nothing short of magical. And his lips . . . the things he could do with that lovely mouth were positively sinful.

Memoirs of a Mistress by An Anonymous Lady

The morning after the masquerade, Daniel sat in his dining room and stared at his uneaten breakfast. His head pounded from a combination of lack of sleep and too much brandy, both of which had proven spectacularly unhelpful in veering his thoughts away from his interlude with Carolyn.

With a groan, he tipped back his head and squeezed his eyes shut. A mistake as far as forgetting her was concerned for she instantly materialized in his mind's eye. An alluring masked goddess who'd fit in his arms as if she were fashioned exclusively for him. Never in his life had he found a waltz so arousing. Her exhilaration, her smile and sense of wonder as they'd circled the floor . . . he couldn't have taken his eyes from her if his very life had depended upon it. She'd utterly captivated him. And without even trying. What the bloody hell would happen to him should she put some effort into it?

He blew out a long sigh, opened his eyes, and reached for his coffee. Damn it, he knew exactly what would happen. He'd lose control, just as he had in the garden.

Bloody hell. He'd meant to simply give her a teasing kiss. A light brush of his lips over hers. A tantalizing taste to make her want more. But the instant his mouth touched hers, his finesse vanished, replaced by a hunger so primal, so deep, so completely overwhelming, he'd been helpless to stem the onslaught. He *never* lost control like that. He'd desired many women, but never once had one of them shattered his command over himself.

Indeed, it was nothing short of a miracle that he'd managed to stop himself from pressing her against the wall, lifting her skirts, and satisfying the unstoppable craving she inspired. He knew, in his heart, that if they'd been somewhere that afforded them a modicum of privacy, he would have given in to the temptation. And given her heated response to their kiss, he didn't doubt she would have allowed it. Welcomed it. She'd felt the same desperate need, the same hot, sharp stab of desire as he. He'd tasted it in every nuance of her kiss. Felt it with every shudder and quiver that had trembled through her.

He'd expected her to affect him strongly, but never, not even in one of his numerous fantasies about her, had he ever anticipated the impact of that single kiss. He'd intended to seduce her slowly. Obviously their encounter, as well as her ardent response, had caught her equally as off guard, because he knew she wasn't the sort of woman to welcome overt advances. Or a quick grope in the garden. No, that certainly wasn't the way to tempt her. Unfortunately, that's precisely what he'd done, and had accomplished nothing save frightening her off. The profound distress in her eyes when she left the terrace was a look he wouldn't soon forget.

Daniel took a deep swallow of his now lukewarm coffee and asked himself the disturbing question that had circled through his mind the entire sleepless night.

Did she know who she'd been with?

Had she known *he* was the highwayman? Known that the man she'd kissed so hungrily, had responded to so passionately, was him?

Deep, dark satisfaction filled him at the thought that she'd known, was fully aware of whose arms held her. Whose lips kissed her. The notion that she hadn't known, however, all but seared him with white hot jealousy—an ugly emotion he rarely experienced, yet its intensity left no doubt as to what it was. The only woman who'd ever inspired the feeling in him was . . . her. Certainly Society was filled with men who were wealthier, more handsome, luckier at the faro tables, had more lovers than he—all of which could inspire jealousy. Yet the only man he had ever truly been jealous of was Edward. And only then because of Carolyn.

Surely she'd known it was he behind the highwayman's mask. Hadn't she? The thought of her kissing another man the way she'd kissed him . . . bloody hell, it made his blood boil beneath his skin to even consider it.

Well, if she didn't know, he intended to see to it that she did. As soon as the hour was more appropriate and this damnable headache abated, he would call on her. And tell her. And allay the concerns that had caused her to flee last night. Whether she cared to admit it or not, she was clearly ripe for an affair, and he had no intention of allowing another man to claim what he wanted.

He lowered his coffee cup and rested his aching head in his hands. Another mistake, as the image that had bedeviled him ever since she left him on that terrace slammed into his mind once again . . . the conclusion of their heated interlude. Her skirts ruched up, her legs wrapped around his waist. His erection buried in her tight, wet heat. Slow, hard thrusts that quickened, deepened, propelling them both over the edge—

A guttural sound rattled in his throat and he shifted in his seat to relieve the growing discomfort in his breeches. Damn it, just what he didn't need—another throbbing ache.

"'Ere ye go, milord." The familiar male voice from directly beside him startled Daniel from his erotic brown study. Samuel, impeccably turned out in his footman's livery, set a tall glass on the mahogany table in front of him. "Nothin' worse than the mornin' after a night spent swillin' blue ruin."

Daniel cast a suspicious eye toward the mud-colored concoction in the glass. "It was brandy, not gin."

"Whichever hogwash ye drank, this'll set ye back to rights."

Daniel frowned at the strapping young man. "Hardly hogwash. This particular brandy was over one hundred years old."

"Still made yer head hurt," Samuel said in his matter-of-fact way that surely should have irked Daniel. He pointed a white-gloved hand at the glass. "Drink," he ordered, as if he were the lord of the house and Daniel the footman. "The sooner ye do so, the sooner ye'll feel better and pinken up. 'Tis a bit pasty yer lookin', milord." At Daniel's scowl, Samuel quickly added, "Beggin' yer pardon for sayin' so."

Bloody hell, he absolutely needed to do something about Samuel's penchant for speaking out of turn. "You should beg my pardon," Daniel grumbled. "You're far too cheeky for your own good."

"Ain't cheeky to tell the truth," Samuel said, his countenance and tone perfectly serious. "I promised I'd never lie to ye, and I won't. Always the brutal truth is what ye'll git from me, milord."

"Thank you, although I think we need to work on making it a bit less brutal." He shot the glass a doubtful look. "What is that?"

"Recipe I learned from the barkeep at a pub in Leeds called the Slaughtered Pig. Weevil were his name. Used to call him Evil Weevil."

"How delightful. However, I made it a rule long ago to not drink things inspired by people named Evil."

"Oh, Evil knew wot he was about, milord," Samuel said in that same serious tone. "You drink that and in twenty minutes you'll be glad ye did. Folks at the Slaughtered Pig swore by it."

"Well, with a recommendation like that, how can I refuse?" Daniel murmured. He picked up the glass then shrugged. Why not? He'd be hard pressed to feel much worse. He took a swallow. And barely refrained from spewing the mouthful across the table.

"Good God," he managed to croak as a shudder ran through him. The look he treated Samuel to should have skewered the lad to the floor. "I've never tasted anything so vile."

"Never said it tasted good," Samuel said, annoyingly impervious to the skewering look. "Suck it right down, milord, all at once."

Not convinced that the cure wasn't going to kill him, Daniel drank the entire contents, then set down the glass with enough force to shatter the crystal. "*Blech.*"

"Ye'll be sayin' 'thank ye' in less than twenty minutes."

"Excellent. However, I intend to say '*blech*' until then."

Samuel shot him an unrepentant grin. "A fresh cup of coffee for ye, milord?"

"Please. Anything that might help chase the *blech* away."

Daniel watched the young man move toward the sideboard, and the area around his heart squeezed with pride. Samuel was certainly not the same destitute, desperate, and physically ill footpad he'd met a year ago on a cold, rainy night in Bristol when the lad tried to rob him. He had easily foiled the attempt, so easily he'd at first thought his assailant, who could barely stand, was intoxicated. But when the young man collapsed at his feet, Daniel realized that in addition to being filthy and dressed in rags, his assailant was burning up with fever. And looked as if he hadn't had a decent meal in months.

Sympathy and whispers from the past he'd refused to acknowledge shoved aside his annoyance at being targeted, and instead of turning the ill young man over to the authorities, Daniel carried him back to the inn where he was staying and summoned a doctor.

The lad hovered between life and death for three days, murmuring in his delirium of abuses he'd apparently suffered, things Daniel prayed hadn't actually occurred. On the fourth day his fever finally broke and Daniel found himself being studied through the narrowed eyes of a weak but lucid patient who, after a bit of coaxing, identified himself as Samuel Travers, age seventeen. It required a great deal of convincing to assure the lad that he meant him no harm, did not plan to turn him over to the authorities, and harbored no designs on him. The assurances Samuel needed convinced Daniel that, sadly, the nightmarish scenario the lad had alluded to during his feverish rantings had indeed happened.

At first Samuel refused to believe that Daniel had helped him "just fer the hell of it" with nothing to gain for himself, but over the course of the next several days he slowly came to accept it as the truth. While Samuel rested and ate and regained his strength, they shared stories of their lives, and a tentative trust was forged between them. Samuel told Daniel of his mother's death when he was five, leaving him with no one save a drunkard uncle to look after him. Of never having a true home after his mother died. Of being forced to steal in order to eat. Of moving from town to town to avoid the law. Of finally running away at the age of twelve and doing his best to fend for himself.

Although their childhoods were vastly different, Samuel's stories brought back a barrage of memories Daniel kept carefully and firmly buried. Of his own mother's death when he was eight, and the painful aftermath. Memories he'd never shared with anyone and couldn't bring himself to reveal to Samuel. But the fact that they'd both lost their mothers was a small bit of common ground upon which they built.

As a result of their conversations, Daniel found himself taking a long, contemplative look at his own life. And not liking what he saw, especially when he realized that a mere accident of birth was all that separated him—a wealthy aristocrat who possessed every creature comfort—from Samuel, a young man who'd been reduced to living by his wits, begging and stealing just to survive.

Daniel's introspection culminated in him finally recognizing that the vague feeling of discontent that had plagued him over the past several years was a sense of ennui, of apathy. Nothing seemed a challenge anymore. Nothing truly captured his interest, although how could it when he had everything he could possibly want? Yet what was he doing with his largess?

Nothing, he realized with no small amount of shame. Nothing save frittering away his time and money on transitory pleasures and shallow pursuits. Not that he had any intention of giving those up, but inspired by Samuel, he decided it was time he put some of his money and time to better use. Toward that end, he offered Samuel a job as a footman, with the stipulation that if Samuel ever again tried to rob him—or anyone else—he would toss him out. Samuel accepted the opportunity, and over the course of the past year had proven himself hardworking, reliable, intelligent, and, as Daniel quickly discovered, brutally honest. And painfully outspoken.

Samuel didn't grasp the normal rigid formality that existed between the master of the house and a footman. Daniel occasionally corrected him, but truth be known, he found their verbal exchanges both enlightening and diverting. He especially enjoyed the way Samuel, while always respectful, never kowtowed to him, a truly refreshing change. Thanks to his title and position in Society, he was normally surrounded by sycophants. He certainly couldn't accuse Samuel of ever saying something simply because he believed it was what Daniel wanted to hear.

In moments of unpainted self-honesty, Daniel had to admit that his unusually informal relationship with Samuel was the result of his own reluctance to curb the young man's outspokenness. In a most surprising turn of events, he'd come to look upon him almost as a younger brother. Certainly he felt closer to Samuel than he did to Stuart and George. Neither of his two dissolute younger half brothers had any use for him—unless they needed money or assistance in getting out of some scrape or another.

No, since Samuel's arrival, Daniel could no longer claim his life was boring or lacked challenge. Indeed, things around the town house—as well as his country estate in Kent—more often than not bordered on disorder, thanks to a habit of Samuel's Daniel hadn't anticipated.

As if the mere thought of Samuel's habit conjured up a physical reminder, Daniel was yanked from his reverie when a ball of pure black fluff jumped onto his lap. He looked down and found himself the object of a one-eyed feline stare.

"Ah, good morning, Blinky," he murmured, scratching the cat behind her ears. Blinky immediately narrowed her one topaz-colored eye and leaned into Daniel's touch. A deep purr vibrated in the animal's throat and she kneaded Daniel's linen napkin with her front paws.

Samuel set Daniel's coffee on the table in front of him, after which he gave Blinky's head a quick pat. Then the footman straightened and cleared this throat.

Uh-oh. Daniel pressed his lips together to contain the half groan, half laugh that threatened to escape. He knew what that throat clearing meant. Knew that *Ye'll never guess wot, milord* would be the next words spoken.

"Ye'll never guess wot, milord," Samuel said, as if cued to do so.

It had taken a bit of getting used to, hearing those words, coming to know what they meant, having his normal routine disrupted. But he couldn't deny that he now anticipated that sentence from Samuel. Of course, he dared not show *too* much enthusiasm, lest his entire household be overrun.

Daniel stared down at Blinky, whose one-eyed, nose-twitching interest was currently fixated on his untouched plate of eggs and bacon. "I can't imagine," he said blandly, as if after a year with Samuel in his employ, he didn't know damn well "wot."

"'Tis a *puppy*, milord." Samuel said the word *puppy* with a hushed reverence normally reserved for members of the royal family. "'Bout six months old, I'd guess."

"I see," Daniel said with a somber nod. "And what malady has stricken the animal?"

"Abandoned, milord. Found 'im, last night, half starved, huddled behind some trash in an alley."

Daniel no longer admonished Samuel about roaming London's dark alleys, as he knew his warnings would fall on deaf ears. Nor was he concerned that Samuel was relieving anyone of their purses. No, his footman was looking for another sort of victim.

"And what do you suggest we call this abandoned canine?" Daniel asked, knowing the name would give a true clue as to the animal's . . . problem.

"Baldy, milord," Samuel said without hesitation.

Daniel considered the ramifications of that while breaking off a bit of bacon for Blinky. The cat gobbled up the morsel then promptly batted at his hand and yowled for another. "Shaved?" Daniel finally guessed.

Samuel nodded. "Had to, milord. To get rid o' the matted hair and fleas."

"Ah." Blinky yowled again, and Daniel absently fed the impatient beast another bit of bacon. "And where is Baldy now?"

"In the kitchens, milord. Asleep. After I shaved and bathed 'im, Cook fed 'im good. Then the wee beastie curled up by the hearth. Probably sleep most of the day, I'd wager."

"Who? Cook?" Daniel deadpanned.

"Baldy, milord." Samuel hesitated, then asked, "So . . . can we keep 'im?"

It never failed to amaze Daniel that after all these months and all these animals, Samuel took nothing for granted and still asked. "I suppose we have room for one more 'wee beastie.'"

Samuel's broad shoulders, which only a year ago had been bony and narrow, sagged with obvious relief. "I were hopin' so, milord. I told Baldy wot ye'd done fer me, wot a fine, decent man ye are."

Bloody hell. A humbling wave of something that felt precisely like embarrassment swept through Daniel, and he found himself at a momentary loss for words, a state of affairs Samuel's gratitude always managed to reduce him to.

"A man shouldn't be praised for doing the right thing, Samuel. For simply helping an abandoned creature."

"Ye're wrong, milord," Samuel replied in his nonkowtowing manner. "Ye may think that kindness is easily found, but I'm tellin' ye, it ain't. And when yer lucky enough to find it, it needs to be recognized. 'Tis a good thing yer doin'. More so 'cause ye don't have to do it. And most likely will end up with more chewed furniture for yer trouble."

"It's actually *your* act of kindness, Samuel."

"'Tis true I find the lost and abandoned, milord, but 'tis you who has the means to help 'em. The means and the heart. I couldn't do nothin' if it weren't for you." His quick grin flashed. "Definitely not, as I'd be in the dirt, pushin' up petunias, that's where I'd be."

"Well, we couldn't have that," Daniel said, forcing a wry note into his voice. "Who else would disrupt my formerly well-ordered household with irreverent conduct and an assortment of mangy animals?"

"No one, milord," Samuel said without hesitation.

True. And that would be Daniel's very great loss.

"No one," he agreed with an exaggerated, put-upon sigh. He shot Blinky a wink. The cat responded with a one-eyed glare that she pointedly shifted from Daniel to the bacon.

Samuel smiled, showing off his slightly crooked front teeth. "How's yer headache, milord?"

"It's . . ." Daniel considered for several seconds, then huffed out a surprised laugh. "Gone."

"Hate to say 'I told ye so . . .'"

Daniel shot the young man a mock scowl. "No you don't. In fact, I believe that that is one of your favorite things to say."

"Glad ye're feelin' better, because . . ." Samuel cleared his throat. " . . . ye'll never guess wot, milord."

Daniel froze. Dear God, two *guess wots* in one day? Since Samuel tended to spring his *I've found us another stray* surprises according to size, Daniel knew that whatever was coming next was larger than a puppy.

"I can't imagine," he murmured, bracing himself

as he scratched Blinky behind her ears. "Horse? Donkey? Camel?"

Samuel blinked. "Camel?"

Daniel shrugged. "Merely a guess. Certainly if an orphaned dromedary wandered about London, you'd find it. And bring it here."

"Naturally, milord. But it's not a camel."

"My relief knows no bounds. Don't tell me. Baldy has five canine friends in tow?"

"No, milord. Far as I can tell, Baldy's all alone in the world. 'Cept fer us now, of course." Samuel cleared his throat, and Daniel noticed that he looked decidedly nervous. And that his skin had taken on a faint greenish cast that matched his livery, although not in a good way.

"It's that . . . ye've a visitor, milord. A Mr. Rayburn."

Daniel's brows shot upward. "Charles Rayburn? The magistrate?"

Samuel nodded. "Aye. He's awaitin' ye in the drawing room. With another bloke, called himself Gideon Mayne."

"I don't know anyone by that name."

"Bloke didn't say so, but I'd peg 'im as a Runner."

Daniel studied his obviously nervous, green-tinged footman. "When did they arrive?"

"'Bout half an hour ago. I were passin' by the foyer when Barkley were lettin' them in. Overheard who they were. After Barkley showed 'em into the drawing room, I offered to tell ye they were here, seein' as how I were comin' to the dinin' room."

"And you're just telling me now?" Good God, he

really needed to discuss Samuel's lack of propriety regarding his duties. He was fortunate he hadn't accidentally strolled into his drawing room three hours from now and discovered the magistrate and Runner still awaiting him.

Samuel shrugged. "We had other business to discuss first, and I wanted to get ye pinkened up before springin' the news that the law were here. Besides, can't say I minded the thought of them blokes waitin' on ye. As they should. Ye're an important man. God-awful hour for them to be disturbin' ye. Especially . . ."

"Especially what?"

Samuel swallowed, his Adam's apple bobbing. Several seconds passed, then he said in a rush, "Wot if they're here 'bout me?" Before Daniel could speak, Samuel rushed on, "I ain't done nothin', milord. I swear it. Upon me life. I promised ye I wouldn't steal and I haven't."

"I don't doubt you, Samuel."

That seemed to calm Samuel a bit, and he jerked his head in a nod. "Thank ye."

"I'm sure whatever they want has nothing to do with you. And if it does, it's obviously a misunderstanding that we'll work out."

Fear clouded Samuel's dark eyes, a look Daniel hadn't seen in many months. One he hated seeing now. "But wot if it's about somethin' I stole before? Before ye helped me? Wot if they want to take me away—"

"No one is taking anyone anywhere," Daniel said firmly. He gently set Blinky on the floor then rose. "I'll go see what they want."

"Ye'll tell me wot it is?" Samuel asked in an unsteady voice. "As soon as they leave?"

He clamped his hand on Samuel's shoulder. "As soon as they leave. Don't worry. I'm sure it's nothing."

He strode toward the drawing room, praying he was right. And knowing he'd protect Samuel with whatever resources necessary.

When he entered the foyer, Barkley straightened to his full height. "Are you ready to be announced to your callers, my lord?" the butler asked in the same dour monotone he'd used for every one of the ten years he'd been in Daniel's employ.

"Yes. I gather they've been waiting quite some time." He cast the butler a sidelong glance. "But I suspect you knew that would be the case when you allowed Samuel to bring me word that they were here."

"Serves them right to wait, calling at such an unfashionable hour." Barkley hoisted his nose upward and gave an elegant sniff. "Especially if they're here about Samuel."

They'll have a hell of a fight on their hands if they are. "One way to find out."

He followed Barkley down the corridor, and after the butler announced him, entered the room. Charles Rayburn, the magistrate, rose from his chair next to the fire. Daniel judged the tall, robust man to be in his mid-forties. He noted that Rayburn's sharp green eyes took in every detail of his appearance.

"Good morning, my lord," Rayburn said. "My apologies for the early morning call." He nodded toward the other man, who stood near the fireplace.

"This is Mr. Gideon Mayne. Mr. Mayne is a Bow Street Runner."

Daniel's initial impression of Mr. Mayne was that he was very tall, very muscular, and very solemn. His face, which sported a nose that had clearly been broken at one time, looked as if it were hewn from stone. Clearly this was not a social call.

After nodding to both men, he indicated the chairs set around the hearth and asked, "Shall we sit?"

Mr. Mayne looked as if sitting was the last thing he wished to do, but he offered no objection. After they were all settled, Daniel asked, "What is the purpose of this visit?"

"It concerns Lady Walsh's masquerade last evening, my lord," Rayburn said.

Daniel allowed only his surprise—and none of his relief—to show. Obviously this wasn't about Samuel. "What about it?"

"You were costumed as a highwayman, were you not?"

"I was."

Rayburn and Mayne exchanged a quick glance. "You were seen in the company of a particular lady last evening, my lord."

An image of Carolyn instantly materialized in his mind. "What of it?"

"I'm afraid, my lord, that lady's been murdered."

Chapter 5

I'd always believed myself a modest person, and, looking back, at the beginning of our liaison, I was. But as our relationship deepened, my mantle of modesty disintegrated. I became bold. Filled with passions and needs I'd never before imagined. I craved him, his touch, his kiss, the feel of his skin, as I imagine one would a drug.

Memoirs of a Mistress by An Anonymous Lady

Everything inside Daniel froze. An icy wind seemed to blow through the hole the magistrate's words punched through him. A silent *No!* screamed through his mind, one he surely would have roared aloud had he been able to draw a breath. An unbearable weight crushed his chest, seemingly collapsing his lungs, shattering his heart.

Carolyn . . . dear God, not Carolyn.

"Lady Crawford's body was discovered just before dawn in the mews behind Lady Walsh's town house," Rayburn said.

The magistrate's words slowly filtered through the numb shock engulfing him like a black fog. He frowned. Then blinked. "Did . . . did you say Lady *Crawford*?"

"Yes, my lord. Appears she was bludgeoned to death. Still wore party costume. Some sort of damsel in distress ensemble. She hadn't been dead long when a rat catcher found her."

His profound relief that the victim wasn't Carolyn rendered him nearly light-headed. Then the ramifications of the magistrate's news about Blythe, Lady Crawford, sank in. "Good God," he said, dragging his hands down his face. "Have you captured the person responsible?"

"No, my lord. Indeed, we've only just begun making inquiries."

Daniel looked at Mr. Mayne. "You're assisting?"

"I've been hired by Lady Crawford's family. Mr. Rayburn has kindly allowed me to be present during his inquiries." He regarded Daniel steadily through eyes so dark it was impossible to discern the pupil from the iris. "You were acquainted with Lady Crawford."

"Yes."

"Intimately acquainted."

It was a statement rather than a question. Daniel kept his expression impassive and studied Gideon Mayne. With his stark features, slightly rumpled clothes, and dark hair that needed a trim, no on would ever accuse him of being classically handsome, although he wasn't unattractive. But he possessed an intimidating air, the sort that suggested he wouldn't hesitate to put his considerable size and strength to use if necessary. Indeed, he looked as if he'd just finished pummeling a dozen or so men into the dirt and wouldn't mind doing so again. Starting with him.

"I'm not in the habit of kissing and telling, Mr. Mayne."

"This is a murder investigation, Lord Surbrooke," said the Runner without the slightest change in his forbidding expression. "Not a digging expedition for gossip fodder."

Not caring for the man's manner, Daniel deliberately waited to the mental count of ten before replying. "Blythe and I are—were—longtime friends." God, it simply wasn't possible that she was dead.

"Just how *friendly* were you?" Mayne persisted.

"I hardly see how that matters," Daniel said, "unless . . ." He lifted a single brow and shifted his gaze to Rayburn. ". . . I'm a suspect."

Mayne didn't deny it, and Rayburn shot the Runner a quick scowl. "We're asking the same questions of everyone who attended last night's party, hoping that maybe someone saw something that will lead us to the killer." Rayburn withdrew a notebook from inside his jacket then asked, "Did you see anything or anyone that might be considered suspicious?"

Daniel considered for several seconds, then shook his head. "No. The party was the usual crush. I noticed nothing out of the ordinary. Do you have reason to believe the culprit was a guest?"

"No reason to believe anything at this point except we've got a dead woman on our hands," Mayne broke in. "We've a witness who says you spoke to Lady Crawford last night."

"I did. We exchanged a few words."

"On the terrace?" asked Rayburn.

"Yes." After Carolyn had departed, he remained outdoors for nearly half an hour, lost in his thoughts. Blythe had stepped outside and approached him, pulling him from his solitary musings.

"What did you talk about?"

"Nothing of consequence. The weather. The party. A musicale we're both invited to next week."

"How long were you together?"

"No more than five minutes. The air was damp and chilly and she grew cold. I escorted her back inside then left the party."

"What time did you depart?"

"I'm not absolutely certain, as I didn't consult my watch, but I'd guess it was approaching two A.M."

"And where did you go?"

Daniel raised his brows. "Here. I came home."

"Can anyone verify that?" Mayne broke in. "Your coachman or house servants perhaps?"

"I'm afraid not. I dismissed my carriage and driver after arriving at the party and therefore walked home. My staff was asleep when I arrived."

"Even your butler and valet?"

"I'm afraid so. Barkley and Redmond are not young men. I do not require them to wait for me to arrive home."

Rayburn made notations in his small notebook

then looked up. "Do you know of anyone who might wish Lady Crawford harm?"

"No. She was a lovely, personable woman. Surely her death is the result of footpads."

"Perhaps," Rayburn said, "although 'tis clear robbery was not the motive."

"Why do you say that?" Daniel asked.

"Because Lady Crawford's jewelry was intact. She wore a very distinctive pearl choker."

An image of a triple strand of perfectly matched pearls flickered through Daniel's mind. "Did the choker have a diamond and ruby clasp?"

Interest flared in Rayburn's eyes. "Yes. How did you know?"

As he had nothing to hide and they could easily find out anyway from a number of sources, including the jeweler, he said, "It sounds like a piece I gave Blythe."

"Quite an expensive bauble to give a mere friend," Mayne remarked. "When did you give it to her?"

"Late last year. And yes, it was quite valuable. Perhaps the killer meant to steal it but was frightened off before he could do so."

"Perhaps," Rayburn said, jotting another notation in his notebook. "Do you know if Lady Crawford was currently . . . involved with anyone?"

He'd heard a vague rumor that Lord Warwick— whom he neither liked nor admired—was Blythe's latest conquest, but since it wasn't his habit to repeat unsubstantiated gossip, he said, "I'm not certain. I just arrived in Town yesterday afternoon after an extended stay in the country. I can only tell you that she wasn't involved with me."

"Currently," Mayne said.

Daniel shifted his attention to the Runner and offered him nothing more than a cold stare. He wouldn't lie, but he'd be damned if he would say anything that might sully a dead woman's memory. Especially to this brusque Runner who was glaring at him as if he'd committed the crime. His affair with Blythe had lasted less than two months—a torrid few weeks that had flared quickly then burned out. He'd soon realized that beneath her stunning beauty lurked a vain, selfish, and not particularly nice woman. It was quite possible she had enemies, although who they might be, he didn't know. Regardless, she didn't deserve the horrible end she'd come to.

"Is there anything else?" Daniel asked.

"Your costume," said Rayburn, "Can you describe it?"

"It was quite plain—black shirt, breeches, boots and mask, and a long black cape."

"The rat catcher saw someone wearing a black cape leaving the mews just as he entered."

Daniel's brows rose. "I'm hardly the only guest who wore a black cape. Perhaps this rat catcher is the fiend you're looking for."

"Perhaps," Mayne said, but in a tone that made it clear he didn't think so. Indeed, everything in the man's demeanor indicated that he considered Daniel a suspect.

"That's all, my lord," said Rayburn.

"For now," added Mayne.

Daniel rose and led the way to the foyer. "Thank you for your time, my lord," said Rayburn at the door.

"You're welcome. Please let me know if I can be of any further assistance."

"We will," Mayne said, accepting his hat from Barkley. He then gave Daniel a curt nod and departed, with Rayburn on his heels. The instant the door closed behind them, Samuel entered the foyer.

"Well?" he asked, his white-gloved hands clenched, his face drawn and pale. "Are they lookin' for me?"

"No." He told Samuel and Barkley about his conversation with Rayburn and Mayne, concluding with, "I cannot believe this has happened. Cannot fathom that Blythe is dead. And that she died in such a horrible way."

A frown furrowed between Samuel's brows. "Ye'd best be careful, milord. 'Tis clear they're sniffin' in your direction for this killin'."

Daniel nodded thoughtfully. "I had that impression myself. Especially from Mayne, who looked as if he wanted nothing more than to cart me off to the gallows. But they said they intended to question everyone who attended the party. I'm not the only man who wore a black cape or who spoke to Blythe last evening." Nor was he the only man with whom she'd had an affair.

But instead of looking relieved, Samuel appeared even more worried. "But the necklace she wore were one ye gave her. I know how these men of the law are, milord. They get an idea in their heads and it don't much matter if they're wrong. I've seen more than one innocent man arrested."

Daniel forced a smile. "Not to worry. They were merely doing their jobs and being thorough. The good news is that their inquiries had nothing to do with you."

Samuel's stiff posture relaxed a bit. "That is good news indeed."

Daniel glanced toward the ormolu clock and noted with relief that it was no longer impossibly early. "I'm going out for a while. When I return, I'll prepare myself to meet Baldy."

In the meantime he had a goddess to see—and now for an even more pressing matter than discussing their terrace interlude. With a murderer on the loose, he needed to make certain Carolyn was protected.

Carolyn stood in her foyer, her feet rooted to the black and white marble tiles as she watched Nelson close the door after Mr. Rayburn and Mr. Mayne. Her brief interview with them had shocked her.

Still stunned, she slowly made her way back to the drawing room, trying to absorb the incredible, horrible news that Lady Crawford was dead. Murdered.

A shudder ran through her. They hadn't been close friends, barely more than acquaintances, but of course she knew the beautiful widow. She'd told Mr. Rayburn and Mr. Mayne everything she knew, which was next to nothing, and answered all their questions, thinking the entire time that some awful mistake must have been made.

After closing the drawing room door behind her, she crossed the Turkish rug to her desk and sat. Picking up her quill, she tried to resume the chore she'd been attempting to accomplish when the magistrate and Bow Street Runner arrived—to write a note to

Lady Walsh thanking her for the lovely party last evening. But now, as before, all she managed to do was stare at the blank vellum. And remember.

Him.

The sound of his voice. The touch of his hands. The scent of his skin. The taste of his kiss. The heat that had poured through her, melting her until she felt as if she'd dissolve into a puddle at his feet.

With an exclamation of disgust, she set down the quill and rose. Paced the length of the room several times, then halted before the fireplace. And looked up. To stare at the handsome face, the beautiful green eyes, of the husband she'd loved so much.

The instant she'd returned home last night, she came to this very room, where she'd remained until dawn, staring at Edward's portrait while tears tracked down her face and guilt ate at her. Not only for what she'd done, but because she had enjoyed it so much. And she'd realized, with no small amount of chagrin, that part of her wished her interlude with Lord Surbrooke hadn't ended so abruptly. Had continued. In a more private setting.

Yet another part of her wanted desperately to forget the encounter, dismiss the shocking, unexpected passion he'd released within her. But she couldn't stop thinking about him. Even as she gazed at Edward's beloved face, the other man infiltrated her thoughts. Wormed his way into her recollections of past waltzes and kisses she'd shared with Edward. And for that she deeply resented him. He'd proven a highwayman indeed, stealing her common sense and her private memories of her husband.

As dawn had broken, leaking streaks of mauve into the quiet room, she finally climbed the stairs to her bedchamber, believing she'd put the episode into perspective. Her aberration in judgment was purely the result of the anonymity of the masque. If not for her costume, she never would have behaved in such an uncharacteristic manner. It was Galatea, not Carolyn Turner, Viscountess Wingate, who'd lost her head. Now that she'd shed her false identity, she wouldn't make such an error again. She wanted to move on with her life, but in the capacity of a sedate widow. Not an adventuress seeking sensual pleasure.

Thankfully, Lord Surbrooke didn't know she was the woman he'd kissed. She just needed to put the encounter out of her mind—and surely after a day or so she'd forget it—and pretend it hadn't happened.

Now, after a few hours' sleep, and with the morning sunshine pouring through the window, the entire episode did seem somewhat of a dream. A feverish dream, one obviously fueled by her avid readings of the *Memoirs*. Readings that had unexpectedly reawakened sensual needs she'd thought long buried. Needs she'd never expected to feel again.

Her gaze lowered to her desk's top drawer, and reaching out, she slowly slid it open. Moved aside several sheets of vellum to reveal a slim, black, leather-bound volume. Ran her fingers over the gold lettering adorning the cover. MEMOIRS OF A MISTRESS.

She'd wanted to toss it into the fire this morning, had attempted to do so, yet something held her back. The same unsettling something that had prevented

her from refusing Lord Surbrooke's invitation to
dance. Or his suggestion that they retire to the terrace. It was something she could neither define nor
ignore. Something that deeply troubled her.

Pulling the book from the drawer, she opened it to
a random page.

> *. . . he sank deeper into our kiss, his tongue*
> *slowly mating with mine, an intoxicating fric-*
> *tion that made me burn for the moment when*
> *his body would finally sink into—*

With a groan she slapped the pages shut, the sharp
snap echoing in the quiet room. After drawing a
shaky breath, she snatched up the book, lifted her
chin and strode with determined, resolute steps toward the fireplace.

She stood on the stone hearth, clutching the book,
the heat of the low burning fire warming her through
her morning gown. Her mind demanded she toss the
volume into the flames, yet still she hesitated.

With a groan, she lowered her head to rest her chin
against the book's edge. Why, oh *why* had she read
it? Before doing so she hadn't questioned her life, her
decisions. She knew exactly who she was—Edward's
widow. She lived a quiet, calm, circumspect existence, and while some might have considered it lacking in excitement, it suited her. Perfectly. She had her
routine. Her correspondence. Her sister and friends.
Her embroidery . . . although she had to admit that she
hated embroidery.

But then she'd read this . . . this damnable book.

She lifted her head to glare at the offending volume. Her fingers clenched it so tightly her knuckles turned white. Now all she could think about was . . . *that*.

That . . . and Lord Surbrooke.

She squeezed her eyes shut and an image of him instantly materialized. Not of him costumed as the dark and alluring highwayman, but as himself, as he'd been at Matthew's house party. His dark blue gaze resting on her, his lovely mouth curved in that slightly crooked grin. A lock of his thick, dark hair falling over his brow.

Her heart rate quickened and she slowly opened her eyes. Stared into the dancing orange and gold flames. And forced herself to face the truth. Her attraction to Lord Surbrooke had taken root well before she'd ever read the *Memoirs*. The seeds had been planted during Matthew's country house party, and now . . . now they'd bloomed into something completely unexpected. Entirely unwanted. Yet totally undeniable.

And roundly unacceptable.

Good Lord, if she was to entertain an attraction to a man—something she'd honestly never considered— *why* was it him? She couldn't deny that from a purely physical standpoint he was extremely handsome, but she'd never been drawn to any man based on mere good looks. Indeed, because of her own upbringing, she tended to avoid such spectacular looking men. She'd been instantly drawn to Edward, who, to her, was extraordinarily handsome, but not in any obvious way. His looks were subdued. Understated. As was his gentle manner. She'd fallen in love with his quiet sense of humor. His intelligence and integrity. His profound kindness and amiability.

Lord Surbrooke, with his stunning looks, heated glances, and reputation as a charming rogue, was not at all the sort of man she'd ever preferred.

Again she looked at the book clutched in her hands. Even though the *Memoirs* may not have struck the match of her unwanted attraction, it certainly fanned the flames with its sensual stories, embedding steamy images in her mind. Images in which Lord Surbrooke prominently figured. Images she wanted, desperately, to banish.

Clearly, ridding herself of this book was the first step toward that end, with the second step being to avoid Lord Surbrooke. Surely that wouldn't be too difficult. He no doubt had dozens of women hanging on his every word to occupy his time. Women with whom he shared all manner of intimacies. Women he kissed passionately at masquerade balls. . .

A heated shiver rippled down her spine, followed immediately by a strange knotting in her stomach. An irritating tension that felt precisely like . . . jealousy.

Her brows snapped downward. Good heavens, what did she care if he kissed other women? Made love to them? She didn't. Not at all. Since he'd had no idea whom he was kissing last night, it had clearly been just another anonymous encounter for him, one he'd most likely already forgotten. One which, thank goodness, he'd had the presence of mind to call a halt to. Surely she would have if he hadn't. Surely, after just another few seconds of kissing, she would have pushed him away. Her annoyingly honest inner voice coughed to life and muttered something that sounded suspiciously like *Not bloody likely*. She managed, with an effort, to ignore it.

Still, a tiny, contrary part of her thrilled at the notion that she'd elicited such a passionate response from him. She hadn't known herself capable of doing so. As ardent as Edward had always been, she'd never incited such a . . . lack of restraint in him. And certainly not at a party. Somewhere they could have been discovered.

A wave of shame washed over her at her thoughts, which she could only label as disloyal. It was both unfair and ridiculous to compare Edward, who had been unfailingly polite and mannerly in every aspect of his life, with a man she barely knew, and what little she did know about him proved he was capable of less than decorous behavior.

Obviously the loneliness that had been plaguing her had gotten the better of her, propelling her to act in a most uncharacteristic fashion last night. While she had no intention of repeating her actions, there was no point in keeping anything that might encourage her to again step outside the cozy cocoon she'd wrapped around herself.

Drawing a resolute breath, she crouched before the fire and slowly extended the *Memoirs. Let it go,* her mind urged. *Toss it in.* It was the right thing to do. Her better judgment, her common sense, knew it.

A knock on the door startled her and she jumped to her feet. A guilty flush scorched her, although she wasn't sure why, and she quickly shoved the book beneath the brocade cushion of the settee. "Come in," she called.

Nelson opened the door, then approached her,

bearing a silver salver upon which sat a calling card. "You've a visitor, my lady," the butler said, extending the polished tray.

Carolyn picked up the card, looked at the neatly printed writing. Her heart performed a quick acrobatic roll then settled into a rhythm of hard, fast beats.

Good God, what was he *doing here?*

"Are you at home, my lady?"

Carolyn swallowed. "Yes. You may show Lord Surbrooke in." The words somehow came out of her mouth in spite of the fact that they were the exact opposite of what she knew she should be saying.

Nelson inclined his head then withdrew. The instant he quit the room Carolyn dashed to the mirror hanging on the far wall. And barely bit back an *Ack!* of dismay. No need to pinch her cheeks to give herself some color—the crimson blush staining her skin made it appear as if she'd stuck her face in an oven. Good heavens, even her eyes appeared a bit red, not to mention somewhat swollen, courtesy of too much crying and too little sleep. Or perhaps it was just a reflection from her glowing cheeks.

She pressed her lips together and frowned. What difference did it make what she looked like? Why, none at all! She had no desire to impress Lord Surbrooke. None at all.

Footfalls sounded from the corridor, and with a gasp she hurried away from the mirror. Halting in front of the fireplace, she barely had time to smooth her suddenly damp palms down her gown when Nelson appeared in the doorway.

"Lord Surbrooke," he announced. After a quick bow, he stepped aside and Lord Surbrooke moved into the opening. And Carolyn's heart performed another tumbling roll.

Heavens, the man looked far too appealing by half. As always, he was immaculately groomed. From his midnight blue cutaway jacket that perfectly matched his eyes and accentuated the breadth of his shoulders, to his snowy white shirt and cravat that fell in a perfect waterfall knot, down to fawn breeches that hugged his muscular legs, to his mirror-shined black boots.

He walked slowly toward her, and Carolyn could do nothing save stare, rendered mute by the predatory grace of his movements. Heavens. He walked well. Danced well. Kissed . . . extraordinarily well.

Heat raced through her and she barely managed to keep from fanning her hand in front of her face. Watching him made her feel as if she were standing next to a blazing hearth. *You* are *standing next to a blazing hearth,* her inner voice reminded her.

Relief raced through her and she moved several steps away from the fireplace. Of course she was. No wonder it was so warm in here. It had absolutely nothing to do with her visitor.

Over Lord Surbrooke's shoulder she vaguely noticed Nelson pulling the door closed. If she'd had her wits about her she would have called out to him to leave the door open, but it appeared she was fully witless. And speechless.

Lord Surbrooke halted, leaving a respectable six foot distance between them—one she felt distressingly tempted to lessen.

He said something—she knew because his lips moved—but his words didn't penetrate because the memory of their kiss inundated her with such intensity, all she could hear was her heart beat thudding in her ears.

There . . . his lips were moving again. Those beautiful, masculine lips that looked so firm and felt so wonderful. Those lips . . . those lips . . . dear God, she'd completely lost the entire thread of the conversation. Not to mention her mind.

Snapping her gaze away from his mouth, she looked into his eyes then cleared her throat to locate her missing voice. "I beg your pardon?"

"I said I was afraid it might be too early to call. Thank you for seeing me."

"Actually, you aren't my first visitor of the day."

"Oh?" His gaze sharpened with interest. "Would your other visitors have been Mr. Rayburn and Mr. Mayne?"

Carolyn nodded. "Yes. They've visited you as well? They mentioned they intended to interview all the party guests."

"They left my home not long ago. A terrible, shocking thing, Lady Crawford's death."

"Dreadful. I hope they catch the killer quickly."

"As do I. But until he is apprehended, you must take extra care. Do not go anywhere unescorted."

"It is not my habit to do so."

"Good."

Silence fell between them. She cast desperately about in her mind for something to say, a difficult task, for the sight of him in her drawing room somehow emptied her mind. And in spite of the room's spacious size, his presence seemed to reduce the area to no larger than a box.

It was he who finally broke the quiet. "Am I interrupting anything?"

She suddenly recalled what she'd been doing when Nelson announced him—preparing to toss the *Memoirs* into the fire. Her gaze darted to the settee and dismay washed through her. The edge of the book protruded from beneath the cushion.

"Nothing," she said quickly. And perhaps a shade too loudly. "You're not interrupting anything. However, I'm curious as to why you're calling." *Yes, please tell me. Quickly. Then leave. So I can start forgetting all about you.*

A smile pulled up one corner of his mouth. "May I sit down?"

No. Tell me then leave. And quit smiling. "Of course." She indicated the wing chair, but instead he settled himself on the settee. Directly over the *Memoirs*. She stared at the cushion in alarm . . . alarm that melted into chagrin as she realized her gaze was now riveted on his groin. His absolutely fascinating groin.

She sucked in a quick breath and lifted her eyes. And found him studying her. In a way that made it clear that she'd been caught staring. At his fascinating groin.

Good God. This visit had barely begun and already it was a disaster. At least it couldn't get any worse.

Pulling herself together, she sat at the opposite end of the settee and managed to say in a perfectly composed tone, "What did you wish to see me about, Lord Surbrooke?"

"I wanted to give you something." He held out a glass jar sealed with wax, filled with an amber colored substance.

Carolyn stared at the offering in surprise. Where had that come from? Clearly he'd been holding it all along and she hadn't noticed. *Because you were so preoccupied staring at his lips. And eyes. And fascinating groin.*

She accepted the jar and held it up to the light. "It looks like honey."

He smiled. "Probably because it *is* honey. From my own bees. I keep a number of skeps at Meadow Hill, my country estate in Kent."

"I . . . thank you," she said, unable to keep the note of surprise from her voice. "I'm very fond of honey."

"Yes, I know."

"You do? How?"

"You mentioned it during one of our conversations at Matthew's house party."

"Did I?" she murmured, far more pleased than she should have been that he'd remember such a minor detail. "I don't recall."

"I wished to give you something, but wasn't certain what it should be. But then you said you'd prefer a gift that reminded me of you. And honey reminds me of you," he said softly. "It is the exact color of your hair."

Her brows pulled downward. Surely she hadn't said anything so . . . forward to him. "When did I say that?"

He reached out and lightly touched a tendril of her

hair. The intimate gesture stopped her breath. "Last night. On the terrace." His gaze seemed to bore into hers. "Galatea."

She actually felt the blood drain from her head, leaving nothing save a buzzing sound in her ears. Good God. Had she, less than a minute ago, believed this visit couldn't get any worse? Yes, she had.

Obviously she'd been very, very wrong.

Chapter 6

I believed myself well acquainted with physical pleasure before entering into my arrangement with Lord X. After only one kiss, however, I suspected I didn't know as much as I thought. After our second kiss, I was sure of it. Because I'd never craved a third kiss so badly.

Memoirs of a Mistress by An Anonymous Lady

*D*aniel watched the color leach from Carolyn's face and his jaw tightened. She was clearly stunned, and not in a delighted way. Disappointment washed through him, followed immediately by a tight grip of jealousy. And something else he couldn't quite name other than to know it made his heart feel as if a piece were torn from it. Based on her reaction, she hadn't known it was him she'd kissed.

Damn it, who the bloody hell had she thought the highwayman was? He didn't know, but was determined to find out. Before he could ask, however, she moistened her lips, and that flick of her tongue distracted him. He hadn't quite recovered when she asked, "How did you know Galatea was me?"

"It wasn't difficult. The way you hold yourself. The curve of your chin. Your laugh. You are . . . unmistakable."

For several long seconds she studied him through those beautiful eyes that reminded him of a cloudless summer sky. Then, without saying a word, she rose and moved toward the fireplace. After setting the jar of honey on the mantel, she kept her back to him and appeared to stare into the flames.

"How long did you know it was me?" she asked quietly.

He hesitated. His pride—dented by the fact she hadn't realized he was the highwayman—demanded he not admit he'd known her identity all along. That he hadn't guessed until after they kissed. If she were any other woman, the falsehood would have slipped from his lips without a qualm. Seduction was nothing more than a series of intricate games—games he knew very well how to play. Just as he knew very well how to keep his own counsel and reveal as little as possible of himself to his lovers. In games of love, information was ammunition. The man who gave a woman too much risked getting shot.

But with this woman, the lie caught in his throat, refusing to be spoken. For the sake of his battered pride, he even coughed once in an attempt to dislodge the falsehood, but it refused to budge, leaving him with only one option: to tell her the unvarnished truth. Completely uncharacteristic, but there was

simply no other alternative. He didn't quite understand *why* he felt this way, why he had no choice in
the matter, and damn it, he detested feeling so confused. But as this was the hand he'd been dealt, he
had no choice but to play it. Bloody hell, no wonder
he'd never cared for card games.

He stood, then crossed to the fireplace, stopping
directly behind her. The faint scent of flowers rose
from her skin, teasing his senses, and he drew a deep
breath. God, she smelled good. Like a garden on a
sunny day.

His gaze riveted on the nape of her neck. That
column of creamy skin, flanked by a pair of honey-
colored tendrils artfully loosened from her upswept
hair, looked so soft, so vulnerable. And so damn
touchable.

"I knew it was you the instant I saw you," he admitted softly. Unable to resist, he reached out and
touched a single fingertip to that tempting bit of
skin, relishing the discovery that it felt as velvety as
it looked.

He savored her quick intake of breath, as well as
the slight tremor that ran through her. "I was completely aware it was you I spoke to," he continued,
lightly trailing his fingertip along the gentle curve of
her nape. "You I danced with." He stepped forward
until his front lightly grazed her back, and brushed
his lips against the skin his finger had just explored.
"You I kissed."

She went perfectly still, indeed, it seemed she'd
ceased breathing, and grim satisfaction filled him.
Excellent. It was a sensation he understood all too

well, and it was entirely her fault. Every time he so much as thought of this woman, the sensual images she inspired made it feel for several seconds as if his lungs forgot how to work.

His arms slid around her waist, and holding her lightly against him, he dragged his lips along her neck and inhaled . . . slowly, deeply, steeping his senses in the soft, floral scent of her. The delicious and almost painfully arousing sensation of holding her in his arms. And as happened every time he was near her, his finesse fled, leaving him struggling to keep from simply snatching her against him. Backing her against the nearest wall. Or bending her over the nearest chair. Or tossing her on the nearest settee. Or just dragging her to the floor. Anywhere to put out this damnable fire that roared through him every time he touched her. A flame that burned even hotter now that he'd tasted her.

The effort not to give in to the craving had him damn near shaking, and he briefly closed his eyes. Forced himself to pull himself together. For God's sake, he'd barely touched her. Never had he experienced such an overwhelming need to have any woman. Still, his inner voice warned him not to move too quickly with Carolyn, lest he scare her off again as he had last night.

Leaning back, he gently turned her until she faced him. One look at her heightened color and languorous expression left no doubt that she was as affected as he. Thank God. Because the next time he kissed her she was damn well going to know it was him doing so.

He reached out and lightly stroked his fingers down her soft cheek. "Who did you think kissed you last night?" he asked, voicing the question that had ceaselessly reverberated through his mind. Hating that he had to ask it.

She studied him with an indecipherable expression, and he dearly wished he could read her thoughts. Then, as if recalling that they stood so close, that his hands rested on her waist, she eased away, putting several feet between them. A space he had to force himself not to erase.

"A dashing highwayman," she finally said. "I'm afraid I got caught up in the excitement and anonymity of the masque and . . ."

Her voice trailed off and she shifted her gaze to the fire. Although disappointed that she hadn't known or guessed his identity, he was vastly relieved that she at least hadn't named another man.

"And you gave in to your desires?" he suggested softly when she remained silent.

She shook her head. "No. I made a mistake."

She turned toward him, and for the first time he realized that her eyes bore traces of redness around the rims and faint smudges beneath. Signs of a restless, sleepless night. And perhaps even tears. The thought of her crying filled him with an ache he couldn't name. Brought to life a need to comfort and protect—a need he hadn't felt for a very long time. A need he'd thought long dead.

It required all his will not to reach for her. "It wasn't a mistake," he said, his voice quiet yet implacable.

A look of resolution and something else—anguish perhaps?—flickered in her gaze and she lifted her chin. "I assure you it was, Lord Surbrooke. I didn't mean—"

"Daniel."

She hesitated, then continued, "I didn't mean for things to go as far as they did. I shouldn't have accompanied you—the highwayman—onto the terrace. I can only reiterate that I made a mistake. And ask for your forgiveness."

"I assure you there is nothing to forgive." No longer able to stop himself, he stepped closer to her. He wondered if she'd back away, and was pleased when she stood her ground. "I suppose I should apologize as well, but I'm afraid I can't. I'm not sorry. Indeed, my only regret is that you left so abruptly."

She shook her head. "Lord Surbrooke, I—"

"Daniel. Please, call me Daniel." He smiled, hoping to coax one from her in return. "After last evening surely we are on a first name basis. At least I hope so . . . *Lady Wingate?*"

When, in spite of the exaggerated questioning tone in which he uttered her name, she didn't issue the invitation he hoped, he added, "At least I hope so . . . my dear *Lady Wingate?*"

Encouraged by the slight twitch of her lips, he continued, "My extremely lovely, very dear *Lady Wingate?*"

The barest whiff of amusement entered her eyes. "How long you do intend to continue in this vein?"

"For as long as it takes . . . my extremely lovely, very dear, and greatly talented *Lady Wingate.*"

She cocked a brow. "Greatly talented? Clearly you've never heard me sing."

"No." He clutched his hands to his chest in a dramatic pose. "But I'm certain the sound rivals that of angels' voices."

"Only if angels' voices sound like out-of-tune squeaking carriage wheels."

He made a *tsking* sound. "I'm afraid I cannot allow you to disparage my friend—the extremely lovely, very dear, greatly talented, and highly amusing *Lady Wingate*."

"At this rate, by the end of the day I'll bear more titles than the entire royal family combined."

"I'm certain that's correct, my extremely lovely, very dear, greatly talented, highly amusing, and extraordinarily intelligent *Lady Wingate*."

She shot him a half-exasperated, half-amused look. "It has clearly escaped your notice, my lord, that I am endeavoring to maintain a bit of propriety between us."

"Daniel. And no, it hasn't escaped my notice." He grinned and waggled his brows. "But clearly it has escaped your notice that I'd like you to stop."

"I believe even a blind man could see that. Yet I'm also endeavoring to politely extricate myself from an embarrassing situation. In a way that will allow us to forget our lapse in judgment last night and continue to enjoy the easy camaraderie we established at Matthew's house party."

"Is that truly what you think last night was? A lapse in judgment?"

"Yes. And one I've no intention of repeating." The words weren't said unkindly. Indeed, he could easily read the apology in her eyes, the plea for understanding.

The problem was, he didn't understand. Nor did he want an apology.

"Can you tell me why?" he asked, his gaze searching hers. "It was clear you enjoyed our kiss as much as I did."

Crimson rushed into her cheeks, and he marveled that a woman over thirty, one who'd been married, could still blush. "That makes no difference."

"I disagree. There is an attraction between us. One I've felt for . . . quite some time."

Surprise, and something else, flickered in her eyes, but it was gone before he could identify it. "You have?"

Since the moment I first saw you. Ten years go. "Yes. And it's something I'd like to explore further. Unless . . . are you saying I'm incorrect? That the attraction is all one-sided?"

Her blush deepened. "Any woman with a heartbeat would think you very handsome—"

"I don't care about what any woman would think. I only care about what *you* think."

"Surely my opinion regarding your attractiveness isn't important, my lord."

"Daniel. And actually your opinion is very important to me." His lips twitched. "Although I really just want you to agree with me."

She gave a surprised laugh, which she attempted to cover with a cough, and he noted that she appeared a bit more relaxed. A whiff of mischief danced in her eyes. "You wish for me to agree that you're attractive? Surely you realize how conceited that makes you sound."

"No. I'm hoping you'll agree that there's an attraction between us. And that you'd like to explore that attraction as much as I would."

She immediately sobered. Pressing her lips together, she averted her gaze. Then drew a breath and faced him again. "I'm very flattered, but—"

Reaching out, he gently pressed his fingers to her lips. "Why don't we leave it for now at 'I'm very flattered'?" He flashed a smile, one he prayed didn't look as forced as it felt, then lowered his hand. "I find that statements that follow the word 'but' are generally not very encouraging."

"But that is just the point. Although my actions of last evening may understandably indicate otherwise, I do not wish to encourage you."

"Me in particular? Or gentlemen in general?"

"Gentlemen in general. But especially not you."

He winced. "Ouch. That loud crash you just heard was my manly ego smashing to bits."

She reached out and briefly laid her hand against his upper arm. If he'd been capable of levity, he would have laughed at the frisson of heat that raced through him at the innocent gesture. "You misunderstand me. I say especially not you because . . . I like you. I don't want to hurt you."

He quirked a brow. "Do you intend to cosh me with an iron skillet? Or perhaps a fire poker? Heavy rock? Shove me down the stairs?"

Her lips twitched. "Of course not."

"Then I fail to see how you could possibly hurt me."

She turned to look at the painting above the mantel, and he followed her gaze. Edward smiled from the canvas, his handsome face frozen in time. A life-sized ghost captured in oil paint.

Daniel pulled his gaze away from the painting to look at her. "I see. You've told me about your devotion to Edward, your wish to never remarry, and I understand." But though he claimed to understand and didn't begrudge Carolyn her feelings, he simply couldn't comprehend that profound depth of love. The sort that owned one's entire heart and soul. "You're afraid that because your heart isn't free, you'll hurt my tender emotions."

She moved to face him, then nodded. "At the risk of sounding horribly full of myself, yes. I've no desire to hurt either of us."

"At the risk of sounding horribly full of *myself,* I do not allow my tender emotions to enter into any of my liaisons." He gave her a quick grin. "Indeed, history has shown that I'm quite lacking in tender emotions, so you need not worry. And like you, I've no desire to marry."

She raised her brows. "What of your title?"

He shrugged. "I suppose I'll have to get leg-shackled someday, but I've no intention of considering it until I'm in my dotage. If I happen to cock up my toes before the deed is done, I have two younger brothers."

Another layer of crimson washed over her cheeks, and he had to fist his hands to keep from cupping her face between his palms and kissing her until neither of them could catch their breath. "You're suggesting we have an affair."

Bloody hell, yes. Starting immediately, if not sooner. "I'm suggesting we see where last night's kiss leads us," he replied cautiously, not wanting to see her sprint from the room in panic, "although I admit I have a very good idea where that will be."

"Which is an affair."

"Yes."

The flash of heat in her eyes told him she was tempted. But then her gaze flicked to the portrait and she shook her head. "I've never . . . I cannot." Another shake of her head. "I'm sorry."

Reaching out, he lightly clasped her hands. "I know how much you loved him. Still love him. He was, in every way, a man to be admired. Do you not think he'd want you to live?"

"Yes, but . . ." Her words trailed off and he could easily see how torn she was.

"I don't require your heart. In truth, I've absolutely no wish for it."

Confusion clouded her eyes. "Then what do you want?"

"Is it not obvious? I want *you.* Your company. Your laughter." He gently squeezed her hands. "I want you as my lover. In my bed. Or your bed . . . or wherever our encounters may take us. Your heart can remain your own. As mine shall continue to belong to me. Your body, however . . ." His gaze skimmed slowly down her form.

"Would be yours?" she asked in a husky whisper.

"Yes." He resettled his gaze on hers. "As mine would be yours."

"For how long?"

"For as long as we wished. Until one of us no longer wanted to be involved."

"Just a temporary, carefree liaison, based solely upon physical gratification." She sounded both skeptical and intrigued.

"Yes. Except you forgot to mention discreet. No one would know except us."

"How do I know you wouldn't tell anyone?"

"First, because I give you my word of honor I wouldn't. And second, I don't like to share. Anything. But most especially the private details of my life."

"I . . . see."

"I would protect you in every way. Including against pregnancy."

Her gaze briefly dipped downward. "That . . . that wouldn't be necessary. After seven childless years of marriage, I finally had to accept that I am unable to conceive."

There was no missing the sadness in her voice, and he gave her hands another gentle squeeze.

"You are a stunning, desirable woman. And passionate as well—something that, based on your reaction to our kiss, I think you've lost sight of."

A frown whispered across her face. "I fear you're reading too much into it. My reaction was an aberration."

"No, it wasn't."

"Yes, it was."

"I see I shall simply have to prove you wrong." And with those words he erased the distance between them with a single step and covered her mouth with his, instantly falling into the same dark abyss of want and need he'd plunged into last night. A fiery, shadowy place where only the two of them existed. A place he never wanted to leave.

Forcing himself to move with a deliberate lack of haste, one in complete contrast to the urgency pounding through him, he released her hands and slid his around her waist, drawing her against him until they touched from chest to knee. For several seconds she remained stiff, then with a soft moan wrapped her arms around his neck and parted her lips.

If he hadn't been so consumed with need, he might have savored the triumph. Instead, he tightened his hold on her and sank deeper into the kiss, his tongue exploring the delicious, velvety warmth of her mouth. With each passing second he felt more and more as if he were being pulled into a carnal vortex from which there was no escape. Not that he wanted to get away. God no. In fact, they weren't nearly close enough.

With a groan he slid one hand down to the small of her back. His palm pressed against the base of her spine and his fingers splayed over the curve of her buttocks, urging her tighter against him. His erection pressed into her and his hips involuntarily flexed, a slow thrust that dragged a growl of pure want from his throat.

He lost all concept of time. Knew only that no matter how long he kissed her it wasn't long enough. Heart hammering, he somehow found the strength to lift his head, but only far enough to trail his lips along her jaw. Down the curve of her fragrant neck. All the while absorbing the sweetly erotic sounds emanating from her parted lips. He glided his tongue along the side of her neck, tasting her warm, flower-scented skin, then gently sucked on the spot where her rapid pulse beat. No woman had ever tasted so delicious.

With an effort that cost him, he finally raised his head. And bit back a groan of intense longing at the sight that greeted him.

With her eyes drooped to half-mast, her cheeks flushed crimson, and her lips parted and kiss-swollen, she looked thoroughly and deliciously aroused. Keeping one arm wrapped around her waist to hold her anchored securely against him, he raised a non-too-steady hand and brushed the backs of his fingers across her warm, satiny smooth cheek.

Her eyes fluttered the rest of the way open and he stared into their deep blue depths. And felt himself drowning all over again.

"Still think last night was an aberration?" he asked, his voice low and rough with arousal.

He didn't recognize the expression that ghosted over her features, but it clearly wasn't happiness. Indeed, it looked more like defeat. "Apparently not," she conceded. "But—"

He cut off her words with a quick kiss. "Remember what I said about statements that follow the word 'but' not being very encouraging?"

She opened her mouth, clearly intending to argue further, when a knock sounded on the door. For several seconds she froze, then with a gasp she pulled away from him, as if he'd burned her, and smoothed her hands over her hair and gown in an agitated gesture.

"You look fine," he assured her, jerking his jacket into place. "Although by 'fine' I actually mean 'perfect.'"

And by God, she did. Perfectly kissed, he decided, as he mentally cursed the interruption. Although, perhaps it had actually come at the ideal time. They'd just shared what he would describe as another extraordinary kiss, and she hadn't had time to raise any objections. Indeed, he should grasp this opportunity to depart and leave her to recall just how incredible their kiss was. And hopefully leave her wanting more.

"Come in," she called.

The door opened and the dour-faced butler who'd shown Daniel in entered bearing a silver salver upon which sat a trio of calling cards. "Visitors to see you, my lady. Lady Walsh, Lady Balsam, and Mrs. Amunsbury. Are you at home?"

Her gaze shifted to Daniel. "I must be going," he said quickly. "I've several appointments scheduled."

She nodded then said to the butler, "You may escort Lord Surbrooke to the foyer, then show the ladies in, Nelson."

"Very good, my lady."

She turned back to Daniel. "Thank you for the honey."

"You're welcome. Will you be attending Lord and Lady Gatesbourne's soiree this evening?" He assumed she would, as their daughter, Lady Julianne, was one of her closest friends.

She hesitated. "I've not yet decided."

And in that instant he knew that *he* was the reason she wasn't certain if she'd attend. Clearly she didn't know if she wanted to see him again. Her decision whether to attend would reveal a great deal, he decided.

Forcing himself not to touch her, he merely made her a formal bow. "I hope to see you there, my lady. And please remember to take care and not go out alone." He then crossed to the doorway and made himself follow Nelson from the room without looking back.

In the foyer, he exchanged greetings with Kimberly, Lady Balsam, and Mrs. Amunsbury, all of whom eyed him curiously.

"And what brings you to Lady Wingate's home?" asked Lady Balsam, brushing away one of her turban's peacock feathers from her cheek.

Daniel forced a smile. The beautiful, haughty countess was one of the most notorious gossips in the ton. "Merely a neighborly visit, as my home is only two doors away. After I heard the shocking news about Lady Crawford's death, I decided to check on Lady Wingate to make certain she was all right."

"Quite the knight in shining armor," said Kimberly, eyeing him with amusement. "Is she all right?"

"I'm happy to report she is fine. And I'm very glad to see all you ladies are fine as well." Curious as to the reason for their visit, as he wasn't aware that any of the ladies were particularly close friends of Carolyn's, he casually asked, "What brings you calling on this lovely day?"

"We were on our way to Regent Street to visit the

shops when Lady Walsh suggested we call upon Lady Wingate to see if she'd like to join us," reported Mrs. Amunsbury. She held her nose hoisted so high in the air, Daniel wondered that she didn't regularly tip backward. "We're all so delighted she is getting out in Society again."

"Yet now we must be concerned about a murderer running about," said Lady Balsam with a sniff. Daniel barely refrained from looking toward the ceiling. God forbid *anything* should have the gall to come between the countess and her visits to the shops. "Terrible business, the murder is," she continued, "but really, whatever was Lady Crawford thinking, lurking about in the mews? Asking for trouble, for a lady to venture there."

Although he agreed, he had no wish to discuss the matter further. After offering the ladies a formal bow, he left. As he made his way down the flagstone steps then the short path leading to the black wrought-iron gate, he pondered Lady Balsam's words and wondered who or what had led Blythe to the mews. Her adventurous spirit wasn't the sort that would lead her to expose herself to unsafe areas. Which could only mean she'd either expected to meet someone in the mews—someone who either hadn't shown up, leaving her at the mercy of whoever killed her—and that person had killed her. Or she hadn't gone into the mews alone, and the companion who accompanied her there killed her. Which meant that the murderer had attended the masquerade. Like everyone else, he could only hope the culprit was quickly caught and brought to justice. And that Rayburn, and especially

Mayne, would turn their attention away from him and concentrate on finding the real murderer.

Yet even as the mystery surrounding Blythe's death circled through his mind, deep inside him another question tied him in knots.

Would Carolyn come to the Gatesbourne soiree tonight?

He supposed the answer depended on the other question that he knew would haunt him all day.

Would she be brave enough to admit she wanted him as much as he wanted her?

Chapter 7

*He approached the tub, wearing only a wicked grin.
"There is nothing quite as captivating as a beautiful
woman taking a bath," he murmured. I could only guess
he hadn't looked in the mirror because I'd never seen
anything as captivating as him—sinfully handsome,
tall and masculine, broad and muscled. And very, very
aroused. . .*

Memoirs of a Mistress by An Anonymous Lady

Holding a glass of lemon flavored punch,
Carolyn stood in the drawing room of Lord
and Lady Gatesbourne's elegant Grosvenor Square
mansion and nodded at whatever Sarah was saying.
Her sister had been chatting for several minutes, and
while Carolyn felt certain that whatever tale she was
relaying was fascinating, she still found her attention

wandering. To the very thing she didn't wish to think about.

Lord Surbrooke.

Blast the man. Why couldn't she simply banish him from her thoughts? The fact that he seemed branded in her mind was both confusing and utterly vexing. It was as if her brain had developed a freakish resistance to doing what she wanted it to do—which was to forget everything that had to do with Lord Surbrooke. His crooked smile. His dark blue eyes. His handsome face.

His devouring kiss.

And its devastating effect on her.

Even now, hours after he'd departed her home, heat crept up her spine at the mere thought of the way he'd held her. Touched her. Kissed her. The unmistakable evidence of his arousal pressing against her, swirling a storm of physical wants and needs through her. Wants and needs that still, in spite of the passage of nearly twelve hours, had not abated one bit. Her skin felt hot and too tight, as if it had been soaked in warm starch.

After she'd declined the kind invitation from Lady Walsh, Lady Balsam, and Mrs. Amunsbury to visit the shops, she'd indulged in a warm bath, hoping to ease her discomfort and relax her mind. She always found a soak in her oversized tub soothing. But not today. No, today her mind had buzzed with images of Lord Surbrooke—naked—approaching the tub. His body sculpted to perfection and perfectly aroused—something he proceeded to make perfect use of. With her. In the tub.

The vivid images had left her in such a state, she'd fled the tub and spent two hours pacing, concluding that she simply couldn't attend tonight's party at Julianne's parents' home. She'd planned to go, had looked forward to spending the evening with Sarah, Julianne, and Emily, but *he* was going to be there.

I knew it was you the instant I saw you. His words filled her with the most confusing combination of guilt and excitement. She hadn't been able to admit to him that she'd known his identity the instant she saw him. To do so would have forced her to acknowledge out loud that theirs hadn't been a chance, anonymous encounter. Her only protection against him, the things he made her feel, was to feign ignorance. Otherwise that anonymous meeting would be changed into a deliberate choice . . . a choice to share intimacies with a man who wasn't her husband. Who wasn't Edward. The man she'd loved, still loved.

But Edward is gone, her inner voice whispered.

Yes. And she was alive. Something Lord Surbrooke had made very evident. But how could she deliberately choose to be with another man? A man who wanted them to become lovers.

And that was why she had ultimately decided to attend the party. Because staying away would be tantamount to admitting she wanted to be his lover but was too afraid to say so. Which was untrue. She wasn't afraid to tell him what needed to be said—that she would not, could not, be his lover. And until such time as she could find a private moment to deliver her decision, she'd adopt an air of cool indifference.

Except she couldn't quite manage to find her air of cool indifference.

The fact that even while standing in this crowded, noisy drawing room she couldn't think of anything save sensual images of her and Lord Surbrooke, naked, in a bathtub . . . well, that didn't bode well at all.

Heat sizzled through her, and she pulled in a deep breath, nodding absently at Sarah while her gaze panned the room. Where was he? Had he decided not to attend the party? She should be glad. She *was* glad. In fact, she was delighted. She'd come and stood her ground and therefore had won the day, staying true to her convictions. This unwanted attraction for him would quickly fade and she'd regain her sensibilities, which he had somehow managed to sneak beneath her guard to steal. Then she and Lord Surbrooke would return to the casual friendship they'd enjoyed before the masked ball. He was clearly looking for a new bed partner. And, of course, that partner would not be her. She simply couldn't become his lover. She wasn't the sort of woman to engage in an affair, no matter how incredibly he might kiss. And make her yearn.

All she had to do now was tell him.

Therefore the least he could have done was show up this evening so she could do so. Once she put this episode behind her and moved on, life would return to normal. Her very fulfilling life did not have room for any man, and most especially not one like Lord Surbrooke, who was so . . . practiced. So much so that he'd made her temporarily forget herself. But she wouldn't allow it to happen again.

He's made you forget yourself twice, her pesky inner voice reminded her.

Annoyed, she shoved the voice aside. Naturally, after hearing her refusal, he would pour on his considerable charm and endeavor to change her mind, if for no other reason than to salvage his pride—she imagined that few, if any, women had ever turned him down. But she was resolute. Determined. She would not be swayed from her decision. No matter how persuasive his kisses. No matter how they made her simply . . . melt. No matter how thoughtful his gift of honey had been.

None of it mattered.

She had to resume the calm, sedate lifestyle she'd carved out for herself. And that certainly did not include a torrid affair with a man who, while unquestioningly attractive, was really nothing more than a spoiled, shallow seducer of women. After hearing her decision, she had no doubt he would immediately turn his attention to someone else. Another woman who would fall willingly into his arms.

That thought filled her with an uncomfortable sensation that made her feel as if her entire body had just twisted itself into a tight knot. She gripped her glass of punch so tight the intricate design cut into her fingers. Damnation, she could almost see him . . . taking some other nameless, faceless woman in his arms. *Making* her *feel all the heated, shockingly pleasurable things he'd made* me *feel last night and this morning.*

"Don't you agree, Carolyn?"

Sarah's question yanked her from her unsettling

thoughts, and she shifted her gaze to her sister, who was staring at her over the rims of her spectacles. "I beg your pardon?" she asked.

Sarah pursed her lips. "I don't believe you've heard a word I said."

Fire raced into Carolyn's face. "I'm sorry. I'm afraid I'm . . . preoccupied."

Concern flashed in Sarah's brown eyes. "Are you all right?

No. I'm overheated and frustrated and confused and it's all that aggravating man's fault. "Yes, poppet, I'm fine."

"Are you certain? You look . . . flushed."

The fact that her inner discomfort showed so plainly on the outside only served to rush more heat through her. "It's just a bit warm in here. What were you saying?"

"Several things. First, that Lady Crawford's murder is on everyone's lips. There's talk of husbands not allowing their wives to go anywhere unescorted. When we arrived, Julianne said her father threatened not to allow her out of the house. Matthew has made me promise half a dozen times not to venture *anywhere* alone."

"I'm glad he's done so," Carolyn said. "Everyone I've spoken to is very concerned." She leaned closer and said in an undertone, "I see that Mr. Rayburn and Mr. Mayne are here. That makes one feel a bit safer."

"Yes," Sarah agreed, "although I'd guess they're here in more of an investigative capacity than a protective one."

A shiver ran through Carolyn. "Surely Lady Crawford's death was the result of footpads, and not someone who attended the party."

"I hope so."

"What else did you say?" Carolyn asked.

"He still hasn't sent me a note."

"He? Note?"

Sarah pushed her glasses higher on her nose, and for the first time Carolyn noticed that her normally imperturbable sister seemed very . . . perturbed. Indeed, she appeared to be in an absolute dither.

Leaning closer, Sarah said in an agitated undertone, "Matthew. And I'm referring to the sort of note we read about in the *Memoirs*. I don't understand why he hasn't. Good heavens, the man thinks nothing of plying me with diamond ear bobs, yet I ask him to send me a one line note and he cannot manage it."

Carolyn's amusement was tempered by Sarah's obvious discomposed state. "Giving you diamonds rather than a note. That beast. He deserves a good thrashing."

Sarah blinked, then a sheepish expression crossed her face. "Point taken. It's just that, well, I'm anxious for him to do so. So I can experience the same excitement the Anonymous Lady described."

The knot in Carolyn's stomach cinched tighter. Those damnable excitements the Anonymous Lady had described were the catalyst that had sent all her thoughts—and actions— running amok. "He's most likely just trying to figure out the perfect time and place, poppet. Don't be so impatient."

"I suppose, but 'tis difficult when I know something so pleasurable awaits me."

She instantly thought of Lord Surbrooke . . . naked, aroused, climbing into her bathtub, the mental picture so vivid her breath caught. She squeezed her eyes briefly shut to banish the image. "I'm certain Matthew will send you a note soon." Then, determined to change the subject, she asked, "Have you seen Emily and Julianne?"

She craned her neck, looking around for her friends. And most certainly not hoping to catch a glimpse of *him*. She noted Mrs. Amunsbury, Lady Balsam, and Lady Walsh standing in a tight group near the fireplace. All three ladies were looking at her, and Carolyn couldn't help but wonder if they'd been discussing her. She inclined her head, a greeting the trio returned, then continued looking about. "There's such a crush of people it's impos—"

Her words cut off when her gaze happened upon Lord Surbrooke. He stood on the opposite side of the large, crowded room, facing her, his head bent to catch the words of a petite blond woman whose back was to Carolyn. As she watched, he laughed at something the woman said. Then, as if sensing the weight of her stare, he glanced up and their gazes met.

Carolyn felt the impact of his regard all the way down to her toes, which promptly curled into her satin slippers. For several frantic heartbeats it seemed as if his gaze bore straight through her. He offered her the briefest of nods, then returned his attention to the blonde.

A heated flush enveloped her entire body, and she

had to force herself not to snatch her sister's fan and wave it furiously in front of her burning face. Myriad emotions assailed her. Disappointment, confusion, and embarrassment all collided. He'd acknowledged her, but in a wholly impersonal manner one would use with a stranger. Certainly not in any way that would indicate to her he'd kissed her senseless. Twice. And not in any way that made it appear he was happy to see her. No, he looked perfectly content to continue speaking to the blonde upon whose every word he clung.

A wave of something that felt precisely like jealousy nearly drowned her, although surely it was just annoyance. Why, the man was impossible! Kissing her as if he couldn't breathe without her one minute, then barely glancing her way the next. The blonde was welcome to Lord Surbrooke.

Lifting her chin, she returned her attention to Sarah. And discovered her sister watching her with a questioning look.

"Are you certain you're all right, Carolyn? You don't seem at all yourself. Would you like to leave? Matthew and I can accompany you home."

She shook her head and kept her attention firmly fixed on her sister. "I'm fine. Truly. Just a bit tired." Yes, tired of thinking of things best forgotten. Tired of searching the room for a man she didn't even want to see, other than to tell him she didn't wish to see him.

"I see you found Julianne. Doesn't she look lovely?"

"Julianne? No, I didn't see her. Where is she?"

Sarah shot her an odd look. "You were looking directly at her. She's speaking to Lord Surbrooke."

Carolyn blinked. Then her gaze flew across the room. And she realized that the petite blonde facing Lord Surbrooke was indeed Julianne. And Lord Surbrooke was still hanging on her every word.

"Lord Surbrooke seems to be hanging on her every word," Sarah commented in an undertone, eerily mirroring Carolyn's thoughts. "They make a handsome couple, don't you agree?"

A vice seemed to be compressing her chest, and she barely managed to force out, "Indeed."

And indeed they did. How could they not? Lord Surbrooke's masculine dark good looks perfectly complimented Julianne's delicate golden beauty.

"Lady Gatesbourne is watching them from near the potted palm," Sarah whispered from the side of her mouth, indicating the plant with a slight jerk of her head. "She's sizing up Lord Surbrooke with the sort of zeal I imagine an undertaker experiences when measuring one for a coffin."

A brittle laugh escaped Carolyn. "If Lady Gatesbourne is expecting to bring Lord Surbrooke up to snuff, she's in for a disappointment. The gentleman has no intention of marrying anytime soon."

"So Matthew has told me." She felt the weight of Sarah's regard. "I don't recall mentioning such to you, however."

Carolyn pulled her gaze away from the striking couple. "Lord Surbrooke told me himself."

"Indeed? When?"

Carolyn hoped her shrug looked less forced than it felt. "During one of our conversations," she said vaguely. Her conscience slapped her for her less than forthcoming answer, but she knew if she mentioned Lord Surbrooke's visit to her home that morning, her curious sister would ask endless questions—questions she had no desire to answer.

Sarah nodded. "Ah, at Matthew's house party. 'Tis a shame he's so set against marriage. He's a very fine man."

Carolyn's brows shot up. She'd always considered Sarah an excellent judge of character. And Lord Surbrooke was nothing more than a shallow, albeit charming, rake. Just a handsome exterior covering a pleasure-seeking shell. "You think so?"

Sarah's vigorous nod sent her spectacles sliding down her nose. "Oh, yes. He's been Matthew's closest friend for years. From everything Matthew's told me, Lord Surbrooke is loyal and honorable and very kind." She waggled her brows at Carolyn. "And he certainly isn't difficult to look at."

"No, he certainly isn't," she concurred, for to do anything else would have sparked Sarah's lively curiosity. She bit her tongue to ruthlessly squelch the barrage of questions about him that begged to be asked. She knew everything she had to—that he wanted to bed her—and she wasn't going to fall in with his tempting, er, unacceptable plan.

"Based on the way Lord Surbrooke is smiling and laughing, he and Julianne obviously aren't discussing the topic on everyone else's lips."

Lips . . . yes, his lips . . . those perfect lips. That had kissed her so . . . perfectly. His lips . . . his lips . . . damnation, she'd once again lost the thread of the conversation. "I beg your pardon?"

Sarah shot her an odd look. "They don't appear to be discussing the murder."

"No." What *were* they discussing? She glanced across the room once more. Humph. Surely a chat about the weather wouldn't cause that twinkle in Lord Surbrooke's eyes. And what was this? He was leaning forward, as if to whisper something in Julianne's ear.

At that precise moment Mrs. Amunsbury, Lady Walsh, and Lady Balsam approached, blocking her view. "Heavens, you both look so serious," said Lady Walsh, her curious gaze bouncing between Carolyn and Sarah. She lowered her voice and asked, "Are you discussing the murder? Why, it's nothing short of a public outcry. Everyone is outraged and frightened for their safety."

Before either Carolyn or Sarah could answer, Mrs. Amunsbury, quizzing glass raised, said, "They weren't discussing the murder. Anyone can see they're discussing the very handsome Lord Surbrooke."

"Yes," agreed Lady Balsam, "who is now leading Lady Julianne onto the dance floor."

Carolyn's gaze flew across the room. Lord Surbrooke and Julianne, both of them smiling, approached the parquet dance floor. Where he would hold her in his strong arms. And gaze at her with his beautiful blue eyes. And Julianne would experience the heady pleasure of whirling around the room with him. Of his attention fixed upon her. Know the feel of her hand clasped in his. His hand resting on the small of her back.

An unpleasant sensation gripped her midsection and she dragged her gaze back to her companions.

"He's been quite busy today," Lady Balsam murmured.

"Indeed," agreed Lady Walsh, a half smile playing around the corners of her mouth. She turned her attention to Carolyn. "First a call upon you, now a dance with one of your closest friends. I wonder who will be next?"

Mrs. Amunsbury lifted a perfectly arched brow and a knowing smile curved her lips. "No doubt the scoundrel saw half a dozen women between this morning's call upon Lady Wingate and now."

"Lord Surbrooke called upon you?" Sarah asked, her brows hiked all the way up.

Carolyn cursed the flush she felt warming her face. "Just briefly, to make certain I was all right after hearing about the murder."

"Very *gentlemanly* of him," Lady Balsam said, her catlike gaze fixed on Carolyn.

Another flush washed through Carolyn. There was no missing the insinuation in Lady Balsam's words, nor the speculation in her eyes. Raising her chin, she replied calmly, "Yes, it was a kind gesture. We *are* neighbors, you know."

"Yes, dear, we know," said Lady Walsh, her tone ripe with amusement. Her gaze shifted, then she said, "We've been searching for Lord Heaton everywhere and I've just now spotted him. Will you excuse us?"

She moved off, Lady Balsam and Mrs. Amunsbury following in her wake. Carolyn watched them melt into the crowd and tried to push away her uneasiness.

It seemed clear they suspected Lord Surbrooke's visit this morning had been less than innocent.

She involuntarily raised her hand and brushed her fingers over her lips while a mental image of him kissing her flickered through her mind.

Fine. It *had* been less than innocent. But it wasn't as if they were having *an affair*.

"There you are!" came Emily's voice. "I've been looking for you everywhere. Have you ever seen such a crush? People say they're concerned about a murderer lurking about, yet rather than staying safely at home they're all here, talking feverishly about the crime." She turned to Sarah. "You might want to rescue your husband. My aunt Agatha has trapped him near the potted palm in the corner and he's far too polite to escape."

Sarah craned her neck in the direction of the potted palms. "I wouldn't worry. He's very adept at such situations. Besides, if he suffers a bit, it's no less than he deserves for not yet sending me the time and place *Memoirs* note."

Carolyn's gaze involuntarily shifted to the dance floor. Lord Surbrooke was smiling down at Julianne as they waltzed in perfect unison. Julianne, her beautiful face flushed a delicate pink, smiled in return. A lump seemed to clog Carolyn's throat and she gave herself a mental slap then forced her errant attention back where it belonged.

"There's speculation that Lady Crawford's death wasn't the result of a botched robbery, but a deliberate act," Emily said. "Perhaps committed by a past or current lover."

"Who told you that?" Carolyn asked.

"I've spoken to so many people. Lord Tolliver perhaps? Gossip has it that Lord Warwick was her latest paramour and that he's been questioned by the magistrate and a Runner."

"Everyone who attended the masque is being questioned," Sarah said.

"Yes," Emily agreed. "But *special interest* is being paid to several people, Lord Warwick among them, although I've heard that he has an alibi." She lowered her voice and confided, "If you ask me, they should question Mr. Jennsen."

"Why do you say that?" Carolyn asked.

Emily raised her brows. "Am I the only one who's noticed the number of strange happenings that have occurred since his arrival in England?"

"Don't be absurd," Sarah scolded. "Just because you don't like the man—"

"I don't," Emily agreed, "and—" Whatever else she was about to add was lost when she suddenly stiffened and puckered her lips. "Botheration, here he comes. If you'll excuse me, I'd rather stare at the wallpaper than make conversation with that man."

With that she turned and stalked away, quickly melting into the crowd.

Carolyn blinked. What was that all about? Emily was normally very genial and good-natured. Could Mr. Jennsen be one of the many people to whom Emily's father was deeply in debt? Could that be the source of her uncharacteristic animosity?

"Good evening, ladies," Mr. Jennsen said, stopping in front of them. His gaze flicked in the direction Emily had just gone, then he offered them both a smile and a formal bow. "I am clearly the luckiest man in the room to find myself in the company of not one, but two such lovely women."

"Don't be fooled," Carolyn said in a loud, teasing whisper to Sarah. "I'm certain he has said that to every group of women he's joined this evening."

"I've done no such thing," Mr. Jennsen said, his dark eyes gleaming.

"Which means he's only just arrived," Sarah whispered loudly to Carolyn.

They all laughed, then after exchanging a few pleasantries, Sarah fanned herself and said, "There are so many people, and it's so warm in here . . . if you'll excuse me, I need a bit of fresh air."

Carolyn studied her sister, noting her pale cheeks, which should have been flushed, given the heat of the room. "I'll go with you," she said.

"I'd be happy to escort you both," Mr. Jennsen added.

"Thank you, but you two stay and chat," Sarah said with a wave of her hand. "Matthew is standing by the doors leading to the terrace. I'll rescue him from his current conversation. Besides, I want to mention the *Memoirs* note to him again." She mumbled the last, and Carolyn wondered if her sister even realized she'd spoken the words out loud.

"*Memoirs* note?" Mr. Jennsen asked as Sarah walked away.

"Oh, nothing," Carolyn said lightly. Yet the half-knowing, half-amused look in Mr. Jennsen's eyes made her wonder if he knew about the latest rage.

His gaze swept over her pale aqua gown with unmistakable appreciation. "You were lovely as Galatea, but you are even more stunning as yourself."

"Thank you," she said with a smile, and wondered why she felt so relaxed in his company. Although not classically handsome, he was undeniably attractive—masculine and powerful—and possessed a darkly sensual edge. So why didn't *he* render her breathless? Why wasn't she imagining *him* naked with her in the bath? Surely if her current flustered state was merely the result of the *Memoirs*, then any attractive man would do.

"I suppose you've heard of Lady Crawford's death," he said.

"Yes. I'm stunned and saddened."

"I'd only just met her at the masquerade."

Recollection tickled Carolyn's memory. "She was the costumed wench admiring your pirate garb. You spoke to her after we talked."

He nodded. "Yes. She was laughing, so vibrant. I can hardly believe she died only a few hours later. I hope you're taking care not to venture off alone."

The music ended, followed by a round of polite applause. Carolyn's errant gaze once again shifted to the dance floor and riveted on Lord Surbrooke escorting Julianne toward her mother. He glanced in Carolyn's direction, but rather than looking at her, his gaze settled on Mr. Jennsen. She watched him bestow a kiss upon Julianne's fingers—a gesture that sizzled an uncomfortable sensation down her spine—then he started making his way toward her. Or perhaps toward Mr. Jennsen, as that's who his attention seemed fixed upon.

Since she had no desire to speak to Lord Surbrooke in front of the very observant Mr. Jennsen, she hastily said, "If you'll excuse me, I see a friend I've been looking for."

Mr. Jennsen made her a bow. "Enjoy your evening, my lady."

Carolyn quickly made her way into the crowd, then circled around, intending to head for Julianne. Enjoy her evening? She hoped to. Because thus far she most certainly had not.

Chapter 8

He led me from the crowded party, down a series of dimly lit corridors. I didn't question where we were going. It didn't matter. He found an empty room, locked the door. Pressed me against the oak panel and lifted my skirts. My knees buckled at the first long, hard, delicious thrust into my wet, overheated sex.

Memoirs of a Mistress by An Anonymous Lady

A moment of your time, Jennsen?" Daniel asked, stopping in front of the American. The question came out in a much more brusque tone than he'd intended, but damn it, he hadn't liked seeing Carolyn standing next to the other man. Hadn't liked the way Jennsen looked at her—in a way that made it patently clear he liked what he saw. Hadn't liked the way Carolyn smiled up at him. No, he hadn't liked any of it.

With the party noises buzzing around them, Jennsen studied him with an unflinching gaze that Daniel suspected didn't miss very much. "Of course. In fact, I was hoping to see you this evening. I've some further information regarding that business matter we discussed several weeks ago."

Business matter? It took several seconds for Daniel to realize he must mean the investment Lord Tolliver had wanted him to make in his shipping venture. It wasn't at all what he wished to discuss with Jennsen, indeed he'd quite forgotten about it, but he supposed it was as good an excuse as any other.

"Shall we retire to a quieter, more private spot?" Daniel suggested.

"Good idea."

Daniel led the way to the French windows and outside into the cool air, where they moved toward the far end of the terrace. There, Jennsen asked without preamble, "Did you invest in Lord Tolliver's shipping venture?"

"No. After reviewing the information you gave me, I decided against it." Daniel tried to dredge up some gratitude but it was damn difficult while recalling the heat in Jennsen's eyes while he'd looked at Carolyn.

"A wise decision, especially since I've just learned that Tolliver's financial situation is even less stable than I thought. Plus, I had the opportunity to examine his materials for building the ships. They're inferior."

Daniel raised his brows. "How did you happen to have such an opportunity?"

Jennsen shrugged. "I hardly see how that matters."

Daniel's jaw tightened. Obviously Jennsen was a man who didn't mind bending—or breaking—the rules in order to get what he wanted. "Have other potential investors besides me backed out?"

"Yes," Jennsen said. "Looks as if Tolliver stands to lose everything."

He recalled his tense exchange with the inebriated earl at last night's masked ball. Facing financial and possibly social ruin had driven more than one man to the bottle.

"Good decision not to invest," Jennsen said. "Certainly if it were my money, I'd have nothing to do with it."

Daniel nodded slowly. He hadn't doubted Jennsen's earlier assessment—which had led him not to invest—nor did he now. According to everything he'd seen and heard, the man was a financial genius, and he certainly had the wealth to prove it. Wealth he'd reportedly built from nothing. Part of Daniel supposed he should voice his appreciation. The other part of him wanted to toss the bastard on his arse.

He cleared his throat. "Thank you," he said stiffly.

There was no missing the amusement that kindled in Jennsen's gaze. "Damn near killed you to say it, didn't it? But at any rate, you're welcome. Now why don't you tell me what you wanted to talk to me about—although I could save us both some time and tell you I already know. The killing stares you shoot my way whenever I'm near her haven't gone unnoticed." He leaned his hips against the stone railing. "If you intend to glare at every man who looks at her, you're doomed to spend your entire life with a scowl on your face."

Daniel's gaze didn't waver. "There are looks, then there are *looks*."

"I see. And I've given her *looks*." Jennsen shrugged. "You can hardly blame me. She's extraordinarily beautiful."

"And unavailable."

Jennsen's brows raised. "Indeed? I've heard no announcement of an engagement. Or are you on the brink of proposing?"

"That is none of your concern."

"Just as my friendship with Lady Wingate, or any other woman for that matter, is none of yours."

Daniel's eyes narrowed. "You seem to have a habit of casting your eye upon women who are—"

"The object of someone else's fancy?"

"That's as good a description as any. A few months ago you were gazing at Lady Wingate's sister in the same manner you now are looking at Lady Wingate."

"Yes. And look how that turned out. Sarah married your friend and is now Marchioness Langston. And before that, as you may have heard, I fancied another woman who married shortly thereafter." A gleam flashed in his eyes. "You may think me your rival, Surbrooke, and in truth I hope to God I am. But I think perhaps I might just be an inadvertent matchmaker." He flashed a grin. "Perhaps I should start charging for my services."

When Daniel's only response was a freezing stare, Jennsen shrugged. "Or perhaps not. Time will tell. Pleasure talking to you." He inclined his head, then walked back toward the French windows as if he hadn't a care in the world and disappeared into the ballroom.

Daniel frowned at the spot where he'd last seen the aggravating man and blew out a long breath. Bloody hell. What had all that meant? Damned if he knew. But one thing was clear—he and Jennsen wanted the same woman.

And Jennsen wasn't going to have her.

He'd tried to give her some space this evening, forced himself not to pounce on her the instant he saw her—as much in an effort not to scare her off as prove to himself he could do it. But it was now far past the time for him to seek out what he wanted and ensure that he got it. She'd already hastened away when he'd approached her and Jennsen. He'd not let her escape again.

Filled with determination, he was about to reenter the ballroom when he experienced a strong sensation of being watched. His gaze searched the dimly lit terrace, the people standing in groups chatting, then the fenced garden and couples strolling the paths, and noted no one looking at him. Bloody hell, now he was imagining things.

Without further delay he rejoined the party. And was immediately waylaid by his hostess, Lady Gatesbourne. Only a lifetime of breeding kept him from shaking off the overbearing woman whose gaze bore an unmistakable matchmaking gleam. And who was dropping extremely unsubtle hints that she'd like to dance. Bloody hell. Resigned to being polite—but only because she was his hostess—he partnered her in a cotillion. Immediately after the dance, however, he made her a formal bow and set about finding Carolyn.

His lungs ceased working in that strange way they had when he finally spotted her. By God, she was lovely, her upswept honey-colored hair gleaming under the dozens of candles glittering in the crystal chandeliers. Her gown was the exact shade of aquamarines, and his imagination instantly conjured him clasping a strand of the pale blue gems around her slender neck. Then removing her gown, leaving her dressed in only his jewels. And a welcoming smile . . . yes, that would be very nice.

He blinked away the sensual image and noticed that just then she did smile . . . but not at him. No, she was once again smiling at that bastard Jennsen. Who was smiling back. With that *look* in his eye. And two other gentlemen hovered nearby, studying her like predatory animals sniffing out a particularly tasty morsel. The same gut-tightening he was becoming accustomed to experiencing whenever matters concerning Carolyn were involved seized him and he quickened his steps. By the time he reached her, he was hot and annoyed and wanted nothing more than to introduce Jennsen, as well as those other two, to the bloody flagstones.

"Good evening, Lady Wingate," he said, halting in front of her and offering a formal bow. He flicked a glance at her companion. "Jennsen."

The warmth that had been in her eyes for Jennsen turned cool as she gazed upon Daniel, and the knot in his stomach tightened further. "Lord Surbrooke," she murmured.

"I have it on good authority that the next dance is a waltz. Would you do me the honor?" A rather brusque invitation, which only increased his annoyance, this time at himself for again lacking finesse.

She hesitated, and appeared about to refuse, but then nodded. "Very well."

After excusing herself to Jennsen, who appeared wholly amused, damn him, she placed her fingertips on Daniel's extended arm. A tingle ran up his elbow in spite of the fact that she touched him with what appeared to be all the enthusiasm one would display toward a poisonous insect.

As soon as the music started, he swept her in to his arms. And breathed his first easy breath of the entire night.

"You look stunning," he said, his heart beating ridiculously fast as his gaze devoured her.

"Thank you."

"I'm very glad you decided to attend the party."

She lifted her chin. "I saw no reason not to. Julianne is one of my closest friends."

He could almost hear her adding in a defiant voice, *And I wasn't about to let you scare me off.* Excellent. He'd known she was brave. She merely needed to assert that repressed aspect of herself more. He certainly hoped she would do so where he was concerned.

After savoring the feel of her in his arms for several turns, he couldn't stop himself from speaking the simple truth. "I've thought of nothing else except you all day."

One elegant brow arched upward and a whiff of amusement entered her eyes. "That is obvious, given your attentiveness this evening."

Hmmm. Did she sound . . . irritated? Satisfaction filled him at the possibility. "You've had my full attention all evening, I assure you." At her look of disbelief, he spread his fingers wider against her back and pulled her several inches closer. Then in a voice only she could hear, he said, "You require proof? Very well. Since your arrival you've eaten four canapés and sipped three glasses of punch. You've chatted with eleven women, including your sister, Lady Emily, Lady Julianne, and five gentlemen, including your brother-in-law and Mr. Jennsen—twice. You've smiled twenty-seven times, frowned eight, laughed fifteen, sneezed once, and haven't danced until now."

Her eyes widened. "You made that up."

"I did not. But I forgot one thing. You are unequivocally the most beautiful woman in the room."

A blush stained her cheeks, and it was all he could do not to lean down and touch his lips to the beguiling color. "For the sake of politeness," he continued, "I danced with my hostess and my hostess's daughter, yet even then you occupied my thoughts. I've been looking forward to this moment, to holding you in my arms, ever since I arrived."

He watched her, wondering if he'd gone too far, if his blatant honesty would frighten her off. He hoped not, because he couldn't seem to stop himself. Couldn't bring himself to prevaricate with her.

Finally she cleared her throat. "Actually, I'm glad for this opportunity to speak with you, my lord."

"Daniel . . . my extremely lovely, very dear, greatly talented, highly amusing, and extraordinarily intelligent *Lady Wingate*." His gaze dipped to her mouth. "Who possesses the most kissable lips I've ever seen."

Her blush deepened and she glanced around, as if to make certain no one had heard his quiet comment. "That is precisely what I wanted to talk to you about."

"Your very kissable lips? Excellent, as it is a subject I'm anxious to explore further."

She shook her head. "That is *not* what I meant." She appeared to draw a bracing breath. "I've considered your . . . offer."

"That we become lovers?"

"Yes. I'm afraid I must decline."

He studied her closely. There was determination in her eyes, but something else. Something that looked like regret. Tension radiated off her, making it clear she expected an argument from him. And God knows he wanted to give her one. Actually what he wanted to do was drag her off to some dark, private quiet corner and kiss her, touch her, until she changed her mind.

But neither arguing nor dragging was in his best interests. No, best to allow her to win this battle. Let her think she was in control. Because he had every intention of winning the war. And making her lose control. In his arms. And in his bed.

Therefore, like every general who'd just lost a battle, he regrouped and prepared to outflank.

He nodded. "Very well. I understand."

Her nonplussed reaction indicated she *had* anticipated an argument. Keeping his expression carefully blank, he added, "Although you've no desire for us to become lovers, I hope we can continue to be what we've been all along—friends."

"I . . . well, yes. I suppose—"

"Excellent. I bid you a good evening." He offered her a formal bow, then walked away, absorbing her stare, which he felt boring into his back. And forced himself not to turn around.

Chapter 9

I didn't know him very well, but that didn't seem to matter much when he glided his hand up my leg. And not at all when his mouth followed the same path.

Memoirs of a Mistress by An Anonymous Lady

When Daniel arrived home, rather than finding his household dark and asleep, lights blazed in several windows and he was greeted at the door by Samuel.

"Ye'll never guess wot, milord," the footman said before Daniel had even removed his hat.

Uh-oh. The fact that whatever animal Samuel had rescued this time merited him waiting up to tell him about it didn't bode well.

"I can't imagine," Daniel murmured, bracing himself. "What have you brought home this time?"

Samuel swallowed audibly. "It's a . . . girl."

"A girl . . . what? A girl squirrel? A girl rabbit?" Good God, he hoped not another girl rabbit. The last one Samuel brought home had promptly given birth to even more rabbits—all of which now resided in the country at Meadow Hill. No doubt the property was overrun with multiple generations of the furry, cotton-tailed creatures.

Samuel shook his head. "No, milord. Just a . . . girl." He cleared his throat. "Of the female person variety."

Daniel stared at his footman, whose cheeks bore twin flags of scarlet. Before he could speak, Samuel said in a rush, "Found 'er huddled in an alley, milord. Cryin' she were. Thought at first I were goin' to hurt her." Samuel's eyes flashed. "She'd already been hurt."

Daniel's jaw clenched. "How badly?"

"Got two blackened eyes, some cuts, and lots o' bruises. She managed to get away before the bastard who grabbed her hurt her worse." His lips pressed into a tight line then his voice dropped to a whisper. "But she'd been hurt before, milord. I . . . could tell."

A knot twisted in Daniel's stomach. Yes, Samuel would unfortunately be able to tell. "Where is she? Does she require a doctor?"

"Curled up on the sofa in the drawing room. Probably someone should look at 'er cuts, but when I mentioned a doctor she got upset and refused. 'Tis clear she don't want a man touchin' her, milord, and I can't blame her none fer that. Took some convincin' to get her to leave that alley with me. But with Cook and Mary already gone home to their families for the night, ain't nobody here but men."

Daniel nodded slowly. "Do you know her name?"

"Katie Marshall, milord."

"And how old is Miss Marshall?"

"Nineteen." Samuel's gaze rested steadily on his. "She's a decent girl, milord. Fell on hard times a few months back when the family she worked for let 'er go. Been tryin' to find work ever since. She'd heard about a family needin' a maid and were on her way to the house when the bastard got hold of her. Stole what little money she had and tried to take more than that." Samuel's eyes flashed. "Fought 'im, she did, and got away."

"Good for her," Daniel said quietly. "I think it best we get someone—a woman—here as soon as possible. Lady Wingate's town house is closest. Go there and ask for her maid to come. After you bring her here, you can go for Cook and Mary. And Samuel?"

"Yes, milord?"

"As luck would have it, I'm certain I'm in need of another maid."

Instead of flashing his normal quick grin, Samuel nodded solemnly. "Thank ye, milord. 'Tis the best of men ye are."

As always, Samuel's gratitude and high opinion humbled him. He wasn't the best of men—he knew that all too well. But maybe, just maybe, with Samuel's help, he was making up for a bit of his past failures.

*W*eary and unsettled after the party, Carolyn was relieved to arrive home. After handing her cashmere shawl to Nelson and bidding the butler good-night, she turned toward the stairway, determined to go to bed and fall into a dreamless sleep.

Alone.

Yes, she was alone.

She frowned. Not alone. Just . . . without him. She had years' worth of memories to keep her company. Not to mention her sister and her friends. Of course she wasn't alone.

Still, the persistent, nagging question floating through the back of her mind plagued her. Had she done the right thing in refusing Lord Surbrooke's offer?

Yes, her common sense insisted.

No, her heart argued.

She was halfway up the stairs when the bell that indicated the front gate had been opened rang. Seconds later the brass door knocker sounded. Surprised, she turned around and looked at an equally surprised Nelson, who stood in the foyer still holding her wrap.

"Who on earth would be calling at such an hour?" Carolyn asked, unable to keep the concern from her voice. Obviously something was wrong—people didn't knock on one's door at one A.M. because all was well.

Before opening the door, Nelson looked out one of the slender windows flanking the oak panel. "'Tis Samuel, Lord Surbrooke's footman," he reported.

Carolyn gripped the banister, her entire body tensing with dread. *Dear God, had something happened to Lord Surbrooke?* "Let him in," she said, forcing the words around the lump of fear lodged in her throat as she moved in jerky motions down the stairs.

Nelson admitted a tall, out of breath, handsome young man who was clearly relieved to see her. He burst into a rapid staccato speech about finding an injured young woman, bringing her home, and her refusal to see a doctor.

"'Tis a woman she needs, milady, if you understand my meanin'. His lordship sent me to fetch yer maid, to see if she could help."

"Of course," Carolyn said, her relief that it wasn't Lord Surbrooke who was injured colliding with her sympathy for the young woman. She turned to Nelson. "Awaken Gertrude. As soon as she's dressed, escort her to Lord Surbrooke's town house. I'll go with Samuel now."

To Carolyn's amazement, Lord Surbrooke opened the door to his town house himself. His normally perfect appearance was more than a bit disarranged. His hair was rumpled, as if he'd plunged his fingers through the dark brown strands. He'd removed his jacket and cravat and rolled back his shirtsleeves, to reveal muscular forearms dusted with dark hair. She'd never seen him so . . . undone. The effect was dazzling and momentarily robbed her of her wits.

A loud meow pulled her from her stupor, and she looked down to see a black cat weaving around Lord Surbrooke's boots. A black cat that looked up at her and blinked. With one eye.

She lifted her gaze back to Lord Surbrooke's and noted he seemed as surprised to see her standing in his foyer as she was to see him. After giving herself a stern mental shake, she said, "Samuel explained the situation and my maid is on her way, but I thought I could be of some help. As a physician's daughter and the older sister of one who constantly scraped herself up, I'm quite adept at these matters."

"Thank you," he said, and tunneled his fingers through his hair. "From what Samuel's told me, Miss Marshall's injuries aren't life threatening, but they should be seen to."

"Of course. Where is she?"

"The drawing room. I've gathered some necessities—bandages, water, and salve—and left them outside the door." He turned to Samuel. "I didn't want to enter and frighten her, so we'll all go in together. After we've been introduced, you can go for Cook and Mary."

When Lord Surbrooke opened the drawing room door, Carolyn saw a young woman curled up on the sofa in front of the hearth. She sat up as they entered. A combination of sympathy and anger rushed through Carolyn at the sight of the dark bruises marring the girl's face. Samuel went immediately to her side.

"That's Lord Surbrooke," the young footman said gently, crouching before her, but not touching her. "There's no reason to fear him, or anyone else in this house. His lordship is the one wot saved me and he's promised to help you, too. Give ye a job right here, in his grand house, as a maid. His friend, Lady Wingate, is a very kind and fine lady indeed. She'll look after ye till her maid arrives. Ye have my word ye're in good hands, Katie."

Katie's wide-eyed gaze shifted to her and Lord

Surbrooke and she jerked her head in a nod. "Th-
Thank ye."

"You're welcome," said Lord Surbrooke.

The three of them brought in the supplies, setting
them on the table next to the sofa. Carolyn noted
that the room, with its pale green silk walls dotted
with pastoral landscapes, rich velvet drapes, and mahogany furniture, reflected understated and excellent
taste. Interesting, and rather surprising, as she would
have guessed a bachelor gentleman's home more
likely to be decorated with stuffed animal heads than
elegant paintings.

Her attention was momentarily captured by the
beautiful large painting above the mantel. It depicted
a woman dressed in a blue gown. Seen from the back,
with only the slightest hint of the curve of her face vis-
ible, she stood on the terrace of what was obviously
a grand manor house. One hand was braced on the
stone balustrade while the other was raised to shadow
the bright sun as she looked out over the extensive
formal English garden, which was in full bloom. An
unseen breeze blew the hem of her gown and a lock
of her light brown hair. In the background, standing
in the garden, was the figure of a gentleman. Carolyn
had the distinct impression that even though the man
was surrounded by the beauty of the garden, the only
thing he saw was the woman on the terrace.

Lord Surbrooke and Samuel departed, leaving her
alone with Katie. She offered the girl a reassuring
smile and did her best to hide the sympathy overwhelming her. Dear God, the poor young woman
was a mess of cuts and bruises.

"My father is a physician, and I learned a great deal from him," she said softly, dunking a clean cloth into a ceramic bowl filled with warm water. "I'd like to clean you up then apply some salve and bandages to the worst of your cuts, if that's all right. I promise to be gentle." She squeezed the excess water from the cloth and held it out. "May I?"

Katie hesitated, then nodded.

Carolyn set to work, first washing away the dirt from Katie's hands. The girl's palms and fingers bore numerous cuts and her knuckles were scraped raw, the nails ripped ragged.

"This happened when you fought off the robber?" Carolyn asked, applying a healing salve to the broken skin on Katie's knuckles. She'd learned from her father long ago that keeping up a light patter of conversation helped take a patient's mind off their injuries.

"Yes, milady."

"You're very brave. And by the looks of these knuckles, you planted the ruffian a few good knocks."

"A few. But it weren't enough. He still made off with all me money, little though it were." As Carolyn continued her ministrations, Katie whispered in a shaky voice, "Do ye think Samuel was right? That Lord Surbrooke will hire me? I can't imagine he would, what with me bein' all cut up and bruised like this." Her swollen eyes welled up with tears. "I looked in the mirror. I know how awful I look."

"I'm certain Samuel wouldn't have said that if Lord Surbrooke hadn't told him so. As for your cuts and bruises, they'll heal."

Katie seemed to relax a bit at that. "I couldn't believe it when Samuel came into that alley. At first I thought he were another footpad, or bent on mischief as men are wont to be. But instead he turned out to be an angel of mercy."

"I heard him say his lordship is the one who saved him. Do you know what he meant?"

"Oh yes, milady. Samuel told me all about it in the hack he hired to drive us here. Talked the entire way, he did. Never in my life have I met a man who talks so much. Usually it's impossible to drag more than a grunt or single word out of 'em."

Carolyn thought of her kindly but taciturn father and smiled. "Men can be frustratingly incommunicative," she agreed.

Katie nodded. "Yes, milady. But not Samuel. Told me all about a cold, rainy night in Bristol, about how he were sick and starvin' and tried to *rob* the earl, if ye can imagine. 'Cept he didn't get any blunt 'cause he collapsed, right at the earl's feet. But instead of turnin' him in, or just leavin' him in the street like anybody else would have done, the earl picked Samuel up and carried him back to the inn where he was stayin'. Ain't that somethin'?"

Before Carolyn could answer that it was indeed, Katie continued, "The earl got doctors for Samuel and saw to it he got well. And when he did, he offered Samuel a job—provided Samuel never stole again. And he hasn't. Not once. Might not believe just anybody who told me that, but somethin' 'bout Samuel inspires trust. Given the way he's helped me, I believe him."

Carolyn looked up from bandaging Katie's hand, her mind swirling with this surprising information. "And now Lord Surbrooke has offered you a job as well."

"So it would seem, thanks to Samuel."

Finished with Katie's hands, Carolyn wet a clean cloth and gently dabbed at the young woman's face. "How long has Samuel been Lord Surbrooke's footman?" she asked.

"'Bout a year. Sang Lord Surbrooke's praises he did. Not only about savin' him, but then there are the dogs."

"The dogs?" Carolyn repeated, bewildered.

"Stubby, Limpy, and Droopy he called them, all named for their . . . problems."

"Problems?"

"Yes, milady. Stubby lost his tail, Limpy's missin' a leg, and Droopy only has one ear that's—"

"Droopy?" Carolyn guessed.

"Yes. All were abandoned or left fer dead. Samuel finds the beasts and brings 'em to his lordship and together they save 'em."

With each passing minute Carolyn's amazement grew. She'd had no idea of this aspect of Lord Surbrooke's character. That he was a man who would not only rescue a former thief, but open his home to the young man, and now to Katie. That he would aid in the rescuing of injured and abandoned animals. She hadn't considered Lord Surbrooke to be anything more than a gentleman of leisure who sought his own pleasures.

Such was her amazement, she couldn't help but

voice it. "I had no idea Lord Surbrooke devoted his time and resources in such a way."

"'Tis a surprise," Katie agreed. Then her expression hardened. "From wot I've seen, not many men in his position would."

She couldn't argue with that statement. "What else did Samuel tell you?"

"That he just found a new puppy and named him Baldy. And there're other dogs but because they'd gotten so many, they live at his lordship's country estate in Kent. Then there are the cats—Blinky and Tippy."

She recalled the one-eyed cat in the foyer. "I believe I saw Blinky. What is Tippy's ailment?"

"One leg shorter than the others, I believe. Besides the cats there've been a few squirrels and a rabbit. Who quickly popped out several more rabbits."

"That must have been a surprise," Carolyn said with a smile, dabbing salve on a shallow cut over Katie's brow.

"No doubt. And then there's the parrot. His name is Naughty. Don't know why he's named that—we arrived here before Samuel could tell me."

"It makes for interesting speculation," Carolyn murmured.

Katie winced when Carolyn dabbed at a bruise on her cheek. "I'm sorry," Carolyn said. "Does it hurt terribly?" The swollen dark purple skin looked tender and painful.

"No, milady. Certainly not in comparison to some of the hurts I've had."

Carolyn's stomach plummeted at the young woman's bleak words. Before she could find her voice, a knock sounded at the door. Lord Surbrooke entered, followed by her maid Gertrude, whose motherly face was wreathed with concern as she looked at Katie.

"Katie, this is Gertrude, my abigail," Carolyn said. "She's taken care of me for years and is one of the kindest people I've ever known."

"I brought one of my own night rails for ye, my dear, so we can get ye comfortable," said Gertrude, tufts of gray hair sticking out of her obviously hastily donned cap. "Then I'll see to cleanin' yer clothes."

Katie blinked her swollen eyes. "Ain't never had nobody wait on me before."

"I've instructed my butler, Barkley, to show you to one of the guest rooms," Lord Surbrooke said. "I'll send up my maid as soon as she arrives and have Cook prepare some broth."

"Don't you worry, my lord, we'll be just fine," Gertrude said, gently helping Katie to stand. "I'll watch over the young lady."

Barkley stood at attention in the doorway. The butler had clearly been warned about Katie's aversion to strange men, for he made no attempt to assist her, rather just led Gertrude and Katie from the room.

Standing next to the fireplace, Carolyn watched Lord Surbrooke close the door after them. The soft click reverberated in the quiet room. For several seconds he remained facing the door, his head bowed, as if by some weight too heavy to bear. Then he turned and their gazes met. All the unexpected things Katie had told her rushed through Carolyn's mind, and she felt as if she were seeing him for the first time.

He dragged his hands down his face and offered her a ghost of a smile. "Quite an eventful evening."

"Yes . . ."

Her reply trailed off as he walked slowly toward her, halting when an arm's length separated them. Her body seemed to strain toward him and she braced her knees to keep from stepping forward to erase that slice of space that simultaneously felt like too much and not nearly enough of a distance. She was about to curl her fingers inward so as not to reach out and brush back the errant lock of hair spilling onto his forehead, when he lightly clasped her hands.

Warmth engulfed her fingers. The sensation of his bare hands on hers rippled tingles of pleasure through her. "Thank you," he said, his serious blue eyes steady on hers. "It was very kind of you to help."

"It was my pleasure to do so. That poor girl. She's very fortunate her injuries weren't more severe." Her gaze searched his. "Are you going to take her on as a maid?"

"Yes."

"Do you *need* another maid?"

He shrugged. "A house this size can always use more help."

His nonchalance proved to her what she'd suspected—that he didn't need another maid at all. Yet he was willing to give an unfortunate young woman a job. Something inside her seemed to shift, but before she could define the sensation, he gently squeezed her hands then released them. She immediately missed the warmth of his skin pressed against hers.

"Would you like to go home?" he asked.

Her common sense told her to leave, that she'd done what she could to help and it was therefore time to go. But her mind buzzed with curiosity, dozens of questions about him she wanted answered. She'd clearly misjudged at least certain aspects of his character. What else had she been wrong about? There was only one way to find out. And she very much wanted to know.

"I'll stay with Gertrude, until your maid and cook arrive," she said.

She couldn't tell by his expression if he was pleased or not. Indeed, a curtain seemed to have fallen over his features. "Can I interest you in a drink?" he asked, walking toward a mahogany end table upon which rested a trio of crystal decanters. "I'm afraid I cannot offer you tea until Cook arrives, but I have brandy, port, or sherry, if you'd like."

More to have something to do with her fidgety hands than because she desired a beverage, she said, "Sherry, please."

After pouring the drinks, he rejoined her and lifted his snifter. "Here's to . . . neighbors. And friendship. You have my gratitude for answering my call for help, especially at such an ungodly hour."

She touched the rim of her glass to his, and the ring of crystal echoed through the room. "'Twas no hardship. I hadn't yet retired."

His gaze skimmed over the aqua gown she'd worn to the Gatesbourne soiree. "So I see. Shall we sit?"

The prospect of sitting with him on the cozy sofa in this cozy room felt far too . . . cozy. And much too tempting. "Actually, I'm feeling . . ." *Far too drawn to you.* " . . . rather restless." True, although the reason had nothing to do with applying salve and bandages, and everything to do with him.

"Restless. Yes, a feeling I share." He hesitated for several seconds, then suggested, "A walk through the conservatory, then?"

That sounded safe enough.

Certainly safer than the quiet, fire-lit intimacy of the drawing room.

After all, what could possibly happen in a room filled with plants?

She offered him a smile. "A walk through the conservatory sounds lovely."

Chapter 10

At one soiree, after a waltz during which he'd blatantly undressed me and made love to me with this eyes, I pulled him into a nearby room and locked the door. And let him finish what he'd started on the dance floor.

Memoirs of a Mistress by An Anonymous Lady

Daniel tossed back his brandy in a single swallow and inwardly grimaced at the fire burning down his throat to his stomach. The last bloody thing he needed was anything else to make him more heated. The mere sight of Carolyn, here, in his drawing room, sipping his sherry, was more than enough to make him feel as if he'd stepped into a roaring hearth.

He watched her delicately sip her sherry. How did she manage to look so beautiful even when doing something as mundane as drinking? His hungry gaze moved lower, drawn to the swell of her generous breasts, which her gown hinted at, then over the flattering aqua garment that perfectly complimented her creamy skin and blue eyes. He'd be hard pressed to name another woman who would have immediately—and personally—answered his call for assistance, not even pausing to change out of her finery. And was willing to act as nurse to a stranger, and actually possessed the skills to do so. Aspects of her besides her beauty to admire. And it suddenly hit him that he didn't require any others. That in fact he quite admired her more than enough already.

He felt the weight of her regard and looked up. And discovered her staring at the vee opening in his shirt. With an expression that indicated she liked what she saw. His shoulders tensed and he tightened his hold on his empty snifter to keep from yanking her into his arms and kissing her until she admitted that she wanted him as much as he wanted her.

She glanced up and their gazes collided. The crimson that rushed into her cheeks made it plain she was aware she'd been caught staring. She took a hasty sip of sherry then set down her glass on the mahogany side table.

After he did the same, they quit the room and headed down the dimly lit corridor leading to the conservatory. From the corner of his eye he noted her twisting her fingers together, a good indication she felt the same awareness, the same thick tension, as he did. A promising sign, as far as he was concerned.

"You're remarkably adept at cleaning and bandaging cuts," he remarked, wading into the silence.

"Sarah was quite the hoyden as a child," she said, her lips curving upward in obvious affectionate remembrance. "I spent many hours doctoring her many scrapes and cuts. And a few of my own."

"You're not the least bit squeamish?"

"No. If I'd been born a boy I would have followed in my father's footsteps and become a physician."

His brows shot up in surprise. He'd never heard an aristocratic woman say such a thing—that she aspired to a profession. But of course, Carolyn wasn't born into the peerage. "You said Sarah was a hoyden. How did you come about *your* scrapes and cuts?"

A smile tugged at her lips. "I have a confession to make."

Interest flared within him. "Oh? Pray don't keep me in suspense. But I find it only fair to remind you—confessions at midnight can be a dangerous thing."

"Then how fortunate for me it's well past midnight." Mischief danced in her eyes, and leaning closer, she confided with a conspiratorial air, "I used to . . . *climb trees.*"

He wasn't sure if he was more surprised, intrigued, or amused. "Never say so."

"I'm afraid it's true. And balance on fallen tree stumps. And jump along the rocks that protruded around the pond near our home. Fell in the water more than once."

A memory attempted to crawl up from where it resided in the depths of his soul and he quickly slammed shut the dungeon door to keep it from see-ing the light of day. "I'm quite certain you're telling me a Bunbury tale, my lady. You're not capable of such shocking behavior."

"I assure you it's true. My mother always insisted my behavior be flawless, yet she put no such restric-tions on Sarah."

"Why is that?"

She hesitated, clearly considering whether to tell him. Finally she said, "Much to my consternation, I was always Mother's favorite. She considered Sarah hopelessly plain and paid little attention to her, pin-ning all her hopes—actually, expectations—on me to marry well. Her favoritism hurt Sarah deeply, and me as well, as I adored Sarah from the day she was born. I escaped Mother's stifling clutches every chance I could, and when I did, I joined Sarah in tree climbing and rock jumping, or whatever grand adventure she was undertaking. Mother would have flown into the boughs had she known, so to cover up those occasions when I'd slip and fall, I learned how to treat my own injuries. And Sarah's as well." She flashed a smile. "Since Father was a physician, it wasn't terribly difficult to figure out. Or to pilfer bandages."

They'd reached the glass doors leading to the con-servatory and he paused. "I must admit I'm taken unawares at this unexpected side of you, my lady."

"I assure you it's true. In fact, I sport a scar on my ankle—a souvenir of one of my less successful tree climbing adventures. I consider it a badge of honor."

He grasped the curved brass knob and opened the door. The air around them was instantly inundated with a floral fragrance layered with hints of freshly turned soil. A silvery beam of moonlight fell upon the stone floor, shimmering down from the glass panels set in the high ceiling. He glanced up and noted a glimpse of a pearly moon set in a black, velvety sky strewn with diamondlike stars.

"How lovely," she murmured, stepping farther into the warm room.

"I thought you might like it."

"I do. Very much." She pulled in a deep breath then smiled. "It must be glorious in the daylight."

"Yes, but I actually prefer coming here at night. I find it very . . ."

"Peaceful?"

He nodded. "Yes. The perfect spot for contemplation."

There was no missing her surprise. "I wouldn't have thought you a man given to quiet reflection."

"Clearly you don't know me as well as you believe."

She gave him a searching look. "Actually, I don't believe I know you very well at all." Before he could assure her that he was delighted to tell her anything she might wish to know, she continued, "Sarah has always had a great love for plants and flowers. Is your interest of a long-standing nature?"

He led her slowly down an aisle of lustrous greenery. "It was actually one of my mother's great passions. This conservatory was her favorite room in the house. It fell into disrepair after she died. When I inherited the house three years ago upon my father's death, I had it refurbished. I maintain it in her memory."

"I'm sorry for your loss," she murmured. "I cannot imagine the difficulty of losing both parents. How old were you when your mother died?"

"Eight." Determined to change the subject, he pointed to the upcoming section of flowers. "The roses," he said. He snapped off a nearby bud, removed the thorns from the stem, then held the bloom out to her. "For you."

"Thank you." She lifted the offering to her nose and inhaled, then held the flower up to examine it in a shimmering ribbon of moonlight. "It doesn't appear to be pure white," she said, slowly turning the stem between her fingers.

"It's a very pale pink, a color my groundskeeper calls 'blush.'" He reached out and stroked his fingertip over the edge of a petal. "This flower reminds me of you."

"Why is that?"

"Because it's delicate. Fragrant. And very, very lovely." He brushed the fingertip that had just touched the rose over her soft cheek. "And because you blush so beautifully."

As if on cue, color rushed into her cheeks, and he smiled. "Just like that."

His compliment clearly flustered her, and she looked down as they continued to slowly walk along the aisle. After several long seconds of silence, she remarked, "You must have left the party early."

"I had no desire to stay after you departed."

Carolyn's gaze snapped to him and her breath

caught at his intense regard. He was looking at her as if she were a sweet confection and he harbored a craving for sugar. *Oh . . . my.* And it wasn't just what he said, but the way he said it, in that low, husky voice. The tension that had gripped her from the moment she found herself alone with him doubled, and her entire body seemed to burst into flame—and he hadn't even touched her. Except for that whisper of a caress against her cheek moments ago, which had left a trail of fire in its wake.

And she realized that in spite of her wish for it to be otherwise, she wanted him to touch her. Very much.

What would he do if she told him so? If she said, *I want you to touch me. Kiss me.*

He'd oblige you, her inner voice whispered.

Yes. And she'd once again feel all the magic she'd experienced on the two other occasions he'd touched her. Kissed her.

She gripped the rose's stem to keep from fanning her hand in front of her overheated face. Desperate for something, anything, to say that didn't include the words *kiss me*, she said, "Katie told me about the interesting array of pets you've saved."

"Ah, yes, they're quite a colorful group—or perhaps 'herd' is a better description."

"Saving abandoned animals . . . it is a surprising and unusual pursuit for an earl."

"Believe me, no one was more surprised than I. It's truly Samuel's enterprise, but when he brought home his first find, a half-starved, sickly, pure black cat missing an eye, I couldn't refuse. Blinky fully recovered and is now an honored member of the household."

She smiled at the pet's name. "I saw Blinky in the foyer when I arrived."

"Only because she prowls the house at night. Beast does nothing but nap before the hearth all day."

His grumpy words were belied by the obvious affection in his voice. "Regardless, not many employers would help their servant in such a way. Or allow them to bring home stray after stray."

"I fear I've little choice, as the need to help those less fortunate is deeply ingrained in Samuel's nature."

"Clearly. It is an admirable attribute. Most likely the result of the kindness you showed him."

He halted at the end of the row and turned to face her. "Obviously Samuel told Katie—"

"Who told me. Yes."

He shrugged. "I did nothing anyone else wouldn't have done."

She raised her brows. Surely he didn't truly believe that. "On the contrary, I think many people would have left a person who'd attempted to rob them where he fell. Or summoned the authorities. You saved his life."

"I merely offered him a choice. He was smart enough to choose wisely."

"A very generous choice, after you'd very generously saved his life."

Again he shrugged. "It just so happened I was in need of a footman."

Why did he insist on making light of what he'd done? She considered asking him, but decided to let the matter rest. For now. But she couldn't deny she was both surprised and intrigued by this unforeseen modest aspect of him—in addition to all the other unexpected aspects she'd learned this evening. The man was full of surprises.

He nodded toward the corner. "Would you care to sit?"

She craned her neck and saw a floral brocade settee set in the corner, surrounded by tall, leafy palms set in porcelain vases. A swatch of moonlight glazed the sitting area in a silvery glow, lending it an almost magical air. Unable to resist the enchanting spot, she nodded and murmured, "Thank you."

After they were seated, she tilted back her head and heaved a contented sigh at the sight of the glittering stars. "This feels like a tiny slice of indoor heaven."

"I couldn't agree more."

Lifting her head, she found his gaze resting upon her. Seated with a slight slouch at his end of the settee, his fingers lightly linked and resting on his flat stomach, his long legs stretched before him, casually crossed at the ankles, he appeared the personification of relaxation. Which was quite vexing, as she felt so very . . . *un*relaxed.

Hoping she sounded as unconcerned as he looked, she asked, "Do you intend to keep all the animals you rescue?"

"I have until now, but given how rapidly their numbers keep growing, I suppose I'll need to consider allowing some to be taken in by others—provided I'm assured the animals would be properly cared for."

"You've never asked Samuel to stop?"

"No. And I've no intention of doing so. He has a

way with animals that I've never seen before. He'd make an excellent veterinarian. I plan to discuss with him the possibility of sending him to school."

She didn't even attempt to hide her surprise. "You'd send your footman to school?"

"If he wished to go. He has a true talent. And a dedication."

"That is very generous of you."

"Not as much as you might think. I have an ulterior motive."

"Which is?"

A hint of mischief danced in his eyes. "I've always wanted a protégé. It's quite fashionable, you know. Of course, now that Samuel has expanded his strays beyond merely animals, I'm thinking I'll need to expand our enterprise to include some sort of employment agency."

Carolyn studied him and inwardly shook her head. She'd always believed herself an astute judge of character, yet in this case it seemed she'd done a poor job of it. Not that she hadn't always liked him—she'd found him personable and charming from the first time they met. But she'd never considered him as anything more than what he appeared—an extremely attractive scapegrace.

Clearly she'd been very wrong. And that was very unsettling. He'd proven difficult to resist when she thought him nothing more than handsome. But now . . . now there were things to admire about him—other than his charm and good looks. Noble things. And that was an attraction she knew would prove even more difficult to resist. And which begged the question . . .

Did she really want to resist?

The voice inside her answered *No!* so quickly, so emphatically, so *loudly*, it almost seemed as if she'd said it out loud.

"No, what?" he asked with a questioning look.

Dear God, she *had* said it out loud. "Nothing," she said, then speedily added, "I recall you telling me that you don't like to share. Yet your actions belie your words, Lord Surbrooke."

"Daniel . . . my extremely lovely, very dear, greatly talented, highly amusing, extraordinarily intelligent, possessor of the most kissable lips I've ever seen, as well as an excellent memory, *Lady Wingate*." He blew out an exaggerated breath. "That is getting to be rather a mouthful, you know. You could put me out of my misery."

She pretended she hadn't heard him say *kissable lips*. "And miss hearing what you'll come up with next? I think not."

"Just my luck. As for my assertion that I don't like to share, I suppose I should clarify my statement. It depends on what I'm sharing." His glittering gaze seemed to burn through her clothing, to scorch her skin. "And whom I'm sharing it with."

And with those few words, a plethora of images bombarded her—of him and her sharing. Heated kisses. Sensual touches. Their bodies.

Myriad wants and needs and emotions swamped her, confusing her, leaving her flustered and completely tongue-tied. She licked her suddenly dry lips, then stilled as he watched the gesture.

She had to swallow twice to locate her voice. "Samuel is fortunate to have found you."

"Actually, I am the fortunate one." He hesitated,

as if debating whether to continue, then finally said, "Before he came to work for me, my life had become . . . unfulfilling. Samuel's charitable endeavors have given me something worthwhile and productive to do. Helping him makes me feel useful. And has brought home the cold, stark reality of the overwhelming number of animals—and people—in desperate need of help."

She nodded slowly, soaking in words she never would have attributed to him. A frisson of shame rippled through her at the realization of how deeply she'd obviously misjudged him. "When you say your life had become unfulfilling, what do you mean?"

"I felt a mounting, frustrating sense of restlessness. Boredom. Emptiness. And really, more than anything, uselessness."

"But what of the earldom? Your properties?"

"That doesn't require as much of my time as you might think. I have an excellent steward who keeps things running so smoothly I'm barely needed. My households are flawlessly run. I could go away for months and not a ripple would occur on the calm water of my earldom." Carolyn noted his eyes were filled with shadows, and wished she knew the cause of them.

Then he flashed a quick smile. "Gets rather tiresome, not being needed. Thanks to Samuel and his animals, I'm feeling a great deal less of that."

"You are very fortunate, my lord. I've suffered from feelings similar to those you described. Unlike you, however, I haven't yet found an activity or cause to alleviate the emptiness." She rarely discussed such things with anyone other than Sarah, yet before she could stop herself, she found herself saying, "I've discovered it's very difficult to go from being needed on a daily basis to not being needed at all."

He straighten his slouched position and shook his head. "You are mistaken. Your sister, your friends, they need you and care for you deeply. I've seen it every time we're all together."

"I know that, of course. However, Emily and Julianne have their own families, and now Sarah is married."

"And you're wondering exactly where you fit in."

Her gaze searched his. "You sound as if you know how that feels."

"Most likely because I do. Precisely. And although I realize you've had to make difficult adjustments I wouldn't wish on anyone, I still find myself envious of the fact that for at least a period of time you felt needed every day."

His words, the sadness lurking in his eyes, rendered her speechless. Before she could even think of a reply, he blinked several times, as if coming out of a trance. A rueful smile curved his lips. "Egad. Pardon me for allowing the conversation to turn so . . . maudlin."

As she wasn't certain how to tell him that she actually found his unguarded words fascinating, she instead forced a light tone and asked, "You'd prefer to discuss the weather?"

"Actually, no. That isn't what I'd prefer at all."

"Oh? And what is your preference?"

Her breath caught at the heated look that flared in

his eyes. His gaze wandered slowly down her form, lingering for several seconds on her ankles before traveling back up. By the time their gazes once again met, his eyes glittered with a combination of heat and mischievous intent that rendered her barely able to pull any air into her lungs.

He reached out and lightly brushed his fingers over the back of her hand. "I would like, very much, to see your tree-climbing scar."

Chapter 11

My lover enjoyed billiards but found a new appreciation for the game when I hiked up my skirts and bent provocatively over the table. He especially enjoyed this new sport when I neglected to don my drawers. Indeed, after two shattering climaxes, I gained a new appreciation for the game myself.

Memoirs of a Mistress by An Anonymous Lady

Carolyn blinked. Out of all the possible things he could have preferred, such as *a kiss*—and after that teasing touch to her hand and the simmering heat in his eyes, which seemed like such promising precursors to *a kiss*—what he wanted most was *to see her scar*?

Damnation. How could she have thought him charming and intelligent when clearly "irritating" and "nincompoop" were far more apt descriptions? Before she could even think up a reply to his request, he lowered himself to one knee in front of her and his fingers slipped beneath the hem of her gown to lightly grasp her left ankle. Warmth raced up her leg, and even as her mind commanded her to move away from his touch, her body refused to obey.

"Is it on this ankle?" he asked, setting her left foot on his upraised knee. He removed her shoe and gently massaged her instep.

A soft gasp escaped her, then she pressed her lips together to contain the moan of delight that threatened to escape at the delicious kneading. Pleasure skittered up her leg, settling low in her belly.

Dear God, she *adored* having her feet rubbed. And he was *so* good at it. And it had been *so* long since she'd felt such exquisite bliss. His caress was going to melt her spine. She'd wilt into a boneless, quivering mass of ecstasy then slither right onto the tiles.

"This ankle?" he repeated.

Not trusting her voice, she merely shook her head.

"Ah, the right ankle, then." But instead of releasing her left foot, his hands slowly moved upward, over her calf, never ceasing their delicious rubbing. Her fingers clutched the brocade cushion as she struggled not to squirm in delight.

When he reached her knee, she watched in shocked, wordless wonder as he slipped off her ribbon garter then slowly rolled down her stocking. The whisper of silk sliding over her flesh tingled heated tremors through her, but they faded to insignificance at the incredible sensation of his hands against her bare skin. After he set aside her stocking, he slowly pushed her gown and petticoat up to her knees.

Her bare toes curled against his muscular thigh. The sight of him on one knee before her, his dark head bent to study what he'd just uncovered, shivered an illicit thrill through her the likes of which she'd never experienced.

"Such lovely, creamy skin," he murmured, his fingers skimming lightly up and down her calf. "So soft. So smooth."

He lifted his head. The heat in his gaze seared her. Trapped in the inferno, she watched him lift her foot and press his mouth to her instep.

Another gasp escaped her, this one followed by a low moan she couldn't contain.

"You're correct." His warm breath whispered over her foot, eliciting a barrage of quivers that tickled over her every nerve ending.

"C-Correct?" she managed, sounding as breathless as she felt.

"There is no scar on this ankle. It is, in fact, the most perfect ankle I've ever seen."

The realization that he'd most assuredly seen plenty of female ankles should have appalled her. Instead she could only take in the breath-stealing reality that he was seeing—and caressing—*her* ankle.

He then kissed his way up her shin. Another shiver of delight trembled through her. After reaching her knee, he set her foot gently on the floor and a groan of protest rose in her throat at the loss. Before she could give it voice, however, he lifted her right foot and afforded it the same sensual treatment he'd lavished on the left. The only sounds in the conservatory were the rustle of material as he pushed up her gown, then slid off her stocking, and her own shallow, rapid breaths.

"Ah, I see the culprit," he murmured, setting the stocking on top of the other one. He minutely examined the inch-long bit of puckered skin just above her anklebone.

"Did it hurt?" he asked, brushing his fingers over the mark.

She'd barely felt the cut, but as she was incapable of stringing together that many words, she merely whispered one syllable. "No."

" 'Tis almost necessary that you have such a minor flaw. Otherwise you'd be absolutely, frighteningly perfect." He studied the scar for several more seconds, then heaved an exaggerated sigh. "I'm afraid this minuscule mark doesn't count and you *are* absolutely perfect."

She licked her lips. "I assure you, I'm nothing of the kind."

"And I assure you, you are underestimating yourself."

He brought her foot to his mouth—his lovely, sensual mouth—but instead of kissing her there, he lightly traced his tongue over the imperfection.

A startled *"Oh!"* escaped her. His eyes darkened at the sound, and he repeated the gesture. What little of her spine remained seemed to evaporate.

"So beautiful," he whispered against her ankle. His hands skimmed slowly upward, caressing her skin, pushing her skirts higher. The heat of his palms touched her through the thin muslin of her drawers.

His mouth followed the same upward trail his hands forged, lightly nipping, kissing. Over her shin, her knees . . . how was it she'd never known that the skin behind her knees was so very sensitive?

An insistent pulse throbbed between her thighs. Her feminine folds felt slick and swollen and heavy. When he urged her legs apart, she didn't resist, and he insinuated his broad shoulders between her knees. The small part of her mind that wasn't lost in the heated fog of stunning arousal tried to interject, warn her that this was not the path she wished to go down, but that small bit was quickly overruled as sensation swamped her.

While his mouth continued its leisurely journey along her inner thigh, one of his hands strayed upward and found the opening in her drawers.

She gasped at the first touch of his fingers against her folds, a sound that tapered off into a long, vaporous sigh of pleasure as he teased her sensitive flesh with a wickedly light, circular motion. Helpless to resist the lure of such tempting pleasure, her head fell limply against the padded back of the settee and her eyes drifted shut. And for the first time in years she allowed herself the luxury of doing nothing save *feel*.

He slipped a finger inside her, and her entire body clenched with a pleasurable spasm. "So tight," he murmured against her thigh. "So hot and wet."

Hot, yes . . . she felt so hot. As if her skin were stretched too tight and consumed with fire. He stroked her with maddening leisure, each caress melting away her inhibitions, dissolving her modesty until she writhed against his hand, impatient for more. He slipped another finger inside her, pumping slowly, drawing a long, ragged moan from her throat.

She felt his other hand at her waist, then his fingers slipped from her body, dragging a soft *"No"* of protest from her. When she felt him tug at her drawers, she lifted her hips and he slid them down her legs.

His avid gaze riveted on her exposed sex, yet rather than experiencing any of the shyness she might have expected, her entire body tensed in an agony of anticipation, awaiting his touch. Instead, however, he plucked the rose from her lap.

"I've dreamed about doing this to you," he said softly, slowly trailing the velvety petals up her inner thigh.

She sucked in a quick breath at the tremor that shimmered through her. "You have? When?"

"Last night." He brushed the flower along the cleft of her sex, and she forgot how to breathe. "And the night before. And the night before that." Another light sweep over her swollen folds. "And numerous nights before that."

He looked up from his wicked ministrations and pinned her with his heated gaze. Then he placed the rose on the settee. "Have you ever wondered what it would feel like for me to touch you like this?" he whispered, slipping a finger deep inside her.

A sigh rushed past her lips, and her eyes slid closed. Dear God, surely he didn't expect her to answer questions when he was making her feel like . . . *this*? As if her insides had turned to a flow of warm honey. As if she were about to simultaneously melt and shatter.

"I've wondered," he said, teasing her most sensitive nub of flesh in a manner that shot liquid fire to her core. "More times than I can count. And still you're more beautiful than I ever imagined."

His fingers once against slid over her folds, inside her, teasing her toward the rapidly approaching climax building at the base of her spine. He pressed his lips to her knee, then kissed his way up her inner thighs, insinuating his shoulders farther between her legs, splaying them wider. And then time seemed to stop as his tongue glided over her aroused sex.

For several seconds her body tensed, but then her initial shocked reaction evaporated into a low groan of helpless pleasure. She forced her eyes open. The sight of his dark head buried between her legs, the sensation of his lips and tongue and fingers caressing her folds, was the most erotic thing she'd ever experienced. The musky scent of her arousal rose in the warm air, mingling with the fragrant flowers. She slumped lower on the settee, and with what sounded like a growl of approval, he lifted her thighs, setting them over his shoulders.

Lost in sensation, she closed her eyes and reveled in the magical torment his mouth and fingers wrought on her, each teasing lick, every relentless stroke touching her deeper, pushing her closer to the brink. When she soared over the edge, a sharp cry escaped her. Her back arched and her fingers bunched in the muslin of her ruched up gown as an intense climax throbbed through her. When the spasms subsided into mere quivers, she collapsed, breathless, limp, and utterly sated.

She felt him trailing light kisses along her inner

thigh, and managed to drag her heavy eyelids open halfway. His eyes burned like a pair of flames. Gazes locked, he slowly lowered her boneless legs from his shoulders. Then he moved closer, leaning over her, until only inches separated their faces.

"Say my name," he demanded in a rough, husky rasp.

She licked her lips and struggled to find her voice. "Lord Surbrooke."

He shook his head and skimmed one palm up her leg, slipping it beneath her to curve over her bare bottom. He pulled her closer, until the hard ridge of his erection that strained against his breeches nestled against her sex. "Daniel."

The feel of him pressed against her so intimately momentarily robbed her of speech. After swallowing, she whispered, "Daniel."

A bit of the tension in his face abated, and with a low groan he slowly lowered his mouth to hers. Her lips parted, welcoming the invasion of his tongue. He tasted of brandy and of her, an utterly foreign combination that intoxicated her. The inner fire he'd stoked and just sated roared back to life, demanding more. Her fingers sifted through his thick hair, urging him closer. He flexed his hips, pressing his erection tighter against her, and at that moment she wanted nothing more than for him to rip open his breeches and thrust all that lovely, hard flesh into her hungry body.

Instead, however, he lifted his head. Confused, she opened her eyes and found him regarding her with that same intense expression.

She blinked several times, then reality returned with a thump. She glanced down the length of her body, taking in the gown bunched up around her waist, the pale skin of her abdomen, the light brown curls at the juncture of her widely spread thighs. His hips nestled tightly against her.

Surely she should be appalled at her wanton behavior, at the liberties she'd allowed him. Liberties her husband had never taken. Or even attempted. Yet instead of appalled, she felt more alive than she had in years. As if she'd emerged from a dark, lonely cave into a sunshine-filled meadow bursting with color and life.

The proper, sedate lady she'd been her entire adult life insisted she tell him this interlude was a mistake. One that could not be repeated. But rather than *mistake,* the only word she wanted to say was. . .

Again.

She could lie to herself, but the irrefutable truth was that she wanted more of the passion they'd just shared. Her mind acknowledged her guilt and tried to list all the reasons she shouldn't allow this to go any further, but she shoved all that aside and listened to her reawakened body, which refused to be silenced. She was attracted to this man. Wanted him—in a purely physical sense. So long as her heart remained uninvolved and they were discreet, there was no reason to deny herself this pleasure. He'd said he didn't want her heart, and had no intention of offering his own. They would share their bodies and nothing more. Just as the Anonymous Lady had done in the *Memoirs.*

"The dogs are barking," he said quietly, brushing his fingers over her cheek. "Which means Samuel has returned."

A frisson of panic rushed through her and she struggled to sit up, but he shook his head and gently pressed her back down. "We have a few moments. Barkley will see to things, and neither he nor Samuel will come in here."

"How do you know?"

"No one is allowed access to this room except me and Walter, my groundskeeper." The pad of his thumb brushed over her bottom lip and he frowned, as if puzzled. "I've never brought anyone here before."

He sounded surprised to have admitted that last bit, and certainly she was surprised to hear it. "Why not? It's such a beautiful room."

"It's private. My . . . sanctuary. I told you I don't like to share." His gaze roamed her face and he looked . . . troubled? "Except, it seems, with you."

His expression cleared and he leaned forward to nuzzle the sensitive skin behind her ear with his warm lips.

"My God . . . you are so beautiful," he whispered, his words ending on a groan. His teeth lightly grazed her earlobe, shooting a barrage of tingles down her neck. "My extremely lovely, very dear, greatly talented, highly amusing, extraordinarily intelligent, possessor of the most kissable lips I've ever seen as well as an excellent memory, and who tastes like flowers . . . everywhere, *Lady Wingate*." He lifted his head and a whiff of amusement entered his eyes. "Do you think we might perhaps be on a first name basis now?"

A heated blush suffused her entire body. "I suppose . . . Daniel."

His smile flashed. "Thank you . . . Carolyn."

The way he said her name, softly, slowly, as if savoring its taste upon his tongue, shivered a dark thrill of delight through her.

With obvious reluctance, he slid his hand from beneath her bottom then reached for her drawers. The ease with which he helped her don her discarded clothing proved he was as adept at dressing a woman as he was at undressing one. And he'd certainly proven he knew what to do once he had her disrobed. She wasn't entirely certain her liquefied knees would ever fully recover.

After he'd slipped her shoes back on her feet, he rose and extended his hand to help her rise. Her gaze riveted on the front of his breeches, which were directly on her eye level. The snug material clearly outlined his thick erection.

Perhaps it was the privacy afforded by this cozy, flower-scented room, illuminated only by silvery skeins of moonlight, that made her daring . . . as daring as she'd felt while wearing Galatea's mask. Or perhaps it was the way he'd made her feel . . . so lush and womanly and shockingly free. But whatever the reason, as she allowed him to help her arise, she boldly dragged her free hand up his muscled thigh and cupped his arousal. He sucked in a quick breath and his eyes seemed to glaze over.

"You pleasured me, yet asked for—and received— nothing in return," she murmured, experiencing a deep surge of feminine satisfaction when he rolled his hips, seeking more of her touch.

"I hardly received nothing. Indeed the pleasure was all mine."

She cocked a brow and shot a significant look downward. *"This . . ."* She lightly stroked him through his breeches. " . . . indicates otherwise."

He wrapped an arm around her waist and pulled her closer, trapping her hand between them. "If you're suggesting you're in my debt—"

"That's precisely what I'm suggesting."

His eyes seemed to breathe smoke. "I believe that makes me the luckiest man in England. Consider me at your disposal."

"A very intriguing offer."

"I'm delighted you think so, especially as you didn't when I first offered."

"I was always intrigued. Just not willing."

"But now you are."

"Obviously."

He rubbed himself against her hand. "I'm extremely happy to hear it."

Her lips twitched. "Obviously."

Clasping her wrist, he dragged her hand up and pressed a fervent kiss against her palm. "Unfortunately, now is—"

"Not an ideal time."

"No. I want to make certain all went well with Samuel's errand and that Cook and my maid are seeing to Katie. Then I'll escort you and Gertrude home." His gaze searched her face. "And as much as I want to continue this right here, right now, I want you to have some time to think. To settle things in your mind. I don't want you to have doubts."

"You're not afraid that after thinking things over I'll change my mind?"

His fingers tightened over hers. "'Afraid' is a lukewarm word for the terror I feel at the possibility. Carolyn . . . the desire between us is the most potent I've ever experienced. I know we would be extraordinary together. But only if it isn't tarnished with regrets."

"I don't regret what we've shared this evening."

"Excellent. I just want to make sure you feel the same way in the morning." He brushed his mouth over hers then continued along the curve of her jaw. "And as hope springs eternal that you will, are you free tomorrow, around noon?"

With his body pressed to hers and his nipping kisses disrupting her thoughts, it was impossible to recall if she had any plans, but if she did, whatever they might be, she intended to reschedule them. "I am."

"Excellent. I'll plan a surprise."

"What if I don't like surprises?"

"You'll like this one. I promise."

A quiver of anticipation rippled through her. After one last lingering kiss, he stepped back. Tucking her hand into the crook of his arm, he led her through the double doors then into the corridor and back to the foyer, where they encountered a pacing Samuel. He halted when he saw them.

"Cook's puttin' a broth together," he reported without preamble, "and Mary's in with Katie and Gertrude."

"How is Katie faring?" Daniel asked.

"She's sleepin'. Gertrude said Katie was sore and

tired, but otherwise fine. If Lady Wingate don't mind, Gertrude offered to stay until Katie wakes up, so she ain't frightened to see a stranger." He looked at Carolyn. "Real thoughtful, your Gertrude is, milady."

"Is that all right with you?" Daniel asked her.

"Of course."

"Samuel will escort her home after Katie awakens." He turned to Samuel. "I'll escort Lady Wingate home now. She has a busy day ahead of her tomorrow and needs her rest."

A blush scorched Carolyn's cheeks at his seemingly innocent words. She quickly said good-bye to Samuel, who handed Carolyn her cashmere shawl and thanked her for helping Katie.

"It was my pleasure to assist you, Samuel," she said with a smile. "And Katie's good fortune that you found her."

She and Daniel left the house. The instant the door closed behind them, he glanced around. After clearly satisfying himself that no one lurked about, he clasped her hand and tucked it beneath his arm. She noted he matched his steps to her shorter stride, for which she was grateful, as she was in no rush to leave his company and the walk to her town house would require less than two minutes.

She was considering asking him into her home but saw a lamp burning in the foyer window, which meant Nelson was waiting up for her. Discretion would hardly be served by bringing her lover home at three A.M.

Her lover.

The words reverberated through her mind. Any

guilt she might have felt was buried beneath the avalanche of anticipation that trembled through her.

"Cold?" he asked.

She looked up at him and shook her head. "No. In fact, quite the opposite."

A slow smile curved his lips. He opened his mouth to speak, but before he could utter a word, a loud bang sounded from across the street at Hyde Park. At the same instant something whizzed past her, mere inches from her nose, then the stone urn on her porch exploded.

Before she could even draw a breath, Daniel yanked her down and shielded her with his body.

"Wh-What was that?" she asked.

"That," Daniel said in a tight, grim voice, "was a pistol shot."

Chapter 12

The uncomfortable jouncing normally suffered while riding in a carriage turned into the most delicious bouncing when my lover's erection was buried deep inside me.

Memoirs of a Mistress by An Anonymous Lady

re you hurt?" Daniel asked, his gaze anxiously searching Carolyn's shocked face.

She shook her head, and his profound relief nearly rendered him light-headed.

"Are you?" she asked.

"I'm fine." Actually, he was nowhere near fine. That shot had barely missed her. Another few inches and—

He cut off the horrific thought. "We need to get inside. Quickly."

He grabbed her hand, and shielding her with his

body, hurried her toward her front door. They'd nearly reached it when the oak panel flew open, revealing
a wide-eyed butler.

"What on earth—"

The butler's words were cut off as they hurried
into the foyer and Daniel quickly closed and locked
the door. Then he turned to Carolyn and grasped her
shoulders.

"You're certain you're all right?" he asked, unable
to shake off the gut-twisting image of that shot actually hitting her.

"I'm fine. Shaken and stunned, but unharmed."

She quickly introduced her butler, who asked,
"What happened?"

"A shot was fired, from the park," Daniel said
tersely. "It nearly hit Lady Wingate."

Nelson's face turned the color of chalk. "Dear
God." He looked Carolyn over, as if to satisfy himself that she truly wasn't injured. Then anger flashed
in his dark eyes. "First Lady Crawford's murder and
now this. Terrible what the world's come to, brig-
ands hurting innocent people, and ladies no less!
'Tis shocking."

"Yes," Daniel agreed. A muscle ticked in his jaw.
Except he suddenly didn't think it was the work
of just any brigand. "The authorities must be summoned," he said to Nelson. "Mr. Rayburn, the magistrate, attended the Gatesbourne soiree this evening.
You might check for him there first."

"Yes, my lord. I'll do so at once," Nelson said, then
looked at Carolyn and hesitated.

"I'll remain here with Lady Wingate until you

return," Daniel assured him. "I'll allow no harm to come to her. And so no harm comes to you, call at my town house and instruct my footman Samuel to accompany you."

"Yes, my lord."

"Are you armed, Nelson?"

The butler leaned down and patted the side of his boot. "Always carry a knife, my lord."

After Nelson left, Daniel locked the door then braced his hands against the oak panel and took several seconds to pull in a calming breath, which unfortunately did nothing to calm him. *Bloody hell, she'd almost been killed.* And it was entirely his fault.

He felt her hand upon his back and turned around. The mere sight of her, standing before him, her beautiful eyes clouded with concern, damn near brought him to his knees. A shudder rippled through him as he relived that shot ringing out, followed by the unthinkable, horrible aftermath of what had nearly occurred.

She reached up and rested her palm against his cheek. "You're so pale, Daniel. Are you certain you weren't injured?"

The sound of his name on her lips, the touch of her hand against his skin, the worry in her eyes, all threatened to undo him.

"I'm not injured." He turned his face to press a kiss against her palm. "But I must talk to you about what happened."

"All right. Let's go to the drawing room." Taking his hand, she led him down the corridor. Once inside the room, they moved toward the hearth, where a low-burning fire crackled in the grate. She sat on the settee, but he felt too restless to join her. Instead he paced the length of the room, every muscle tense, his mind whirling.

As he passed her, she reached out and grabbed his hand. "Daniel, what's wrong?"

He looked down at her and the lump of fear and fury that had lodged in his throat when that shot rang out threatened to choke him. "What's wrong," he said in as calm a tone as he could manage, "is that you were nearly killed."

"As were you." She offered him a shaky smile. "Luckily the only casualty was my urn. Surely it was an accident. A shot gone astray. Fired by some intoxicated reveler."

He shook his head. "I don't believe it was an accident, Carolyn. I'm certain that shot was meant for me. And it nearly killed *you*."

She frowned. "What do you mean? If someone had meant to rob you, they'd hardly shoot at you from across the street."

"The person wasn't trying to rob me. I'm quite certain he meant to kill me."

Fear and horror widened her eyes. "Who would do such a thing? And why?"

Unable to stand still, he slipped his hand from hers and continued to pace while telling her about his aborted investment with Lord Tolliver. "He threatened me at the masquerade ball, but I shrugged off his words as the ramblings of a drunkard." He halted in front of her and fresh anger raced through him. "Based on tonight's shooting, however, Tolliver's threats weren't empty. And you were nearly the victim of his vendetta against me." Bloody hell, if Tolliver had harmed so much as a hair on her head, he would have hunted the man down and killed him without a moment's remorse. As it was, it required a great effort not to do so and to instead allow the authorities to go after the bastard.

Daniel sat beside Carolyn on the settee and clasped her hands, entwining their fingers. He wasn't a spiritual man, hadn't uttered a prayer since the age of eight when he'd painfully learned that no higher being listened to his invocations, yet he couldn't stop the mantra reverberating through his mind: *Thank you for sparing her. Thank you for not taking her away.*

His gaze devoured her and he had to swallow to locate his voice. "I'm sorry, Carolyn. Sorry that something so ugly has touched you. Sorry that it's my fault. That I underestimated Tolliver. I had no idea he'd be so reckless, so bold. It's a mistake I assure you I won't make again. And you have my word I won't allow any harm to come to you."

"Daniel . . ." She slipped one hand from his then reached up to brush back his hair where it had fallen over his forehead. How was it possible that such a simple, innocent gesture from her shuddered more pleasure through him than the most erotic caress from any other woman ever had?

"You are not responsible for the actions of other people," she said softly. "Only for your own. Whatever Lord Tolliver chooses to do is in no way your fault." She trailed her fingertips slowly down his

cheek, then along his jaw. "Please don't blame yourself."

He captured her hand and pressed it against his
chest, right over the spot where his heart thudded hard
and fast. Her words . . . bloody hell, weren't they a
lovely fairy tale? He knew all too well the hell his actions were capable of causing. The images he always
battled away crowded his mind and he forcibly shoved
them aside. One death already weighed heavily on his
conscience. He couldn't bear another one.

"I would never forgive myself if any harm came
to you." The words felt ripped from his throat. They
sounded raw. Edgy. Not a big surprise, he supposed,
as that's precisely how he felt. Uncharacteristically
so. But there was no denying that the mere thought
of Carolyn being hurt, especially because of him,
pushed him toward the very brink of reason.

"As you can see, I am perfectly fine," she said.
"And to my very great relief, so are you—although
I must say, you look as if you could use a brandy.
Unfortunately I don't have any."

He forced a half smile at her obvious attempt
to lighten his mood, but his emotions remained
shrouded in a swirl of darkness. "I don't want a
drink."

No, what he wanted was to gather her close, bury
his face in that warm, fragrant spot where her neck
and shoulder met and simply breathe her in. For
hours. Days. Until the image of that shot whizzing
by her face was erased.

Splaying her fingers against his chest, she said,
"I'm frightened for you. You must promise me that

you'll be very careful and take extremely good care of yourself." She glanced down at her hand and her bottom lip trembled. Then she looked into his eyes and he felt as if he were drowning. "I can't have any harm coming to my . . ."

"Friend?" he supplied when she hesitated.

"Yes. My friend. And . . . lover."

He briefly squeezed his eyes shut, savoring her words. Then he lifted her hand and pressed a fervent kiss against her palm. "And you must promise me the same, my most treasured friend. And lover."

"I promise."

No longer able to resist the craving gnawing at him, he gathered her into his arms. He meant to give her nothing more than a brief kiss, but the instant his lips covered hers, all the fear and worry spiraling inside him seemed to detonate. His mouth claimed hers in a hard, deep kiss that felt desperate. Out of control. And utterly lacking in finesse. His hands, usually so steady, shook as they clasped her to him, unable to let go. Or hold her close enough.

The fact that he'd nearly lost her kept echoing through his mind, fueling an urgent demand to hold her closer, kiss her more deeply. Something wild raged through him, something he couldn't name, as he'd never felt it before. Something that writhed beneath his skin and filled his very bones with the need to hold her. Protect her.

In some distant corner of his mind it registered that she was saying his name. Pushing against his chest. Lifting his head, he pulled a breath into his burning lungs. She stared at him, wide-eyed, her lips red and swollen from his frantic kiss, her hair mussed and bodice askew from his impatient hands.

And sanity returned. Bringing with it a healthy shot of self-disgust at his lack of control.

"I'm sorry," he said, forcing his arms to loosen around her. "I didn't mean to . . ." *Give in to something I'm at a loss to explain.*

"Kiss me until my bones melted? Believe me, there's no need to apologize."

She touched her fingertips to her lips, and he inwardly cursed himself. "Did I hurt you?"

"No. I . . . I simply had no idea I could inspire such unbridled passion."

Curiosity struck him at her words. Did she mean she didn't know she could inspire such passion in *him*—or in any man?

Surely just in him. Because surely Edward had taken every opportunity to show her just how much passion she could inspire with a mere look.

Hadn't he?

He frowned, but before he could ponder further on the question, she rose and hastily smoothed her hair and gown. "As much as I didn't want to stop you, I heard the front gate bell ring. Which means Nelson has returned."

Daniel instantly rose, slipped his knife from his boot and moved to the door. Every muscle alert, he cautiously peered into the corridor, then relaxed when he saw Nelson entering the foyer. After closing the door, he slipped the knife back into his boot then turned to Carolyn and ran a hand through his hair. Bloody hell, he hadn't heard a bell. Hadn't been aware of anything save her. Tolliver could have entered the damn room and he wouldn't have known the man was there until the bastard shot him.

"Do I look . . . undone?" she asked, smoothing her hands over her gown.

"You look . . . perfect."

And she did. Like a demure lady. A demure lady whose rosy flush and slightly swollen lips lent her an air of a ripe peach begging to be plucked. For the sake of discretion, he hoped the dimly lit foyer would hide the color staining her cheeks.

He followed her from the room. Nelson stood in the foyer along with Charles Rayburn and, to Daniel's surprise, Gideon Mayne, the Bow Street Runner.

"Where's Samuel?" Daniel asked.

"He returned to your residence, my lord, to make certain the ladies there were safe," Nelson reported. "We assured him you and Lady Wingate were in good hands."

Daniel nodded then turned a questioning gaze toward Mayne.

"I was still with Rayburn at the Gatesbourne residence when your man arrived," Mayne said in response to Daniel's look.

He noticed Mayne's sharp eyes taking in every aspect of Carolyn's appearance and his muscles tensed. There was something about this man and his brusque manner he didn't care for.

"I came here with Rayburn," Mayne said, "to ascertain if tonight's shooting might be connected in some way to the Lady Crawford matter."

Daniel's brows shot upward. "Why would you think that?"

Mayne's inscrutable gaze gave nothing away. "Just a hunch."

"Have you discovered who killed her?"

"Not yet," said Mayne, treating Daniel to a piercing stare, "but I'm confident the matter will soon be resolved."

"I don't believe her murder and tonight's shooting are connected," Daniel said.

"Why is that?" Rayburn asked.

"Let's retire to the drawing room, gentlemen," Carolyn broke in.

Mayne looked as if he wanted to argue, but he gave a tight nod. Nelson showed the group to the drawing room, then departed. As soon as the door closed behind him, Mayne said to Daniel, "You and Lady Wingate left the Gatesbourne party separately. How was it that you were escorting her home?"

Daniel didn't care for the speculation in the Runner's voice. "One of my female staff took ill. I sent my footman to Lady Wingate's home to see if her maid could assist. Lady Wingate was kind enough to come as well."

"And where was her maid during your walk home?" Mayne asked, his gaze never leaving Daniel.

"She offered to remain and I gratefully accepted."

"Tell us about the shooting," Rayburn urged.

Daniel repeated the story of their near miss, then related what had transpired between him and Tolliver.

When he finished, Mayne said, "If Tolliver is responsible, he might target other investors besides you, as well as Mr. Jennsen. Since Jennsen advised you not to invest, he might have done the same for others. Who else was involved in this investment?"

"I know Tolliver was hoping to interest Lord Warwick and Lord Heaton, but I've no idea the outcome of those discussions."

"We'll look into it," Rayburn said. "I'd advise you to be very careful, Lord Surbrooke, until we're able to clear up this matter. Glad neither of you were hurt."

As their business was concluded, Carolyn walked them all into the foyer. "We'll see you safely home, my lord," Rayburn said, "then Mayne and I will head into the park to see what we can find."

The last thing Daniel wanted to do was leave, but to argue would only lead to speculation that he and Carolyn were . . . involved. And while he personally didn't care who the hell knew, he'd promised her discretion.

Still, it rankled that he couldn't kiss her good-bye. Wasn't free to offer her anything other than a tepid good-night. Couldn't say the words that unexpectedly all but burned his tongue. *I'll miss you.*

Bloody hell. He'd never, not even once, felt the desire to utter such a thing to a woman. Perhaps it was best they weren't alone, lest he'd be tempted to spew all sorts of drivel. Yet drivel though it might be, he couldn't deny it. He hadn't even left her home and already he missed her. Missed talking to her. Touching her. Kissing her. And now nine long hours stretched before him until he could see her again.

Offering her a formal bow, he thanked her again for her assistance, reiterated that he was grateful she wasn't harmed, then bid her good-night.

He had to force his legs to walk away from her.

Force himself not to turn around in hopes of gaining a glimpse of her during the short walk back to his town house accompanied by Rayburn and Mayne.

Samuel opened the door to admit him, and the instant the oak panel closed behind him, his clearly nervous footman asked why the magistrate and Runner had accompanied him home. Daniel quickly explained the situation, concluding with, "Hopefully, Rayburn and Mayne will find that bastard Tolliver." His hands clenched. "If they don't, I'll simply have to locate him myself."

"Ye can count on me to help with that, milord," Samuel said, his dark eyes flashing with anger. "Anybody wot tries to harm ye will have to get through *me* first."

As always, Samuel's loyalty humbled him. "Thank you, but hopefully that won't be necessary. Rayburn and Mayne seem very capable. And determined." Yes, determined that he was a suspect in Blythe's murder. "Now tell me, how is Katie?"

"Still asleep. Gertrude's with her."

"Then she's in good hands. You should go to bed, Samuel. Get some rest."

"I'll go to bed, milord, but I doubt I'll be gettin' any rest. Can't stop picturin' Katie in my mind."

As he couldn't stop picturing Carolyn in his mind, Daniel doubted he'd get much sleep, either. After bidding Samuel good-night, he climbed the stairs to his bedchamber, but instead of heading toward his turned-down bed, he poured himself a brandy then stood before the fireplace and stared into the remnants still glowing in the grate.

And all he saw was her. Her smile. Her beautiful face. Her gorgeous, expressive eyes. How many hours would he need to stare at her before he'd tire of looking at her? Hundreds? Thousands? A humorless sound escaped him. Somehow he suddenly couldn't envision *ever* growing bored of looking at her. Hearing her laughter. Listening to her voice.

Good God, he was going daft. When the bloody hell had the mere look of a woman, the sound of her laughter and voice, ever been enough to give him such a deep sense of satisfaction?

Never, his inner voice instantly answered.

His intense desire for her seemed to grow with each passing moment. He closed his eyes and recalled her in his conservatory. Gown bunched up, legs splayed, sex glistening with need. He swelled against his breeches and groaned. Bloody hell, he could still taste her on his tongue. And God knows he longed to have her beneath him, over him, wrapped around him.

Yet, also strong was this unfamiliar desire to simply *talk* to her. Spend time with her. Dance with her. Hold her hand. Be in the same room with her. Tell her things he'd never told anyone else. He'd never experienced such a thing before, and he wasn't sure he liked it. Sex, desire, lust were purely physical and ultimately uncomplicated. These unprecedented . . . *feelings* Carolyn inspired felt so extremely complicated. And dangerous. As if he were navigating rough seas without benefit of a boat.

With a sigh he glanced at the mantel clock.

Only eight hours twenty-seven minutes until he saw her again.

He groaned and performed a quick calculation in his head. Then, for the second time that evening, he found himself praying, this time that the next five hundred seven minutes would pass very, very quickly.

Chapter 13

I'd always thought chess a boring game until my lover and I played a version where an article of clothing is discarded every time a piece is captured. Since I became naked before him, he named me the loser. Given the way he pleasured me with his mouth and tongue, however, I declared myself the winner.

Memoirs of a Mistress by An Anonymous Lady

As was her habit following breakfast, Carolyn retired to the drawing room to enjoy a second cup of coffee. Normally she sat at her desk near the window and tended to her correspondence, or if it were sunny, just enjoyed the warmth of the rays streaming through the glass panes. Today, however, she paced, too restless, too stirred up from the tumultuous events of the last few days. First a murder,

then taking Daniel as a lover, the fright of nearly being shot, the knowledge that Daniel was the intended
victim. . .

She drew in a shuddering breath. It was little wonder she could barely sit still. And all her churning
thoughts circled around a single word.

Daniel.

After another lap around the Turkish rug, she
paused before the hearth. Clutching her copy of the
Memoirs to her chest, she looked up at Edward's
portrait.

As it did every day, his handsome face regarded
her with that same gentle expression. Not a trace of
condemnation showed in his eyes.

"Do you understand?" she whispered around the
lump clogging her throat. "I pray you do, although
I'm not certain how you can since I barely comprehend what's happening myself."

Edward merely continued to gaze down on her
with benign affection.

"You own my heart," she continued. "You always
will. But Edward, I'm so desperately lonely. I didn't
know how much until he kissed me. I hadn't realized
how deeply I wanted, needed, to be desired in that
way again. How much I missed being touched . . .
and touching in return. How much I truly wanted to
live my life to the fullest until that shot nearly ended
it all."

She looked down at the book she held, at the single blush-colored rose Daniel had given her, now
pressed between the pages. The things he'd done to
her last night . . . Her breath caught at the memory

of the shocking, stunning pleasure. There was no use lying to herself. She'd wanted that pleasure. Had craved it.

And she wanted it again.

Was her reading of the *Memoirs* the only reason she felt this way? If so, why had these feelings manifested themselves with this particular man? She couldn't explain it, but they had, and they were impossible to ignore. Even more so now, given all she'd discovered last night about Daniel—the kind, caring, and generous side of him she'd known nothing about. A side she found both intriguing and very attractive. And again, impossible to ignore.

She raised her gaze to the portrait. "I'm stunned by my reaction to him," she whispered to Edward's image. "I never thought . . . never expected . . . but I cannot deny I desire him. Of course I won't let him touch my memories of you. Will never allow him to come between what you and I once shared."

Yet even as she said the words, she wondered if it were truly possible. Feared it might already be too late. That at some point the reality of making love with Daniel would overtake the memories of what she'd shared with Edward. Ever since Daniel had kissed her at the masquerade ball it was *his* face that haunted her dreams. Conjuring Edward's image in her mind's eye was proving increasingly difficult with each intimacy she shared with Daniel.

Unless she stood here . . . gazing up at Edward's portrait. But even then, she sometimes couldn't quite recall the exact timbre of his voice. The precise cadence of his laugh. The actual way his hair

and skin felt beneath her fingertips. Although those
lapses in her memories had started before she'd
been reacquainted with Daniel during Matthew's
house party, there was no denying they'd increased
since the handsome earl had come on the scene.
No, she couldn't deny that the reality of Daniel's
touch was more thrilling than the fading memory of
Edward's—a fact that, in spite of her determination
to move on, dismayed and frightened her and filled
her with a profound sense of guilt.

Yet, despite the dismay, fear, and guilt, she simply
could no longer ignore the fact that she hadn't died
along with Edward. Or ignore the way Daniel made
her feel, which she could sum up in one word.

Alive.

In so many ways. He made her laugh. Dear God,
she hadn't laughed in so long. He made her *want*.
And *need*. Things she'd never thought to want and
need again. He made her feel young. And desirable.
Made her want to spread her arms and simply twirl
in circles of delight, for no other reason than knowing she could. And that he would take her hands and
circle about with her. He made her feel. . .

Not alone.

Yet just when she discovered all this, she'd nearly
lost her life. And his was in danger. *Please, God, let
that madman Tolliver be caught quickly. . . .*

She drew a deep breath, then told the portrait,
"I've felt nothing save emptiness for three years."
Hot moisture pooled in her eyes and she blinked.
"Please, please, don't hate me, Edward. This . . .
arrangement between Daniel and I is nothing more

than physical. And only temporary. I never wanted to be here without you, but since I am . . . I'm just so tired of being alone."

Carolyn, my darling . . . I love you. Be happy.

Edward's last words, uttered with his final breath, whispered through her mind. She wasn't certain what happiness was anymore and certainly doubted she'd find it with this affair, but she knew it would ease the loneliness. Fill a small part of the emptiness. And until Daniel moved on to his next conquest, as she knew he would as soon as he tired of her—which, given his reputation, wouldn't be long—she'd enjoy his company and their time together. And when he moved on, so would she—reenergized and ready to do something worthwhile with her time.

With that settled in her mind, she crossed to her desk to slip the *Memoirs* into the top drawer. Before doing so, however, she ran the tip of her index finger over the gold lettering on the black leather cover, and images inspired from the book flickered through her mind. All mental pictures she wanted to turn into reality. With Daniel.

A knock sounded and she quickly slid the slim volume beneath several sheets of vellum. After closing the drawer, she called out, "Come in."

Nelson entered, carrying a square silver foil box decorated with an ivory ribbon. "This just arrived for you, my lady." He held out the attractive box, which was just a bit larger than her hand.

Her heart skipped a beat. A present from Daniel? "Thank you, Nelson."

After the butler withdrew, she hurried to her desk,

set down the box, then untied the ribbon. She lifted
the top, picked up the small note card resting on top
of the silver tissue paper, and squinted at the brief
message that must have been hastily written, as the
ink was badly smudged.

I hope you enjoy these, Daniel.

Smiling in anticipation, she unfolded the tissue paper to reveal a half-dozen pieces of marzipan nestled
inside, perfectly formed and decorated in the shapes
of miniature fruits. A strong scent of slightly bitter
almonds rose from the candy, and she involuntarily
wrinkled her nose. Although almond was not her favorite flavor—something Daniel would have no way
of knowing—her heart melted at the thoughtful gesture. It had been a long time since a man had sent
her candy.

In spite of not particularly liking marzipan, she
reached for a piece, in the same spirit she used to
slather butter on slices of black-bottomed bread from
the loaves Sarah would burn while she perfected her
baking skills. Before she could decide between the
strawberry or the peach, another knock sounded on
the door.

At her bid to enter, Nelson opened the door and
walked toward her, this time bearing a silver salver
upon which rested a card. "You've another delivery,
my lady. In the foyer. This came with it." He extended
the salver.

Another delivery? She put the cover back on the candy then slipped the box in the middle drawer. Pluck-
ing the folded vellum from the small tray, she broke
the wax seal and scanned the neatly scripted words.

For Galatea, from the Highwayman. Because they remind him of you.

Heavens, Daniel had had a busy morning. She read the words again and warmth suffused her. This note was far more personal than the first one, and far more mystifying. She followed Nelson down the corridor. When she stepped into the foyer, she gasped. An enormous bouquet, the largest she'd ever seen, sat upon the cherrywood lanterloo table. The flowers were arranged in a stunning, huge cut crystal vase.

Every single bloom was a blush-colored rose.

Good heavens, there had to be at least ten dozen of them. The man must have beheaded every single rosebush in his conservatory. It was ridiculous and excessive and extravagant.

And wildly romantic.

They remind him of you. . . .

Heat flushed through her entire body. Reaching out, she touched one of the delicate blooms and breathed in the heady fragrance scenting the foyer. A lovely, thoughtful gesture, the second one this morning, from a man she was coming to think of as just that—lovely and thoughtful.

As well as full of surprises. Indeed, she recalled that his plans for them this afternoon were also to be a surprise. Which meant he'd be providing *three* surprises in one day. And her providing none.

Not a very even score.

An idea formed in her mind and her lips curved upward in a secret smile.

She turned toward Nelson. "Lord Surbrooke will be calling at noon today. I'll receive him in my private sitting room." The drawing room wouldn't do at all for what she had in mind.

"Yes, my lady."

She slid one long-stemmed rose from the vase then headed toward the stairs.

It was time *she* surprised Daniel. And evened that lopsided score just a bit.

ady Wingate will join you shortly," Nelson said to Daniel after showing him into a cozy, tastefully furnished, yet feminine chamber that was clearly Carolyn's private sitting room. Daniel thanked the butler, who then left, closing the door quietly behind him. Surprised, he looked around at Carolyn's inner sanctum, wondering if there was any significance to her receiving him here rather than the drawing room. Not that he minded the extra privacy, especially given the news he had to share with her. He also couldn't deny he was relieved not to have that huge portrait of Edward staring down at them.

Turning in a slow circle, he took in his surroundings. Pale yellow silk covered the walls, which were decorated with gilt-framed watercolors of various plants and flowers. He suspected they were the work of her sister Sarah, who he knew possessed a great talent for such drawings, and upon closer inspection of one noted her signature in the corner.

A floor-to-ceiling bookcase was flanked by tall, dark green velvet draped windows through which skeins of sunshine slanted. A dainty reading and writing table sat in the corner near the window, positioned to perfectly capture the light. In the other corner was a Recamier couch, its rounded contours upholstered in a soft yellow and green stripe. His gaze fell upon a slender silver vase on an inlaid table next to it. The vase held a single flower—one of the blush pink roses from his conservatory. Surely that was a good sign.

A pair of overstuffed wing chairs set before the white marble fireplace in which a fire burned provided a cozy seating area. A large, ornately carved mirror hung above the mantel, upon which an unusual collection of small porcelain birds flocked. Combined with the moss green carpet decorated with pale pink cabbage roses, he felt as if he stood in the midst of an enchanted indoor garden. He breathed deeply and caught a hint of the subtle floral fragrance she wore. A Carolyn-scented indoor garden.

Carolyn . . . bloody hell, she hadn't been out of his thoughts for so much as a second since he'd left her last night. *Since you left her last night?* his inner voice echoed in an incredulous tone. *She hasn't been out of your thoughts for an instant for a lot longer than that.*

He tipped his head back and closed his eyes. *Oh, all right, fine.* She'd haunted his thoughts a hell of a lot longer, which was uncharacteristic of him. As was the way he'd lost control last night when he'd kissed her. Damn it, he *never* lost control like that. And as the result of a mere kiss? Unheard of.

Last night wasn't the first time you lost control with her, his inner voice reminded him slyly.

Oh, bloody well all right, fine. But he certainly wouldn't behave like that today. He had the afternoon carefully planned. Today was for getting to know more about her—an enjoyable outing followed by a leisurely seduction. He wouldn't rush her, and he certainly wouldn't pounce upon her like a green lad with no command over his passions.

He heard the door open and turned, a greeting upon his lips, which evaporated, along with his ability to speak, at the sight of her leaning against the oak panel.

Her honey-colored hair was loose, a shiny curtain that fell over her shoulders, the curling ends brushing her hips. And she wore . . . bloody hell, she wore an ivory satin robe, tied at the waist. And based on the way the material clung to her curves and outlined her pert nipples, that's all she wore. His stupefied stare wandered all the way down to her bare feet, then back up again, where he encountered her gaze, one that simmered with such sensual heat he felt as if his breeches had been lit on fire.

"Hello, Daniel," she said in a warm, sultry tone. He was about to open his mouth to reply, only to discover that at some point his jaw must have dropped because his mouth was already open. If he'd been able to tear his eyeballs away from her, he would have looked on the floor to see if his jaw had fallen to his feet.

She reached behind her and the click of the lock turning reverberated through the quiet room. The only sounds were the crackle of the fire and his own labored breathing. If he'd ever in his life seen anything more arousing than Carolyn in that robe, looking at him as if she wanted to toss him onto the nearest couch and have her wicked way with him, he couldn't recall what that thing might be.

Again he tried to speak, but again she robbed him of the ability when she pushed off from the door and moved toward him with a sway of her hips that could only be described as sinful. He was helpless to stop his body's swift reaction, and he inwardly shook his head. Hard as a damn brick and she hadn't even touched him. She halted when an arm's length separated them, and if he'd been capable of moving, he surely would have snatched her against him.

"I believe I was the last one who spoke," she said, sounding faintly amused.

He had to swallow twice to locate his voice. "No doubt because you've rendered me speechless. You look so . . . so . . ." Once again his gaze skimmed down her form and a groan rose in his throat. "Like a wicked angel."

"You sent me some lovely gifts this morning."

"If this is your way of thanking me, I'll empty my conservatory of flowers every day."

Mischief danced in her eyes. "I haven't even begun to thank you."

The aplomb she'd momentarily stolen returned—thank God, because she'd reduced him to a slack-jawed gawker—and he erased the distance between them in one step. Sliding his arms around her waist, he drew her closer, until they touched from chest to knee. He lowered his head until his lips hovered just above hers then asked, "What did you have in mind?"

"If I tell you, it will ruin the surprise." She entwined her arms around his neck and rose up on her toes to brush her mouth against his.

A shudder ran through him, and it required every ounce of his strength not to simply back her up against the wall and drive himself into her. Bloody hell, the way she repeatedly stripped him of his mastery over himself, reduced him to such a state and so damn quickly completely unsettled him. Although there was no denying that this playful, seductive side of her delighted as well as surprised him.

Yet even as it did delight him, he couldn't help but wonder if she was truly thinking about *him*, seeing *him*—or if he were simply a stand-in for Edward.

A spurt of unreasonable jealousy rippled through him at the thought of her thinking about Edward while she kissed him. Then he shot himself an inward frown. Bloody ridiculous to be jealous of a dead man. He didn't want her heart and soul. Only her body. And clearly he was going to have his wish. He couldn't ask for anything more. He didn't care if she pictured Edward in her mind.

Did he?

No, of course not.

He lifted his head and wondered if something of his thoughts showed on his face because a small frown creased her brow. Leaning back in the circle of his arms, she asked, "Are you displeased?"

His gaze lingered on the generous curve of her breasts pressed against him. "Hardly. In fact, I'd be willing to wager that I am currently the most pleased man in the entire kingdom."

"Excellent." She stepped back and his hands fell

to his sides. He locked his knees to keep himself in place. As much as he wanted to drag her to the floor, strip off that robe, and touch and taste every inch of her skin, he also very much wanted to see what she would do next.

He didn't have long to wait.

His gaze dropped to her waist, where her fingers played with her robe's knotted sash. "Your plans for us this afternoon—were they urgent?" she asked.

"Nothing that can't wait."

"Do you like my robe?"

"Very much."

"Would you like me to take it off?"

His gaze lifted to hers. *Only more than I want to draw my next breath.* "Very much."

Mischief glittered in her eyes and she nibbled on her bottom lip. "The only problem is I'll be . . . naked."

"Personally, I fail to see how that's a problem."

"Well, it is in so far as you *won't* be."

"My very dear Carolyn, are you asking me to . . . *disrobe*?" He said the last word in an exaggerated, shocked tone.

"If you wouldn't mind too terribly."

"Not *too* terribly, I suppose—if it will please you."

"Oh, it will please me very much. Although there is one thing that would please me more."

"Hmmm. I'm beginning to think you're rather demanding."

Her lips curved upward in a teasing smile. "Wait until we're both undressed."

A quick laugh that turned into a groan of pure lust escaped him. He'd known from the first time he kissed her that a passionate woman lurked beneath her very proper exterior, but he hadn't anticipated this delightful creature standing before him, her eyes gleaming with wicked impishness. "I cannot wait. What is your request?"

"I'd like to help you undress."

He blew out an exaggerated sigh. "A truly monstrous demand, but I'll endeavor not to complain overly much."

She reached out and traced the outline of his erection with a single fingertip, a whisper of a caress that nearly stopped his heart.

"Good," she said, her voice a sensual purr. Her fingers glided upward, to lightly tug at his jacket. "Would now be convenient?"

"Now is perfect."

She helped him off with his jacket, then carefully laid the dark blue garment over the back of one of the wing chairs. When she applied herself to his cravat, he offered up a quick mental thanks that he hadn't employed a complicated knot.

Still, she seemed to be having trouble, and after several aborted attempts her fingers stilled and she looked up from her task. All traces of mischief in her eyes had been replaced by a serious and suddenly unsure expression. "I . . . I haven't done this in a very long time," she whispered.

He gently took her hands and lifted them to his lips. "I know. Take your time. There's no need to rush." He gave her a light, teasing nudge with his pelvis. "All physical evidence to the contrary, I'm not in a hurry. I love the feel of your hands on me."

"But what if . . ." That look of uncertainty grew more pronounced. "What if I don't please you?"

If she hadn't looked so utterly worried, he would have laughed at the absurdity of the question. Releasing her hands, he framed her face between his palms and brushed his thumbs over her smooth cheeks. "Carolyn, there is no possible way you could displease me. If you have any concern, it should be that I will keep you in this room for the next fortnight. Or two. Possibly even three. Maybe more." He leaned down and rested his forehead against hers. "Don't stop. And if your hands shake a bit, know that mine are shaking as well. From wanting you so very much."

She lifted her head, and he was relieved to see her eyes no longer held traces of concern. "How do you always know the right thing to say?"

"I don't. You simply inspire me." He glanced down at his cravat. "Care to continue what you started?"

"Will you help me?"

"With pleasure."

While she worked on his cravat, he removed his waistcoat and pulled his shirt tails from his breeches. He then settled his hands at his sides and forced himself to wait patiently while she finished. When she finally completed her task, he helped her pull his shirt over his head. The garment sailed to the floor and she settled her hands on his chest. That first touch dragged a low groan from his tight throat.

"Oh, my," she whispered, slowly smoothing her hands upward, over his shoulders.

Oh my, indeed. Her gentle explorations were driving him mad. "I've fantasized about you touching me like this," he said, a shudder running through him.

"You have?"

"More times than I can count." Surely he shouldn't have admitted that, but he couldn't seem to help himself. "The fantasy was always good, but the reality is much more pleasurable than I ever imagined."

Her fingers lightly skimmed over his abdomen, and his muscles jumped in response. "You're very . . . nicely made."

He settled his hands on her hips and lightly squeezed. "So are you."

She traced the line of skin just above the waist of his breeches. "I'd very much like for these to come off."

"We are in complete agreement." Taking her hand, he led her to the couch, where he sat and pulled off his boots and stockings. Then he stood and together they unfastened the front placard of his breeches. He quickly skimmed them and his smalls down his legs then stepped out of the garments.

The relief he experienced by freeing himself from the constricting confines of his breeches instantly evaporated when she brushed her fingertips over the head of his erection. His eyes slammed shut and he sucked in a hissing breath, one he held when his lungs ceased to function as her fingers slowly glided up and down his length.

Just when he didn't think he could take any more, she stopped, which left him on the brink of begging her to continue. Forcing his eyes open, he watched her pluck the rose from the silver vase. The look she gave him made him feel as if fire licked beneath his skin.

"You demonstrated a new use for roses last night." She slowly circled the velvety flower around the head of his erection. "Turnabout is only fair."

A low groan escaped him. "Turnabout is going to drive me mad."

"I have a confession to make," she whispered, wrapping her fingers around his shaft while she continued to tease the flower around the head.

He locked his knees and released a slow, careful breath. And once again had to recall how to speak. "Confession?" he managed.

"Yes. And it's nowhere near midnight."

"I'm afraid I won't make it that long. Especially if you keep doing—*aaaahhhh* . . . that."

"Just as well. You told me confessions at midnight lead to danger."

"Danger. Yes." Which precisely described his current situation—he stood in imminent danger of losing the remainder of his rapidly vanishing control. He gritted his teeth against the intense pleasure her touch and teasing strokes of the rose inflicted upon him. He endured the sweet torture until the need to climax approached overwhelming. Then with a shuddering breath he reached out and lightly grasped her wrists.

"If by danger you mean I'm at risk of arriving unfashionably early to the party." He placed the rose on the table, set her hands at her sides, then reached for the sash on her robe. "You said earlier that it would be a problem if you were the only one who was naked. Now I'm afraid I must say the same thing to you."

"You want me naked?"

He flicked a pointed look at his erection. "Obviously."

A devilish gleam lit her eyes. "How much?"

If she had any idea how much, it might very well scare her. God knows it scared him. The knot came free and he slipped his hands inside the satin and skimmed them up her smooth back.

"I'd be hard pressed to think of anything I want more at the moment," he said, slowly easing the material off her shoulders.

"A million pounds?" she suggested in a teasing voice.

The satin slipped down her arms and pooled at her feet with a quiet *shush,* and Daniel's avid gaze roamed. Over smooth, creamy skin. Full breasts topped with aroused coral nipples that seemed to beg for his touch. The gentle curve of her waist and indent of her navel. A triangle of honey-gold curls at the apex of lush thighs that tapered down to slim ankles and the dainty arch of her bare feet.

"Once again, I believe it is your turn to speak," she said.

"I would, except it appears I'm completely out of words. Except to say that you are the most beautiful woman I've ever seen." Reaching out, he cupped her breasts. "The softest I've ever touched." He stepped forward then leaned down and touched his lips to the curve where her neck and shoulder met. "You smell so good." His fingers caressed her taut nipples. "Feel so good." He ran his tongue over her plump bottom lip. "Taste so good."

"That's quite a few words. All of which I liked . . ."

Her words drifted off into a vaporous sigh when he leaned down and drew a nipple into his mouth. While he'd spoken the truth, it would have been far more accurate to say no woman, ever, had felt so good. Tasted so delicious. Ever.

She threaded her fingers through his hair and arched her back, offering more of herself, an invitation he instantly accepted. He drew the tight bud of her nipple deeper into his mouth while his free hand skimmed down her back to cup the enticing curve of her bottom, urging her closer. His hand wandered lower and hooked beneath her thigh, lifting her leg and settling it high on his hip. His fingers glided over her sex and a growl vibrated in his throat.

Lifting his head, he looked at her flushed face and closed eyes. "You're so wet." He slipped two fingers inside her and she gasped, then groaned. "So tight and hot."

And he was so damn hard and she felt so damn good and he'd wanted her for so damn long. He simply couldn't wait any longer. Bloody hell, he was practically shaking. Slipping his fingers from her body, he scooped her up in his arms then gently laid her on the couch, following her down with his body. Settling himself between her splayed thighs, he propped his weight on his forearms and leisurely rubbed the head of his penis along her wet cleft, watching every nuance that passed over her flushed face.

"Open your eyes, Carolyn."

She dragged her lids upward and their gazes met. Her eyes were glazed with arousal, but she somehow seemed more focused on the act itself rather than who was making love to her. And he wanted her aware, very much aware, of who was making love to her.

"Say my name," he demanded, his voice hoarse, muscles straining with the effort to hold back.

She blinked, then studied his face. After several long seconds she finally whispered, "Daniel."

Something that felt like relief washed through him. He slipped just inside her, then paused. "Say it again."

"Daniel."

He glided in another inch. "Again."

She reached up and sifted her fingers through his hair. "Daniel." Arching beneath him, she repeated, "Daniel . . . Daniel."

With a groan, he thrust deep. His gaze never leaving hers, he slowly withdrew, gritting his teeth against the erotic, tight pull of her body. Then he stroked her deeply once more, the slow, slick glide into her wet heat peeling away another layer of his control. Again and again he sank into her, each thrust deepening, quickening. She wrapped her arms and legs around him, meeting his every movement. His lungs burned with his rapid breaths, every muscle straining with the effort he expended to hold off his release until she climaxed. The effort damn near killed him.

The instant she arched beneath him, it felt as if lightning struck him, sizzling and exploding through his entire body. Shudders racked him as he drove hard and deep, pounding into her, spilling what felt like his entire soul into her pulsing heat. Tremors still shook him when his head fell limply into the warm curve of her neck and he fought to catch his breath. He wasn't certain how long it took him to find the strength to lift his head. A minute, or perhaps an hour, he didn't know. Couldn't consider anything beyond absorbing the incredible feeling of remaining buried deep inside her snug heat. And another sensation he couldn't name other than to know it felt as if he'd been punched. In the heart.

Finally he lifted his head to look down at her. And froze.

She lay beneath him, staring up at seemingly nothing, tears running from the corners of her eyes.

Guilt smacked him like a brick to the head. Bloody hell, he'd done it again. Completely lost all control. Only this time he'd—

"Carolyn . . . God, did I hurt you?" He made to move off her, but her arms and legs tightened around him, holding him in place.

She shook her head. "No."

Unconvinced, he gently brushed away the moisture beneath her eyes, but it was instantly replaced by a fresh supply. "Why are you crying?"

Instead of answering, she said, "Thank you."

"Thank you? For making you cry?" Damn it, he felt like a first-class cad.

She nodded. "Yes. I . . . I never thought I would make love again. Never thought I would want to. You made it . . . extraordinary. And for that, I thank you."

Relief nearly overwhelmed him, and everything inside him seemed to shift. "Extraordinary," he repeated softly, his gaze roaming her face. "That describes it—and you—perfectly." Indeed he couldn't recall ever speaking truer words. Because making love with Carolyn was . . . different. He'd surrendered a part of himself, of his control, to their lovemaking that he'd never given up before. A part of himself he hadn't even known existed until it was no longer his.

In the past, after his passion was spent, he was never eager to linger. But with Carolyn, he felt as if he could stay on this couch, buried inside her the entire day. And just look at her. Brush back her shiny hair from her face. He felt a bond with her that he'd never before experienced. An unfamiliar warmth of . . . something that confused him. But that nonetheless couldn't be denied.

Bloody hell, how was it that this one time with Carolyn had reduced every other sexual encounter he'd ever experienced into an emotionless physical act? A sordid imitation of what it was supposed to be? How was it possible that out of all the affairs he'd engaged in, he'd missed out on *this* . . . whatever it was?

"Daniel?"

He blinked away his thoughts and refocused his attention on her. "Yes?"

Her bottom lip trembled. "You've brought me back to life."

His heart seemed to perform a somersault. He searched for his normal lighthearted postcoital persona and came up empty. "Which is precisely what is supposed to happen to Galatea," he said in as breezy a tone as he could muster. "The pleasure was all mine."

"No, it wasn't." She stretched beneath him and flashed a smile. "I feel absolutely marvelous. But I'm famished. Might your plans for us this afternoon include something to eat?"

"As a matter of fact they do. Now that you've had your wicked way with me, shall we get dressed and commence with *my* plans?"

"All right, although I'm rather disappointed that your plans require us to get dressed."

"You won't be when you see where we're going and what I've planned. But about that getting dressed bit?"

"Yes?"

He dropped a quick kiss on her lips. "Don't bother to wear drawers beneath your gown."

Chapter 14

Given the fiery nature of our passion, I thought it would burn out as quickly as it flared. But I soon discovered that the more I saw him, the more I wanted him. And no matter how much I saw him, it wasn't nearly often enough.

Memoirs of a Mistress by An Anonymous Lady

*D*ear lord, she wasn't wearing drawers.

Carolyn tried to concentrate on the bustling scenery as Daniel's elegant carriage traveled down Park Lane, but all she could think about was that she sat across from her lover and lacked undergarments. She stared at the people strolling through Hyde Park, yet saw none of them. Instead, she visualized closing the carriage's maroon velvet curtains, ensconcing them in privacy, then begging him to put out the relentless fire he'd lit within her.

What on earth was happening to her? She'd enjoyed a deeply passionate relationship with Edward, yet at the moment those memories seemed almost lukewarm when compared to this craving she felt for Daniel, which bordered on . . . *ravenous*.

"I have some news for you."

His voice yanked her from her erotic brown study and she turned to look at him. Rather than regarding her with his usual teasing warmth, his dark blue gaze was serious.

"What sort of news?" she asked, forcing aside her lascivious thoughts.

"Gideon Mayne called upon me earlier today. He and Rayburn located Tolliver last night at his town house. The earl reeked of liquor and was passed out in his study. He was holding a pistol. They took him into custody."

"Thank goodness." Carolyn pressed a hand against her midriff. "He really did try to shoot you." A mixture of fear and nausea roiled through her at the thought of Lord Tolliver succeeding.

"Yes. And he nearly killed you instead."

She recalled the sensation of the bullet whizzing by her and shuddered. "Has he confessed?"

"No. He's insisting he's innocent. Says he never left his house last evening. Claims the pistol was meant for himself, to take his own life." A muscle ticked in Daniel's jaw. "According to Mayne, none of Tolliver's servants saw him leave the house, but as they all retired around eleven, neither can they verify that he didn't depart after that."

"It's hardly surprising that someone as unethical

as Lord Tolliver has shown himself to be would lie about shooting at you," Carolyn said.

"I agree. I'll still keep my guard up, but I think it's clear we've got our man. I'd meant to tell you as soon as I saw you, but . . ." His eyes darkened. " . . . you distracted me."

She hoisted a teasing brow. "Hmmm. That sounds distinctly like a complaint."

He leaned forward and lightly clasped one of her gloved hands. Warmth skittered up her arm. "My only complaint is that we're not so occupied right now." He brushed his fingertips against the sensitive skin of her inner wrist, just above the edge of her glove. "You are . . . amazing."

"A word I could just as easily use to describe you, my lord."

He made a *tsking* sound. "Surely you haven't already forgotten that such formality is no longer necessary." As if to prove his point, he slipped one long finger beneath the edge of her glove to slowly stroke her palm.

She sucked a quick breath at the intimacy of the gesture and shook her head. "I haven't forgotten," she said in a shaky whisper. Dear God, if she lived to be one hundred she'd never forget what they'd shared.

"Of course if you *had* forgotten," he continued, his heated gaze locked on hers, "I suppose I'd have to remind you." He heaved an exaggerated sigh. "A heinous task, but I'd endeavor to take it like a man."

Determined not to allow him the upper hand, she leaned forward and set her free hand on his knee. "I

assure you I'm in no danger of forgetting, Daniel."
She glided her hand slowly up his leg. "However, I
would welcome you reminding me. Any time you'd
care to do so. And as for taking it like a man . . ." She
brushed her fingers over the bulge in his breeches, enjoying his quick intake of breath. " . . . I greatly antici-
pate discovering exactly how much you can take."

His eyes seemed to breathe smoke. "Just as I an-
ticipate discovering the same thing about you."

"How nice that we are in agreement."

"I believe that 'nice' is a rather tepid word to describe anything that will transpire between us, my
lady, but I suppose it will do. For now."

"'My lady?'" She copied his earlier *tsking* sound
and repeated his words. "Surely you haven't already
forgotten that such formality is no longer necessary."

"I haven't forgotten. Indeed, should I live into the
next century I'll never forget what we've shared."

His words so closely mirrored her earlier thoughts
she ridiculously wondered if perhaps he could read
minds.

"In your sitting room, you said you had a confession to make," he said, his finger continuing to
lightly stroke beneath her glove with a leisurely,
drugging rhythm, "but you never told me what it
was. I would have asked you at the time, but I was,
um, distracted."

She skimmed her hand along the inside of his
thigh. "I stole your breeches."

His muscles contracted beneath her touch and he
shot a pointed look at her hand on his leg. "Clearly
you haven't. Unfortunately."

She laughed. "Not these breeches. And not today.

It was during Matthew's house party. The ladies devised a scavenger hunt of sorts. My mission was to procure a pair of your breeches. I entered your bedchamber when I knew you wouldn't be about and just like that . . ." She lifted her hand from his leg to snap her fingers. " . . . I made off with your breeches."

He grabbed her hand and settled it right back on his leg. "Fascinating. If I'd suspected you were going to skulk about in my bedchamber, I never would have left."

She lifted her chin. "I wasn't skulking. I was . . ." Her voice trailed off as she searched for a less incriminating word.

"Lurking?" he suggested. "Prowling?"

She hiked her chin higher. "I was merely doing my duty to the game."

"I see. I didn't notice I was missing a pair of breeches."

"I returned them before the house party ended. So I didn't really steal them—I merely borrowed them."

"Ah. So you visited my bedchamber *twice* without my knowledge during the house party."

"Yes."

"And what did you do with my breeches once you'd borrowed them?"

Feeling outrageously daring, she decided to be absolutely honest with him. "I brought them to my bedchamber. I held them against me and thought of you. Of how you looked wearing them. And imagined how you would look without them." Heat suffused her at her admission, a truth she'd stubbornly refused to acknowledge at the time.

Unmistakable interest flared in his eyes and he slid

his finger from her glove. Leaning down, he grasped her ankle and lifted her foot onto his lap. After removing her shoe, he massaged her stockinged foot, eliciting a low groan of delight from her.

"Have I mentioned that I adore having my feet rubbed?" she asked as all her muscles turned to the consistency of porridge.

"You didn't say so, but it was fairly easy to ascertain." His fingers performed some form of magic on her instep and she moaned. His wicked grin flashed. "The moaning and groaning is a bit of a giveaway."

"I imagine, *oooohhh myyyyy . . .* that it is."

"Tell me, how did you imagine I would look without my breeches, Carolyn?"

A long purr vibrated in her throat and she regarded him through eyes drooped half closed with the pleasure radiating upward from her foot. "Wonderful. But the reality proved even better than my imagination, which was quite fertile, I assure you."

His expression turned grave. "I must admit your confession disappoints me."

A frisson of embarrassment shivered through her. "I know it was wrong of me to do, but—"

"I'm not disappointed at what you did but rather at your timing. I wish I'd been present when you came into my bedchamber. Twice."

God help her, but part of her had wanted him to be there as well—something she hadn't been able to admit to herself at the time. "What would you have done if you had been present?" she asked in a breathless voice.

Fire ignited in his gaze, but before he could reply,

the carriage jerked to a halt. He glanced out the window. "As we've arrived, I'll have to tell you later," he said, slipping her shoe back on then gently setting her foot on the floor. "Or better yet, I'll show you."

She barely resisted the urge to demand that they return home at once so he could show her *now*. Instead she adopted a sedate manner completely at odds with the inferno burning within her and looked out the window. And realized where they were.

"Gunter's?" she said, staring at the sign marking London's most famous confectioner's shop at number seven Berkeley Square. A smile curved her lips. "I adore Gunter's!"

He smiled in return. "As do I. It's my favorite London shop."

"Even more so than your tailor?" she teased. "You do have a reputation for being meticulous about your clothing."

"Gunter's is my favorite shop, bar none," he said, his voice perfectly serious. "It appears I have a weakness for fruit flavored ices." His gaze skimmed over her. "Among other things."

How she could still blush after the intimacies they'd shared, she had no idea. To hide the heat suffusing her cheeks, she picked up her reticule in preparation for exiting the carriage. "Edward and I used to . . ." Her voice trailed off awkwardly and she looked at the ground. Surely she shouldn't be speaking of Edward to her lover. Doing so smacked of disloyalty, to both Edward and Daniel. And reminded her of her lingering feelings of guilt at taking a lover—feelings she'd prefer to ignore.

She cleared her throat and finished, "We frequented Gunter's whenever we visited London."

"Carolyn."

He said her name so softly, so kindly, a lump lodged in her throat. When she looked up, she noted his eyes held the same kindness as his tone. "I don't begrudge you your memories of Edward, nor do I want you to feel that you cannot talk about him with me." He hesitated then added, "I knew you'd come here with Edward at least once, as I saw you."

She couldn't hide her surprise. "You did? When?"

"About five years ago. I was across the street and saw you and Edward leaving Gunter's. You were both smiling. You looked very happy."

"Is that why you brought me here—because you knew I'd like it?"

"Partly. But also because in keeping with our conversation at the masquerade ball, the highwayman wanted to give Galatea something that reminded him of her."

"And that something is a fruit-flavored ice?"

"Yes."

"Because I'm so . . . tart and frosty cold?"

His gaze remained serious. "No. Because when I touch you with my tongue you melt."

Oh, my. She recalled the delicious sensation of his tongue touching her, and her heart seemed to trip over itself. He did indeed make her melt. In a way that made her not only want to experience that magic again, but to also affect him the same way.

Before she could respond, he reached out and lightly squeezed her hand. "Would you prefer to go somewhere else?"

Good heavens, he could make her melt even without benefit of his tongue. Clearly all he had to do was look at her. Touch her hand. "No, Daniel. I'd prefer to go to Gunter's. It's been a very long time since I've enjoyed a flavored ice. I think it's time to make some new memories." She squeezed his hand in return. "With you."

What looked like relief flashed in his eyes. "I look forward to sharing those memories with you." Then one corner of his mouth curved upward in a sinful grin. "I'll do my utmost to see that you're not disappointed."

After helping her alight from the carriage, they entered the shop. The delectable scents of sweetmeats, pastries, and fresh baked biscuits assailed her.

"Is an ice your pleasure?" Daniel asked. "I see that they're featuring blueberry today. Or would you prefer something else?"

She offered Daniel a smile. "A blueberry ice sounds divine."

They sat at a small round table in the corner of the shop and enjoyed their frozen treat. After spooning a small bit into her mouth, Carolyn confided in an undertone, "This is so delicious. I want you to know that it's requiring a great deal of self-control for me not to moan out loud with every taste."

Daniel's leg shifted beneath the table and his knee pressed against hers, shooting a spark up her leg. "I want you to know that it's requiring *all* of my self-control not to press you up against Gunter's counter and really give you something to moan about. Suffice it to say that I intend to hear those delightful sounds you make as soon as possible."

Heat whooshed through her with such force she was amazed she didn't burst into flames. And how did he manage to appear so calm and collected when she felt incinerated by the furious blush scorching her entire body?

She glanced around at the other patrons, relieved that none of them appeared to be paying any attention to them. "If you keep looking at me like that, people will suspect that we're . . ."

"Lovers?"

"Yes."

"And how am I looking at you?"

"Like you'd rather be licking me than your blueberry ice."

Not a hint of repentance gleamed in his eyes. "I *would* rather be licking you." After spooning up another bit of ice, he added, "I think you'd prefer that as well."

The degree to which she'd prefer that actually frightened her. "You're melting my blueberry ice," she warned with a breathless laugh.

"Good. The sooner it's gone, the sooner we can leave." He pressed his leg more firmly against hers. "And the sooner I can make you melt."

She spooned a bit of the delicious ice between her lips, reveling in the rapt manner his avid gaze devoured the movement. Something about the contrast of their outwardly polite demeanor and the sensual undercurrents throbbing between them excited her in a way she'd never before experienced.

After she swallowed, she said softly, "And the sooner I can make *you* melt."

He went perfectly still, his spoon suspended midway between his bowl and his mouth. He drew in a slow, deep breath, then carefully set his spoon back in his still half-full bowl. "Let's go."

"Go?" She adopted her most innocent air and batted her eyelashes. "But I haven't finished my ice."

"I'll buy you another one tomorrow." He stood and held out his hand. The smoldering look in his eyes left no doubt that he wanted her as much as she wanted him. And as soon as possible.

She intended to see to it that he didn't have long to wait.

She gave her lips a dainty pat with her napkin, then placed her hand in his to arise. Surrounding herself with her usual air of proper dignity, she allowed him to escort her to his carriage. With his gaze never leaving hers, he took the seat opposite then gave the driver the signal to depart. As soon as they began to move, he flicked the velvet curtains closed.

"Come here," he said, his voice a low growl.

Instead of complying, she reached out and unfastened his breeches. He watched her through half-closed eyes, his chest rising and falling with his rapid breaths. When the buckskin placard opened, she wrapped her fingers around his erection and gently squeezed.

He sucked in a harsh breath. "Carolyn . . ."

A pearl of fluid glistened on the tip, and with a single fingertip she slowly spread the moisture over the head. Never had she behaved in such a bold manner outside the bedchamber. But something about this man and his passionate reactions to her brought out a daring, adventurous spirit she hadn't previously known she'd possessed. An untouched spirit whose emergence was clearly aided by the sensual images her readings of the *Memoirs* had embedded in her mind. The Anonymous Lady had described, in detail, the joys of making love in a moving carriage. According to the *Memoirs,* it was an experience not to be missed, and Carolyn had no intention of doing so.

Keeping her gaze locked with his, she brought her finger to her lips and brushed her tongue over the tip, tasting the salty tang of his essence. Her womb clenched at the fire that blazed in his eyes.

"Carolyn . . ." Her name was a harsh groan filled with need and want. "Come here."

This time she complied, and rose from her seat. Before she so much as blinked, his hands slipped beneath her gown and skimmed up the backs of her thighs to cup her bare bottom and draw her closer. She gasped at the contact, at his kneading, caressing fingers. Bracing one hand on his shoulders, she straddled his thighs, used her other hand to guide him to the opening of her body, and slowly rubbed the velvety head of his erection along her wet, swollen folds. The musky scent of her arousal and his heat filled her head, along with his low growl of pleasure.

Unable to wait any longer to feel him inside her, she sank down, a slow, slick impalement that pulsed sweet, hot pleasure through her. When he was buried to the hilt, so deep she swore he touched her heart, his splayed fingers clenched on her bottom, pressing her tighter against him.

"Carolyn . . ."

The way he said her name, a cross between a prayer and a growl, touched something deep inside her. And there was only one response.

"Daniel." She shifted against him. "You feel so . . . oh, my." Her words dissolved into nothingness when he flexed his hips and embedded himself deeper.

"You feel so . . . incredibly good," he whispered, leaning forward to graze her neck with his teeth.

Spurred on by his words, she slowly rose, then sank down again, her movements aided by the gentle rocking of the carriage. And then she was lost in the pleasure of her downward strokes and his increasingly demanding upward thrusts. Their pace quickened, both of them straining, panting, seeking the deep next stroke. Her climax exploded, and with a cry she couldn't contain, her body arched as the tremors throbbed through her. With a fierce groan, Daniel ground his hips into hers and she felt him pulse inside her.

Limp and breathless, with delightful ripples still shivering through her, Carolyn melted against him. She rested her forehead against his, and their rapid breaths mingled, fanning her overheated face.

"I give you my word," he said, his words husky and unsteady, "that I will, very soon, seduce you slowly. I swear it has been my intention, but you keep disrupting all my fine plans."

"Are you scolding me?"

"Yes, although by 'scolding' I actually mean 'don't ever stop.'" He slipped his hands from beneath her gown and framed her face between his palms. He looked into her eyes with an expression she couldn't decipher, then slowly leaned forward. Their lips met in a deep, passionate kiss that tasted sweet and delicious, flavored with blueberry ice. He ended the kiss as slowly as he'd started it, then lifted an edge of the curtain to cast a quick look out the window.

"We'll be home soon."

She heaved a sigh and wriggled against him. "Which means I have to move."

His lips twitched. "Not necessarily. My staff knows not to open the door until I draw back the curtains."

His words stilled her. She knew he meant them only to reassure her that they wouldn't be caught in dishabille, but they also made it patently obvious that while making love in a carriage was a new experience for her, it wasn't for him.

A jolt of something that felt exactly like jealousy stabbed her, and she inwardly scowled at the ridiculous sensation. She knew he'd had previous lovers—many of them, according to everything she'd heard. She also knew he'd have more lovers after their liaison ended—a realization that seized her insides with an uncomfortable sensation that resembled a cramp.

She tried to shove aside her thoughts as she moved off him. Accepted his proffered handkerchief to wipe away the evidence of their spent passion. Rearranged her skirts while he realigned his clothing.

Yet her disturbing thoughts continued and a frown puckered her brow. It didn't matter how many women came before her, or how many would come after her. Or if he made love to them in his carriage. It didn't matter at all. Not one bit. This was nothing more than a temporary affair. Edward was the love of her life. Daniel—and the *Memoirs*—had merely brought her passions back to the surface, and naturally they'd be strong at the moment, after having been suppressed for so long. Her mind knew it, yet somehow the area surrounding her heart still felt . . . bruised.

"Carolyn? Is something wrong?"

She blinked away her unsettling musings and looked at him. Noticed the concern clouding his blue eyes. And before she could stop herself, she said, "You've done this before."

The instant the words passed her lips, she wished she could recall them. It was none of her concern, and truth be known, she didn't want to know. Especially if she and their tryst lacked in comparison.

His gaze searched hers then he said slowly, as if carefully choosing his words, "As I've no desire to lie to you, I won't deny I've . . . had relations in a carriage before." Then he leaned forward and grasped her hands, squeezing them tightly, his serious eyes pinning her in place. "But I've never wanted any woman as much as I want you, Carolyn. I said that I make you melt, but the truth of the matter is that you make me melt. Every time you touch me." He raised her hand and pressed an ardent kiss against her palm. "Please do not ever compare yourself to any other woman, because you are absolutely incomparable. In every way."

To her mortification, hot moisture pooled behind her eyes. She blinked it away then gave a quick laugh, one comprised mostly of relief. "Even though I disrupt all your fine plans?"

He smiled. "Actually, *because* you disrupt all my fine plans. In the most delightful ways."

Of course he tells every woman that, her inner voice taunted. She shoved aside the irritating voice with another forceful reminder that this was nothing more than a temporary arrangement with a very charming man who would soon move on to the next woman who caught his fancy. So she'd concentrate only on the here and now and enjoy her time with him while it lasted.

"In that case," she said, "do you have any plans for the next hour or so?"

"All my plans for the rest of day involve only pleasing you." He waggled his brows. "What did you have in mind?"

She couldn't help but laugh at his exaggerated lascivious expression. "Do you ever think of anything besides . . . *that*?"

"Of course. Only a moment ago I was wondering what you wore to bed at night."

She tried to suppress a laugh and failed. "I'm afraid that qualifies as a sensual matter."

"No, that is a *clothing* matter." His gaze wandered over her. "So . . . what *do* you wear to bed?"

"I couldn't possibly tell you. After all, a woman must have her secrets."

"You realize you're enticing me to find out."

She hoisted a teasing brow. "From what I can see, you are excessively easy to entice. Now about your plans for the next hour or so—I have a request."

He reached out and brushed the backs of his fingers over the outward curve of her breast. "Whatever it is, I shall do my utmost to oblige you."

"Without even knowing what it is?"

"Yes."

"What if I were to make an utterly outrageous demand?"

"I would do my utmost to oblige you. Does your utterly outrageous demand include removing our clothing?"

She gave his arm a playful swat. "See? Another sensual matter."

"No, another *clothing* matter. But whatever your request is, rest assured, you've only to ask."

Even under their lighthearted banter, she had the impression that he was completely in earnest. "You must be taken advantage of quite frequently by making such generous offers."

"On the contrary, I've yet to be taken advantage of because it isn't an offer I make frequently."

His words, spoken in that soft, serious voice . . . that voice . . . that deep, sensual voice . . . *Botheration, where was I?* Oh, yes her request.

She cleared her throat. "I'd like to discuss Katie with you. And meet your family."

A wary expression crossed his features, then his expression went blank. "My family? I'm afraid that's impossible, as they are traveling on the continent."

"I meant your animal family. Your pets."

"Ah. *That* family," he said, sounding relieved. He lifted her hand and pressed a warm kiss on the sensitive skin of her inner wrist. "I'd be happy to discuss Katie or any topic you wish. As for my pets, it would be my honor and pleasure to introduce you, although I must warn you, they are an unconventional lot."

The carriage jerked to a halt and Daniel flicked

back the curtains. "Ready?" he asked with a smile.

"Ready," she agreed.

But was she? To enter his home, yes. But her inner voice shouted a warning that she wasn't in the least bit prepared for what entering into this affair with Daniel would ultimately entail. What continuing it would mean to the carefully constructed existence she'd built for herself. And in spite of her best efforts to tamp down that voice, it continued to whisper through her mind.

Chapter 15

*Everyday items took on entirely new and sensual mean-
ings with my lover. Jam and honey spread on skin made
for delicious midnight snacks. And my silk stockings
made perfect ropes for tying my lover to the bed. . .*

Memoirs of a Mistress by An Anonymous Lady

The instant Barkley opened the door and Daniel and Carolyn entered the foyer, they were
besieged by his "family," all of whom barked or
meowed in assorted octaves with varying degrees of
loudness. He wondered if his pets' less than perfect
outward appearances and near deafening greeting
might repulse her as they had the last several women
he'd invited into his home. But rather than backing
away from the healed-over infirmities and chaos,
Carolyn grinned and waded right into the fray.

The cats wound between his boots, while his four rambunctious dogs proceeded to welcome him with an enthusiasm that would suggest he'd been away for weeks. They clearly approved of Carolyn, who, after a few preliminary sniffs, they greeted as if she were their long-lost best friend. Every bark and meow seemed to ask him, *Who is this delightful creature you've brought us?*

He looked at Carolyn's bright smile and his chest seemed to constrict. *She's Carolyn. And you're going to adore her.*

Daniel crouched down and was immediately the recipient of a surge of joyful canine affection that nearly upended him. Carolyn laughed at the frenzy and crouched beside him. And was instantly showered with enthusiastic doggie affection and feline purrs.

"They're wonderful," she managed to say between breathless laughs as she petted and scratched and dodged canine kisses.

"They're insane," Daniel corrected, unable to keep from chuckling in spite of his exasperated tone. "Allow me to introduce you," he said, raising his voice to be heard above the din. He patted the shaggy-haired mud-colored dog of dubious ancestry that had no tail. "This is Stubby." He then nodded toward a medium-sized tan dog missing a hind leg who was trying mightily to lick Carolyn's chin and said, "That flirtatious fellow is Limpy."

"I'm guessing this is Baldy?" she said, scooping up the soulful-eyed, hairless puppy that squirmed with panting delight.

"Correct. And this little devil is Droopy," he said, picking up a small black and white, wiggling puff of fluff that sported only one spiky ear, the top of which flopped over. He then nodded toward the pair of cats who now sat sedately several feet away, tails curled around themselves, watching the proceedings with haughty feline disdain that clearly indicated they viewed such canine goings-on as undignified. "Blinky is the pure black one with one eye," Daniel said.

"Yes, I saw her last night."

"Tippy's the calico. She's the only reserved member of this wild bunch and is missing part of a front leg. The pair of them believe this is their house. They kindly allow me and the servants to reside here, but only so long as we continue to feed them. I'm convinced they spend all the time they aren't sleeping plotting ways to get the dogs to move out."

He set Droopy down then rose and extended his hand to her. Carolyn placed Baldy on the marble floor, then slipped her hand into his, a simple action that surely shouldn't have sped up his heart as it did.

Once she stood beside him, he stared down at the prancing quartet of dogs and commanded, "Sit." Recognizing the Voice of Authority, Limpy, Stubby, and Baldy instantly obeyed. Droopy, however, continued to stand and wag his moplike tail.

Carolyn chuckled at the small dog who gazed up at her through adoring black button eyes. "He appears to need a bit more training."

"She," Daniel corrected. "And I'm afraid there's a bit more needed than simple training."

"What do you mean?"

"She doesn't speak English."

Carolyn blinked. "I beg your pardon?"

"I suppose I should say she doesn't *understand* English. Samuel found her outside a building where he heard voices yelling in French."

"I've never heard of such a thing. Perhaps she has suffered some hearing loss due to her injury."

"Oh, she hears fine. Especially when food is mentioned."

"Have you tried speaking French to her?"

"Unfortunately my French is abysmal and I've yet to make inquiries of anyone who speaks the language regarding appropriate doggie commands." He shot her a hopeful look. "I don't suppose you speak French?"

"Only a bit, and not with any proficiency, I'm afraid. Still, I could try." She looked down at Droopy then cleared her throat. *"Asseyez-vous!"*

Droopy's bottom instantly plopped onto the marble tile.

Daniel stared for several seconds then laughed. "You're a genius!"

Carolyn grinned. "Hardly that. And my accent is awful."

"Nonsense. It's perfect. And now, my lovely genius, can you please tell her to stop chewing my boots? And my furniture? And my walking sticks?"

"I'm afraid I don't know how to say any of that."

"My boots, furniture, and walking sticks are devastated. But please, try something else."

"All right." She pursed her lips then said, *"Me parlez."*

Droopy answered with a series of nonstop, enthusiastic barks.

"What did you say?" Daniel asked over the noise.

"'Speak to me.'"

"Excellent." When Droopy continued to bark in a deafening fashion, he added, "Hopefully you know how to say 'be quiet.'"

She looked down at the yapping ball of fluff. "*Calmez-vous, s'il vous plaît.*"

Droopy instantly fell quiet.

"Brilliant," he said. "I must write down those commands. You have my eternal gratitude."

"Perhaps you can teach her English by saying both the French and English commands together."

"See? I told you you were a genius."

She laughed. Looking at her, bathed in a swath of sunlight pouring through the window that seemed to surround her in a golden halo, her eyes alight with merriment, she literally stole his breath. His ability to speak. Indeed, his ability to do anything other than stare at her.

He wasn't certain how long he stood there doing just that before she asked, her voice laced with amusement, "Might your eternal gratitude include a cup of tea? There's still the matter regarding Katie I'd like to discuss with you."

Her words broke through his befuddlement and he gave himself a mental slap. Bloody hell, one look at her and he completely forgot himself. "Of course. Tea. Perhaps even some biscuits."

At the mention of biscuits, Droopy barked twice. Daniel looked down at the tail-wagging dog. "Ah, yes, you understand 'biscuits,' don't you?"

Droopy barked again, and this time Limpy, Stubby, and Baldy joined in. Carolyn laughed. " 'Biscuits' is apparently part of a universal language."

"Apparently," he agreed. He turned to Barkley, who stood at his post near the door. The butler's gaze rested upon Carolyn with a sappy expression that indicated that he, too, found her enchanting. Good God, did there exist a man with a pulse who didn't fall under whatever spell she cast? Apparently not, because as far as Daniel knew, Barkley was quite impervious to feminine wiles. At least while he was on duty.

"Tea in the drawing room, please," he said to the butler.

Barkley blinked, as if coming out of the same sort of trance that had claimed Daniel. Indeed, he looked so befuddled, Daniel was tempted to laugh. "Yes, my lord."

"How has Katie fared in my absence?" he asked.

"Very well, my lord. She's up and about and feeling much improved. Mary has remained with her and is instructing her on the workings of the household. Samuel is watching over her as if she were the crown jewels."

Yes, Daniel had noticed his footman's attentiveness this morning. It seemed clear Samuel's attention was more than simple concern—the young man was smitten.

Smitten . . . his gaze rested on Carolyn. *I know exactly how he feels.*

He frowned at his inner voice's whisperings. Bloody hell, what rubbish. He wasn't smitten. Smitten meant one's heart was involved, and his most assuredly was not. He was merely . . . in lust. Granted, *deeply* in lust, but nothing more. Absolutely not. Only a fool would fall for a woman whose heart belonged to another man.

Shaking off all ridiculous thoughts of being smitten, Daniel escorted Carolyn down the corridor to the drawing room. The dogs pranced after them, followed by the cats, who strolled along at a more sedate pace.

"So is this all of your family?" she asked.

"All the furry sort who reside here. There's a feathered fiend by the name of Naughty, but he's not presentable enough to meet a lady."

"Oh, yes. I recall Katie mentioned a parrot. I'm most curious as to why he's named such. I'd like to make his acquaintance."

Daniel coughed to hide his horrified laugh. "I'm sorry, but I'm afraid you cannot meet Naughty."

She lifted her brows. "This from the man who said he'd grant any request I made?"

"You do not want to meet Naughty. He used to reside in a pub frequented by very unsavory sorts who taught him very inappropriate phrases. I assure you he is very aptly named."

She halted, bringing them to a stop, and planted her hands on her hips. He heard a muffled tapping sound and realized it was the toe of her shoe hitting the carpet. "I've never heard a bird talk before. I'm sure he's delightful."

"He's a menace."

"Consider me duly warned."

"You'll be shocked."

"I'm not as delicate as you think. Perhaps I can teach him some manners."

"Doubtful. He's very set in his ways." Noting the determined glint in her gaze, he narrowed his eyes. "Are you always this stubborn?"

She lifted her chin a bit higher. "Occasionally. When I want something."

"Would you like to know what *I* want?" Without giving her a chance to reply, he snatched her against him and covered her mouth with his. She gasped, effectively parting her lips, and he deepened the kiss, his tongue exploring the delicious warm silk of her mouth. She melted against him, entwined her arms around his neck and mated her tongue with his. A groan vibrated in his throat. Bloody hell, how had he survived the last quarter hour without kissing her?

He pulled her tighter against him, lost in the feel and scent of her, and kissed her as if he were famished and she a twelve-course meal. His body hardened and he settled one hand over the luscious curve of her bottom and slowly rubbed himself against her. By God, she just tasted and felt so damn *good*.

A series of barking sounds broke through the haze of desire engulfing him, and he slowly raised his head. And moaned at the sight of Carolyn's flushed face and moist, kiss-swollen lips. She blinked her eyes open and he stared into their aroused depths. He then flicked a scowl down at his quartet of dogs, all of whom stared up at him with curious gazes. Part of him wanted to banish the beasts for interrupting his kiss, but he grudgingly admitted that if they hadn't, he would have pressed Carolyn against the corridor wall, lifted her skirts, and shocked the entire household.

Damn it, what was wrong *with him?* The way she robbed him of his control was both troubling and irksome, and becoming more of a pressing problem. How did she make him forget all sense of time and place like that?

"Heavens," she murmured, reclaiming his attention. "You're very good at that."

He swallowed the humorless sound that rose in his throat. Gratified as he was to hear her say so, he felt like an uncouth, groping green lad. "I could say the same to you."

She seemed to suddenly recall where they were and stepped back. As much as he didn't want to release her, he forced himself to do so. If for no other reason than to prove to himself that he could.

"Since you're determined, shall we go see Naughty?" he asked.

Her lips twitched. "I thought I just had."

"I meant the parrot."

"Oh. In that case, I accept."

They continued down the corridor, dogs trotting at their heels. When they entered the library, they were greeted by a loud squawk. Blinky and Tippy settled themselves at the base of Naughty's large dome-shaped cage and stared at the colorful bird with the zeal a highwayman would bestow on a money-stuffed purse.

"Lady Wingate, this is Naughty. Please do not say I didn't warn you."

"Hello, Naughty," she said.

Naughty sidestepped around his cage then fixed his beady, black-eyed gaze on Carolyn. "Lift your skirt, hussy."

Daniel pinched the bridge of his nose and shook his head. He'd known this was a mistake.

"Goodness, you are naughty," Carolyn said.

"Drop your drawers, strumpet," suggested Naughty.

"I'm afraid I cannot," Carolyn said in a perfectly calm voice, "as I'm not wearing any."

Daniel nearly choked on his laughter. Carolyn threw him a sideways glance. "Are you certain he learned these things in a pub and not from you?"

Daniel placed his hands over his heart. "I swear. I would have taught him useful phrases."

"Hmmm. I'd think you'd consider 'lift your skirt' and 'drop your drawers' very useful."

He moved to stand behind her and slipped his arms around her, encircling her waist. "Is that an offer?" he asked, nuzzling her fragrant neck with his lips.

"Certainly not. Especially since, as I just pointed out to your parrot, I'm not wearing any drawers."

He lightly bit her earlobe, and absorbed the slight tremor that ran through her. "If you keep reminding me of that, we won't get out of this room until some-time tomorrow."

She turned in his arms and he looked down into eyes filled with an intoxicating mixture of arousal and mischief. "But you promised me tea. And biscuits."

The word *biscuits* brought a sharp yap from Droopy.

"There are other things I'd much rather give you,"

he said, giving her pelvis a light nudge with his.

"Oh? Diamonds? Emeralds? Pearls?"

He raised one hand and cupped her breast. "Among other things."

She leaned into his touch, her nipple pebbling beneath her gown. "Now who's being Naughty?"

"Beautiful lady, beautiful lady," squawked the parrot.

Daniel smiled into her eyes. "Now that's the smartest thing he's ever said. And he says plenty, believe me."

"So I've gathered."

"Give us a smooch," said Naughty.

"You heard the parrot," Daniel said in a perfectly serious tone. "'Give us a smooch.'"

With a laugh, she raised on her toes. "If you insist."

His lips brushed over hers and he fought against the urge to deepen the kiss. Forced himself to keep the contact light—if for no other reason than to prove he could remain in control.

"Let's have a tup, lady."

Daniel raised his head and shot Naughty a glare. It was definitely time to get Carolyn away from his chattering bird. "Time for tea," he said, taking her hand and leading her toward the door.

"What's a 'tup'?" Carolyn asked.

Daniel dragged his free hand down his face and tugged her out of the room. "It's an . . . unladylike term."

"For what?"

"Carnal relations." Instantly, a plethora of images bombarded him. Of him and Carolyn, naked bodies entwined, engaged in carnal relations. A film of sweat coated the base of his spine and he clenched his jaw.

When they reached the drawing room, he deliberately kept the door open—just to prove to himself that he could. That he didn't need to touch her. Or kiss her. That he was perfectly capable of not doing so. That he could win the struggle to retain the gentlemanly restraint she so effortlessly stripped from him.

So instead of giving in to the overwhelming desire to lock the door and drag her to the floor, he went to his desk and withdrew a piece of vellum. "What were those French phrases that will save me?"

She'd just finished repeating them when Katie entered bearing the tea tray. Daniel noted that although the young maid's lip was still swollen and bruises still marred her face, she looked much better than she had last evening.

"How are you feeling, Katie?" he asked.

"Much improved, milord, thank ye," she answered, setting the tray on the table in front of the settee.

"Are you certain you feel well enough to be working already? There's no need to rush."

"I'm fine, milord. And wouldn't dream of takin' advantage of yer generosity." She straightened and clasped her hands in front of her. "I'm grateful not only for ye seein' my injuries treated, but fer givin' me this position." She swallowed. "I'd 'bout given up on thinkin' there were still decent people in this city." She shifted her gaze to Carolyn. "And my thanks to you, too, my lady. Ye were so kind to me." Her bottom lip trembled. "And Gertrude as well. She reminded me so much of my mum. Died last year, my mum did. I miss her somethin' awful."

"I'm so sorry for your loss," Carolyn said. "And I'm glad you're feeling better."

"Thank ye." She offered a quick curtsy then quit the room, leaving the door open, as she'd found it.

"Shall I pour?" Carolyn asked.

"Thank you." His gaze drifted to his dogs, who sat lined up on the hearth rug like pigeons upon a branch, their gazes riveted on the plate of biscuits. "You have a rapt audience," he said with a chuckle.

After serving them both—and tossing each dog a biscuit—she sipped her tea, then stared into the hearth at the low-burning flames. Daniel's gaze roamed over her, taking in her glossy hair, delicate features, and lovely pale green muslin gown. Bloody hell, she was stunning. Literally, as she completely stunned him, not only with her beauty, but her wit. And intelligence. And that devilishly mischievous streak. And the passion that sizzled beneath the surface of that perfect, ladylike exterior.

He was just contemplating how she would react to him pulling her onto his lap when she turned toward him.

"I have a proposition to offer you," she said.

"Yes," he said without hesitation.

"Yes what?"

"My answer is yes. To your proposition."

She blinked. "You don't even know what it is."

"I cannot fathom not liking anything you might suggest. Especially if it's anything like what I was thinking."

"And what were you thinking?"

"That I'd like to drag you onto my lap and slip my hand beneath your gown."

She looked toward the ceiling, but a smile teased the corners of her mouth. "Again you're thinking of sensual matters."

"Not at all. Clearly you didn't hear the word 'gown,' which makes it, once again, a clothing matter."

"Certainly an activity ripe with appeal and possibilities. However, my proposition—at least this one— concerns Katie and her employment situation."

"You mean her position here?"

"Yes. Daniel, I suspect you do not really require another maid. That you offered the job to Katie simply out of kindness. And if that is indeed the case, well, *I'd* like to hire her."

His brows rose. "You're in need of a maid?"

"Not exactly."

"Then why? You think her unhappy with her position here?"

"Not at all," she said quickly, shaking her head. "But I thought about this all morning, wondering if I should broach the subject with you. Seeing Katie just now convinces me my idea is sound. She's obviously grateful to you, and your offering her the position was very kind and generous. But considering her circumstances, I wonder if she might not feel more comfortable in a woman's household. Plus, she clearly took a strong liking to Gertrude, as Gertrude did to her."

She paused, looked down into her steaming cup, then again raised her gaze to his. "Plus, those things you said, about feeling useless and unfulfilled and how helping those in need has lessened those sentiments . . . I know all about feeling useless and unfulfilled, and have yearned for an enterprise to help chase them away. I find your efforts with your animals and now with helping Katie very admirable. Honorable. And I'd like to be a part of them. I thought offering Katie employment in my household could be a first step." Uncertainty flashed in her eyes. "That is, if you wouldn't mind my help."

For several seconds Daniel simply stared at her, stilled by the unexpected emotions her words elicited. After clearing his throat, he said quietly, "It's been a very long time since anyone has used the words 'admirable' and 'honorable' to describe anything I've done, Carolyn."

"I find that difficult to believe."

"You shouldn't. They certainly haven't always described me. I'm not certain I deserve them now."

Her gaze searched his, a frown marring her brow. "Based on your actions, on what I've observed, *I'm* certain you do. And I'm certain Samuel would say the same. And Katie. And all your animal friends, if they were able to do so."

She set aside her teacup then reached out to lay her hand on his. Heat rushed up his arm, and his heart ridiculously skipped at the simple touch. "You should be proud of what you've done, Daniel. Of what you're continuing to do. And I'd be proud and honored to help you. In any way you'd allow me to do so. And I'd be delighted . . . and relieved . . . to be doing something useful."

He looked down and studied her pale, slim hand resting on his. Bloody hell, he liked the way it looked atop his, so small and delicate. Liked the way it felt, so warm and soft. Liked the way it seemed as if it belonged there. A displaced piece of a puzzle that he hadn't even known was missing.

He rarely found himself at a loss for words, but this woman had a way of tying his tongue into knots. Of flooding him with such unexpected emotions he couldn't even begin to figure them out, let alone verbalize them. She'd spoken to him as if she considered him some sort of hero—a huge error on her part, as he knew damn well he wasn't. But how could he tell her that? He'd never told anyone. . . .

He dragged his gaze up to hers, and realized by her high color and embarrassed expression that he'd remained silent too long.

"I beg your pardon," she murmured, slipping her hand from his. "I didn't mean to—"

He grabbed her hand and pressed it between his palms. "I'd be honored to have your assistance, Carolyn. Your offer to employ Katie is very generous and your reasoning is both sound and wise. We can put the proposition before her and allow her to decide. As for the animals, you may be sorry you've offered once your calm household is overrun with crazy canines, felines, and the odd rabbit or two. Or twelve. Believe me, chaos will reign."

Her smile was tentative at first, then bloomed fully, and he felt as if the sun had emerged from behind a cloud. "My household could use a bit of chaos. And I'm very fond of animals."

"Excellent. Shall we start you off with four dogs, two cats, and a very mouthy parrot?"

"If I thought you'd part with any of them, I'd take you up on that offer. But 'tis obvious you adore them."

He heaved a sigh and glanced at his four dogs and two cats, which all lay in a huddle on the hearth rug, heads resting on each others' backs and rumps. "Don't know how that motley bunch managed to get under my skin," he grumbled.

"It's because you've a soft spot inside."

"More like a soft spot in my head."

She smiled, and he felt as if he were slipping into a stupor.

Bloody hell, it seemed that he also had a soft spot right where he didn't want one. And had never before had one. Right in his heart.

Well, he'd have to shore up that unexpectedly vulnerable point very quickly because this interlude with Carolyn was nothing more than an affair. A lighthearted, temporary liaison. To even for one moment consider it something more would be the height of foolishness. Her heart belonged to her husband's memory—she'd made that patently clear. His heart was his own—and he'd be wise to keep it that way.

A lighthearted, temporary liaison.

Yes, that's what this was supposed to be.

So why did it suddenly feel so . . . *un*lighthearted? So . . . intense? Or *was* it sudden? Had it *always* been so all-consuming? Bloody hell, he didn't know. And why, when he tried to imagine himself with a woman other than Carolyn, did his insides seem to curdle in protest? Why did no other woman's face materialize in his mind?

Again, he didn't know. And damn it, he was afraid to examine those questions too closely for fear of what he'd find.

Chapter 16

Sometimes our lovemaking was slow and leisurely, which
I *always* found enjoyable. But those other times, when
it was frantic and wild, when we dragged each other to
the floor and yanked at our clothes as if possessed by
demons, when he lost all control and the memory of his
hard thrusts could still be felt hours later . . . those were
the times I liked best.

Memoirs of a Mistress by An Anonymous Lady

When Carolyn arrived home after tea with
Daniel, she was greeted by Nelson, who in-
formed her that Sarah, Julianne, and Emily, as well
as the trio of Lady Walsh, Lady Balsam, and Mrs.
Amunsbury had called during her absence. Carolyn
nodded absently, her attention caught by the gorgeous display of roses decorating her foyer. Drawing

a deep breath, she closed her eyes and absorbed their heady fragrance.

A blush suffused her at the memory of her sensual carriage encounter with Daniel, and she had to press her lips together to contain her secret smile. The Anonymous Lady's retelling of such a liaison in the *Memoirs* had captivated her, and while the reading of it had been highly stimulating, it couldn't compare to the thrill of the actual experience.

The *Memoirs* . . . yes, they'd inspired some very heated thoughts. Thoughts she'd very much like to share even more of with Daniel.

An idea occurred to her, a wicked idea so tempting that after a moment's pondering she realized she couldn't resist. She hurried to the drawing room and retrieved her copy of the *Memoirs* from her desk. The strong scent of almonds wafted up from the box of marzipan she'd put in the drawer, and she wrinkled her nose even as guilt hit her. The candy was such a thoughtful gift, even though she much preferred the roses.

After removing the bloom she'd pressed between the pages of the *Memoirs*, she penned a quick note on the back of her calling card, then carefully wrapped the slim volume and card with several sheets of tissue paper that she secured with a piece of satin ribbon.

Daniel had given her a number of gifts. It was time she returned the favor.

She made her way back to the foyer and handed Nelson the package. "I'd like this delivered to Lord Surbrooke as soon as possible."

"Yes, my lady. I'll see to it personally."

"Thank you." She was about to head for her bedchamber to decide what to wear to Lord and Lady Exbury's soirée that evening when the bell rang, indicating the front gate had been opened.

"'Tis the American gentleman, Mr. Jennsen," Nelson reported after a discreet peek out the slender window flanking the door.

Carolyn didn't ask how Nelson would recognize Mr. Jennsen—her butler seemed to know everyone in town.

"Are you in, my lady?"

Carolyn nodded, curious as to what would bring Mr. Jennsen calling. "Yes. You may show him into the drawing room, then deliver the package to Lord Surbrooke."

She headed down the corridor to the drawing room, where she checked her appearance in the gilt framed mirror. Heavens, she was practically glowing. Thank goodness the weather was good, so she could blame her vivid coloring on the sun, should Mr. Jennsen even notice.

A knock sounded, and at her bid to enter, Nelson opened the door. "Mr. Jennsen to see you, my lady."

The butler stepped back and Mr. Jennsen entered the room. Dressed in buff breeches, a Devonshire brown jacket, and polished black boots, he looked masculine and robust, and the room seemed to somehow shrink due to his commanding presence. His thick, dark hair appeared ruffled, either by his fingers or the wind, lending him a slightly undone air that suited him. She glanced in surprise at the bouquet of vivid pink peonies he held.

"Good afternoon, Lady Wingate," he said.

"Mr. Jennsen, how nice to see you."

"Please call me Logan." He crossed the carpet and extended the bouquet. "For you."

She buried her face in the colorful, fragrant blooms. "They're lovely. Thank you, Logan." She nodded toward the grouping of chairs around the fireplace. "Would you like to sit down?"

"Thank you."

As they settled themselves on the settee, she asked, "Shall I ring for tea?"

"Thank you, Lady Wingate, but I cannot stay long."

"Carolyn, please," she said, placing her flowers on the end table then offering him a smile. "To what do I owe the honor of this visit?"

"I heard about the shooting incident outside your home last evening and was concerned."

"Who told you?"

He made a vague gesture with his hand. "Servants talk. You know how quickly gossip travels."

"Well, then you must have also heard that I wasn't injured."

"Yes." He smiled. "But I wanted to see for myself. Between that and Lady Crawford's murder, I was concerned for your safety. Besides, those flowers desperately wanted to belong to a beautiful woman." He leaned closer and confided, "They told me so."

"Talking flowers? How unusual." A smiled tugged at her lips. "I wonder what they'll tell me about you?"

He shot the flowers a mock glare. "Only good things, I hope."

"I'm certain of it," she said with a laugh. "Well, as you can see, I'm no worse for the wear for my mishap last evening."

"No worse indeed," he agreed, his gaze wandering over her. "In fact you're positively . . . glowing."

His words raced heat directly into her face. Before she could find her voice, he went on, "I understand Surbrooke was with you last night and he wasn't hurt, either."

Heavens, gossip did indeed travel quickly. "One of his servants fell ill, and my maid and I went to his home to offer assistance."

"I didn't realize your maid was with you. I hope she wasn't injured."

Carolyn felt her blush deepen. "She remained at Lord Surbrooke's home through the night. Lord Surbrooke was kind enough to escort me home."

He nodded slowly. "I see."

His dark eyes studied her intently, as if she were a puzzle he were trying to figure out. She took the opportunity to study him as well. His face was a fascinating landscape of stark panes, softened only by his full, sensual mouth. Although he wasn't classically handsome, he exuded an undeniable masculine appeal and was very attractive. As if his dark good looks weren't enough, the air of mystery that surrounded him—no one knew very much about him or his past in America—coupled with his fabulous wealth, made him the object of great interest amongst the ladies of the ton, despite his undesirable colonial heritage. She had no doubt that many a female heart sped up whenever he entered a room.

Which suddenly begged the question: Why didn't he make *her* heart speed up? She liked him and had enjoyed his company at Matthew's house party and on the few occasions she'd seen him since returning to London. He was wry, witty, intelligent, attractive . . . so why didn't he affect her the same way Daniel did? When she fantasized about the erotic writings from the *Memoirs,* why was the man in her imaginings always Daniel and never Logan?

"Carolyn . . . I wonder if you could possibly be thinking the same thing I am?"

His question yanked her from her thoughts, and she gave a self-conscious laugh. She was about to assure him that she was certain they weren't thinking the same thing, but the words died in her throat, when he captured her upper arms in his large hands. Drew her close. And settled his mouth on hers.

Her body stiffened with shocked surprise, but after several seconds it became obvious that Logan Jennsen knew how to kiss a woman. Since she suddenly found herself very curious, she allowed herself to relax. And quickly realized that although Logan's technique was exceptional and his kiss perfectly pleasant, it didn't come close to affecting her the way Daniel's did. Indeed, Logan couldn't do to her with a masterful kiss what Daniel was able to do with a mere look.

Oh, dear.

He leaned back, and she opened her eyes and found him regarding her with a half-puzzled, half-surprised expression. His hands slid slowly from her shoulders, then he cleared his throat.

"Do you wish to slap my face?" he asked.

For some reason a bubble of amusement rose in her throat, one for which she was grateful, as it pushed aside her unsettling thoughts. "Do you want me to?"

"Not particularly."

"I'd prefer an explanation."

"As to why I'd wish to kiss a beautiful woman? It is not difficult to figure out." A frown bunched his brow and he tapped his index finger against his bottom lip, as if to make certain it was still there. His intense gaze settled on hers. "What did you think?"

Not quite sure how to answer without wounding his feelings, she hedged, "What did *you* think?"

He drew a deep breath, then said, "I'm not good with pretty words the way you Brits are so I'll just spit it out. I've missed my opportunity with more than one woman I've admired since coming to England, and I didn't want to let another one get away. But our kiss wasn't . . . what I expected."

"What had you expected?"

"Pyrotechnics." A sheepish look crossed his face. "I like you too much not to be perfectly honest with you. I didn't feel any . . . spark. I'm sorry." He dragged a hand through his hair. "I think you *should* slap my face."

She couldn't help but laugh. "I like *you* too much not to be honest. I didn't feel any spark, either."

He blinked, then smiled. "Really?"

"Really."

"Well." He blew out a sigh of obvious relief then chuckled. "I suppose my manly pride shouldn't allow me to be so happy about that."

"Nor my womanly vanity." She grinned. "You can bear it if I can."

He chuckled. "Agreed. It would appear we are destined to only be friends."

"So it would appear." And while she was happy

for his friendship, she was deeply troubled by what was now patently clear—that what she felt for Daniel obviously ran deeper. She held out her hand. "Friends?"

"Friends." He lifted her hand and brushed a kiss across the backs of her fingers. "*Mon ami*."

Carolyn blinked in surprise. "Do you speak French?"

"As a matter of fact I do."

"Fluently?"

"Yes." His eyes took on a teasing gleam. "Shall I dazzle you with some verb conjugations?"

She pushed aside her troubling thoughts and instead recalled a button-eyed Droopy. "Actually, there are several phrases I'd like very much to learn."

"I'm sorry I missed seeing you this afternoon," Sarah said, after greeting Carolyn that evening with a tight hug when they found each other at the crush that was Lord and Lady Exbury's soiree. "I'm very relieved you're all right. What a horrible, frightening episode. Thank goodness Lord Tolliver is in custody and cannot hurt anyone else." Sarah released Carolyn, studied her for several seconds, then pushed up her spectacles and blinked. "I must say, you're looking none the worse for your fright. Indeed, you're positively glowing."

Good heavens. Little had she known that her tryst with Daniel would cause her to still glitter like a candle. She looked at her sister and, after a pause, said, "I could say the same about you, Sarah. You look as if you're lit from within."

Her sister's coloring deepened. She grabbed Carolyn's arm and pulled her into the nearby corner of the crowded drawing room, bypassing snippets of conversation dominated by Lady Crawford's murder.

"Can't believe the killer hasn't yet been apprehended—"

"Surely it won't be long . . ."

"I heard they think a former lover—"

"—and now another shooting last night—"

Once ensconced in the privacy provided by the dimly lit corner, Sarah said in an undertone, "I know why *I'm* glowing, and it is entirely the fault of that husband of mine, who finally sent me one of those 'time and place' notes described in the *Memoirs*."

"Clearly it worked remarkably well."

"You have no idea." Sarah lifted a brow. "What is your excuse?"

It is entirely the fault of your husband's best friend, who demonstrated the "carriage lovemaking" described in the Memoirs.

Unwilling to say that aloud, Carolyn hesitated. She'd never kept secrets from Sarah, but how could she expect her sister to understand something that she barely understood herself? An attraction so unexpected, yet so powerful it had her acting in ways she never thought herself capable of? An attraction she was beginning to fear might be turning into something more—with a man who'd made it clear he wanted nothing more than an affair.

And what if she told Sarah and her sister disapproved? She didn't think she could bear to see censure in Sarah's eyes. Yet, she couldn't bear the thought of lying to her, either.

Deciding her best recourse was to offer a bit of the truth and gauge Sarah's reaction, she said, "My excuse is that I've been . . . kissed."

Rather than appearing aghast, Sarah's eyes sparkled with interest. "Indeed? Based on your glow, it must have been a most excellent kiss."

"It was." She barely refrained from heaving a gushy sigh. "Most excellent."

"And who, may I ask, is this excellent kisser?"

Carolyn shook her head, confused. "You're not shocked? Disappointed?"

"Heavens, no. I'm delighted." She moved closer. "So, who was it?"

Humph. While she hadn't wanted to upset Sarah, the very least her sister could have done was act a bit surprised. "Why aren't you scandalized?"

"Because I think you're a beautiful woman who deserves to be kissed and who hasn't been in a very long time."

Sarah's quiet words swelled Carolyn's throat. "In that case, I suppose I must confess that I was actually kissed by *two* men today."

Sarah's brows shot upward, but instead of appearing appalled, her eyes twinkled. "Heavens, you've had a busy day. So, who are these two extremely intelligent, discerning gentlemen of impeccable taste?"

"How do you know they're intelligent, discerning, and possess good taste?"

"Because they chose *you* to kiss."

Some inner devil prompted Carolyn to hike a single brow and ask, "What makes you think I didn't choose *them* to kiss?"

"If you did, that only serves to prove my point, as

you'd hardly choose to kiss a man who didn't possess intelligence, discernment, and impeccable taste. Now, are you going to tell me who they are before I expire of curiosity, or must I locate a fire poker with which to prod you?"

Carolyn shook her head, half in disbelief, half in amusement. "When did you become so *un*shockable?"

"It is completely the fault of that husband of mine. In a scandalously short period of time he's completely stripped me of all my maidenly modesty."

Just as his best friend has done to me.

Sarah nudged her with her elbow. "Do I need to fetch the fire poker?"

"No." She stepped closer to her sister and whispered, "Kiss number one was from Daniel . . . Lord Surbrooke."

"Ah," Sarah said, a smile that could only be described as knowing playing at the corners of her lips. "And how was it?"

Incredible. Delicious. Amazing. "Nice."

"Just nice?"

"Very nice. Botheration, why aren't you surprised?"

"Because I've seen the way he looks at you when he thinks no one is looking."

"And how is that?"

"Like he wants to kiss you. No, actually like he's dying to kiss you. Very thoroughly. For starters."

Oh, my. And he had. Very thoroughly. For starters.

"And kiss number two?" Sarah asked, with another elbow prod.

"Was courtesy of Logan Jennsen."

This time Sarah's brows rose. "Interesting."

"But not surprising?"

"Not particularly, as I've also observed the way he looks at you."

"And how is that?"

"Like you're a bowl of cream and he's a very thirsty cat. And how was Mr. Jennsen's kiss?"

"Also nice."

Sarah stared at her over the rim of her spectacles. "It's not like you to be so uncommunicative, Carolyn." Her expression turned to one of concern. "Is something wrong?"

Carolyn shook her head. "No." Then she nodded. "Yes." She frowned. "I . . . don't know."

A trio of ladies walked by, and Sarah drew her deeper into the corner. "Something's amiss. Please tell me."

Her sister's concern lodged a lump in her throat that she had to swallow twice to dislodge. "Nothing's wrong, exactly. I'm just confused."

Sarah nodded. "Because both men are very attractive, yet you felt something from Lord Surbrooke's kiss that you didn't from Mr. Jennsen's."

Carolyn simply stared. "When did you become clairvoyant?"

"I'm no such thing. I'm merely observant and I know you very well." She clasped both Carolyn's hands in hers. "I've also seen the way you look at Lord Surbrooke when you think no one is looking."

Oh, dear. "And how is that?"

"Like a woman who is captivated by what she sees." Sarah studied her for several seconds through serious eyes. "He makes you laugh."

She nodded. "Yes. And feel and want things I'd never anticipated feeling or wanting again. I thought those yearnings were strictly the result of reading the *Memoirs*. That the sensual nature of the book made me long for the sort of physical closeness Edward and I shared." She paused, not quite sure how to continue.

Sarah nodded slowly. "You thought that like the Anonymous Lady, any of several men could satisfy those physical longings. Yet after kissing two men, both of whom are very attractive, you realize only one of them will do."

Perhaps her sister truly was clairvoyant. "I'm afraid so. And that is most unsettling."

"Because you feel you're being disloyal to Edward's memory?"

"Partly."

"Why else? Lord Surbrooke is a good man."

"Yes." Indeed, he was proving a much better man than she'd thought.

"Yet somehow you don't sound happy about that. Has he done something to offend you?"

"Actually, he sent me candy. And flowers."

One corner of Sarah's mouth quirked upward. "That fiend. I should set the dogs on him."

A laugh escaped her and she shook her head. "Danforth and Desdemona? I'm afraid your dogs, in spite of their imposing size, would simply lick him to death."

"You're right. Clearly I need to purchase some vicious dogs."

"It wouldn't matter. Dogs like him."

"Then you should be happy. Dogs are very good

judges of character. A man beloved by dogs is a man worth having."

"But that is the problem. I don't want to have him."

Sarah's expression turned soft with understanding. "I think, in your heart, you do. And that is what is causing your turmoil."

She shook her head. "My heart belongs to Edward." Didn't it? The fact that she would question something she'd always been so certain of truly alarmed her. "And even if it didn't, Daniel's made it clear he doesn't want my heart. He is only interested in me in a physical sense."

"Is that all you're interested in?"

Yes. No. I don't know. She thought she knew, but she just didn't anymore. The fact that all these changes and feelings had occurred in such a short time span only added to her confusion. "Y-Yes."

"Then I fail to see the problem. You both want the same thing." Sarah squeezed her hands again. "And you both should have it."

Carolyn searched her sister's eyes. "You're encouraging me to have an affair."

"I'm encouraging you to do whatever is going to make you happy. You've been unhappy for so long, and I want you to live again. I'll not find fault with anything you do, Carolyn." She hesitated, then said, "You've already begun an affair with him."

It wasn't a question, and was stated with such kindness and understanding, tears pooled in Carolyn's eyes. "I . . . I'm not quite certain what's come over me. I thought I had everything all figured out, but after Logan kissed me and it didn't elicit the same sensations as Daniel's kiss . . ." Her voice trailed off, then she drew a deep breath and continued. "This interlude with Daniel was supposed to be lighthearted. Carefree. And uncomplicated. And suddenly it doesn't feel that way."

"Because feelings are very difficult to contain. And predict."

"Which is very unsettling and vexing."

"Yes. But it can also be wonderful."

Yes. Or heartbreaking.

Sarah gave her quick hug. "Enjoy yourself, Carolyn. Bask in everything that makes you glow. If you concentrate on making today the best it can be, tomorrow will fall into place."

Carolyn leaned forward and kissed Sarah's cheek. "Thank you."

"You're welcome." She lowered her voice. "Don't look now, but Lord Surbrooke is across the room speaking to . . ." She craned her neck. " . . . Lady Margate. He's just caught sight of you and—oh, my, what a look came into his eyes. Like a flare of fire upon dry kindling."

Carolyn couldn't help but look. Her gaze locked with Daniel's across the room, and it seemed as if everything between them—the guests, the noise, the music, the clink of crystal glasses—all faded away. Myriad questions bombarded her and it was all she could do to remain in place and not rush across the room to ask him. *Did you read the book? My note? Are you as anxious to be together again as I am?*

"Julianne and Emily are about to descend upon us," Sarah said from the corner of her mouth. "I'm going to leave you in their very capable hands while I locate my husband, who promised me a dance."

Wondering how long it would take Daniel to approach her, Carolyn offered him a discreet nod, one he returned. Then she forced her attention to Emily and Julianne, who were demanding to hear the details of last night's shooting. When she glanced back to where she'd last seen Daniel, he was gone, as was Lady Margate, to whom he'd been speaking. Was he on his way across the room? Her heart quickened with the notion. But after a quarter hour had passed in conversation with Julianne and Emily and he'd yet to approach her, her spirits sank.

Where was he, and why hadn't he come to her?

Chapter 17

Some women enjoy the confines of marriage, but I embraced the freedom of widowhood, having no one to answer to but myself. I was free to concentrate my attention on one lover, or, if I so desired, allow my attention to wander to more than one gentleman.

Memoirs of a Mistress by An Anonymous Lady

njoying the party?"

The question pulled Daniel's attention away from Carolyn, who stood near the punch bowl on the opposite side of the crowded room, and he turned. Matthew stood next to him, champagne glass in hand.

"Of course I'm enjoying the party." A complete lie. He'd done his duty, chatting and mingling with the other guests, including Gideon Mayne and Charles Rayburn, who were in attendance, still hoping to find a lead in Blythe's murder. More than once he'd felt their stares boring into him.

But now that he'd fulfilled his social obligations, he wanted nothing more than to leave. With Carolyn, who, despite his best efforts, he hadn't been able to erase from his thoughts for so much as an instant. Especially after reading the explicit book she'd sent him. The brief words she'd written on the accompanying card were burned into his brain: *I want all of this.*

And God knows, he wanted to give it all to her. And had decided to begin right away, by employing a method used by one the Anonymous Lady's lovers. At a party they both attended, the lady's lover had purposely kept his distance, building an air of anticipation. And now he was doing his damnedest to remain aloof, but the effort was costing him. Perhaps he'd be better served to employ a different method described in the book—that of spiriting his lover away to the nearest empty room, locking the door, and proceeding to show her how much he desired her. But given the gossip he knew was already circulating regarding them being together during last night's shooting, he decided for her sake to err on the side of discretion.

Although, spiriting her away might be a better plan since that bastard Jennsen was now talking to her. And smiling at her. And damn it, she was smiling back. In fact, they were chatting like the best of friends.

"I must say I'm surprised you're enjoying the party," said Matthew, "because you don't look as if you are. Your countenance resembles a storm cloud."

Bloody hell. He wiped his expression clean then

tossed back a swallow of his brandy. "The party is delightful."

"Glad you think so. Personally, I cannot wait to get my lovely wife home and out of that very lovely gown she's wearing. Do you have plans for later this evening?"

Yes. I'm going to toss that bastard Jennsen into the nearest privet hedge. Then make love to the most beautiful woman I've ever known. "Why do you ask?"

"Just making conversation." He paused, then said, "Striking couple."

"Who?"

"Carolyn and Jennsen."

Daniel's fingers tightened on his snifter. "They're not a couple," he said, proud of how nonchalant he sounded.

"I hadn't thought so, but something my wife told me not a quarter hour ago changed my mind."

"Oh? What did she tell you?"

"Jennsen kissed her—'her' being Carolyn, of course. Not my wife. If he'd kissed my wife, I assure you he wouldn't be capable of attending a party."

Everything inside Daniel froze. He slowly turned toward Matthew. "I beg your pardon?"

"I said, 'If he'd kissed my wife—'"

"Not that part."

"Ah. Jennsen kissed Carolyn."

Feeling as if he'd been stabbed, Daniel asked tersely, "When?"

"Today."

He shook his head. "You're mistaken." He had to be.

"I assure you I'm not."

"Where?"

Matthew frowned. "Sarah didn't say, although if I had to guess, I'd say probably in the drawing room."

"I meant where on her body did he kiss her? Her hand? Her cheek?" While he hated the idea of it, he supposed he could refrain from tossing Jennsen on his arse for kissing her hand or cheek. He supposed.

Matthew shook his head. "Oh, no. On her lips. According to Sarah it was *quite* a kiss."

He felt as if his pores were about to spew steam. "What the bloody hell does that mean?"

Matthew cocked a brow at his tone. "Surely you've had ample enough lovers to know what sort of kiss 'quite' a kiss is."

A red haze seemed to dull his vision. That bastard had kissed Carolyn. *His* Carolyn. He was going to do worse than toss Jennsen on his bloody colonial arse—he was going to kick it all the way back to America. He opened his mouth to speak, but in his fury no words came forth. He'd never, in his entire life, been so angry. Or so sickly jealous.

Which was ridiculous. He held no claim on Carolyn. Like all his previous lovers, she was free to do whatever she wished with whomever she wanted. As was he. The problem was that, unlike all his previous liaisons, he didn't want anyone other than her. And the possibility that she might want someone other than him, might share with someone else the intimacies that she'd shared with him, all but cleaved him in two. Clearly Jennsen was attracted to her. Was she attracted to Jennsen as well?

"What was her reaction to Jennsen's kiss?" He had to force the words past his tight throat.

"I've no idea. But she doesn't appear to be angry with him. And clearly she didn't blacken his eyes." Matthew leaned closer. "I was under the impression you were interested in the lady. If so, you'd best stop fannying around."

"What makes you think I'm fannying around?"

"The fact that she's standing over there chatting and smiling with Jennsen and you're here with me is evidence enough."

Daniel watched Jennsen hand Carolyn a fresh glass of punch and tried to banish the gut-wrenching image of that bastard kissing his woman. Tasting her. Touching her skin. Making love to her.

She isn't your woman. She's your lover. Nothing more. Yes. Which is what he'd wanted—his usual shallow affair. And what she'd wanted—because her heart remained devoted to Edward. Christ, it was bad enough he had to compete with her dead husband's memory—a man she set on a pedestal so high as to render him a near deity. Now he had to compete with Jennsen as well? A very much alive man who clearly had no qualms about taking what he wanted. And a man who, based on the way she was smiling at him, she obviously liked.

Well, Daniel didn't have any qualms about taking what he wanted either, something Jennsen was going to discover before this evening was over.

Beside him, Matthew said in an undertone, "Well, I wouldn't worry about it if I were you. I distinctly recall you telling me that all women look the same in the dark, so based on that theory, any woman will do as far as satisfying your lustful urges. Certainly there are a bevy of lovely females to choose from right here in this room."

Were there? He hadn't noticed. The only woman he'd paid the slightest attention to all evening was Carolyn. Even while speaking to other women—such as Kimberly and Gwendolyn, Lady Margate, with both of whom he'd once been intimate—he'd been completely aware of Carolyn. Where she was, with whom she spoke. How many times she looked in his direction. And he clearly needed to rethink his "all women look the same in the dark" theory since Carolyn had pulverized it into dust.

Matthew made a *tsking* sound. "Oh, how the mighty have fallen."

"What are you talking about?"

"You, my friend. I'm talking about you. A very short time ago you told me you only wanted an affair and that your heart remained your own."

Daniel dragged his gaze away from Carolyn and Jennsen to glare at his friend. "Your point?"

"I believe you've been hoist upon your own petard." He clapped his hand on Daniel's shoulder. "Having recently been through the gut-twisting experience of losing my heart, not to mention my soul, you have my sympathies."

Daniel actually felt himself go pale. "I've done nothing of the sort."

"I've been observing you, my friend, and you most certainly have."

"Since when have you taken to observing me so closely?"

Matthew flashed a smile. "Since you became so very interesting to watch. Consider me at your disposal should you need an ear to listen—or a shoulder to cry on."

"I'm hardly going to burst into tears."

Matthew gave an approving nod. "Keep that stiff upper lip. Good plan. As for me, I'll just wait for the moment until I can say 'I told you so.' And perhaps even collect on that fifty pound wager we made. In the meantime, I'm off to find the love of my life, take her home and get her into bed. I suggest you do the same. I wish you luck."

His thoughts in turmoil, Daniel watched his friend walk away. Could Matthew be right? Had he foolishly lost his heart? Bloody hell, he certainly hoped not, because if he had, he'd done so with a woman who'd made it plain she didn't want it.

He looked toward Carolyn, who now stood chatting with her friends Lady Julianne and Lady Emily. A quick scan of the area showed that bastard Jennsen moving toward the French windows leading to the terrace.

Jaw tight, Daniel headed after him. When he stepped outside, Daniel saw his quarry standing alone in the corner, staring out into the small garden.

"A moment of your time, Jennsen."

Jennsen turned toward him and raised his brows, most likely at his peremptory tone. Daniel didn't give a damn.

After muttering something that sounded suspiciously like *This should prove entertaining*, Jennsen inclined his head. "You resemble a teakettle about to spew steam, Surbrooke."

Most likely because that's precisely how he felt. "You kissed Lady Wingate."

Jennsen's brows rose and he looked slightly amused. "I don't see how that's any of your concern."

"It is very much my concern. You are casting your amorous attentions in the wrong direction."

"As far as I can tell, I'm free to cast them in any direction I please." He gave a short laugh. "Unlike you aristocrats, I'm not enslaved by a title or stringent rules regarding romance and marriage or the pressing need to provide an heir to some centuries old pile of rubble."

"And yet you aspire to win the favor of a viscountess."

"You know as well as I that Carolyn isn't like the other women in there." He jerked his chin toward the drawing room. "She only married into that title and has, thank God, retained the goodness from her more humble beginnings."

Daniel's hands fisted at Jennsen's familiar use of her first name. "Which makes her far too good for you."

"And perfect for you, I suppose."

"That is none of your business. Suffice it to say the lady is not available."

"Surely that is for her to decide." Jennsen narrowed his eyes. "Are you betrothed?" Before Daniel could answer, Jennsen added quickly, "No, of course you're not. Your aversion to marriage is well known." His lips curved upward in a slow smile. "I myself harbor no such aversion. I merely need to find the right woman."

"I assure you that woman is not Lady Wingate." He stepped closer to Jennsen and took satisfaction that he stood just a bit taller than the American. "The lady has made her choice, and it's not you."

Jennsen regarded him steadily. Finally he said, "I'm aware of that."

Daniel barely managed to hide his surprise at Jennsen's capitulation. He wanted to ask Jennsen how he knew—right after he planted the bastard a facer—but thought better of it. It didn't matter how he knew so long as he knew. A bit of the tension eased from his shoulders.

"Nor, as it happens," Jennsen continued, "is she my choice."

Another layer of tension dissipated. "Excellent."

"But know—the only reason I told you is because I've no wish to cause Carolyn any difficulties." His gaze flicked over Daniel. "If she had to choose someone else, I'm glad it's you."

"And why is that?"

"Because it's very clear you care for her. And she deserves to be cared for."

Daniel kept his expression impassive, but only with an effort. Bloody hell, first Matthew, now Jennsen. When had he become so transparent? Well, of course he cared for her. He'd desired her since the first moment he saw her. And even though Jennsen's assessment vaguely annoyed him, he appreciated the man's honesty. In fact it occurred to him that so long as Jennsen stayed away from Carolyn, he could possibly, maybe, perhaps, someday actually come to like the man. Just a little.

He cleared his throat. "As for you finding the right woman, Jennsen, for all your disparaging remarks about us aristocrats, I wager you'll fall arse over heels for an English girl." A laugh escaped him. "Oh, the irony of that."

Jennsen made a scoffing sound. "If I do, you can bet your arse she won't be some nose-in-the-air Society chit. I'd rather marry a barmaid."

"And yet at Matthew's house party you cast your eye upon Lady Wingate's sister, and then toward Lady Wingate."

"Neither of whom were 'to the manor born.'"

Daniel pondered for several seconds then asked, "Care to make it interesting?"

"What do you mean?"

"I've fifty pounds that says you'll fall in love with a Society chit."

"Done," said Jennsen without an instant's hesitation. "Easiest fifty pounds I'll ever earn. Care to make it even more interesting?"

"You'd prefer to lose one hundred pounds?"

"Oh, I have no intention of losing. I meant another fifty-pound wager. That you, too, will fall in love with a Society chit."

Daniel inwardly chuckled. Since he'd already made nearly the identical bet with Matthew, why not collect twice? Jennsen had no way of knowing that having reached the age of three and thirty without falling prey to the manacles of love, he was obviously quite impervious. While Carolyn might have managed to steal a tiny piece of his previously untouched heart, that hardly meant she owned it all. Or that he'd allow himself to get leg-shackled. His heart, as always, remained his—albeit with the minuscule nick currently in it.

"Agreed." He smiled and rubbed his hands together. "I'm going to enjoy relieving you of your hundred pounds, Jennsen."

Jennsen chuckled and shook his head. "You'll never see it. There will be no Society chit for me, and your neck is already in the noose, Surbrooke, with the hangman's hand on the trapdoor lever. But still, I wish you luck." Still chuckling, Jennsen walked away, disappearing into the drawing room.

Annoyed, yet not quite certain why, Daniel looked through the French windows into the drawing room. His gaze found Carolyn, and as if she felt the weight of his stare, she turned toward him. Their gazes met through the glass, and it felt as if the flagstones beneath his feet shifted.

Both Matthew and Jennsen had wished him luck, and he suddenly didn't doubt that he'd need it.

Chapter 18

I had only one steadfast rule regarding my affairs, and I
was extremely careful not to break it: I never allowed my
heart to become involved. For to do so would only bring
pain and misery, and I wanted none of that.

Memoirs of a Mistress by An Anonymous Lady

Dressed in an ice blue, lace trimmed negligee
and matching robe, Carolyn paced the confines
of her foyer. She paused to glance at the clock on
the corner table. Just past two A.M. She'd last seen
Daniel an hour earlier in Lord Exbury's foyer as
she'd departed the soiree. *I'll see you very soon,* he'd
murmured. Before she could ask him to clarify what
"very soon" meant, he'd vanished into the crowd.

Hopeful that he meant later that night, she'd sent
Nelson off to bed as soon as she arrived home, raced
up to her bedchamber and changed into her finest

•

negligee. For the past half hour she'd kept up her vigil in the foyer, praying for the front gate bell to jingle, indicating he'd come.

She pressed her hands to her midriff to calm her inner flutters, and anticipation quickened her breathing, the same sense of expectation that had heightened her senses all evening. She'd spent very little actual time with Daniel at the Exbury soiree. They'd shared one waltz, during which she'd barely been able to speak, what with the inferno consuming her as he'd undressed her with his eyes. Indeed, about all she'd managed was to ask him if he'd received her gift. His eyes had blazed and he answered yes. And then he spoke the words that had whispered through her brain the rest of the evening: *I want to give you all that, Carolyn. And more.*

After that, they'd had only a brief conversation, and numerous glances across the room, ending with his cryptic, *I'll see you very soon.*

Yet their lack of actual contact had only served to elevate her yearning for him. She'd been painfully aware of Daniel every second, barely able to concentrate on anything or anyone other than him. And found herself more than a little jealous every time a woman claimed his attention. Lady Walsh, Lady Balsam, and Lady Margate—all beautiful women.

She'd wanted to slap every one of them.

After another quarter hour of pacing the foyer, she finally accepted the disappointing realization that "very soon" had not meant "later tonight." Heaving a sigh, she climbed the stairs and headed for her bedchamber, even though she knew sleep would elude her.

She entered her room and closed the door behind

her. Tipping back her head, she closed her eyes and leaned her shoulders against the wood panel, every fiber of her being torn between missing Daniel and fervently wishing she didn't. Finally, she listlessly raised her head and opened her eyes. And stilled. And stared.

At Daniel, who lay atop her counterpane, his back propped up against the headboard cushioned by her lace-trimmed pillows, his arms raised and casually linked behind his head.

Daniel, who wore nothing except skin.

And who was obviously very happy to see her.

"You should probably lock the door," he said softly.

Unable to take her gaze off him, she reached behind her and fumbled with the lock. As soon as it clicked into place, he slowly rose from the bed and walked toward her, reminding her of a dark jungle cat who'd spotted its prey.

She couldn't have moved or spoken had her life depended on it. Her breath caught at the sight of him, so strong, muscular, and so very aroused. The heat smoldering in his gaze threatened to incinerate her where she stood.

The fire burning in the grate cast the room in a warm, golden glow that illuminated his body in a captivating pattern of shadows and light. When he reached her, he drew her into his arms and lowered his head. The feel of his body pressing against hers, of his bare skin beneath her hands as she ran them up his chest to encircle his neck, rendered her light-headed. Their lips met and hers parted on a sigh of pleasure. Unlike their last kiss, which had been wild and frantic, this one was slow. Deliberate. Deep. Intoxicating. And liquefied her knees.

He lifted his head, ending the kiss as slowly as he'd initiated it, leaving her breathless for more. His gaze simmered with an intensity she hadn't seen before, one that made her wish she could read his thoughts. One that sizzled a heated tremor to her core.

Brushing his fingers gently along her jaw, he said softly, "Carolyn."

In response, she whispered the one word that had trembled on her lips all evening. "Daniel." Then she swallowed and asked, "What are you doing here?"

"Waiting for you. For what seemed like forever, by the way. Where have you been?"

A sheepish grin quirked one corner of her mouth. "In the foyer."

His gaze swept over her attire. "Wearing a negligee?"

"I was waiting for you, as I'd hoped your 'I'll see you very soon' comment meant I'd see you tonight. How did you get in here?"

"I couldn't possibly tell you. After all, a man must have his secrets."

Realizing he'd repeated the exact words she'd said to him earlier, she tossed his own reply back at him. "You realize you're enticing me to find out."

"I'm delighted to hear you're enticed. I will tell you that my method of arrival is in keeping with my highwayman persona. And that the lock on your bedchamber window is not all it should be, but I managed to fix it while I waited for you."

Her gaze flew to the French windows that led to a

small balcony. "You came in through the *window*? However did you climb up to the second floor?"

"As I said, a man must have his secrets, although I will admit I was fully dressed when I arrived. Since you wouldn't tell me what you wore to bed, I decided to find out for myself." His hot gaze skimmed over the cream lace outlining her breasts. "I like it very much. And in the spirit of full disclosure, I thought it only fair to let you see what *I* wear to bed."

Her gaze traveled over his broad shoulders and chest. She licked her lips. "I like it very much."

She wanted to press herself against him, feel the magic of his kiss again, but instead he took her hand and led her toward the bed. Rather than tossing her on the mattress as she'd hoped, he lifted a slim wrapped package from her night table. "For you."

"Another gift?" she asked, surprised yet undeniably pleased. She took the offering, which based on its shape and size she suspected was a book. Dear God, him showing up in her bedchamber naked was gift enough. "If you're not careful I'm going to start expecting presents every time I see you," she teased.

"It will be my pleasure to provide them."

"Shall I open it now?"

"Only if you want to see what it is."

Even though it was nearly impossible to concentrate on anything other than his nakedness, she managed to untie the ribbon and pull away the tissue paper, to reveal a slightly worn, leather-bound volume. She ran her finger over the gilt title letters. A CONCISE COLLECTION OF GREEK MYTHOLOGY.

"Galatea told the highwayman that rather than jewels, she'd prefer a book from a gentleman's own collection. Since you gave me one from yours, I thought it fitting to give you one from mine." He touched a bit of blue ribbon emerging from one of the pages. "I've marked the passages relating to Galatea."

"Thank you."

"You're welcome." One corner of his mouth lifted. "Not quite as stimulating as the book you gave me."

"Nevertheless, I'll treasure it."

"I'm glad." He took the book from her and set it on the nightstand. "And speaking of treasure, it's about time the highwayman collected his bounty." He lightly clasped her waist and his gaze wandered down to her feet then slowly back up. "You're stunning."

"As are you."

"Except you're overdressed."

"So I've noticed." She glided her hands across the breadth of his chest. "Will you help me correct that?"

"Never have I received a more tempting invitation."

While he untied the sash to her robe, she pressed her lips to the center of his chest, closed her eyes and breathed in his scent. The smell of him, warm and clean, with a hint of sandalwood and starched linen, made her head spin. Made her want to simply burrow into his skin and do nothing save breathe him in.

She kissed her way across the broad expanse of his chest, absorbing his low growl of approval, while he slipped her robe from her shoulders. It fell to her feet in a whisper of silk, then his hands slowly unraveled her single braid, to sift through her hair. Her fingers traced his ridged abdomen then moved behind him to lightly circle the small of his back. When she flicked her tongue over his nipple, he sucked in a quick breath.

Tension all but radiated from him, proving he was holding himself in strict control, determined not to lose his command over himself. Unfortunately—or perhaps fortunately—she was equally as determined to see him lose that mastery. In that heart stopping manner that made her insides dissolve.

"You're distracting me from my task," he said, touching his lips to her throat.

"What task is that?"

"Getting you naked."

"*Ohhhhhh* . . ." Her voice trailed off when he cupped her breasts and teased her nipples through the silk of her gown. His hands skimmed upward to hook beneath the thin straps. Her breath stalled when he glided the garment off her shoulders. The cool material washed over her heated skin and pooled at her ankles to join her robe.

"Stunning," he murmured again, his gaze feasting on her. He feathered light kisses down her neck, across her collarbone, then down her chest until his tongue drew lazy circles around her nipple. While one hand palmed her other breast, his other roamed down the center of her spine, over her buttocks, then brushed along the sensitive cleft between.

She pulled in a deep breath, releasing it on a long moan when he drew her nipple deep into the warmth of his mouth. Her fingers sifted through his thick hair while everything inside her raced and throbbed, filling her with an edgy tension that demanded relief. She spread her legs, a silent invitation for him to touch her swollen, wet sex, but instead he continued his unhurried teasing and laving of her breasts, his leisurely caresses of her bottom.

She reached between them to touch him, but he lifted his head and captured her hand.

"Not yet." Bending his knees, he scooped her up in his arms. A startled gasp escaped her, and she wrapped her arms around his neck as he headed for the corner of the room.

"I'm perfectly capable of walking," she felt compelled to say even while reveling in his strength.

"I know. But I'm completely incapable of keeping my hands off you." He gently set her down in front of the full-length cheval glass then moved to retrieve the round, velvet-padded seat from her dressing table. After setting the small chair at her feet, he moved to stand behind her, his erection nestling against her back.

In their reflection, Carolyn saw his large hands come around her waist to cup her breasts.

"I want to make love to you here," he said softly, his lips brushing her temple, his intense gaze on hers in the mirror, "so you can see not just me, but both of us. Together. Me caressing you." His fingers lightly played with her pebbled nipples. "Kissing you." He trailed his lips along her ear. "Tasting you," he murmured, then ran his tongue down the length of her neck.

A barrage of tingles erupted under her skin, and she leaned into his touch, closing her eyes.

"Look at me," he said in a gruff voice. "Don't close your eyes."

She blinked her eyes open and her gaze collided

with his. Never had anyone looked at her with such fervent, focused heat. Such avid intensity.

"I want you to see me touching you, Carolyn." One of his hands skimmed down her torso, over her hip, then down to hook under her thigh. He lifted her leg and set her foot on the padded chair cushion.

An all over blush suffused her at the sight of herself so exposed, but any embarrassment she might have felt evaporated with the first brush of his fingers over her glistening sex.

A long *"Oooohhhh"* of pleasure escaped her and she arched her back in a silent plea for more.

"You're so beautifully soft," he said to her reflection, one hand lazily playing with her breast, while the fingers of the other slowly caressed her swollen folds. "So wet." He buried his lips against her hair, breathed deep, and gave a low groan. "And you smell so incredibly good. Feel so incredibly good."

She lifted her arms up and back to encircle his neck. "You make me feel so incredibly good," she whispered, darkly fascinated at the wickedly arousing sight of his hands pleasuring her.

He continued his slow but relentless assault on her body, slipping two fingers inside her, slowly pumping while pressing his palm against her sensitive nub of flesh with just enough pressure to make her tremble but not give her the relief her body desperately craved.

Her breathing turned shallow, rapid, and with a groan of desperation she undulated against his hand, seeking, needing, more. Panting, her head lolled against his shoulder. Lost in a fog of need and sensation, her eyes drifted closed.

"Open your eyes, Carolyn. Look at me."

His voice was a low, harsh command, and she did as he bid. His gaze, hot and intense, met hers in the mirror. "Say you want me."

She licked her lips, fought to find her voice. "I do. You know I do."

His fingers touched her just a bit deeper. "Say it."

"I . . . want you." Dear God, couldn't he tell? Couldn't he tell she was one touch away from wilting?

"I want you, *Daniel*," he said, his gaze never leaving hers.

"I want you, Daniel," she whispered, feverishly pressing against his hand, seeking relief from this brink of madness where he dangled her.

"Again."

"I want you, Daniel." She slid one hand from around his neck and insinuated it between their bodies to wrap around his erection. "I want you, Daniel. So much. Now. Please."

Dark satisfaction glittered in his eyes. Without a word he slipped his fingers from her and sank to his knees, settling his backside on his heels. He then urged her down with him until she knelt, straddling his thighs. Still facing the mirror, he positioned the head of his erection at her wet opening.

Watching in the mirror, while his hands cupped her breasts, Carolyn sank slowly down, dragging a long groan from both of them.

For several seconds neither moved. All she could do was stare into his eyes in the mirror and absorb the incredible sensation of him pressing deep inside her. Looking at him, and at herself. At them. Together. It was such a moving, stirring, beautiful, and deeply intimate sight her throat swelled.

She rested her hands on top of his where they cupped her breasts. And whispered, "Daniel."

A groan that sounded ripped from his throat echoed in her ears. "Carolyn. My God, Carolyn . . ." He rolled his hips and she moaned as he surged deeper inside her. She turned her head and their mouths met in a deep, lush, tongue-mating kiss. He stroked inside her with increasingly demanding upward thrusts, each one pushing her closer to a pinnacle of pleasure that remained just tantalizingly out of reach, building a ferocious need in her the likes of which she'd never before experienced.

Breaking off their kiss, with his gaze fastened on hers, he grazed the fingers of one large hand down her torso, over her abdomen and between her thighs. He tormented her exquisitely sensitive nub of flesh, his touch perfect and magical and relentless. Her climax didn't merely throb through her, it attacked her, bombarding her with an intense pleasure that had her crying out. Her fingers raked over his thighs and she drowned in the waves of her release as they washed over her. Her breaths were still coming in rapid puffs when Daniel's body stiffened behind her and through glazed vision she watched his release overtake him, his face taking on an utterly beautiful intensity as she felt his body throb and spill into hers.

"Carolyn."

Her name, sounding like a heartfelt prayer, whispered by her ear. Then he rested his forehead against her temple. His skin glistened in the firelight and his ragged breaths blew over her flushed skin.

She lifted one limp hand and skimmed her fingers through his mussed hair. "Daniel."

Their gazes met in the mirror. A surge of tenderness raced through her, so strong it shook her, and she trembled.

His arms tightened around her. "Carolyn, I—"

His words broke off and he swallowed. Twice. Something that looked like confusion ghosted over his features. Then his expression returned to its normal teasing warmth. "I think that will last me. For a few minutes."

"For a few minutes," she agreed.

"But the night has just begun."

Anticipation shivered through her and she latched onto the sensation. And firmly pushed aside the unexpected and unwanted tenderness that threatened to undo her. She knew very well where tenderness could lead, and that was a path she could not, would not, allow herself to travel down with this man. Tenderness had no place in their temporary affair. And so long as she remembered that, all would be well.

But as her gaze held his in the mirror, she very much feared that she stood in mortal danger of forgetting.

Chapter 19

I found the best way to keep my lover interested was to maintain an air of mystery—to have my little secrets, make certain he knew I had them, but never quite tell him what they were. And, of course, finding clever ways and locations to make love also ensured he didn't grow bored.

Memoirs of a Mistress by An Anonymous Lady

Reclining on a blanket beneath the shade of a century-old willow, with skeins of afternoon sunshine dappling through the breeze ruffled leaves, Daniel closed his eyes and heaved a contented sigh. He'd never before considered what would comprise a perfect day, but today had met—nay, exceeded—any criteria he might have dreamed up.

Earlier, when the first mauve shades of dawn had streaked across the sky, indicating it was time to leave Carolyn's bed, he found it nearly impossible to do so. He didn't care for the thought of not seeing her for even several hours. And after spending such a perfect night with her, wrapped in the private cocoon of her bedchamber, where they'd been free to talk and laugh and make love, he craved more of the same.

Although he told himself he could spend the next night with her, he simply didn't want to wait that long. He wanted to spend the day with her. Talking. Laughing. Walking. Touching. And he wanted all that away from the prying eyes of London society.

He wanted her all to himself.

And so before leaving her bed, he'd invited her to spend the day with him at Meadow Hill, his country estate in Kent, a three hour journey from London. She'd accepted, and they left directly after breakfast with plans to return to London after dinner. And thus had begun the most perfect day he ever could have imagined.

Holding Carolyn as she slept during the carriage ride, snuggled against him, her head nestled on his shoulder, one hand resting on his chest, right over the spot where his heart beat. Arriving at Meadow Hill, where he'd given her a tour of the house, including his bedchamber, as it had been more than an interminable five hours since he'd made love to her. He'd never brought a woman to his country home before, had never considered doing so. But bringing Carolyn had been . . . right. The instant she stepped into the foyer, she'd filled his home with sunshine, chasing away darkness he hadn't even realized dwelled there. She'd taken the familiar—that which he'd lived with for years—and made everything seem bright and new again.

After arranging for a light picnic lunch, they'd made their way to the stables, where he introduced her to the rest of his rescued pets while their horses were saddled. His animals fell in love with her, and it was clear the feeling was mutual. Then they rode around the vast grounds, his favorite part of the estate. When he dismounted to pick her a bouquet of wildflowers, she'd thanked him by opening the front placard of his breeches, sinking to her knees, and proving that she could indeed melt him with her tongue. He'd proven the same to her, and he knew that for the rest of his life wildflowers would remind him of her. And this perfect day.

Afterward, they'd continued their ride. He hadn't intended to stop at the small lake on the property, but she caught a glimpse of the sparkling water through the trees and was enchanted. When she suggested they set up their picnic beneath the willow near the shore, he'd had to clamp his jaws together to keep from uttering a harsh no. He hated the water, and the lake was the last place he wanted to be. But seeing the eagerness in her eyes, he'd been unable to refuse her.

By sitting with his back to the water, he'd almost forgotten it was there, and was able to enjoy both the casual meal and her company. And now, full and sleepy, his spine settled against the willow's trunk and Carolyn's head resting in his lap, he lightly played with a tendril of her silky hair.

Bloody hell, the thought of this day ending filled him with a sense of loss that confounded him. One that had him flailing in a quagmire of completely unfamiliar emotions—emotions he'd valiantly but unsuccessfully fought all day to keep at bay.

He kept hoping sanity would slap him, stop him from this seemingly unstoppable headlong plunge into the emotional abyss yawning before him. But it seemed he was helpless to halt his descent. Helpless to stop wanting her. Touching her. Simply being with her. And completely unprepared to know how to navigate such previously unchartered emotional waters.

He looked down and watched her study a tiny yellow flower she'd plucked from the grass. Such a simple act, yet one that utterly enchanted him. There was something so natural about her. She didn't possess the haughty demeanor of so many women of his class, no doubt because she wasn't born into the peerage. She was a viscountess now, yet in spite of her status, retained an air of easygoing charm that utterly captivated him. The look of wonder that entered her eyes at the sound of a wren's warble or the sight of a butterfly or a tiny yellow flower intoxicated him.

"You don't take things for granted." He hadn't meant to say the words out loud, but when he did, Carolyn lifted her chin and gazed up at him.

She studied him through serious eyes for several seconds then nodded. "I try not to. I've been given more than I ever thought to possess. More than I deserve. But I've also lost a great deal. When the thing you love most in the world is snatched away from you . . ." Her voice trailed off and she frowned, then returned her gaze to the yellow flower.

She meant Edward, of course, the man she'd loved,

and continued to love, so deeply. He was unprepared for the profound frisson of envy that ripped through him. How would it feel to be so adored? For someone to consider you that which they loved most in the world?

A frown bunched his brow. He'd never before wondered such a thing. He supposed it must feel good, although he had no way of knowing. Certainly no one had ever loved him that way.

"I do my best to appreciate what I still have," she said softly, "although it's been a difficult journey."

Her words made him realize how often he took his own privileged life and position for granted, and shame filled him. "You've inspired me to follow your example and be more appreciative," he said.

Her gaze flew to his and there was no missing the surprise in her eyes. "*You* are the inspiring one, Daniel. The way you've helped Samuel and Katie and those poor animals." She shot him a quizzical look then shook her head. "You don't have any idea how wonderful you are, do you?"

He was prevented from voicing the incredulous sound that rose in his throat by the lump that settled there at her question. The oddest sensation flowed through him, one he couldn't name, as he'd never felt it before. One that made it seem as if he'd been wrapped up in a warm, velvety blanket on a cold, winter night.

Bloody hell, again she was gazing up at him as if he were some sort of hero. And while he couldn't deny that having her look at him like that made him feel so damn good, neither could he deny the guilt that nipped at him for not correcting her. Because she was incredibly wrong.

He managed a weak smile and skimmed his hand lightly over her soft hair. "I'm glad you think so."

She smiled, then settled her head more comfortably in his lap and closed her eyes. "I know so."

He shut his eyes as well, allowing himself a few minutes to recover from the emotions welling inside him. But that few minutes, coupled with almost no rest last night, lulled him into a much needed sleep. The next thing he knew, his backside was numb and he realized he must have dozed off. He moved his hand to touch Carolyn and felt nothing. Blinking his heavy lids open, he saw he was alone under the tree.

"Carolyn?" Not seeing her wandering amongst the copse of trees in front of him, he turned to look behind him, toward the lake. And froze.

Carolyn, her back to him, wearing only her thin chemise, stood in the lake, the water lapping at her hips. Chilled fingers of icy fear raced up his spine to wrap around his throat—terrifying glimmers emerging from the dark place he kept them ruthlessly buried. As he watched, she moved forward, the water rising to her waist.

The rational part of his mind told him she was fine, but the memories he'd locked away so long ago bombarded him, mixing the past with the present, rushing sick, cold dread through him, twisting his insides into a painful knot.

With his heart beating so hard it felt as if each thud bruised his ribs, he rose on shaky legs and pulled in an unsteady breath.

"Carolyn!"

Her name sounded rough and hoarse, and he heard the panic gripping him. She turned at the sound, and unlike all those years ago, he was offered a sunny smile. A cheerful wave. But then his vision seemed to waver and instead of loose honey-colored hair he saw a dark braid. And eyes, so empty and bleak.

He blinked, and Carolyn's bright smile again swam before him. Her lips moved, saying something to him, but he couldn't hear above the roar in his ears. She waved again then turned and waded deeper into the water. He started forward on unsteady legs and shouted at her to come back, but just then she lost her footing. Her arms flailed and with a cry she went down. And disappeared beneath the water's glasslike surface.

God Almighty, not again. Not again.

The words reverberated through his mind, a blood-curdling mantra. Everything inside him turned to ice, and for a single stuttering heartbeat he vividly relived what he'd spent years trying to forget. Then, with a jagged cry that seemed rendered from the very depths of his soul, he roared, *"No!"* and ran into the lake, frantic to reach her. He swam toward her, desperately fighting his past and his memories but failing.

Carolyn's head popped above the surface, and with a sputter she spit out a mouthful of lake water. A huff of incredulous laughter escaped her and she brushed at the tangled strands of hair plastered to her face. How clumsy could she be? Good heavens, her feet had gone right out from underneath her.

Shaking her head at her lack of grace, she struggled to rise. She'd just gained her balance when strong hands grabbed her upper arms and roughly turned her around. Blinking away the lake water clinging to her lashes, she looked up at Daniel. A self-conscious laugh escaped her and she again shoved at the hair clinging to her face.

"Can you believe I . . ."

Her words trailed off, as did her grin, when she saw his expression. His face was the color of chalk and his haunted eyes looked as if they'd been burned into his pale skin. His mouth was drawn into a tight, white-edged line and he radiated tension. Those burning eyes raked her face.

"Are you all right?" he asked in a low, harsh voice she didn't recognize. Before she could even open her mouth to answer, he gave her a quick shake. "Tell me you're all right."

"I'm fine. Wet and clumsy but completely fine."

His fingers tightened on her arms. "You went under the water."

She nodded. "I slipped." Because he seemed so undone, she offered him another smile. "I realize I must look a fright, but it's nothing a towel and a hairbrush can't correct."

Instead of smiling back, he snatched her against him. His arms banded around her like a vise, molding her to him. The hard, fast beats of his heart knocked against her, and with a groan he buried his face in the curve of her neck. At first she thought he was merely overreacting to a simple accident, thinking, as men tended to, that women were composed of fragile glass and would easily break—or in this case, dissolve. But after about ten seconds she realized he was shaking.

"Daniel?" She squirmed in his tight hold and he finally lifted his head. His ravaged expression stunned her. And worried her. Never had she seen such a desolate look in anyone's eyes. And although he was staring at her, it almost seemed that he didn't see her.

She framed his colorless face between her wet hands. "Clearly I scared you. I'm so sorry. But there's no reason to be concerned. I'm fine, Daniel. Absolutely fine." She brushed her thumbs over his cheekbones. "Although it wasn't necessary, I appreciate you dashing into the water to save me."

The dazed expression in his eyes faded a bit, but she was still worried. The man looked as if he'd seen a ghost. Taking his hand, she said, "Let's get out of the water."

He jerked his head in a barely perceptible nod, and with his hand tightly gripping hers, they made their way to the shore. By the time they emerged from the water, he was shivering badly, increasing Carolyn's concern since the day was warm with bright sunshine and the water wasn't cold. She walked to the willow, snatched up the blanket, then led him into the sun.

"Let's sit," she said softly.

He sat down hard on the grass, as if his legs had given out. She wrapped the blanket around his shoulders then knelt in front of him and clasped his hands. His fingers were icy cold, his skin still deathly pale. "Daniel," she said softly. "What's wrong?"

He didn't answer for so long she thought he meant to ignore her. He simply stared out at the water, looking so shaken her heart ached for him. She gently rubbed his chilled hands between hers. And waited.

Finally a bit of color returned to his cheeks and he cleared his throat. "I don't like the water," he said in a voice that sounded as if he hadn't used it in several years.

"So I've gathered. I'm sorry I suggested we eat here. If I'd known your aversion, I never would have—"

"It's not your fault. No one knows. I've never told anyone."

She waited for him to continue, but another long silence ensued. It was obvious he was struggling with something, something that profoundly pained him. Finally she lifted his hands and pressed her lips to his cold fingers. "You don't have to tell me, Daniel."

He turned and looked at her, and her throat swelled at the bleakness in his eyes. His normally perfectly put-together exterior had cracked, breaking the shiny facade to reveal a man who deeply grieved something.

"She died. In the water." The whispered words seemed ripped from his depths. He drew a shuddering breath. "I tried to save her. But it was too late. By the time I dragged her out, she was dead."

Carolyn's breath caught and a flood of sympathy washed over her. "Oh, Daniel. How awful. I'm so very sorry."

His gaze searched hers, as if looking for understanding, then words just poured out of him in a dry rasp. "I'd gone to the lake at Surbrooke Manor. I laid down in my favorite sunny spot and fell asleep. When I woke up, I saw her. In water up to her waist. I called to her, but she kept wading out deeper. Deeper. I couldn't

understand why she didn't answer me. I screamed.
Louder. Begging her to stop, to look at me.

"Finally she turned. And I saw it in her eyes. I
knew what she planned to do. I don't know how I
knew, but I knew. I ran into the water, yelling, plead-
ing. I told her I loved her. That I needed her. More
than anyone else in the world. But it didn't matter.
She turned from me and kept walking. The lake there
drops off sharply in the middle. I saw her go under.
But I was a good swimmer. Thought I could save
her. But I failed. The stones—" His voice broke and
he cleared his throat. "She'd weighted down her skirt
with stones. I eventually found her. Pulled her up.
But it was too late."

Dear God. He'd witnessed a woman he loved kill
herself. Had tried to save her, but couldn't. And
clearly blamed himself.

Something wet plopped onto her hands, which still
tightly held his, and she realized it was a tear. From
her. They dripped from her eyes and silently coursed
down her cheeks. "Daniel . . . I'm so sorry."

His eyes bored into hers. "After our meal today I
fell asleep, and when I awoke, you were gone. I saw
you in the water, walking in deeper, and then going
under. . . ." A tremor ran through him. "It was like
reliving my worst nightmare."

Guilt and self-reproach stabbed her and she
squeezed his hands tighter. "I'm so sorry I frightened you. Like you, I dozed off. When I awoke, I
felt hot and uncomfortable and the water seemed so
inviting. You were sleeping so soundly, I didn't want
to wake you. I planned to just take a quick dip to
refresh myself." She'd also planned to entice him to

join her if he woke up, not realizing that there was no chance of that.

She bent her head and rested her cheek against their joined hands. "Even though I'm well acquainted with grief, I don't know what to say to you except to express my sorrow that you suffered such a heartbreaking loss. Was your loss . . . recent?"

Something flicked in his eyes then he shook his head. "No. I was eight. Carolyn, the woman was my mother."

For several long seconds Carolyn could only stare in stunned disbelief. She'd assumed he'd been an adult. Had lost a woman he was in love with. Which was horrible. But for a young boy to witness his own mother's suicide. . .

"Dear God, Daniel." Now she understood those shadows that clouded his eyes. The pain that lurked in their dark blue depths.

"She'd had another child before me," he said, his voice raw, distant. "A boy. He was stillborn. It sent her into a deep melancholy from which she never fully emerged. I came along about a year later, and although I think she tried to take an interest in me, she simply . . . couldn't."

"What of your father?"

"He thought I would cheer her spirits, but when I failed to do so, he wanted nothing to do with me. He eventually remarried and had two more sons with his new wife. Sophie never cared for me—if not for me, her eldest son would be the heir. Nor do my half brothers hold me in any esteem, mostly for the same reason. We rarely see each other. They only contact me when they need something, most often money."

His gaze shifted back to the water. "Until his dying day my father blamed me for my mother's death."

Pity for Daniel, for all he'd suffered, and anger at his father's thoughtless cruelty, collided in Carolyn. Certainly it wasn't necessary for his father to blame Daniel for his mother's death—clearly Daniel blamed himself more than anyone else ever could.

She touched his chin and waited until he'd turned back to her. "Do you recall I told you the other day that we cannot control other people's actions—only our own?" After he gave a tight nod, she continued, "Your mother's death was not your fault, Daniel. The sadness that drove her to take her own life had nothing to do with you."

Deep regret and naked desolation clouded his beautiful eyes. "I couldn't stop her sadness."

"But you didn't cause it." She brushed a stray dark lock from his forehead. "This . . . this is difficult for me to say, as it's something I've never told anyone. Not even Sarah, from whom I have no secrets." She drew a slow, bracing breath, then said softly, "For months after Edward died, I thought of taking my own life. I would sit for hours, staring at his portrait, feeling so alone and hopeless, unable to see a way to go on without him. Not wanting to go on without him."

The memory of those hideous, dark days swept through her and she shuddered. "But something inside me wouldn't, couldn't, allow me to end my life. I don't know what that something was. Perhaps an inner strength I'm unaware of. To this day I don't understand how or why I had it. . . . My point is, my decision had only to do with me, not anyone else. If I'd been determined to end my life, no one—not even my beloved sister—could have talked me out of doing so or prevented it. Anymore than you could have prevented your mother from doing so."

A long silence swelled between them. Then he finally said, "I wish my mother had possessed that inner strength you spoke about."

"So do I. But it's not your fault that she did not."

He slipped one hand from hers, reached out and softly traced his fingertips over her face, as if trying to memorize her features. "I'm very glad you had it."

"So am I, although I wasn't at the time." She kissed his fingertips as they passed over her lips. "Thank you for confiding in me."

"Thank you for listening. And confiding in me." He cupped her cheek in his palm. "I hadn't intended to tell you, but having done so, I feel . . . better. Relieved. As if a great weight has been lifted."

"Keeping feelings locked inside can be a great burden."

"Yes. I don't often speak from the heart." One corner of his mouth lifted in a humorless half smile. "Some would say that's because I don't have one."

"And they would be wrong, Daniel." She laid one hand against his chest, her palm absorbing the steady thud there. "You have a kind, generous heart. Don't ever think otherwise."

Yes. And he was a kind, generous, honorable man who hid an enormous amount of pain behind the facade of a charming rogue. She'd known him for years, yet hadn't really known him—the real him. Until now. Until he'd shown her his heart.

A wave of warm tenderness inundated her, overflowing her own heart with a sensation that made

her go utterly still. Because she recognized it. Very
well. Because she'd felt it. Once before. With Edward. It was—

Love.

Dear God, she loved Daniel.

For several seconds she couldn't breathe. Couldn't
take it in. She tried to deny it, but no, there was no
mistake. She loved him.

But how had this happened? She barely knew him.

You've known him for years.

But not well.

You've gotten to know him very *well recently.*

But not enough to love him.

*You must recall that it only takes the heart a single
beat to* know.

Yes, she recalled. And therefore knew there was no
mistaking her feelings.

She realized they must have been building over
the last few months, ever since she'd seen him at
Matthew's house party. It was undeniable. Even
though she never thought she'd fall in love again,
she loved him.

A man who'd made it perfectly clear he didn't want
her heart and who had no intention of giving his.

And even though she never thought she'd contemplate another marriage, she suddenly realized that
the thought of marrying the man she loved filled her
with a contentment she hadn't believed she would
experience again.

Daniel hadn't made any attempt to hide his aversion to marriage. Given his wealth and holdings, the
only reason he would need to marry was to provide

an heir, something he could do decades from now. And given her lack of success in conceiving, even if he changed his mind and decided to marry now, she couldn't provide him with that heir. He had not one but two brothers who could inherit the earldom, but she knew every man wanted a son to be his heir.

She squeezed her eyes shut and cursed the irony.

"Carolyn?"

She opened her eyes and looked into his concerned depths.

"Are you all right?" he asked.

No. I've foolishly fallen in love with you. And I don't know what I'm going to do about it. She attempted a smile but wasn't certain she succeeded. "I'm fine."

"I think we should get back to the house. Prepare for our return to London."

"Very well."

She made to arise, but he held her in place and slowly leaned forward. Settled his mouth on hers. And kissed her with a tender passion that swelled her throat and pushed hot moisture behind her eyes. Then he gathered up their belongings while she quickly donned her clothing.

An hour later saw them refreshed and on their way back to London. Not trusting her voice nor certain what to say, she spent the ride snuggled against him, resting her head against his chest. They spoke little, and she wondered what he was thinking. Hoped he was taking her words to heart that he was not to blame for his mother's death. And prayed he hadn't guessed the depth of her feelings for him.

She'd known their affair would eventually come to an end, but now realized that she'd need to end it as soon as possible. There was no point in confessing her feelings to a man who'd made it clear he only wanted an affair. To tell him would only embarrass them both, and no doubt horrify him.

Yet she couldn't continue their liaison feeling as she did about him. She knew from experience her feelings would only deepen, which meant that the longer she delayed in ending their affair, the more painful ending it would be.

Still, she couldn't even contemplate telling him now. Not when all his raw emotions and memories of his mother's death had so recently surfaced. And she wanted, needed, to be with him one more time. Make love with him one more time. And then she'd let him go. And once again start her life over.

When they arrived in London, the carriage stopped in front of her town house. Daniel escorted her to her door, where he lifted her hand and kissed her fingers.

"Thank you. For a beautiful day I will never forget."

Emotion clogged her throat, cutting off her words. She swallowed and managed a husky, "I'll never forget it either, Daniel."

And then he was gone.

And she climbed the stairs to her bedchamber on leaden legs.

Minutes after leaving Carolyn at her town house, Daniel, mentally drained and exhausted, approached his own home. Barkley and

Samuel awaited him in the foyer, the latter pacing the marble floor.

"Ye'll never guess wot, milord," Samuel said the instant Daniel entered the foyer.

Bloody hell. He wasn't certain he had the strength for any further drama today. "I can't imagine."

"Those two blokes are back. The magistrate and the Runner. Been 'ere nigh on two hours waitin' on ye. We told 'em we didn't know when ye'd be returnin' but they insisted on waitin'."

"Did they say why?"

Samuel shook his head and swallowed nervously.

Daniel clapped a reassuring hand on the young man's shoulder. "No doubt they've made a breakthrough in Lady Crawford's murder. I'll see what they want."

"Just in case they're here about young Samuel, I showed them into the library, my lord," Barkley intoned. "I thought perhaps they might enjoy Naughty's company."

Good God. Two hours with Naughty? He doubted either man would be amused.

He entered the library and was relieved to note that Naughty was sleeping. Rayburn and Mayne rose, and after greetings were exchanged, Mayne said in his brusque manner, "You've been out all day, Lord Surbrooke?"

"Yes. I arrived home just now."

"Where have you been?"

"I visited my country home in Kent."

Mayne's brows rose. "Rather a long trip for one day."

"The weather was good and I enjoy the journey."

Rayburn cleared his throat. "You must have gotten an early start this morning. What time did you leave?"

"Around seven." His gaze shifted between them. "Gentlemen, I'm weary and would like retire, so perhaps you could get to the point of this visit. Is it regarding Tolliver? Or Lady Crawford's murder?"

"Now why would you think we're here about Lady Crawford's murder?" Mayne asked sharply.

"I can only assume you're here about one or the other, as I can't see that we have anything else to discuss."

"I'm afraid we do," Rayburn said, his deep voice serious. "Tell me, Lord Surbrooke, what time did you depart Lord Exbury's party last evening?"

"I'm not exactly certain, but I'd guess around one A.M."

"Did you come straight home?"

"Yes."

"Did you remain at home?"

He hesitated for single beat, during which he shoved his conscience aside. "Yes." He had. For about twenty minutes before leaving to go to Carolyn.

Mayne's eyes narrowed with clear distrust. "Rayburn and I observed you talking to Lady Margate at the Exbury soiree last evening."

Daniel thought for several seconds then nodded. "We exchanged a few pleasantries."

"What is your relationship with her?"

"We are friends."

"We've heard from several sources that as recently as last year you were more."

"It's no secret that Gwendolyn and I had a brief affair."

"Did you give her any jewelry, as you had Lady Crawford?" asked Rayburn.

"Yes. A bracelet."

"Sapphires?"

Daniel nodded. "As a matter of fact she was wearing it last evening." A frisson of unease snaked down his spine. "Why do you ask?"

"Because, Lord Surbrooke," said Rayburn, "Lady Margate was found dead early this morning, in the mews behind Lord Exbury's town house. She was bludgeoned to death—the same method as your other previous lover, Lady Crawford. And you, my lord, are the one common link between the two murders."

Chapter 20

A woman should never be afraid to take the initiative in lovemaking. I never had a lover complain that I was too forward or wanton, but plenty of them complained about their wives who did little more than lay immobile beneath them and cringe. Which is, of course, why those gentlemen sought me out in the first place.

Memoirs of a Mistress by An Anonymous Lady

Daniel stared at the two men and forced his outward demeanor to remain calm—a marked contrast to his inner turmoil. He could barely comprehend that Gwendolyn was dead, let alone that Mayne and Rayburn suspected him of murder. They'd been suspicious after Blythe's death, Mayne especially, though he hadn't been overly concerned. But now. . .

He lifted his brows. "You really believe me capable of committing such crimes?"

"Given the right provocation, any man is capable of murder, my lord," Mayne said, his dark eyes never shifting from Daniel's face.

"Yourself included?" Daniel asked, his own gaze not wavering.

"*Any* man," Mayne reiterated.

"And what could possibly motivate me to kill two women, both of whom I was fond?"

"Perhaps you weren't as fond of them as you'd like us to believe," Mayne stated.

"You'd have a great deal of trouble proving that, especially as it isn't true. While the evidence seems to point to me—"

"There's no 'seems to' about it," Mayne broke in. "It *does* point to you. Only you."

"Very conveniently so," Daniel said. "*Too* conveniently. Surely it's occurred to you that someone is trying to make me look like the guilty party."

"That's what you said about Tolliver," Rayburn said. "He couldn't have murdered Lady Margate, as he's in custody."

"But he certainly could have killed Lady Crawford," Daniel said, striving to keep his annoyance in check. "And shot at me. Unless you think I shot at myself. Perhaps Tolliver arranged for someone else to kill Lady Margate in the same way as Lady Crawford. The man threatened me, wanted revenge on me. What better way than to see me ruined and hanged for murder?"

Rayburn frowned. "Then why try to shoot you?"

"Impatience perhaps?" Daniel suggested. "I've no idea the workings of a madman's mind."

"Who stands to inherit your title and properties should you die?" Mayne asked.

Daniel hesitated at the abrupt question, then said, "My younger half brother, Stuart. And after him, his younger brother, George."

"Half brothers?" said Rayburn.

"My father remarried after my mother's death."

"And how is your relationship with them?"

"Strained," Daniel admitted. "However, neither could be responsible, as they're on the continent. Have been for the past several months."

"And your stepmother?"

"Is with them."

"Inheriting an earldom is certainly motive," Mayne pointed out. "Any one of them could have traveled back to England."

"Very unlikely," Daniel said. "Their last letter to me arrived only a few days ago from Austria. They were having a delightful time and planned to journey to Italy from there."

"Sounds like a friendly letter considering your strained relationship," remarked Rayburn.

"They're always friendly when asking me for money," Daniel said dryly. "While both they and my stepmother are greedy and shallow, they're not murderers."

"Any other enemies?" Rayburn asked.

"None that I'm aware of, but it seems quite clear I have one. I trust you'll keep trying to discover his identity. As will I." Daniel rose. "If there's nothing else . . ." he said, glancing pointedly at the door.

Rayburn and Mayne departed, although it was obvious to Daniel that Mayne wanted nothing more than to confine him in shackles and drag him off to the hangman's noose. He guessed Mayne suspected he'd bent the truth about leaving the house last night, and that didn't bode well. The Runner clearly thought him guilty. Which meant that Mayne would be spending his time looking for evidence against him rather than searching for the real killer.

Bloody hell.

A disturbing thought tickled the back of his mind, and with a frown, he paced before the hearth. It was glaringly clear that someone was trying to frame him for murder. But who? And why? Both victims were previous lovers. His frown deepened. Actually, they were two of his most recent lovers. The only women he'd been with since Blythe and Gwendolyn were Kimberly and—

Carolyn.

He halted as if he'd walked into a wall. Was his enemy specifically targeting his former lovers? It seemed so—and what better way to cast suspicion on him? In which case, both Kimberly and Carolyn could be in danger. The thought of Kimberly in danger angered and concerned him. But the thought of Carolyn in danger—

He felt as if his heart stopped beating. The thought of Carolyn in danger chilled him to the bone. Did his enemy know of his relationship with Carolyn? And then another thought hit him—one that froze his blood.

What if that shot the night before last wasn't meant for him but for Carolyn?

For several seconds his lungs ceased to function. He had no proof, but the churning in his gut told him he was right. Perhaps his earlier lovers might be in danger, but based on the pattern of the last two crimes, Kimberly and Carolyn were the next logical victims. He ran into the foyer and quickly told Samuel and Barkley about his conversation with Rayburn and Mayne.

"Wot bloody idiots, thinkin' ye could hurt those ladies," Samuel said, his eyes flashing.

"I agree, but that's not what's important right now. I need to warn Lady Walsh and Lady Wingate they might be in danger due to their . . . connection with me. Samuel, I want you to locate Rayburn and Mayne and tell them what I've told you. I don't know where they were going, but they'll eventually end up back at the Bow Street office."

"Yes, milord."

They left together, heading in opposite directions. When Daniel arrived at Carolyn's town house, Nelson said, "Lady Wingate is not at home."

Sick fear gripped Daniel. "Where is she?"

"At her sister's town house. Marchioness Langston called twice today, most anxious to speak with Lady Wingate. Lady Wingate remained at home only long enough to change clothes then departed."

"Are you certain she arrived safely?"

Nelson blinked. "Yes, my lord. She sent the carriage back, saying Lord Langston would see her home."

Relief loosened some of the tension gripping Daniel. He quickly related his concerns regarding Carolyn's safety to Nelson.

When he finished, the butler drew himself up to his

full height and determination filled his eyes. "I'll inform the rest of the household, my lord. Rest assured we'll allow no harm to come to Lady Wingate."

"Excellent. I'm off now to warn Lady Walsh."

"But who will protect *you*, my lord?"

"I'm armed. And this bastard doesn't want to kill me—he wants me to hang for murder." And based on his interview with Mayne and Rayburn, if he didn't act quickly, the bastard would most likely succeed.

Daniel left and climbed into his carriage. Although he wanted to go immediately to Carolyn, his rational mind told him she was safe with Matthew. Kimberly's home was on the way to Matthew's town house, and she needed to be warned as well. After giving his coachman Kimberly's direction, he sat back and prayed he was wrong about the danger. But everything inside him told him he was right.

When he arrived at Kimberly's town house, he was relieved to find her at home. He was greeted warmly by her butler, Sanders, and as on his previous visits, was shown to her private sitting room. She entered several minutes later, wearing an exquisite cream lace negligee and matching robe.

"How lovely to see you," she said with a warm smile, holding out her hands. "I called on you earlier today and was sorry to have missed you. At your club, were you?"

He squeezed her hands then released them. "No. A quick jaunt to the country. Kimberly, there's something I must tell you."

"Then by all means, let us sit." She waved her hand toward the oversized sofa in front of the hearth. "Would you care for a brandy?"

"No, thank you. Nor do I wish to sit." He tersely told her everything, and watched her eyes widen with each sentence he spoke. When he finished, he asked, "Who is here to protect you besides Sanders?"

"James, and you know what a strapping young man my footman is."

"Good. Inform them both and do not go anywhere unescorted." He lightly clasped her upper arms. "Anywhere."

"I won't, but darling, you're scaring me." She reached and brushed her fingers over his tense jaw. "I'd feel much safer if you stayed with me."

He gave her shoulders an encouraging squeeze then released her. "I'm sorry, but I must go. I've every confidence in James and Sanders."

After extracting her promise to be careful, he departed, instructing his coachman to make haste to Matthew's town house. When he arrived, he was assured by Matthew's butler, Graham, that Lady Wingate was indeed there, visiting with Lady Langston, Lady Julianne, and Lady Emily in the marchioness's private sitting room. Daniel was about to demand to see her when Matthew strolled into the foyer.

"Seems to be our evening for visitors," he said with a smile that faded as he drew closer to Daniel. "Are you all right?"

Daniel shook his head. "I need to speak to Carolyn."

Matthew hesitated. "She's with Sarah, who's been very anxious to speak with her all day. Emily and Julianne arrived just before you." He turned to Graham. "When the ladies come downstairs, please tell them Lord Surbrooke and I await them in the drawing room."

"Yes, my lord."

Daniel was about to protest, but decided that since Carolyn was clearly safe, he could take this opportunity to fill Matthew in on the latest developments.

Matthew led him into the drawing room, and after closing the door behind them, immediately asked, "What's wrong, Daniel?"

He listened carefully while Daniel told him everything, concluding with, "Now I must warn Carolyn. If anything were to happen to her . . ." His voice trailed off and he shook his head, unable to contemplate such an outcome. "I want her safe. At all costs."

Matthew made no reply. Instead, he walked to the decanters and poured two generous brandies. After handing a crystal snifter to Daniel, he said, "I agree with your assessment that someone's trying to frame you, and is killing your former lovers in order to do so. But *who* is doing it and why?"

Daniel dragged his hands down his face. "I don't know. Since Gwendolyn's murder couldn't have been committed by Tolliver, I'm wondering if he either hired someone to commit the crime or perhaps had a silent business partner who is also facing financial ruin. Someone who would blame his difficulties on me for backing out of the deal."

"Perhaps." Matthew's gaze met his. "Have you considered your family?" he asked quietly. "There's no love lost between you, and they would certainly benefit from your demise."

A humorless sound escaped Daniel. "Mayne and Rayburn suggested the same thing. Perhaps if they were in London I'd be inclined to suspect them, but they're in Austria."

Matthew nodded slowly. "The suggestion of Tol-liver having a silent partner is a good one, one we should have Rayburn and Mayne look into."

"Samuel is searching for them. As soon as I speak to them, I'll let them know." He pulled in a deep breath then admitted, "I wasn't entirely truthful with Mayne earlier, and I suspect he knows."

"About what?"

"He wanted to know my whereabouts last night. I told him I was home."

"But you weren't?"

"No."

When he didn't elaborate, Matthew said, "You were with Carolyn."

It wasn't a question and there was no point deny-ing it, as Matthew knew him so well. He gave a tight nod then said, "I promised her discretion and had no intention of telling them something that is none of their business."

"Surely they'll guess the nature of your relationship once they learn you believe her to be in danger."

"Perhaps, but there's no way around telling them that. Still, I don't plan to admit to them that Carolyn and I are anything more than close friends, which is perfectly true. Anything else is none of their damn business."

"You were with Carolyn today as well?"

"Yes. I took her to Meadow Hill."

Matthew's brows rose at that. "I see. And how was your visit there?"

Emotional. Frightening. Cathartic.

Perfect.

"Enjoyable," he murmured. Not wishing to answer

any more questions on that topic, he said, "Sarah was anxious to speak with Carolyn. Nothing is amiss, I hope."

"On the contrary, everything is wonderful. I'm going to be a father."

Based on his expression, there was no doubt Matthew was ecstatic. Daniel smiled and held out his hand, happy for his friend, but aware of a vague sense of emptiness tugging at him. "Congratulations."

"Thank you."

"You seem very calm."

"Actually, I've been a frenzy of anxiety ever since the doctor confirmed the pregnancy this morning. Both Sarah and the doctor assure me she's perfectly fit, and Sarah has *forbid* me to worry. She said if I intend to pace the floors until the babe arrives, she'll cosh me over the head with a skillet."

"Quite the violent streak your wife has."

"Apparently. Of course, even the threat of bodily harm won't keep me from worrying. I'm afraid worrying comes with the territory of loving someone." Matthew looked at him over the rim of his brandy snifter. "As you're finding out."

Daniel's own snifter halted halfway to his lips and his brows collapsed in a frown. "What do you mean?"

"Do you truly not know?"

"Know what?"

Matthew looked toward the ceiling then pinned his gaze on Daniel. "You're in love, you idiot."

An immediate denial sprang to Daniel's lips, but when he opened his mouth no sound came forth. In love? Surely not. But the instant he tried to deny it, he realized with stunning clarity it was true. *That's* what this bone-deep wanting, needing, and yearning was. This unfamiliar aching, twisting, gut wrenching plethora of emotions that ran the gamut from happiness to misery.

He was in love.

The knowledge hit him with the force of a plank upside his head. Good God, this was worse than he'd thought. Had he believed he was only losing a small bit of his heart to Carolyn? What a jest! He'd lost the entire thing. And his soul as well.

He set down his brandy then walked to the sofa, where he sat down heavily. Tunneling his fingers through his hair, he looked up at Matthew and said in a dazed voice that seemed to come from very far away, "Bloody hell, you're right."

"That you're in love? I know."

"That I'm an idiot." Daniel rested his head in his hands and groaned. "How did this happen? And how do I make it go away?"

Matthew chuckled. "I imagine it happened in the usual manner—you discovered someone who . . . completes you. As for making it go away, I know from experience that you can't. It's not dyspepsia after all." He settled himself in the wing chair across from Daniel. "And why would you want to? Carolyn is a lovely woman."

Daniel raised his head. "Yes, she is. But she isn't in love with me. She still worships her dead husband. Her heart will always belong to him. She's made no secret of that." A humorless sound escaped him at the irony. He'd never before wanted a woman's heart, and had certainly never intended to give his away. And what happened? He lost his heart to a woman who didn't want it and had no intention of giving him hers.

He blew out a long breath. "What a bloody mess."

"Perhaps she'll change her mind," Matthew said.

Daniel shook his head. "No. Edward was the love of her life. She adored him. Still does. No man could aspire to scale the pedestal upon which she's put him."

"It's obvious she cares for you."

"Yes, I'm sure she does, but in a lukewarm way compared to her feelings for Edward."

And he knew, in his heart, that would never be enough for him. He could accept her loving memories of Edward—he wouldn't begrudge her the things that made her happy—but neither could he bear not to be first in her affections. To know that Edward's ghost always stood between them. That comparisons would always be made and he would always come out lacking.

For his own sake, he needed to end his affair with her. Now. Before he did something stupid and made an ass of himself. Like telling her he loved her. Or asking her to marry him. Or worse, *begging* her to do so. The only thing he could think of that was worse than not seeing love in her eyes would be seeing pity in them.

"Damn it all, why would anyone actually *want* to fall in love?" he asked.

"It's an incredible thing when you find the right person," Matthew said softly.

Yes, the right person being someone who loved

you as deeply as you loved them. Unfortunately that hadn't happened to him. And this unrequited, one-sided emotional hell was nothing short of torture.

"We're going to have to rename our group the Ladies Literary Society—Plus One Baby," Carolyn said, giving Sarah a hug after her announcement that she was expecting a child. Sarah's happy news had enabled her to shove aside her own sadness over foolishly allowing herself to love a man who wanted no part of love. "I cannot wait to be an aunt."

"Neither can I," Julianne and Emily said in unison.

"Well, you're all going to have to help me keep Matthew in check," Sarah said, pushing up her glasses, "because I can already see he's going to render us both insane. He didn't even want me to climb the stairs!" She looked toward the ceiling. "If I don't nip his masculine panic in the bud right now, this is going to be a very long pregnancy indeed."

Carolyn reached out and squeezed her hand. "Be happy that the man you love is so devoted and caring, Sarah. There is no greater gift." *And no greater pain than when you are in love alone.*

"Speaking of great gifts," said Julianne, "did anyone happen to notice that Mr. Gideon Mayne, the Bow Street Runner, attended Lord and Lady Exbury's soiree last evening?"

"Yes," said Emily. "He was there with Mr. Rayburn."

"They are hoping to find clues regarding Lady Crawford's murder," added Carolyn. "But what does Mr. Mayne have to do with great gifts?"

Julianne looked around the room, as if making certain no one else was present to hear what she was about to share. Then she said, her eyes glowing, "Ever since he came to our home to question me and Mother after the masquerade, I . . . well, I haven't been able to stop thinking about him."

"A Bow Street Runner?" Emily said, her eyes agog with shock. "Good heavens, Julianne. Your mother would succumb to apoplexy, and for once I'd have to agree with her. A *Runner*? He is completely unacceptable. So common. And so coarse and hard-looking. Why he's almost as bad as that dreadful Mr. Jennsen."

Julianne raised her chin. "*I* think Mr. Mayne looks dashing and dangerous and exciting."

"He most likely is dangerous," Sarah broke in. "Certainly his occupation is."

Carolyn patted Julianne's hand. "While there's no denying he's attractive, it would be most unwise to entertain romantic thoughts about a man with whom you could never have a romance." She inwardly winced at the irony of her advice. "Personally, I think it's our reading of the *Memoirs* that has us all in a dither. I think for our next book selection, we need to choose something of a less salacious nature."

Sarah grinned. "Now what would be the fun in that?"

Carolyn smiled in return, but in her heart she couldn't help but feel that reading the *Memoirs* had set her on this disastrous path that led straight to heartbreak.

A wave of weariness washed through her, exacerbated by her emotional day and lack of sleep. She rose and said, "I don't wish to break up this gathering, but I'm exhausted."

Sarah looked at her and frowned. "You look tired. Are you all right?"

No. Everything hurts. My heart most of all. She forced a smile. "I'm fine. Just in need of sleep. Will I see you all tomorrow at Lady Pelfield's soiree?"

"Matthew and I will be there," Sarah said.

"Me, too," both Julianne and Emily said.

After giving hugs and kisses, Carolyn quit the room and made her way down the stairs. When she arrived in the foyer, Graham said, "His lordship is in the drawing room, Lady Wingate. This way, please."

She'd expected the butler to simply tell Matthew she was ready to leave, but obviously he wanted her to follow him. Pressing her fingers against her temple to ward off the headache brewing there, she walked down the corridor. After Graham announced her at the door to the drawing room, she entered, saw Matthew and smiled, hoping she didn't look as tired as she felt.

"Sarah told me the happy news," she said, offering her brother-in-law her hands then leaning in to kiss his cheek. "I'm so happy for you both."

"Thank you." He looked over her shoulder and she turned. And stilled at the sight of Daniel standing before the fire.

"Hello, Carolyn," he said, both his expression and tone grave.

Her heart turned over in that same way it always seemed to whenever she laid eyes on him. "Daniel.

Are you here to share in Matthew and Sarah's good news?"

"No. I'm here to talk to you."

Before she could express her surprise, Matthew said, "If you'll excuse me, I'm going to see if there is anything my lovely wife requires. Daniel has offered to escort you home. Is that all right? It would allow me to remain with Sarah."

"Yes, of course." She offered him the best smile she could muster. "But there's no need for concern. She's not doing anything more strenuous than talking to Julianne and Emily."

"Good. That means I can cease worrying for perhaps thirty seconds." He quit the room, closing the door quietly behind him.

Daniel walked toward her, and anticipating a kiss, her heart sped up. It wasn't until he drew nearer that she noticed the lines of fatigue and worry etched around his eyes. Recalling how emotional he'd been earlier, sympathy tugged at her. "Are you all right?" she asked.

He shook his head. "No. We must talk." He took her hand and led her to the sofa. She relished the warmth of his palm touching hers and fought back the encroaching pain that threatened to overwhelm her at the realization that soon she would no longer be holding his hand.

After they were seated she listened in stunned disbelief as he told her all that had transpired after he'd left her at her town house. When he finished she remained silent for a full minute, taking it all in.

Two of Daniel's former lovers dead. Daniel suspected of committing the crimes. His belief she was in danger. Finally she said, "I cannot believe Lady Margate is dead." She pressed her lips together. "Or that those two nincompoops think you could possibly be responsible."

A tired smile lifted one corner of his mouth. "I appreciate your outrage on my behalf."

She clasped his hand between hers. "Daniel, as much as I appreciate you trying to keep my name out of this, you must tell Mr. Mayne where you were last night."

He shook his head. "The only thing he needs to know is that I wasn't off killing anyone."

She raised her chin. "I don't want him to have any reason to doubt you. If you don't tell him, *I* will."

His gaze roamed her face and she wished she could read his thoughts. "You realize that if you do so, word of our affair most likely will leak out."

"Then so be it. That is certainly preferable to having the magistrate and Mr. Mayne believe you guilty of murder. And given your determination to protect me, they'll surely guess."

"But will only *know* that my concern for you springs from our close friendship. It's not necessary to bring your name into this and subject you to gossip. Rayburn and Mayne won't find evidence to charge me with crimes I didn't commit."

"Whoever is trying to frame you will no doubt try to fabricate some sort of evidence against you. The killer has already managed to cast suspicion upon you." She shook her head. "Your intention to protect me, while honorable, is unacceptable. When Mr. Rayburn and Mr. Mayne come to interview me, as I know they shall, I'm going to tell them the truth, Daniel."

He didn't look pleased, but to her relief he didn't argue further. Instead he said, "We need to ensure your safety. I want your word that you won't go anywhere alone until the killer is apprehended."

"I promise I won't." She rose. "But I want to leave here. Now. If I'm truly in danger, I don't want to risk it following me to Sarah's home."

He rose as well, and for the space of several heartbeats they looked at each other. Less than an arm's length separated them. He looked so tired and troubled. Everything in her cried out, wanting to hold him, touch him. Be held and touched by him. She'd planned to make love with him once more, but now realized she simply couldn't. For if she did, she'd never be able to let him go. Would never survive walking away. Would do something foolish like beg him to love her. And stay with her forever.

Her better judgment told her to resist touching him, that every caress would only make saying good-bye that much more difficult. But need overwhelmed her, and she leaned toward him.

With a low groan that sounded agonized, Daniel jerked her against him and crushed his mouth down on hers. His kiss tasted of desperation and fear. Worry and frustration. And deep, hot desire. She clung to him, pressing herself closer, branding in her memory the feel of his hard body tight against hers. The warm, intoxicating taste of his kiss. The thick, silky texture of his hair. The delicious, unforgettable scent that belonged to him alone.

Where she found the strength to pull away, she'd never know. How she wished she were like the Anonymous Lady and able to keep her heart free! They looked at each other, both breathing hard, and she knew that for her own self-preservation she had to tell him. Tonight.

Once they were seated in his carriage and on their way to her home, she licked her suddenly dry lips and said, "Daniel, I've been thinking about our . . . arrangement."

Sitting across from her, he regarded her through hooded but watchful eyes. "Yes?"

And she forced out the words she knew she had to say. The words that would break her heart nonetheless. "I . . . I think it best if we don't see each other in . . . that way anymore."

The loudest silence she'd ever heard filled the carriage. His expression remained completely blank, but then something flickered in his eyes and for one insane moment she wondered if he might refuse. Might tell her that he wouldn't, couldn't, consider such a thing because he'd unexpectedly fallen in love with her. And couldn't imagine not being with her.

Instead, he simply asked, "Why?"

Because I love you and I can't bear that you don't love me. Because I have to try to protect whatever tiny piece of my heart you haven't stolen. "While I've no qualms admitting to the authorities that we were together last night, I have no wish for my life to be gossip fodder, and if we continue, you know it shall be." She attempted a lighthearted expression. "Our affair had to end eventually. Given the circumstances, this is that time."

Again silence swelled between them and she held her breath. Then he jerked his head in a quick nod. "You're right, of course. Our affair had to end eventually."

His words ruthlessly extinguished that foolish flicker of hope. That he accepted her decision so lightly proved that in the end she'd meant nothing more to him than another sexual conquest. And proved beyond any doubt that she'd made the right decision. Still, being right didn't mean she didn't hurt. Pain and a deep despair she'd hoped never to experience again sawed through her.

Something must have shown on her face because he asked softly, "What are you thinking?"

As she'd done so many times in the past, she pushed her heartache to the back of her mind, to be taken out and examined later, when she was alone. And could cry.

"I was thinking about Edward," she answered honestly.

A shutter seemed to fall over his eyes, and he said nothing in reply.

They arrived at her town house a few minutes later and he escorted her inside. Nelson reported that nothing untoward had occurred in their absence and that he would keep watch at the front door through the night.

"I'll arrange for someone to guard the back of the house," Daniel told her. "You'll recall your promise not to go anywhere alone until this madman is apprehended."

"You have my word."

He looked as if he wanted to say something more,

and her breath caught. He reached out and raised her hand to his mouth. Brushed his lips against the back of her gloved fingers. And then he did say something else.

"Good-bye, Carolyn."

Without another word he turned and left. And her heart shattered into a million brittle fragments.

Chapter 21

Although I attempted to remain friends with my former lovers, it unfortunately didn't always work out that way. It is a sad fact of life that sometimes affairs just end badly.

Memoirs of a Mistress by An Anonymous Lady

*H*idden from view by a row of neatly trimmed privet hedges, Daniel sat on the damp ground with his back resting against the stone wall that separated Carolyn's small garden from her neighbor's. Clouds obscured the moon, and the air felt thick and heavy with rain. He'd taken up his post within minutes after leaving Carolyn, going home only long enough to see if Samuel had returned. His footman had awaited him in the foyer and reported that he'd been unable to find the magistrate but finally located Mr. Mayne, who hadn't seemed overly impressed with his tale but nonetheless promised to call in the morning.

After instructing Samuel to keep guard at home, Daniel had stolen into Carolyn's garden and taken up his vigil. Armed with a pistol and his knife, he had no intention of allowing anyone to gain access to her house. If anyone had any designs to hurt her, they'd damn well have to accomplish the task over his lifeless body.

Lifeless . . . He blew out a long, slow breath. Bloody hell, that's exactly how he felt. Lifeless and numb. Defeated. Gutted.

Our affair had to end eventually. Her words echoed through his mind, cutting another oozing wound in his battered heart. Hadn't he intended to tell her the same thing? Yes, although he had to wonder if he actually would have been able to utter the words if she hadn't said them first. When she had, he wanted nothing more than to grab her and shake her. Force her to put the past behind her and stop worshipping a ghost.

I was thinking about Edward. . .

He briefly squeezed his eyes closed. He wanted to hate the man, but how did one hate a dead man? A man who'd been a friend? A man he'd liked and admired? A man who hadn't deserved to die at such a young age? He could understand that Carolyn would always love Edward, but why did she have to love *only* Edward?

When she'd told him their affair must end, his first strong, primal instinct had been to argue, but he forced himself not to. It was for the best, especially now, that he keep his physical distance from her, as he didn't want to bring danger her way. Perhaps, after all this was over, he could try to convince her—

He ruthlessly sliced off the thought. What was the point? She'd made her choice and had chosen her husband's memory. For him to try and convince her to prolong their affair would only humiliate them both. Rather than trying to accomplish the impossible task of finding a way to make her forget a man she'd never forget, he would be much better served to try to find a way to make himself fall out of love.

A tight, bitter sound clogged his throat. God, if only he could do so. Somewhere the gods must be laughing at him. That after a lifetime of scoffing at the notion of love, it had reached up and grabbed him, body and soul, and left him with nothing but a numb, empty space where his heart used to beat.

His gaze lifted to Carolyn's bedchamber window. To the small balcony over which he'd tossed a rope then scaled to enter her room. Had he truly thought he'd merely desired her body? Had wanted nothing more from her than sexual games? Had felt nothing beyond lust? He thunked his head against the cold, rough stone. What a bloody idiot he was.

He kept his vigil all through the night, senses on alert, ears attuned to any strange sounds, eyes ceaselessly scanning, but nothing suspicious occurred. It began to rain around three A.M., at first softly, but then more steadily, until the drops fell in a cold, silent sheet that plastered his hair and clothing to his chilled skin. By the time dawn broke, a barely discernable gray streak in the dreary, opaque sky, the rain had tapered off to a light drizzle.

Suddenly, a soft glow illuminated Carolyn's bedchamber window. He instantly pictured her lighting a lamp. Rising from bed. Brushing her hair. Getting dressed. And wished with everything in him that he was in that room with her.

An hour passed before the light went out, a sign that she'd left her bedchamber, most likely to go to breakfast, and he realized that the rain had finally stopped. In a perfect match to his mood, the sky remained gloomy and overcast. He rose stiffly, his cold, cramped muscles protesting. He pushed his damp hair back with both hands and grimaced at the feel of wet clothing sticking to his skin. He'd go home and change his clothes then resume his vigil.

When he entered his foyer a few minutes later, Samuel and Barkley reported all was well. "Not a peep o' disturbance, milord," Samuel said.

"Excellent. I want you to keep watch in Lady Wingate's garden while I change clothes."

"Yes, milord. Got me knife right here," Samuel said, patting his boot. "Won't nobody get by me."

He departed through the rear of the house, and Daniel started up the stairs.

"Shall I arrange for a hot bath, my lord?" Barkley asked.

"No, thank you. Just breakfast and coffee." He'd made it halfway up the stairs when the brass door knocker sounded.

Barkley peeked through the side window. "'Tis Mr. Mayne, my lord," he reported in an undertone.

"Show him into the dining room and offer him breakfast. I'll join him shortly." He took the remainder of the stairs two at a time, anxious to change, complete his business with Mayne, then resume his watch in Carolyn's garden.

Ten minutes later he strode into the dining room, noting that Mayne was only drinking coffee. After exchanging greetings with the Runner, Daniel asked, "Where's Rayburn?"

Mayne frowned. "He said he had other matters to attend to. I'll report to him later."

While helping himself to eggs, ham, and bacon from the sideboard, Daniel reiterated what Samuel had told the Runner last night. As he took his seat at the head of the table, he concluded by saying, "I warned Lady Walsh of possible danger. Lady Wingate as well."

Mayne's impassive face didn't show a flicker of emotion. "Lady Wingate . . . is she the reason you lied about your whereabouts the night before last?"

Daniel clenched his jaw. He didn't want this man to know of his affair with Carolyn, but since she clearly intended to tell him herself, there was no point in prevaricating. "I didn't precisely lie. I did come home. But then I left. And went to Lady Wingate's town house. I didn't tell you, as my private life is none of your business, nor did I want Lady Wingate to become gossip fodder."

"You were there all night?"

"Until dawn, yes."

"And Lady Wingate will vouch for this?"

"Yes."

Mayne's gaze settled for several seconds on Daniel's still damp hair. "Where were you *last* night, Lord Surbrooke?"

Annoyance rippled through him at the man's silky tone, and he made him wait for his answer while he chewed then swallowed a forkful of egg. "In Lady Wingate's garden. Keeping watch."

"And will Lady Wingate vouch for that as well?"

"She doesn't know I was there."

"Did anyone see you?"

"No. But my butler and footman know I was."

"Because they *saw* you there—or merely because you told them that's where you'd be?"

"Are you insinuating I was somewhere else?"

"If you're asking if I've discovered another body of one of your former lovers, the answer is not yet." He lifted his china cup and looked at Daniel over the rim. "The day is young, however."

"Your time would be better served trying to come up with a plan to capture the true killer."

"Do you have any suggestions?"

"As a matter of fact, I do. As you know, both murders occurred during or after a party I attended. I'm scheduled to attend a soiree at the home of Lady Pelfield this evening."

Interest flickered in Mayne's dark eyes. "So you think it possible our man may strike again tonight. Will Lady Walsh and Lady Wingate be in attendance?"

"I'm not certain about Lady Walsh, although as it's a huge soiree, she probably will. I know Lady Wingate plans to attend."

"So we could use one of them as bait."

"No." The word came out harsh, forceful. "Absolutely not." The thought of a murdering madman so much as touching Carolyn twisted his insides into a painful knot. "I was thinking we could employ extra help and all be extra vigilant. Keep a careful eye on both ladies. Have one of us within arm's reach at all times. As soon as someone tries to lure either of them off alone, we'll have our killer."

Mayne said nothing for several seconds, just looked at him through his dark, inscrutable eyes. Finally he murmured, "And what if this is a case of the fox guarding the chicken coop?"

"Meaning what if *I'm* the one who will attempt to lure one of them off alone?" Daniel leaned forward and narrowed his eyes. "And what if, Mr. Mayne, *you* are the fox?"

Something flickered in those dark eyes, then Mayne inclined his head. "Appears this will be an interesting evening."

Daniel took a swallow of his coffee, tapped his napkin to his lips, then rose. "If there's nothing else, I wish to return to Lady Wingate's garden."

Mayne rose. "I'll go with you. I'd like to speak to Lady Wingate myself."

They'd just entered the corridor when Daniel heard the front door open. Seconds later Samuel yelled to Barkley, "I must speak to his lordship at once!"

His anxious tone shivered a chill down Daniel's spine, and he took off at a dead run toward the foyer, Mayne hot on his heels. As soon as Daniel saw Samuel, his dread grew at the sight of the young man's wide eyes and pale face. His footman was breathing hard and clearly agitated.

"What is it?" Daniel asked tersely. "Lady Wingate?"

"She's gone, milord."

Daniel felt the blood rush from his head. "What do you mean, gone?"

Samuel's words poured out in a rapid flow. "I were watchin' Lady Wingate's garden, just like ye told me. After a bit Katie came outside. Seen me through the window, she had, and wanted to say hello. We got to talkin' and then she asked me what I were doin'. When I told her I were guardin' the back o' the house in case the murderer were lurkin' about, she says, 'Oh, no need to worry about that, the murderer's been caught.'"

"What?" Daniel and Mayne asked in unison.

Samuel nodded. "That's wot she said. When I asked her how she knew, she said because Lady Wingate had received a note from Lord Surbrooke tellin' her so."

The floor seemed to shift around Daniel's feet. "I sent no such note. Where is Lady Wingate now?"

"Katie wasn't sure, she only knew Lady Wingate went out. I told her to get Nelson and find the note. I ran here to tell ye."

Daniel grabbed his pistol from the foyer table where he'd left it on his way up the stairs. His gaze flicked between Samuel and Mayne. "Let's go."

Carolyn made her way along the winding path in Hyde Park and pulled her shawl tighter around her shoulders to ward off the damp, chilly breeze. Ghostly fingers of smoky fog rose from the ground, while the dismal sky, gloomy with low-hanging clouds, threatened to spew rain at any moment. As a result the park was deserted.

She hurried along, anxious to reach the spot where Daniel's note had indicated that she would meet him and Mr. Mayne. Thank goodness they'd apprehended the killer. She looked forward to giving the Runner a good dressing down for suspecting Daniel.

The path curved just ahead, which led to the small U-shaped area surrounded by a thick copse of elms and hedges where Daniel had asked her to meet them. She veered off the path and entered the break in the tall hedges. A lone figure stood in the far corner of the small fog-shrouded clearing, and Carolyn called out a greeting.

The figure approached and Carolyn blinked in surprise. "What are *you* doing here?"

A smile. And an odd glitter in green eyes that stilled Carolyn and raced an icy shiver down her spine.

A black gloved hand raised a pistol and pointed it at the center of her chest. "I'm here to see you, Lady Wingate."

Carolyn stared at the pistol, trying to make sense of what was happening. She drew an unsteady breath and raised her gaze back to those eyes she now realized gleamed with madness. "Surely that weapon isn't necessary."

"Oh, but I'm afraid it is. If you cooperate, only you will die. If you move or scream, I'll kill you, then make certain your sister dies next. Do you understand?"

Heart pounding so loud she could hear its echo in her ears, Carolyn managed to nod. "Yes."

Dear God. Surely someone—Nelson, Katie, Daniel, *someone*—would soon realize she'd been lured away on false pretenses. She just had to remain calm and stay alive until they found her. Her gaze flicked to the pistol, which didn't waver at all.

She lifted her chin. "Obviously the note wasn't from Daniel and I am to be your third victim . . . or have there been others, Lady Walsh?"

A cunning smile curved Kimberly Sizemore's lips. "Only Lady Crawford and Lady Margate. After you're gone, I'll have what I want."

"And what, precisely, is that?"

The smile disappeared and cold, stark hatred kindled in Lady Walsh's eyes. "I want Daniel ruined. As he ruined me."

Carolyn nodded slowly, as if that made perfect sense. "I see. And how did he ruin you?"

The hatred burned brighter. "He courted me, flattered me, seduced and charmed me. I fell madly, passionately in love with him. Just when I was certain I was on the verge of winning him, he cast me aside like day-old trash to attend a house party at Lord Langston's country estate. Oh, he was very civil about ending our liaison, but it still amounted to being thrown away."

Her glittering eyes narrowed. "I'd planned to regain his favor when he returned to London, but he came back a different man. Every time I approached him, he put me off. And I realized he'd taken another lover. All I needed to do was find out who so I could best plan how to win him back."

Her gaze raked over Carolyn with ill-concealed disgust. "I saw the two of you the night of my masquerade ball. On the terrace. I couldn't credit that he'd chosen *you*—a boring, timid widow who'd *nev-*

er be able to please him as I had. Surely you didn't think you could keep a man like Daniel satisfied."

Anger over the destruction this madwoman had caused pushed aside a portion of Carolyn's fear and she lifted her brows. "Perhaps I'm not as boring and timid as you think."

Lady Walsh's eyes turned to slits. "He would have returned to me if not for you. I tried to tempt him back, but he stubbornly refused. And turned my love to hate. That's when I decided that if I couldn't have him, no one would."

"Then why didn't you simply kill him?"

Her lips curved up in a travesty of a smile. "But that's exactly what I'm doing. Shooting or stabbing him would be too quick, and Daniel must suffer. Must be ruined. So I decided to frame him for murder. Of his former lovers."

"How did you kill them?" Carolyn asked, straining her ears, praying she'd soon hear footsteps coming along the path.

Pride now gleamed in Lady Walsh's eyes. "I lured them to their deaths by sending them the sort of time and place lover's notes that are currently all the rage. I disguised my handwriting to resemble Daniel's and asked them both to wear pieces of jewelry to their liaison that he'd given them. After you're found dead, his fate will be sealed. Especially after I plant the notes he sent to Lady Crawford and Lady Margate where the authorities will find them."

"Why didn't you just leave the notes on the dead women?"

"I'd planned to send one to you on the night you

would be killed, and I didn't want you afraid to answer the missive." Her expression turned cunning. "That's if you didn't die sooner."

"You mean the shot you fired?"

A sly smile curved her lips. "Perhaps."

"Why this change in your plans?"

Lady Walsh frowned. "Because Daniel decided both you and I were in danger. Did you know he came to me last night, to warn me to be careful? I almost felt sorry for my plan to ruin him, and I might have halted it had he accepted my invitation to stay. But instead he left." She glared at Carolyn. "To go to you, I'm sure."

"Yes."

"That final rejection sealed his fate, and forced me to act sooner than I'd planned. I knew he'd see to it that you were never out of his sight." Another sick smile. "But I fooled him. And you. And now here we are. And you're going to die."

A cold fury unlike anything she'd ever known rose in Carolyn. "You already failed when you shot at me the other night," she said with a sneer.

"I won't miss this time."

Realizing it was now or never, Carolyn sprang at her attacker with a feral scream that cut through the chilled air. Shock, then profound hatred, registered in Lady Walsh's eyes as they struggled over the pistol. Carolyn fought with every ounce of her strength to keep the muzzle pointed away from herself, but Lady Walsh was demonically strong, and as determined as she. Fear and fury forced Carolyn to keep struggling. Sweat broke out on her skin, and her every muscle trembled with her efforts.

Yet despite her valiant attempt, Lady Walsh managed to jam the pistol's muzzle directly beneath her breast. *Dear God, I'm going to die. At the hands of this madwoman.*

No sooner had the thought whispered through her mind than Lady Walsh cried out and stiffened. Her eyes went wide and her grip slackened on the pistol. Carolyn grabbed the weapon and scurried back, away from her. Shaking, she pointed the pistol at Lady Walsh, fully prepared to squeeze the trigger, but to her astonishment, the woman fell to her knees. A trickle of blood oozed between her lips and a thin line of scarlet trailed over her jaw. Her eyes were rapidly dimming, but they remained focused on Carolyn.

"I'll have my revenge," she whispered. "Even from the grave I'll see you dead." She collapsed forward then, and Carolyn stared with disbelief at the hilt of the knife protruding from her back.

Dazed, she looked up and saw Daniel standing in the opening in the hedges. Before she could move, he ran to her. "Are you hurt?" he asked, gently removing the pistol from her suddenly nerveless fingers.

"I . . . I'm fine." Although fine didn't precisely describe the shakiness attacking her limbs.

He passed the pistol to Mr. Mayne, who'd entered the clearing along with Samuel and Nelson, who held a knife in one hand and brandished a fire iron in the other.

She blinked at her very proper butler. "Good heavens, Nelson, what are you doing here?"

"Came to help rescue you, my lady."

For some reason, that filled her eyes with tears. "Thank you. All of you."

Daniel wrapped an arm around her then led her away from the body. She glanced at it over her shoulder and shuddered. When they stopped walking, she turned to face him. He cupped her cheeks between his hands and his anxious gaze raked her face.

"You're certain you're not hurt?"

She nodded. "Yes."

Before she could utter another word, he crushed her to him in a hug so tight she could barely breathe. She clung to him, grateful for his strength, because her legs still felt decidedly wobbly.

"My God, Carolyn," he whispered against her hair. "I've never, in my entire life, been so frightened."

"She was going to kill me," she mumbled into his chest.

A shudder racked his frame. "Yes, I know."

She lifted her head and leaned back just enough to look into his eyes. "Did you kill her?"

"Yes."

"You made an excellent throw with that knife. I'm very relieved you didn't miss."

"There was no possible way I was going to miss. Not with all that was at stake."

"I wasn't going to let her shoot me. Not without a fight."

He brushed back a loosened tangle of her hair. "I'm very relieved to hear it. I didn't know you were so fierce."

"Neither did I."

"You're a veritable tigress."

"Apparently. But I certainly hope I never have to prove it again in such a manner."

"As do I. Do you feel able to walk?"

"I'm a bit unsteady, but I'd rather walk home than stay here."

Keeping his arms around her, Daniel looked over her shoulder. "I'm going to escort Lady Wingate home, Mayne. Do you need me to send for anyone?"

"No. Samuel's offered to fetch Rayburn, and Nelson can stay with me, if that's all right with Lady Wingate."

"Of course."

When she and Daniel reached the opening in the hedges, Carolyn couldn't stop herself from taking one final look behind her at Lady Walsh.

"What did she say to you, at the end?" Daniel asked.

"'I'll have my revenge . . . even from the grave I'll see you dead.'" A shiver ran through Carolyn, and Daniel wrapped his arm more firmly around her shoulders. "I have no idea what she meant."

"It doesn't matter. She's dead, and can do nothing to hurt you or anyone else ever again."

Twenty minutes later a frantic Katie opened the door to Carolyn's town house. After assuring the maid that her mistress was well, Daniel instructed her to arrange for a bath. Then he lifted Carolyn in his arms and strode down the corridor toward the drawing room.

"I'm perfectly fit," she felt compelled to point out, even as her arms gratefully twined around his neck.

"Of course you are. You are a fierce tigress. Carrying you is a completely selfish act on my part."

He entered the drawing room and pushed the door

firmly closed with his boot. Then he walked directly to the fireplace and gently deposited her on the settee. He sat beside her and took her hands.

She slipped one hand free and brushed her fingers over his cheek, almost giddy from delight in touching him. "You're pale."

He gave a weak smile. "I don't think I'm quite recovered from my fright. Actually, I don't know if I'll ever fully recover." He brought her hand to his mouth and pressed a fervent kiss against her fingers. "I almost lost you. I cannot even begin to describe how I felt when I realized you'd been lured into the hands of the killer. When I didn't know if I'd reach you in time. When I saw you struggling with that madwoman. I haven't prayed in a very long time, but I called upon every saint I could recall." He pressed her hand against his chest. "And my prayers were answered."

The steady beat of his heart beneath her palm brought a lump to her throat. Dear God, she loved him so much. And they'd nearly lost each other, a shocking reminder of how precious life was. And love. And how neither should ever be wasted. She loved him. And even though he didn't love her, even though she risked making a fool out of herself, she had to tell him.

Not quite sure how to begin, she cleared her throat. "You saved my life."

"I can only be grateful I wasn't too late and had the chance to do so."

"You have my deepest gratitude."

He frowned. Hesitated. Then said, "I don't want your gratitude, Carolyn."

"Oh," she said in a small voice. This wasn't going particularly well.

"I want your love."

It was her turn to frown. "I beg your pardon?"

"I want your love." He drew then released a deep breath. "Carolyn, I love you. So much I can barely sit still." He gripped her hands and looked at her through such serious eyes she realized with a shocked jolt that he was in dead earnest.

"I recall the first instant I saw you," he said softly. "Something happened to me in that moment. I wanted you, but there was something more . . . something I couldn't name because it had never happened to me before. You were the most exquisite woman I'd ever seen. Your smile, your laugh, captivated me, and I wanted nothing more than to spirit you away from the crowd and have you all to myself." A half smile quirked one corner of his lips. "That was the night you and Edward announced your engagement."

Carolyn felt her eyes widen. "I . . . I had no idea."

"Well, thank goodness," he said dryly. "As you know, we saw each other occasionally over the years, but I made a concentrated effort to stay away. Edward was my friend, and I didn't like myself for desiring his wife. For being unable to keep from doing so."

He reached out and brushed his fingers over her cheek. "But even though months or years would go by between the times I saw you, I never forgot you. Do you recall the painting in my drawing room?"

"Over the fireplace? The woman in the blue gown looking out at the garden?"

"Yes. I bought it because it reminded me of you.

Of that first time I saw you. You were wearing a blue dress, and I always liked to imagine myself as the man in the painting, the one you were looking for. The one who was waiting for you."

Hot moisture stung her eyes. "I had no idea your regard was of such long standing."

"Actually, neither did I. Carolyn, I have a confession to make."

"Even though it's nowhere near midnight?"

"Yes. I attended Matthew's house party because I knew you were going to be there. I knew I desired you, but once I saw you again . . . it was just like that first time. Like I'd been struck by lightning. It took me quite a while to figure out what was happening to me because I had nothing to compare it to. I always thought my heart was my own, but I was wrong. I lost it ten years ago to a girl I didn't even know who announced she was marrying another man."

He leaned forward and brushed his lips lightly over hers. "I know you said you didn't want my heart, but it's yours just the same." A sheepish smile touched one corner of his mouth. "It appears it always has been."

A half laugh, half sob escaped her. Wrapping her arms around him, she buried her face in his neck and bawled.

"Bloody hell," she heard him say, and she sobbed even harder. "Good God, I didn't mean to make you *cry*." She could feel him frantically patting his jacket in search of his handkerchief.

"Here," he said, pressing the square of white linen into her hand. "I'm sorry. I shouldn't have told you, at least not now. After all you've been through today—"

"Don't you dare . . ." She gave her nose a mighty blow. " . . . apologize. Or even think of taking back what you said. Because I won't let you."

He studied her for several seconds then nodded. "You have that fierce look about you again."

"I should hope so. What sort of man tells a woman he loves her and then *apologizes* for it?"

He pondered, then said, "I'm stumped."

"Actually that was a rhetorical question, but no matter. The point is that I love you, too."

He went perfectly still. He swallowed audibly then said quietly, "Carolyn, when I said I wanted your love, I meant I wanted you to give it freely. Not feel coerced into saying you love me because I said it to you."

She framed his face between her hands. "My darling Daniel, I give you my love freely. Without reservation. I wanted to tell you how I felt but was too afraid. I had a wonderful marriage with Edward and honestly never thought I could find that depth of feeling again with anyone. But you proved me wrong. My attraction to you, my feelings for you, began at Matthew's house party and have grown and flourished since then. In fact, I have a confession of my own. I knew it was you I danced with at the masquerade. You who kissed me."

He turned his head and lightly kissed her palm. "I'm delighted to hear it."

She hesitated, then said, "I'll always cherish what I had with Edward, but I want to make new memories. With you."

He kissed her palm again. "Please know I don't resent your love for Edward, Carolyn. I'm just deeply grateful and thankful that there's room in your heart for me as well."

"Edward owned my heart when he lived. But now I give it to you. Freely and completely."

Her breath caught at the flare of love that blazed in his eyes. "And I will cherish it. Always." Without another word, he lowered himself to one knee before her. "Carolyn, will you marry me?"

Her heart filled to overflowing and she wanted nothing more than to accept. But first she had to remind him. "I . . . I can't give you a child, Daniel."

The tenderness in his beautiful blue eyes melted her. "I don't care. And I have two greedy younger brothers who will be delighted to hear it." He raised her hands to his lips. "*You* are what is important to me, Carolyn. Children are a lovely gift, but not absolutely necessary. You, however, are like air—absolutely essential."

Her lips trembled. "You do always seem to know the right thing to say."

"Does that mean the answer is yes? You'll marry me?"

Another half laugh, half sob, escaped her. Throwing her arms around him, she said, "Yes!" Then proceeded to bawl all over his cravat.

"Good lord, I can see I'm going to need a larger supply of these," he teased, again pressing his handkerchief into her hand. "I'll arrange for several dozen as a gift for you—at the same time I pay off my debts."

"Debts?"

"Yes. Seems I owe both Matthew and Logan Jennsen fifty pounds."

"Whatever for?" she asked, mystified, even more so as he didn't appear the least bit upset about losing such large sums.

"A man must have his secrets," he said with a lopsided smile.

"I see. Well, as for gifts, you've already given me far too many," she protested, wiping at her wet eyes. "Which reminds me . . . I hope you won't be offended, but I'm afraid I don't care for marzipan."

"Why would I be offended? I don't particularly care for it either."

"Well, I thought since you'd sent me some . . . but for future reference, I much prefer chocolate."

He frowned. "What do you mean? I never sent you marzipan."

She frowned right back. "Of course you did. I have the box, along with your note in my desk."

He shook his head. "Carolyn, I never sent you marzipan."

An odd chill swept through her, and without a word she rose and crossed the room. Daniel followed her. After opening the top drawer and removing the box of candy, she set it on her desk and handed him the note.

"This is similar to my handwriting," he said, his voice grave, "but it's not mine."

"I thought the card seemed oddly impersonal, but I never suspected it wasn't from you." Their gazes met and realization hit her. "Do you think Lady Walsh sent the candy?"

"I suspect so. Let me see it."

She removed the lid and wrinkled her nose at the strong odor of bitter almonds. "They smell odd," she said. "I thought so the first time I opened the box."

A muscle ticked in Daniel's jaw, and he replaced the lid then clasped her shoulders. His eyes were dark with emotion.

"I'm guessing the candy is poisoned. Given the smell, most likely cyanide. The marzipan's almond paste would help mask the bitter almond odor."

Carolyn felt herself pale. "That's what her final words meant. How she'd get her revenge from the grave."

"Yes." He briefly squeezed his eyes shut. "Thank God you don't like marzipan," he said in a rough voice.

A chill rippled through Carolyn and she stepped into the circle of Daniel's strong arms.

"So now it's truly done," she said, weak with relief. "Completely over."

"On the contrary, my extremely lovely, very dear, greatly talented, highly amusing, extraordinarily intelligent, possessor of the most kissable lips I've ever seen, as well as an excellent memory, keeper of my heart, and soon to be *Lady Surbrooke*," Daniel said, his eyes brimming with love. "This is only the first of a lifetime of memories we are going to make together."

Good Girls <u>Do</u>

Just because a woman is brought up a proper lady, doesn't mean she isn't harboring some very improper desires. And just because a lady may have led a more . . . *colorful* life, doesn't mean she hasn't got a heart of gold. In fact, we're willing to bet that within the hearts of the most well-intentioned beauties beat the kind of passion that conventional society cannot contain . . . and only a rare gentleman can capture.

In the coming months, Avon Books brings you four captivating romances featuring heroines who live by their own rules when it comes to matters of the heart. Turn the page for a sneak preview of these spectacular novels from best-selling authors Jacquie D'Alessandro, Christina Dodd, Victoria Alexander, and Samantha James!

Coming January 2008

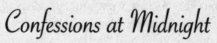

Confessions at Midnight

a brand-new *Mayhem in Mayfair* novel
by *USA Today* bestselling author

Jacquie D'Alessandro

Though Carolyn Turner can't believe the Ladies Literary Society of London would choose an erotic novel as their reading selection, she also can't help but read the tantalizing Memoirs of a Mistress *at least a half dozen times! Suddenly the lovely widow is tempted to surrender to her newly fueled fantasies when in the company of roguishly sexy Lord Surbrooke, a man no proper lady should be seen talking to, much less kissing. . . .*

*A*re you warm enough?" he asked.

Dear God, ensconced with Lord Surbrooke in the privacy provided by the potted palms, Carolyn felt as if she stood in the midst of a roaring fire. She nodded, then her gaze searched his. "Do . . . do you know who I am?"

His gaze slowly skimmed over her, lingering on the bare expanse of her shoulders and the curves she knew her ivory gown highlighted—skin and curves that her

normal modest mode of dress never would have revealed. That openly admiring look, which still held no
hint of recognition, reignited the heat the breeze had
momentarily cooled. When their eyes once again met,
he murmured, "You are Aphrodite, goddess of desire."

She relaxed a bit. He clearly didn't know who she
was, for the way he'd said "desire," in that husky, gruff
voice, was a tone Lord Surbrooke had never used with
Lady Wingate. Yet her relaxation was short-lived as that
desire-filled timbre pulsed a confusing tension through
her, part of which warned her to leave the terrace at
once. To return to the masquerade party and continue
searching for her sister and friends. But another
part—the part held enthralled by the darkly alluring
highwayman and the protection of her anonymity—
refused to move.

To add to her temptation was the fact that this anonymous interlude might afford her the opportunity to
learn more about him. In spite of their numerous conversations during the course of Matthew's house party,
all she actually knew of Lord Surbrooke was that he
was intelligent and witty, impeccably polite, unfailingly charming, and always perfectly groomed. He'd
never given her the slightest hint as to what caused
the shadows that lurked in his eyes. Yet she knew they
were there, and her curiosity was well and truly piqued.
Now, if she could only recall how to breathe, she could
perhaps discover his secrets.

After clearing her throat to locate her voice, she said,
"Actually, I am Galatea."

He nodded slowly, his gaze trailing over her. "Galatea
. . . the ivory statue of Aphrodite carved by Pygma-

lion because of his desire for her. But why are you not Aphrodite herself?"

"In truth, I thought costuming myself as such a bit too . . . immodest. I'd actually planned to be a shepherdess. My sister somehow managed to convince me to wear this instead." She gave a short laugh. "I believe she coshed me over the head while I slept."

"Whatever she did, she should be roundly applauded for her efforts. You are . . . exquisite. More so than Aphrodite herself."

His low voice spread over her like warm honey. Still, she couldn't help but tease, "Says a thief whose vision is impaired by darkness."

"I'm not really a thief. And my eyesight is perfect. As for Aphrodite, she is a woman to be envied. She had only one divine duty—to make love and inspire others to do so as well."

His words, spoken in that deep, hypnotic timbre, combined with his steady regard, spiraled heat through her and robbed her of speech. And reaffirmed her conclusion that he didn't know who she was. Never once during all the conversations she'd shared with Lord Surbrooke had he ever spoken to her—Carolyn—of anything so suggestive. Nor had he employed that husky, intimate tone. Nor could she imagine him doing so. She wasn't the dazzling sort of woman to incite a man's passions, at least not a man in his position, who could have any woman he wanted, and according to rumor, did.

Emboldened by his words and her secret identity, she said, "Aphrodite was desired by all and had her choice of lovers."

"Yes. One of her favorites was Ares." He lifted his hand, and she noticed he'd removed his black gloves. Reaching out, he touched a single fingertip to her bare shoulder. Her breath caught at the whisper of contact then ceased altogether when he slowly dragged his finger along her collarbone. "Makes me wish I'd dressed as the god of war rather than a highwayman."

He lowered his hand to his side, and she had to press her lips together to contain the unexpected groan of protest that rose in her throat at the sudden absence of his touch. She braced her knees, stunned at how they'd weakened at that brief, feathery caress.

She swallowed to find her voice. "Aphrodite caught Ares with another lover."

"He was a fool. Any man lucky enough to have you wouldn't want any other."

"You mean Aphrodite."

"You *are* Aphrodite."

"Actually, I'm Galatea," she reminded him.

"Ah, yes. The statute Pygmalion fell so in love with was so lifelike he often laid his hand upon it to assure himself whether his creation were alive or not." He reached out and curled his warm fingers around her bare upper arm, just above where her long satin ivory glove ended. "Unlike Galatea, you are very much real."

Priceless

the classic novel
by *New York Times* bestselling author

Christina Dodd

One of the celebrated Sirens of Ireland, spirited Bronwyn Edana is known for stunning titled society with her courageous exploits. But once betrothed to nobleman Adam Keane, she finds herself at the center of a shocking conspiracy that could rock the British realm. Now she faces her most daring adventure yet: risking it all for the only man she would ever love. . . .

Adam drew her outdoors, into the heated darkness. A great bonfire leaped in the middle of the square, answering the flames atop the hill, calling in the summer. On a platform, a swarm of instruments—violin, flute, and harmonica—squalled. The players cajoled off-key bits of melody, then whole bars of music, and at last, inspired by the occasion, a rollicking song. Although Bronwyn had never heard it before, its concentrated rhythm set her foot to tapping.

With a tug of his hand, Adam had her in the center

of a circle of clapping villagers. "I don't know how to dance to this," she warned.

"Nor do I," he answered, placing his hands on her waist. "Have a care for your toes."

She had no need to care for her toes, for Adam led with a strength that compensated for his limp. He kept his hands on her waist as he lifted her, turned her, swung her in circles. Under his guidance, she relaxed and began to enjoy the leaping, foot-stomping gambol. The community cheered, not at all distressed by the innovative steps, and the whole village joined them around the bonfire.

Girls with their sweethearts, men with their wives, old folks with their grandchildren, all whisked by as Adam twirled Bronwyn around and around. Bronwyn laughed until she was out of breath, and when she was gasping, the music changed. The rhythm slowed, the frenetic pace dwindled.

She saw Adam's amused expression change as he drew her toward him. His heavy lids veiled his gaze, and she knew he'd done so to hide his intention. She wondered why, then felt only shock as their bodies collided.

Shutting her eyes against the buffet of his heated frame against hers, she breathed a long, slow breath. The incense of his skin mated with the scent of the burning wood, and beneath the shield of her eyelids fireworks exploded. She groaned as her own body was licked by the flames.

Before she was scorched, he twirled her away, then back, in accordance to the rules of the dance.

There were people around, she knew, but she pretended they weren't watching their lord and lady. She pretended Adam and Bronwyn were alone.

Ignoring the proper steps, Adam wrapped himself around her, one arm against her shoulders, one arm at her waist.

Her hands held his shoulders. Her fingers flexed, feeling the muscles hidden beneath the fine linen. She could hear his heart thudding, hear the rasp of his breath and his moan as she touched his neck with her tongue. She only wanted a taste of him, but mistook it for interest, for he scooped her up.

Her eyes flew open. He'd ferried them to the edge of the dancing figures, planning their escape like a smuggler planning a landfall. A whirl and they were gone into the trees. Looking back, she could see the sparks of the bonfire, like a constellation of stars climbing to the sky.

This was what she wanted, what she dreaded, what she longed for. Since she'd met Adam, she didn't understand herself. His gaze scorched her, and she reveled in the discomfort. His hands massaged her as if he found pleasure in her shape; they wandered places no one had touched since she'd been an infant, and it excited her. Even now, as he pulled her into the darkest corner of the wood, she went on willing feet.

He pushed her against the trunk of a broad oak and murmured, "Bronwyn, give me your mouth."

She found his lips and marveled at their accuracy. His arm held her back, his hand clasped her waist; all along their length they grew together, like two fevered creatures of the night.

Coming March 2008

The Perfect Wife

the classic novel
by *New York Times* bestselling author

Victoria Alexander

*When the Earl of Wyldewood decides he is looking for
a proper wife, Sabrina Winfield bargains for the position of his convenient bride. This fiery beauty will do
anything to protect her family, even if it means playing
into Nicholas Harrington's arrogant ideas about how
a woman should behave. But the passion in the infuri-
ating earl's touch shatters any illusions Sabrina has of
keeping her heart safe. . . .*

*S*abrina stepped forward and gazed up at him. The
glittering heavens reflected in her eyes, and Nicholas had to stop himself from reaching for her.

She drew a steady breath. "Since this is to be a marriage of convenience only and privately we shall continue to live our separate lives, and since you already
have an heir, I will expect you to respect my privacy."

"Respect your privacy?" he blurted, stunned. "Do

you mean to say you will be my wife but you will not share my bed?"

"That's exactly what I mean," she said earnestly. "I shall be everything you want in a countess. I shall be the perfect wife. But I shall not share any man's bed with other women, and I shall not give my favors to a man I do not love."

She stepped back. "I suspect you would never wish the public spectacle of a divorce; therefore, if we do not suit, we can have the marriage annulled, or we can do what so many do and live completely apart from one another. If these terms are unacceptable to you . . ." Sabrina tilted her head in a questioning manner. "Well, Nicholas, what's it to be?"

He stared, the silence growing between them. He had thought she'd be the appropriate wife for his purposes the evening they first met. But now he wanted more. Much, much more. The light of the moon cast a shimmering halo about her hair, caressing her finely carved features, her classically sculpted form. She was a vision in the misty magic of the black and silver shades of the night. He could only remember one other time in his life when his desire for a woman had been this overpowering. Irrational, instinctual and, ultimately, undeniable. He would take her as his wife, terms, conditions and all.

"I have a condition of my own," he said softly. "If we decide we do not suit, it must be a joint decision. We must agree to separate."

"Is that all?"

The moonlight reflected the surprise on her face.

Nicholas smiled to himself. Obviously, she did not think he'd accept her outrageous proposition. He nodded.

"Then as acting captain of this vessel, Simon can marry us. Is tomorrow acceptable?"

"More than acceptable." He pulled her into his arms.

"Nicholas," she gasped, "I hardly think this is an auspicious start to a marriage of convenience."

"We are not yet wed," he murmured, "and at the moment I find this wonderfully convenient." He pressed his lips to hers.

The pressure of his touch stole her breath and sapped her will. She struggled to fight a sea of powerful sensations, flooding her veins, throbbing through her blood. How would she resist him? If he could do this to her with a mere kiss . . . she shuddered with anticipation and ignored the distant warning in the back of her mind; it was not to be.

He held her close, plundering her lips with his own. Instinctively, he sensed her surrender, knew the moment of her defeat. Satisfied, he released her. Lifting her chin with a gentle touch, he gazed into eyes aglow with the power of his passion.

"Until tomorrow."

It took but a moment. Nicholas noted Sabrina gathering her wits about her. Noted her transformation into the cool, collected Lady Stanford. She was good, his bride-to-be, very good.

"Tomorrow." She nodded politely, turned and walked into the darkness. He rested his back against the rail and watched her disappear into the night. Her scent lingered in the air, vaguely spicy, hinting of a long-forgotten memory. A smile grew on his lips and he considered the unexpected benefits of taking a wife.

Nicholas, Earl of Wyldewood, was a man of honor, and he would abide by their bargain, abide by their terms.

All, of course, except one.

Coming April 2008

The Seduction of an Unknown Lady

an exciting new novel
by *New York Times* bestselling author

Samantha James

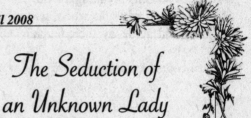

Fionna Hawkes values her independence as much as she does her privacy. Which is why she must resist Lord Aidan McBride, despite his persistent desire to know her better. Fiona not only has her secret identity as horror writer F. J. Sparrow to protect, but her family as well. But who will protect her from this bold nobleman's charms?

*Y*ou are the talk of all the neighbors, Lord Aidan—"

"Please," he interrupted. "It's Aidan. Just Aidan. The formality is not necessary. After all, we've been in each other's company in the dark before."

Fionna gasped.

"Miss Hawkes, you surprise me. I didn't think you were a woman easily shocked."

His eyes were twinkling. Fionna's narrowed. "I think you meant to shock me."

He chuckled. "I do believe I did."

For a fraction of an instant, his gaze met hers with that boldness she found so disconcerting. Then, to her further shock, his eyes trickled down her features, settling on her mouth. Something sparked in those incredible blue eyes; it vanished by the time she recognized it. Yet that spark set her further off guard . . . and further on edge.

Fionna we her lips. If he could be bold, then so could she. Her chin tipped. "I should like to know what you're thinking, my lord."

His smile was slow-growing. "I'm not so sure you do, Miss Hawkes."

"I believe I know my own mind." Fionna was adamant.

"Very well then. I was thinking that I am a most fortunate man."

"Why?" she asked bluntly.

Again that slow smile—a breathtaking one, she discovered. All at once she felt oddly short of breath. And there it was again, that spark in his eyes, only now it appeared in the glint of his smile.

"Perhaps fortunate is not the best way to describe it." He pretended to ponder. "No, that is not it at all. Indeed, I must say, I relish my luck."

"Your luck, my lord? And why is that?"

"It's quite simple, really. I relish my luck . . . in that I have found you before my brother."

Fionna's cheeks heated. Oh, heavens, the man was outrageous! He was surely an accomplished flirt—but surely he wasn't flirting with her.

"And another thing, Miss Hawkes." He traced a fingertip around the shape of her mouth, sending her heart into such a cascade of rhythm that she could barely breathe.

Nor could she have moved if the earth had tumbled away beneath them both.

He dared still more, for the very tip of that daring finger breached her lips, running lightly along the line of her teeth. "I am immensely delighted," he said mildly, "to discover that you are most definitely *not* a vampire."

No, she was not. Still, Fionna didn't know whether to laugh or cry. Ah, she thought, if he only knew . . .